The Passenger

The Passenger is about my first year in Portland. I worked in a hotel; I don't know if you've ever had a similar job, but you're kind of a ghost. **a novel of Old Portland** you're kind of a spirit, most people don't see you...you're a spectre, a voyeur **by Izaak David Diggs** that was another ghost year for me---I haunted the hotel, I haunted bars © **2021 Izaak David Diggs** ISBN: **978-1-7345428-7-5** where I wrote alone, drifting over barstools like mist **All rights reserved by the author including the reproduce in part or in its entirety** i put an apple on the cover because, initially, Portland was like Eden **cover photo by ike james, cover design/ composition by Faera Lane** but after experiencing part of it I was ready to move on...and I did. **Released 9 Sept. 2021 (MW/LH)**

I0635609

It's not too late to change your mind...

My mother insisted on waiting with me for
the train. It was cold out and the station was deserted.
Across the tracks was the one part of Lodi that could be
considered dangerous after dark. A security guard was
circling the station but she looked soft and drowsy. I was
convinced that the town wouldn't let me escape so easily; I
imagined it rousing one of the homeless vets who slept
nearby, filling their head with sparks and sending them into
a violent fury. I had been feeling trapped and anxious so
long that my mind couldn't accept that freedom was
possible. My mother kept talking and I kept nodding and
smiling even though I wanted her to go: I needed to make a
clean break from her and that town. I had known for some
time that Lodi was no good for me and that leaving was a
matter of survival.

I love my mother and will always be grateful for her
putting up with me when I was at my worst. Nevertheless, I
cannot live with her; in some ways we are very different.
February of 2013 marked eleven months under her roof. I
was itching to get out, to be *anywhere* else; my mother
would have been happy if I had stayed with her the rest of
her life. I envy her kindness and generosity. I envied her
fine qualities even as they were driving me nuts. She was
telling me that I could still change my mind even as the
train pulled up. I couldn't give her the response she wanted;
all I could do was hug her one last time and carry my bags
towards the open door. The conductor stepped out of the

train and looked surprised to see someone with baggage waiting on the platform.

"I'm going to Portland," I said.

"I guess it's good we stopped then."

He accepted the ticket I was holding out and logged it in using his iPhone. As he motioned me inside I looked over my shoulder to make sure Mom had gotten back to her car safely. She was still watching from the platform, probably still hoping that I would change my mind.

I sat next to a window and looked out at the lights in the distance. It was that time of night where it is neither one day nor the one that follows it; you're just floating in a void, confused from lack of sleep. A middle aged guy was telling an even older man that he was visiting his dying father in Eugene. The older man said that he would pray for both of them.

"Thank you" the middle aged man smiled. "I haven't been back to Eugene in a long time."

The old man thought about that for a moment; he could tell by his face that he was being drawn back into his own memories.

"It's funny what draws us back to places we once knew," he replied softly.

"I don't know if I ever knew Eugene," his companion said in a jovial tone. "All I knew was that I wanted to leave there when I was younger."

The lights receded as the train moved on into the darkness between towns. A father and son were roughhousing on a couple of seats. I followed the reflections of their changing shapes in the window as Lodi disappeared behind me.

I was glad to be out of Lodi but understood there were no guarantees in Portland. I had a room for a couple of months---three or four at the most---and beyond that there was just chance and maybe luck. I had failed to find a job the year before and had been forced to return to Lodi after running out of money. 2012 had been a crazy year and not all of it had been the good variety of crazy. My best friend Noah had been following my blog; picking up my descent into madness and refusing to stand by. I was hesitant to accept more of his generosity after accepting so much of it in the past. On the other hand, I also knew that I needed to do *something*, and Noah's offer was the only "something" that had presented itself.

The train pulled into Sacramento at half past eleven. Disembarking, the passengers discovered that the train north would be delayed for two hours. All of us shuffled like zombies down a series of ramps and tunnels into the heart of the station. Being there brought back memories of when I was a kid and we had taken Amtrak to Portland or Reno. They still had the wooden benches with built-in heaters but there were also flat screens with arrival and departure information. The room was full of scaffolding and exposed metal trusses which gave the place a weird feeling of being in flux, the past sharing the same space as the present and future. We were all in limbo: Between trains, between days, between destinations.

Most of the people in the waiting room appeared to be passengers but there were a few homeless people asleep on the benches. I busied myself writing and sketching in a notebook in an attempt to turn the hours into minutes. I was thinking about Noah, how good a friend he had always been. I always worried that he was getting the short end of the stick with regards to our relationship. Our friendship had always been one of the few things that I could depend on and I never took it lightly. I thought about our past, found myself getting sentimental, and went back to drawing.

At half past one there was an announcement that our train was pulling into the station. We grabbed our bags and shuffled back up the tunnels and ramps. In Portland the train boardings had been well organized and proceeded smoothly. In Sacramento, however, they were chaotic and reminded me of the last helicopter taking off from the roof of the American Embassy in Saigon.

My seatmate appeared to be in his mid-forties with a weathered face and duff-colored goatee. He reeked of spent Pall Mall cigarettes and a stained duffel bag lay on the floor between his feet. My suitcase wouldn't fit in the overhead so I wrestled it into the space in front of my legs. He asked me where I was going and I told him.
"Portland is a pretty good town," he frowned. "But it was better twenty years ago before it got so expensive."
"Where are you going?"
"Seattle."
"Isn't Seattle pretty expensive?"
"I guess, but I have a buddy who owns a boat. I'll be staying with him for a while."

I was going to ask what sort of boat but he got a text and the conversation ended. The train was pulling out of Sacramento and people were still settling in. Children, excited to be up in the middle of the night, were running up and down the aisles and overwhelming their weary parents. It made me think about my own mother. I felt guilty, she was hurt that I had left---I felt guilty but I knew that I wouldn't have been any good to her if I had stayed; I wouldn't have been good to anyone including myself.

I didn't get much sleep on the train. I'd nod off for a few minutes only to wake up with a jolt. Light began filling the sky north of Redding and the train began a slow turn to skirt the north side of Mount Shasta. A light snow was dusting the trees that stood on the edges of the desolate valleys we passed through. Coming off Shasta the train dipped into the high desert and the snow became thin and weary like the ground it was settling on. The train had grown quiet and there was a stark poetry to the light out there. It was looking to be a beautiful morning and I felt optimistic for what lay ahead.

The next town of any size that we came across was Klamath Falls. It reminded me of Bakersfield: A poor city with lots of shanties and old trailers on desolate lots. The train stopped and people filled the corridor on their way out to smoke or stretch their legs. Some kids were talking about a Swedish House Mafia gig they went to in San Francisco. They interspersed their stories about buying sweatshirts and posters with memories of all the homeless people hitting them up for money.

"The worst was when we went to this convenience store for food," one of the kids recounted. "We thought it would be okay because it was only three blocks away from the theatre but these guys ran up to us and were literally trying to sell us meat."

I forced their stories into the background and stared into the distance. One of the shacks had an old camper parked behind it. I tried to imagine all the places it had been, all the adventures it had been a part of. That was my ideal life; just traveling around in some old camper and writing, just getting by. After four years of tough going my expectations in life had changed. Not lowered, I didn't see it that way, but changed drastically from when I wanted a house and furniture and all those things adults are supposed to want. Now I just wanted a simple life, just enough to get by.

The train passed through more snowy mountains before following the shore of a broad river. People left in the morning and afternoon to take meals in the dining car and allowed their children to run amuck. After lunch, a man with a Middle Eastern accent came over the PA to inform us that a harmonica had been left in the bar. It was sunny by the time we got to the Willamette Valley. All the lush green reminded me of Portland; the closer we got to the city I could feel my emotions coming to the surface. I saw the bridges and the river I had walked along a year before. The train cut through downtown and when I saw all the old buildings I felt like I had come home.

2

Noah was waiting out front in his diesel VW Golf. I dropped my bags in the back and we picked up on the long, eccentric conversation we've been having for over thirty years. We had both grown up poor kids in a wealthy place, what we did with that childhood is one of the few ways that we are different. He was always focused, logical, and responsible; I was always eccentric and impulsive. Somehow we worked as friends, maybe because we saw the world as if we were looking at it through the same eyes and processing it with similar brains. We picked up cat food and then went to his house in one of the older neighborhoods between Hawthorne and Belmont. Later I would learn that I was staying a block from where Elliott Smith had lived. It was fascinating to think that I was walking the same sidewalks he had; probably frequenting the same bars as well.

The house was as I had remembered it: So well decorated that it belonged in a magazine. *New Yorkers* and *Scientific Americans* in tidy piles. Clean kitchen. I was determined to tread lightly and make myself scarce. Anne was working that night so Noah and I went to a local bar to drink strong beer and talk politics. All around us were gentle, soft-focus Portland people with their mismatched clothes and polite ways. They seemed as alien to me as I must have to them. I couldn't help but like them, though, something about the town was putting the electricity back in my blood and throwing light in my dark corners.

The night was still at our heels so we walked to the Safeway on Hawthorne to get more beer. We took it down to the basement where Noah keeps his office and musical instruments. I saw his old Les Paul and thought about Chase. I wanted to ask him if he had been playing---the guitar didn't have any dust on it---but it always had been a touchy subject.

"I picked it up a few days ago." I guess he had caught me looking.

"Cool. I miss doing music myself." Did that sound like a hint? It felt like I was always suggesting that we work on music together and worried that I was becoming a pest.

"Maybe we can do something when I get done with this project," he said.

I nodded and took a drink from my beer. Noah worked too much: It had always been that way and I worried about him.

"I played the Album a couple of days ago." There was no emotion in his voice, none in his eyes either. In his heart? Probably.

"Yeah?"

He said nothing, just took a drink from his beer. I thought of Chase again; I never really liked him, another of the few differences between Noah and I. Out of respect I had never spoken badly about him, Noah had always been sensitive about that sort of thing. It didn't matter if it had been twenty years; something's don't have an expiration date.

We had polished off the six pack by the time we heard Anne's boots upstairs. She looked skinny and there were streaks of silver in her hair that hadn't been there the year before. Noah gave Anne a quick hug and I averted my eyes, thinking of the guitars downstairs and consequently Chase. How much did she know about that situation? After the embrace she focused on me with a warm smile.

"Good to have you back in town," she said.

Looking into her eyes I could see that she meant it. I showed my gratitude by bidding them goodnight and making myself scarce.

3

Normally I can drink six beers without a problem but those weren't normal beers. I woke up feeling my age and then foolish when I remembered that I had an interview with a temp agency at eleven. It was my first morning back in Portland. Through the hangover, I was feeling an indefinable but undeniable sense of optimism. The world was bleary yet still beautiful.

Noah was already downstairs working, Sigur Ros coming up through the kitchen floor as I made coffee.
I played the Album a couple of days ago.
All of us were in our mid-twenties then. When the bassist left the band I offered to fill in for him in the studio and instantly regretted it; I felt like by offering that I had put Noah on the spot. I wasn't good enough, not as *locked in* as Noah envisioned the bass parts. He wouldn't have told me that, he would have given me a chance even if it cost thousands of dollars and many hours of studio time. I laughed off the suggestion a few seconds later and N looked relieved. In the end, he played all the bass parts. I was there when he laid down the tracks, still wishing I could have played them but respecting how clear his vision was.

I returned to the present as Noah switched from Sigur Ros to Radiohead. My coffee was done so I took it downstairs to check the news on the iMac my friend kept for recording. I looked around at the piano and all the guitars. There was a picture of Noah and Chase on top of the piano. They had been in their mid-twenties then; the singer would always remain there.

On the bus downtown that morning I saw an elderly person with a marijuana leaf on their cap. I couldn't tell if Leaf Cap was a man or a woman; that sort of gender confusion would become a normal occurrence for me during my time in Portland. The ambiguous person with the cap disembarked at the first stop on the west side of the river. Unsure of my bearings, I followed them off the bus. I had forgotten my way around the Downtown streets and was lost for a few minutes. Everything was fuzzy and aching, a reminder of my age, of foolish things that I should have left behind many years before. Noah had quit music when the Album went nowhere. People who don't know him think it was because Chase died and maybe it was to some degree, but that wasn't the only reason. Noah wanted stability, a career that wouldn't leave him scratching for a meager living when he was forty-five like I was doing. Why hadn't *I* given up? Why was I still trying to make it as a writer after so many years of failure? Was Noah the smart one for knowing when to quit? Or, was this the way our lives were supposed to be from the beginning? I had no idea; it fascinated me and I had posed that question countless times, but the answer had never come.

I found Indenture-Temps with less than five minutes to spare. The receptionist gave me forms to fill out and told me that a staffing manager named Tammy would meet with me when I finished them. Half of my attention was on the paperwork and half on the young woman behind the desk. She looked like Natalie Merchant from 10,000 Maniacs, same earnest, wide face and large breasts. Finding myself getting preoccupied and inappropriately turned on, I forced myself to focus on the minutiae of past job experience and educational background. I handed the forms in at the same moment Tammy walked up from somewhere in the back of the office. She looked right at me and smiled brightly. I forced a smile in return that felt fake and cheesy---why was I still putting myself in that position at 45? Did I look as old and hungover as I felt? If I did, Tammy's expression didn't betray it. She was nice enough and somewhere in her mid thirties with bleach blonde hair, a checked jacket, and jangly sort of red jewelry that looked like plastic. We went into a small office where she asked me questions and I somehow answered them. Tammy was left handed and I found myself staring at her hand as she wrote southpaw. Fifteen minutes passed, we exchanged another set of smiles, and then I made my way out of the office and back into the crisp, February morning.

I walked several blocks to a street that I knew the 15 ran down. There was a Prince impersonator waiting at the bus stop. He had the same skin color, lack of height, and pencil thin mustache as the singer; faux Prince even had similar facial expressions. His outfit, however, was off the mark: Sky blue leggings, brown jacket, and a porkpie hat. A prisoner transport truck pulled up across the street and was surrounded by half a dozen sheriffs' deputies. They kept their hands close to their sidearms and were constantly scanning the surrounding area. Next to where the truck was parked, a steel shed that looked to be roughly four by eight rose out of the sidewalk; most likely a secret entrance to the courthouse. Judging by the seriousness on the cops' faces, whoever was riding in that truck must have been pretty important. I took a cautious step closer to them to get a better look but the bus came before I could see who all the fuss was about.

I had a phone interview at two o'clock for a hotel job. The only downside of Noah and Anne's house was that my phone did not work there; I had to walk two blocks before I could check my messages or make a call. I always walked down to Taylor Street to get a signal; the sweet spot being in front of a house where Elliott Smith's girlfriend had lived. I would look at the basement windows and wonder if *that* was where Elliott had recorded *Roman Candle*. He had come from Texas and died in Los Angeles but Elliott Smith seemed to belong in Portland; a sensitive hunched over figure making his way through the rain. I imagined Elliott fishing for a pack of cigarettes in the pocket of his hoodie right where I was standing. Catching myself daydreaming, I turned my attention from the house to the street. There was a van with Alaska plates that was usually parked next to where I used my phone. Judging by the heavy curtains I assumed that someone was living in it that beat up Econoline and that observation made me think about how I had been trying to buy a van back in Lodi and how my life would have been different if I had made that happen.

4

It was cold out the next morning. I made coffee for us and went down to the basement to look for work on-line. My hope was that either the agency would find me a gig or something would come of the previous day's phone interview. I walked down to Taylor Street to check my voicemail every hour and a half. Seeing the moss on the roofs and feeling the dampness in the air made being back more real. The eleven month block of chaos since I had left town was fading into insignificance, the weight I had been bearing through the wilderness rising from my shoulders. It felt like I was slowly coming back to life after a long hibernation full of unsettling dreams.

My plan for the day was to take the train out to IKEA; IKEA is always a good place to fill up on cheap hot dogs and look around. In the evening, I would find a dive bar to write in. I was determined to be a good guest; in my mind that meant being away from the house as much as possible. Down in Lodi I had started a list of cheap or even free things to do in Portland like visit IKEA or explore the places that I hadn't gotten around to seeing the year before.

Every time I went out to check my voicemail it felt like I was braving the cold for nothing. The day had started off so good but the darkness still had a way of finding me. Getting an email rejection from a literary agent didn't improve my frame of mind. I had collected nearly two dozen of them since the previous summer. You try to be strong, maybe you even *feel* strong from time to time, but it wears at you: Always struggling to make it, living out of a suitcase as you bounce from guest room to guest room. Alternating between frozen burritos and Top Ramen like someone twenty years younger. I had a good feeling about Portland, that things would change for the better, but I was still a long way from healed.

I took the MAX out to IKEA. My camera bag was over my shoulder with my notebooks inside. Among the families in their nice Banana Republic or REI clothes, I felt like a nomad or even a voyeur. Upstairs, I found the orange loveseat Teresa and I had coveted back in Phoenix at another IKEA in another life. It was weird to think that something deep that both of us thought was for life had just evaporated like a dream. We had a nice rental house, cats, and plans for future children and now we would probably never see each other again. It felt weird, but not bad weird, just strange that something so intertwined in one's life could just vanish. I thought about that as I checked out that orange loveseat, alone. Maybe I was better at going solo through life, free to do whatever I felt compelled to do without dragging anyone into my artistic, threadbare life.

The night prowl started at the Bare Bones Bar a few blocks from the house. It seemed more like an IKEA demo kitchen than a dive bar. Every detail seemed scientifically calculated to draw hipsters in: Low-fi rock music. Three dollar Olympia tall boys. Free wi-fi. At least the bartender was cute. I flirted with her a little but she wasn't having it. I sat at a table next to the windows so I could watch people passing on the sidewalk. Forcing myself to stop checking out the bartender I eventually got some writing done. A cute brunette walked in; she was short with a nice figure. Looking from her to the bartender I found myself wishing that it was easier for me to talk to women. I have always been useless at that sort of thing; I don't have a relaxed, easy way of talking to people and have always envied people who possess that quality. It looks so easy for them---how can it be so easy?

By the time I finished my beer I was ready to move on. Four blocks down Belmont was a bar I had heard of that was known locally as the Vern. The story was that one rainy night a bus driver hit the "Tavern" sign and knocked off the first two letters. The bartender had *Impractical Jokers on* the TV which reminded me of a friend of mine. I texted her only to find that she was being treated for cancer. Beyond feeling bad for JB the news made me scared; here was someone ten years younger than myself with cancer. There I was, out in the weather and drinking too much without health insurance---what would happen to me if I got sick? The selfish things that pop in our heads when we get bad news.

I managed to get some writing done until the smell from the men's room and my concern about JB derailed me. I walked back to the house to eat a little and use the bathroom. The mood had been going from dark to light and back all day---why couldn't I just focus on being back in Portland? Maybe the four years since the Crash had worn me down to a patch of thin skin criss-crossed with raw nerves. Before the Crash, things had been going good: Teresa and I had the best jobs of our lives and a nice rental house in an older part of Phoenix. We lost it all and moved back to her mother's house in Sacramento. Our marriage didn't survive it, that crashed, too. Sitting in Noah's guest bedroom, I found myself dwelling on things that were pointless to dwell on. Needing a distraction, I decided to walk over to Chopsticks II on Burnside for some karaoke.

The cute girl who had KJ'd the previous year wasn't there. Wednesday had been her night but some guy with a soul patch had taken her place. Noah showed up and we drank beer and watched people sing. One guy sounded like a cross between Frankenstein and a rusty hinge; I remembered seeing him every time I had gone to Chopsticks the year before. The other regular was a girl whose name I always forgot. She seemed the sort of person who would have forty cats, each with a cute name and a sweater. Catgirl sang okay, certainly better than a lot of the drunks that were there, but there was something desperate about her. The later it got the more people filtered in; they were still showing up at 12:30 when we left.

Noah had ridden his bike over so I walked back down 28th alone. I was a little drunk but it was a beautiful night inside my head and out in the world. Things seemed so different than in Lodi, it felt like anything was possible and that I was where I belonged. N was in the kitchen washing some pans when I got back. Seeing him, I was reminded of a scene outside of Chopsticks as he unchained his bike. A couple of music nazi sort of hipsters had been talking about records and one of them mentioned the Album.

"Oh, now you're just being obscure for the sake of being obscure," his friend had laughed.

Noah had ten feet away putting the chain in his backpack; he *had* to have heard them talking. His face gave nothing away so I pretended like the conversation hadn't happened. This is one reason we have been friends so long: I try to be respectful of N's privacy, try not to bring up things that I know have scarred him. Watching N scrub a pan, I thought of those hipsters talking and how I could have sworn that I saw a flash of darkness on my friend's face, just a momentary twitch, something that only a close friend would recognize. It reminded me how much I love him and would do anything for my friend.

"You want a beer?" I asked.

"Nah, I'm about to head off to bed."

"Alright, have a good night."

"You, too, see you tomorrow."

I grabbed a beer and climbed into bed to read an article on Venezuela in the latest *New Yorker*. I fell asleep between the pages and dreamt about nothing.

5

For my fourth day back in Portland I went to Foster Burger
for lunch. I had always wanted to go there the year before
but hadn't felt that I could justify spending ten dollars on a
burger plate. Spending a few dollars on alcohol a night
didn't bother me, but I was saving Foster Burger for a
special occasion. My plan the year before had been to go
there in celebration of when I got a job. I applied to
everything from Taco Bell to $70,000 a year gigs that I
would have had to bullshit my way into. In the end, I ran
out of money and left town on a day of ceaseless rain.

The year before I had lived near 65th and Holgate,
experiencing and embracing the cliché of the struggling
artist. My room was cold and I was sick for a week but it
will always be a time that I look back on fondly---a time
rich in creativity and experience. I wrote and drew on giant
sketch pads that I had picked up at a nearby dollar store.
The landlord was overly earnest and left his smelly towels
in the bathroom but he was also decent and kind. Most of
the thirty nights I lived in his house I ended up walking to
Foster Liquors to get a forty or a cheap bottle of wine. The
owner was an Asian man in his sixties who always looked
sad, maybe he saw lots of down on their luck people buying
shitty booze and it got to him. Or, maybe he had been in
some Asian war started by Americans and had seen a lot of
people die horrible deaths. I always tried to imagine his
past when I walked back to the house with another brown
paper bag. Once I was in my room I would get lost in being

creative---writing and designing houses and composing music. Maybe I *was* living the cliché of the starving artist but it felt really good at the time; I truly felt that I was leading the life I was meant to lead. When I was married it had always seemed selfish to just lose myself in art, just follow the whirlpool into my own head. Finally I was as free to be as weird and creative and selfish and random as I wanted to. I was happy, maybe the happiest I had been in my life.

The appearance of the sun was a surprise after a storm earlier in the day. That morning the rain and wind had started when I was on my way to a job interview downtown. I put on a button-down shirt and slacks and did my best to convince the interviewer that I could be the maintenance guy in their hotel. The interview went well and I was told that they'd be calling me by the following Wednesday. Leaving the hotel, the wind kept turning my umbrella inside out. It was bitterly cold and every time I saw a homeless person I was reminded of how close I was to being among their ranks; it made me feel vulnerable and small.

Welcome to Portland: The weather hates you. The weather is not your friend. The weather probably wants to kill you.

I turned that interview over and over in my mind as I rode the bus down to Foster. Not wanting to obsess about it, I tried to plan what I'd be doing that night to get out of the house. Foster Burger was even better than I'd heard. I considered getting a beer but it was still early so I settled for a glass of water. I paid the check and waited for the next

14 bus. At Division and 50th, I disembarked and just started walking west as I listened to Elliott Smith. He wrote a lot about Division and I had to wonder if I was seeing the same things that he had twenty years earlier. There were a lot of newer buildings, expensive places, but there were still signs of the older Portland that I had heard stories about. A girl was sitting next to a dumpster singing to herself; I took out my earbuds to listen but didn't recognize the tune. She was small and faded like a shrinking ghost. I put my earbuds back in and continued walking.

None of the taverns on Division struck my fancy so I went to the Bare Bones Bar. I drank a $1.50 draft PBR and inscribed the postcards that I had bought for JB. The bartender was really cute and reminded me of Britney Murphy; not the Britney Murphy of *Eight Mile*, more like how she looked in *Clueless*. I didn't talk to her that night; I was worried that I'd come across as just another creepy customer hitting on her. Instead, I just sat at a corner table and tried to write. After sitting there for half an hour and getting nothing done I moved on to the next bar.

I was unemployed and staying in a guest room of the only people I knew in town. Despite that, I felt alive again, like something amazing was happening and anything was possible. I kept thinking about all the people I had been around at a miserable temp gig back in Stockton. It was a stressful job but they had to stay because of their mortgage or car payments. I, on the other hand, was free---I had nothing, but I also had no obligations. Nights like my fifth one in Portland I felt like the luckiest guy in the world.

I had another $1.50 PBR at the Vern and got some writing done. A Timberwolves game was playing in the background and some of the regulars were shouting at the television. There was a nerdy cute sort of woman in a black tank top but she was there with a chubby guy in a Misfits t-shirt. Some guy at the bar had a red mohawk and a bunch of notebooks next to his drink and I wondered if he was a writer. Aside from one or two women the bar was a sausage fest so I decided to move on.

It was bitterly cold out for the first three blocks I walked down Belmont. My idea of staying out of Noah and Anne's hair was not going back to the house before eleven. It was hard, though, when the nights got cold like that. Bar number three was Mulligan's at Hawthorne and 36th. It seemed as if they were trying to come across as a dive bar like so many other bars on Hawthorne. There was a neon sign with a shamrock and hipsters smoking out front. They all watched me approach and I suddenly felt out of place and awkward, nervously pulling at the strap on my bag as I went inside.

There were some loud drunks in the bar. I got a Hamms for $2.25 and got some writing done. I also got a whiskey for $3.25---I just asked for the cheapest whiskey they had. It was embarrassing but I had been spending too much money. The guy behind the bar looked at me like I was a schmuck and maybe he was right: I was spending too much money and I was also drinking too much, I couldn't decide which was worse.

6

The following morning the sun was insinuating through the blinds, something that rarely happens in Portland before March. I walked to the Belmont library and got a replacement library card. None of the books there seemed appealing so I decided to go to the Central Library downtown. At the bus stop there was a cute girl reading a book and a homeless guy. I looked at that hobo and realized the only difference between us was that I had a place to sleep that night. Could I make Portland work the second time around? Could I get a job and a room in a couple of months? What if I couldn't? I knew that going back to Lodi wasn't an option. Noah and Anne wouldn't just kick me out. In fact, they would insist on my staying as long as it took, but I was drawing a line in my head, a timeline; I was determined to survive on the streets before taking advantage of our friendship.

Portland's Central Library was as beautiful as it was old, reminding me of an opera house with its perilous marble stairs that mocked my shoes. It took me forever to find the music section. Wandering around I overheard an ugly conversation coiled between bookcases. A man was hissing some venom at his female companion, his voice like a drawn back fist.
"I don't know what's fucking wrong with you," he said. "I have no idea what to do with you, you are completely fucked up."

I crept away and went to look in a part of the library that I hadn't covered. When I went back to check on the man and woman they were gone.

Walking down 6th past Pioneer Square I saw a Seth Rogan look alike with a clipboard and prayed that he wouldn't make eye contact. He did, stepping towards me and extending his free hand.
"What's your name?" He beamed.
"Joe." I responded tersely.
I left my hands in my pockets and kept walking.

I wanted to take a picture of the Yamhill Pub where JB and I had hung out the year before. As I was looking over a man with a long feather in his hat and an elaborate mustache walked out of the bar; he eyed me suspiciously until I walked away. SW Taylor and 2nd was like a ghost town and felt spooky. I passed the time waiting for the bus looking at all the old buildings, imaging all the stories that had played out in them. A homeless guy with curly, blonde hair was staring down at the sidewalk. He bore a strong resemblance to Chase in his last days, right before the singer had fallen through the skylights of a warehouse; the resemblance was strong enough that I almost went up to him. It was stupid: I had nothing to say to Chase when he was alive, why would that have changed now that he was dead?

On the 15 there was this old homeless guy who had stacked a whole bunch of clothes on a couple of the seats. He was furiously messing with his long, gray hair as if he had mange or something. Not scratching at it, but running his fingers through it passionately, distractedly. I was distracted as well, thinking about twenty years earlier when I wasn't Noah's only deeply creative irresponsible friend. Maybe that's why Chase and I never got along, we were sharing a place in Noah's life. They had been friends first, back to sixth grade, in fact. I would have loved to have been the Jagger to Noah's Richards but I didn't have the right voice. In fact, I couldn't even sing back then---Chase could and he was charismatic. He was a great front man; it took me forever to admit that.

I decided to visit my old neighborhood again so I took the 14 down to Foster-Powell. Getting off in front of the Round Table, I walked past the international meat shop and Foster Liquors where I stuck my head in to see if the sad old man was there. An Asian woman in her forties watched me suspiciously from behind the counter. I tried to look friendly and offered an explanation.
"I used to live around here and shopped here a lot."
"Lots of people shop here," she replied tersely.
Her gaze was as unyielding as the asphalt surrounding the shop. My smile died friendless and I walked back out into the false spring.

The house where I rented the room looked the same so I took a picture. From there, I walked a few blocks over to Foster and took some shots of this amazing old flatiron building that I had coveted the year before. I would stand in front of and stare at it almost every day. Some days I'd walk over and look up at it and think of all the things that could be done with the building. I imagined dressing for dinner and entertaining ghosts, standing on the roof and drinking martinis on mild summer nights. I'd stand on that sidewalk between the dollar store and my cold room and redraw the world around me.

On the bus back I decided that I wanted to walk up Division a bit. I walked ten blocks, passing a school and a Dairy Queen. It felt like I had to wait forever for the next bus but I was tired of walking. When the bus finally came I sat a few seats behind a homeless guy who looked like a character out of a Crumb cartoon. He wore an overcoat and a beard that was all salt and pepper fury like a storm. This old lady sitting next to him kept looking at me with this creepy old lady smile. I jotted some notes down, braved another couple of miles, and then signaled the driver to stop.

I got off the bus and walked through the Ladd Division neighborhood to the Burgerville on Hawthorne. I had a cheeseburger for lunch and drew a couple of cartoons. After my creativity had petered out I started to read the bio of Kate Bush that I had checked out. The manager was this huge woman in a blue shirt with a happy smile; she was giving her employees reviews out in the dining room. One of the staff was a sad faced girl with short hair. I could see her struggling to smile as she got her review, I could tell that she understood that she was supposed to smile but the emotions behind it were alien to her. I understood that someday she would be a character in a book or movie I would write, too drab to be beautiful yet too compelling to ignore.

My plan was to hit the first bar at six, nurse a beer for an hour and a half, and then move on to the second bar. The bar I wanted to stop at had a DJ playing that night and the last thing I wanted to do was listen to dubstep. I kept walking, crossing over the hill between Hawthorne and Belmont and ending up at the Bare Bones Bar. I got my PBR draft for $1.50 and mostly read while I was there. People met up and laughed and drank pricey drinks. My favorite bartender wasn't behind the counter. In her place was a hard faced blonde somewhere in her late thirties. I saw white powder on mirrors in her past, a credit card chopping through it as life had cut deep lines into her face.

As I nursed my beer I went over my texts. I had decided to get back into photography and was meeting my first model the following afternoon. Photography had brought me a lot of enjoyment the previous summer and I had always intended to pick it up again. My Craigslist ad had gotten maybe a dozen responses and I understood that for every twenty emails I got maybe one would pan out.

After the Bare Bones I walked down Belmont. It was freezing out and the first few blocks were murder. There was a different bartender at Mulligan's, a girl in her mid twenties with long, black hair and an Italian or Spanish face. She was at the other end of the bar talking to some guy I assumed was her boyfriend. I started sketching and going over the plot points of the story I was working on.

After ten minutes I was able to make the connection and started writing at a furious pace. When I stopped I felt self-conscious; I knew that it had to be weird to see some strange guy scribbling away so intensely. When I write longhand I am putting words down as fast as my hand can manipulate a pen, only stopping every few minutes to take a sip of whiskey or water. I got through a chapter, put my stuff in my bag, and made my way back out into the night.

7

It was five in the afternoon and raining lightly when I left the house. It had been a bad day full of self-doubt darkened further by a nagging hangover. Like the sky outside the day was gray and lost well into the afternoon. My moods might have been swinging back and forth but at least there were highs.

I figured I'd hit the first bar a little after six and then move on to Chopsticks in time for karaoke. I got some cough lozenges from Fred Meyer and then went to Powell's on Hawthorne to kill some time. Dee from the Hotel Glass called when I was flipping through a book on deep sea life. It took a few moments for me to understand that she was calling to tell me that I had the job and orientation would begin on Friday. After hanging up I put the book back on the shelf and wrote myself a reminder note. Had that really happened? Did I really have a job after being back in Portland for eight days? I was standing in the middle of Powell's on the verge of tears, grateful that what had been a shitty day was turning out so amazing.

I texted Noah to let him know the good news as I walked to the Bare Bones for a celebratory martini. After all the well liquor the Bombay tasted decadent and life felt good. I read as I drank, giving myself a night off from writing. At Chopsticks, I drank whiskey and got sloppy and still kept trying to sing well past midnight.

8

The following morning a night of celebrating still colored my blood like a gentle curse. On one of my short walks to check my voicemail I saw a condom on the sidewalk that didn't appear to be used. Had it fallen out of a car or a pocket? Had a couple indulged in feverish sex against a tree? Or, had someone simply dropped it out of carelessness? I must have stared at that thing for close to a minute imagining all the possibilities.

It was misting when I left the house at five. Walking down Madison I saw a middle-aged woman with Downs Syndrome being helped by her caregiver; both of them were carrying grocery bags. I passed them and then they passed me when I stopped to take pictures of a house that had been raised.

I went back to the first dive bar I had found after returning to Portland. The Langano was down in a basement with DJ turntables and a drum kit that had a teddy bear stuffed in the kick drum. That bar never seemed to have more than three or four people in it; maybe it was because the bartender kept disappearing. There was graffiti everywhere aside from the main room. I got two chapters done on the book and when the inspiration dissipated I looked around to see how my surroundings had changed. I had no interest in sticking around any longer but it was only 6:15 and I was trying to hold off hitting the second bar until eight. I used the restroom and took a few pictures of the cartoons and scribbled non-sequiturs that covered every surface.

I left the bar and walked up a street that runs parallel to Hawthorne. It cut through a beautiful neighborhood that reminded me of the 40s in Sacramento with its scores of hundred year old houses that had been lovingly restored. It was 6:45 and I contemplated hitting the Bare Bones Bar for happy hour so I could get a $1.50 PBR. Turning west down 17th, I picked up my pace. The Bare Bones was full so I didn't even go in. I walked over to this place called Claudia's that I had been curious about but had that bar, some poker tournament going on and a vibe I wasn't digging. A couple of women were smoking outside and watched me pass. Their gazes were not out of longing but curiosity and reminded me that I was still a stranger in that town and might always be.

At Mulligan's the cheap whiskey was no longer so cheap. Since the last time I had ordered it the price had gone up a dollar and a half. I sipped my drink and a glass of water and wrote another chapter of the book. There were times where I was pretty sure that I was doing the best writing of my life. I also understood that in order to keep doing so I had to confront things in myself I rarely acknowledge. Looking at that mess head on brought my emotions to the surface; I found myself on the verge of tears sitting alone in a bar surrounded by groups of laughing strangers. I must have looked forlorn because the bartender walked over to my table. She was somewhere in her late twenties and white as me but with dark hair.
"You're all alone--what are you doing? Writing?" She asked.

"Yeah. I like writing in bars."

"You looked lonely and I saw your drink is almost gone, do you want another one?"

"No, thank you. I'll probably be taking off in a few minutes," I replied.

"I know a couple of writers; they say that writing can be really lonely."

"Sometimes. On occasion it feels like you're on a desert island teasing the sun with mirrors."

She smiled but there was awkwardness to it. A second later she was walking away to chat with some people a few tables closer to the bar. I had opened my mouth, some weird stuff had escaped, and I had scared off another attractive woman.

I finished writing at 7:40. It was too early to go back to the house so I walked down to the Vern and got a cheap pint. There weren't any free seats in the bar so I went back to the room with the pool tables. Done writing for the night, I dug out a biography on Sam Cooke and divided my time between reading and observing. They were playing 80s metal and when "Rock You Like a Hurricane" came on it brought back memories of my attempting to break dance to that song at a party. I had been 18 and had given myself alcohol poisoning, throwing up on expensive rugs and passing out in a bathroom. It was the first time that I had been stupid with respect to drinking and certainly not the last.

There were a lot of women at the Vern but they are all with guys or in large groups. Under one of the pool tables was a box labeled Ore Ida Tater Tots. I have no idea why but that box fascinated me. I was alone with a drink and my weirdness and yet the world made perfect sense.

9

Three days after my new boss called to offer me a job, I spent the entire afternoon going through orientation. Dee seemed like she would be a good manager, open minded and maybe even a little eccentric. The two of us got along well which I took to be a good sign. She told me about all the perks I'd be getting and the opportunity to learn skills like brewing. The century old Hotel Glass was two blocks down the street from Powell's. Over the years it had been everything from a speakeasy to a gay bath house with "glory hole booths" which Dee told us about during the tour. All the rooms in the hotel were named after songs by bands that had played in the Glass Ballroom down the street. Because the hotel was wedge shaped all the rooms had interesting angles as did the hallways. It seemed like a fascinating place and I was hoping to see some ghosts.

Dee confided that the training would take a few days before my regular schedule started. The two of us got to talking after the other trainees had left. She wasn't conventionally pretty but still sexy with full, natural breasts. I thought she might have been checking me out but maybe it was just wishful thinking.
"What brought you up to Portland, Ike?" She asked.
I told her the story of how I had discovered the town while helping my sister move from Colorado to Oregon. Then, I told her about Noah and how he had offered his guest room a month earlier. Before I knew it, I had told her about his band and the one album they had made.

"I have never heard of them, sorry," she smiled.

"They never became big, it was the tail end of grunge when the album came out and there was a glut of bands playing grungy sort of music."

"And your friend quit music after that?"

"Yeah." I didn't tell her about Chase dying; it seemed a dark place to go with one's boss.

Someone came up with invoices that Dee needed to review. She apologized, told me when to come back for more training, and we shook hands. Looking at her breasts straining through her shirt had given me an erection; part of me wanted her to see it but I also understood that would have been a bad idea.

"I'm just going to finish my water if that's okay," I said.

"Of course, I'll see you in a couple of days."

I finished my water and went downstairs to a restroom to deal with my arousal. After composing myself I left the hotel and started coming up with a game plan for that night.

Noah texted me. Anne was visiting friends of hers so he suggested we walk down to the Green Dragon. He was waiting out front when I got back to the house. After a few blocks had fallen behind us we got to talking about music.

"I've been thinking about Chase the past few months," he said.

There it was, *out there*. I was prepared to just listen to whatever he wanted to say but he had left an opening.

"Yeah, me too," was my response. "In fact, I thought I saw him a couple of days ago."

I was subtly watching his face, looking for any signs of pain that may have been a cue to change the subject.

"Things are good, you know?" He said. "I know you worry about how I took it back then, that I blamed myself."

"Are you past that?" I asked carefully. "I mean, have you stopped blaming yourself?"

He had to think about that.

"I don't know if I ever blamed myself, even then I understood how self-destructive he was."

Noah trailed off. We passed a side street with two Citroens parked on it. It was another half block before he continued.

"I think I was angry with myself for being selfish; he was the perfect singer for what I was doing back then. When he died, I knew it was over and I didn't want it to be."

"That album was amazing," I said. "I mean, people still talk about it."

"Four hundred satisfied customers," he smiled before looking thoughtful again. "Some of the things you wrote last summer," Noah added. "They reminded me of how Chase was."

I felt guilty about that, unintentionally opening old wounds---whatever they were.

"It was stupid; I know I made a lot of people worry."

"You did, that's why I invited you up here. That, and I enjoy spending time with you."

Things had gotten too serious; both of us felt an awkwardness surrounding us like the late winter bite to the air. I launched into one of my impressions; Noah laughed and added to the ridiculousness with an impression of his own. The Green Dragon came into view and we were once again just two more friends in a city full of friends going to bars.

10

The following morning I went downstairs with my shoulder bag and a cup of coffee. I spent a few hours typing up what I had written in my notebooks. At half past two, I walked over to Hawthorne and waited for the next bus across the river. A man sitting in his car across the street rolled down his window and spit into the road. A beautiful young woman walked up and stood next to the shelter. She looked like a Portland version of Veronica Lake and her lipstick was perfect, red as blood when it escapes a wound.

The 14 was crowded all the way down the aisle. We rode it across the calm river and the tires made the bridge plates hum. I disembarked near Pioneer Square and walked down Sixth Avenue. My boots drummed the cement as I passed a celebration of bad sculpture and a shoelace masquerading as a worm. I found the bus stop I was looking for but the line didn't operate on Saturdays; I tore up my plans and walked on. Crossing into the Pearl District I covered block after block with the gray afternoon wrapped around me. There were gorgeous old buildings to look up at that had been built by men that time had turned into ghosts. I imagined them watching passersby through the leaded glass windows and thought of the girl who looked like Veronica Lake in a flannel shirt. Where had she ended up? Why had she looked so sad? Knowing we would never cross paths again I put her out of my mind and walked on.

My revised plan was to end up in the basement bar of the Hotel Glass but it seemed too early to be drinking beer--- especially at my new workplace. Hungry and broke, I stopped in the McDonalds up Burnside; the only Mickey D's between the Pearl and Trendy-Third, it seemed to be a refuge for all the homeless people in the area. The guy in front of me was only in his mid-twenties but on the path to death. He was either drunk or really stoned and struggling through his order. I got my cheeseburger and walked until the crowds fell away and I was alone. Pulling the burger out of the bag, I stared at a parking lot that was once one of the most beautiful homes in Portland as I ate.

It still felt too early to stop by the bar but I needed a bathroom so I went into Powell's. The restroom was full so I browsed the medical section and found a fascinating book on the history of opium. Still needing a bathroom, I left the bookstore and walked up eleventh; I must have walked a mile just killing time. Deciding that four would be an okay time to get a beer, I went back to the hotel bar only to order ice tea. The bathroom had these funky old urinals that had been around since the days of Al Capone. I closed my eyes and tried to time slip but got nowhere.

I spent maybe an hour in the bar and then walked up to Salmon to catch the 15 with no destination in mind. It had become a game I played of just hopping from bus to bus and seeing where I ended up. I alighted at Belmont and Grand in an area that was trying to look industrial but was actually pricey and geared towards hipsters with money.

Looking at the menus on restaurant windows I was reminded of that shoelace masquerading as a worm.

It was misting but I had already gotten in that Portland frame of mind where you ignore the weather. I walked down Hawthorne to 25th and then over to Division. Seeing the Reel 'M' Inn Tavern, it seemed as good a destination as any. The bartender was an attractive woman in her mid twenties wearing a gray t-shirt. She wasn't beautiful like a model; her beauty was casual like her clothes. I alternated between PBR and water and got three chapters written. A large group of people were eating and the food smelled really good; it smelled like the sort of greasy, meaningless food that you crave after walking all day. The men's bathroom was tiny, the toilet being in an area the size of a phone booth. Someone had written "Does anyone shit here?" and I realized that I had wondered that as well. Back at my table I finished my beer and understood that it was time to move on.

It was dark out and lightly raining. The streets shined like dark mirrors you look into when everything is going in circles. A guy walking the other way had looked at me funny so I listened for his footsteps changing direction. Walking up Division I passed more windows full of happy people eating expensive food and felt like a ghost. My path led down a shortcut through a park; it was poorly lit but I didn't feel unsafe.

The rain had stopped by the time I turned up Hawthorne. I walked west to use the bathroom at the new Safeway.

Relieved, I crossed the hill only to end up at the Vern again. There was a beautiful woman in a black dress standing near the bar. She wasn't beautiful like a model or a trophy wife who used to be a model, she was just cute like a girl you see across a room or a co-worker you have a crush on but never figure out what to say to them. I sipped my whiskey and then sipped a beer and then sipped another beer. Every so often I'd look over at that girl in the black dress talking to her friends and find myself wishing I was someone else, someone who can just talk to people and not come across as awkward or weird. I was not that person and I understood that maybe I would never be.

I didn't get any writing done at the Vern. Instead, I drank too much and then went back to the house to drink some more. My dreams were weird and made even less sense than usual.

11

The next morning should have hurt more than it did. I slept
in late out of indulgence, not over-indulgence. I left the
house around three and walked down Belmont. The
hipsters were out en masse to enjoy the sunny afternoon.
The young woman behind the wheel of the 15 bus was
really cute and had a nose stud. I rode down to the
Washington/Stark neighborhood not far from 82nd. There
was nothing interesting on Washington, just some industrial
buildings and a store that sold foam. I continued down to
82nd which had been one of the main north-south highways
through town before it was made obsolete by Interstate 205.
The used car lots and cheap restaurants were the only signs
that it had once been a valued thoroughfare; everything
looked run down and shabby. The immigrants had taken
advantage of the marked down real estate and made their
livings with a determined wariness. I looked up and down
the street for a couple of minutes before walking up Stark
to where there were a few interesting shops and bars.
Caught up in the joys of discovery, I felt twenty years
younger than I was and forty years younger than I had felt
in Lodi.

I walked up Yamhill through the residential neighborhoods
on the north side of Mount Tabor. At the top of the hill, I
caught the 15 down Belmont to a liquor store with a sign
that I had been meaning to photograph. The light was
wrong to get the shot so I settled for going inside to buy a
bottle of water. There was an Al Stewart song coming over

the cheap PA that I had always meant to use in a movie and the clerk behind the counter looked too young to sell beer. I walked out singing "Year of the Cat" to myself, opening my mind to all the weirdness and magic laying beautiful traps in the future.

The streets south of Belmont were narrow and reminded me of pictures of European cities. Coming to Hawthorne, I decided to take the 14 down to check out the food carts on Foster. A girl wearing a scarf covered with peace signs was interviewing people at a bus stop for a college project. She asked me a couple of questions about Mount Tabor but since I hadn't been in town that long I didn't have much to say. The girl was willowy and pale; she was talkative but it seemed more a nervous habit than natural friendliness. Silences seemed to bother her: Those moments when the conversation died she'd look out into the distance for the bus; I tried to be thoughtful by doing the same.

Getting off the bus I was feeling awkward as if that girl's nervousness had rubbed off on me. Walking around the food carts, I thought about checking out the menus but that would have required getting close to the carts which may have led to the people inside talking to me. Feeling deflated, I walked up to Taco Time. The cashier had an enormous afro that was easily a foot high. I sat in a booth and looked across the parking lot at a topless bar that had been painted purple. After finishing my soft taco I jumped back on the 14 heading west. The willowy girl was on board and smiled when she saw me. I didn't sit next to her; I could tell that she was just being friendly and didn't want to be presumptuous by sharing her seat. I got off at Division and walked a couple of blocks down the road to a transit stand. The buses were running late so I walked for a bit, waited a bit, got bored, and kept walking. When the bus finally came I took it ten blocks south before disembarking to walk west through more old neighborhoods.

The Clinton district was tiny, comprising two bars and half a dozen shops. Two people were kissing outside of the bar I had been thinking of checking out. Not wanting to break their moment, I kept walking south. I ended up at the Reel 'M' Inn but it was happy hour so the place was packed. I was concerned that if I walked in there wouldn't be any place to sit and there'd be nothing left to do but stand there looking lost before walking out like a fool. I looked up at the sign for a few moments before continuing on. It was getting dark by that point. After using the bathroom in Safeway I walked over the hill to the Bare Bones Bar. It was still happy hour so I was able to get a cheap beer and a small table to make plans at. The hard blonde bartender was working that night. Something about the way she treated me made me feel small; it was nothing she said or even did, it was just a feeling. Some people just make you feel small or maybe they're just a hard surface reflecting how you see yourself. I don't know why I kept going back to the Bare Bones, especially since it was too dim for reading or writing. There was the bartender who looked like Britney Murphy but she didn't seem to work that often. I hung out there for an hour or so, squinting at a Sam Cooke biography as I sipped my beer.

It was still too early to go back to the house so I walked over to Mulligan's. The gorgeous bartender was there, not the Spanish Italian looking one but the white one. I was going to try and get some writing done but *The Walking Dead* was on and I got sucked in. I was back at the house around nine. Part of me wanted to keep drinking until I went to bed but I struggled against that desire. I had a small glass of wine and then forced myself to make herbal tea to sip in bed as I read myself to sleep.

12

I woke up around four thirty and understood that closing my eyes would be futile. How much sleep had I actually gotten? Four hours? I started reading a library book and fell asleep after maybe twenty minutes. The next time I looked at the clock it was nearly nine and I could hear the piano through the vents. I couldn't remember the last time I had heard Noah play---had it been ten years? I wanted to go downstairs to hear it better but didn't want to intrude. I know in the past that he has played music when his mind is blocked; I've done the same when I can't write. Noah was working by the time I brought him coffee, the piano closed up and put in the past. I wanted him to be a musical genius again; it made me sad that such a great gift was allowed to lie dormant. Some people are engineered for music and my best friend was one of them.

Three hours later I was walking into the hotel for another shift. My new job was very physical: Wrestling with dumpsters, mopping, and going out in the rain to sweep up dozens of cigarette butts. The worst chore involved a machine I called the Backpack of Peril. It was a vacuum that you wore using shoulder straps so you could sweep the stairs. It only weighed about ten pounds but felt heavier after half an hour of climbing staircases while vacuuming and wrestling with a fifty foot extension cord. I also had thirteen bathrooms to clean; I quickly learned that wearing plastic gloves was not optional.

My third day was the first time that I heard fucking in one of the rooms. It excited me and I wanted to linger near the door but my trainer showed up unexpectedly. There was a moment of embarrassment while I wondered if she understood what I had been doing. Kate's expression was unreadable as I tried to play it off as if I was shocked and disgusted by the sounds coming from the room. She shrugged and got a towel from the closet.

"You'll hear a lot of that," she said. "Better get used to it."

During the eight hours I was there I only had one five minute break. Kate was a hard worker, didn't take breaks herself, and consequently I didn't take them either while she was training me. On the plus side, I got a set amount of money towards food depending on how many hours I worked. Since I had worked a full shift I got enough to buy a cheeseburger and fries. When my order came up I took it to a booth by a window and watched the tourists walking by as I ate.

13

The days I worked the morning shift always started with me wrestling dumpsters onto the lift. My fourth morning on the job, someone from the kitchen had dumped a couple of gallons of sour cream in the compost bin. It took Kate and I an hour to clean that rancid sour cream out. My body was slowly adjusting to the physical demands of the job--- slowly. I definitely felt my age the first week or two. I had to wake up at 5:30 and usually ended up running the five blocks to the bus stop. I brought in the dumpsters, swept the cigarette butts off the sidewalks, and ran up and down stairs all day. We cleaned bathrooms and mopped; I had forgotten how physical mopping is. Three hours into the shift I was always ravenous; hungry like I have been few times in my life. The first couple of weeks I only ordered a cheeseburger and fries and always sat in the same booth by the window.

Back then, I was still in love with the Hotel Glass and enjoyed all the eccentric decorations and angles. The history of the building was unusual and told by pictures that had been hung all over the hotel: Underworld figures. Drag queens. Hippies with proto hipster beards. People having sex in a Jeep parked in the basement. Some of the pictures were quite risqué and I was amazed to be working for a company that would put them up.

Wresting the dumpsters through the basement was always an awful chore. The space was very tight and you had to move things to allow them passage. Despite that and trying to sweep up cigarette butts in the rain and the overused elevator, I still fell in love with the job. Realizing that scared me when I remembered what had happened with jobs that I had fallen for in the past. Maybe things would be different working for the hotel, maybe my life was turning around; I wanted to think so.

As we worked Kate would tell me horror stories about drunk people vomiting and shitting where they shouldn't--- things she promised that I would eventually face...
"It will happen to you, Ike; you'll see. You'll be checking a stairway or a room and there will be shit on a wall or in a waste basket. I had that happen a couple of times and on both occasions they put the trash can in the stairwell--- maybe they didn't like it stinking up the room."
I would smile and laugh at her stories but inside I was shuddering and hoping that sort of thing *wouldn't* happen on my shifts.

The free meals were nice but I was even more pleased that I got along with all of my co-workers, even Willy Gilly. WG was surly and acted old enough to have been around when hair was invented. He didn't look that old, he just *seemed* old like a rock reluctantly coming to life to express its doubts and opinions. His voice was like gravel being pushed through molasses by a bullfrog; I struggled not to laugh every time I heard him talking down the radio.

Since I hadn't slept much the night before I was dead on my feet by the end of my fourth shift. Despite that, I was

49

determined to get some writing done before the night was through. There was a bar called Holman's that I had passed many times while walking down 28th. During the walk there I listened to Stevie Wonder and kept looking up at the darkening sky. On the corner of 28th and Anekey, I saw a drunk guy in a leather jacket talking to a woman with a dog.

"Is that a yellow lab? Is that...a yellow lab?" He slurred. The woman was smiling but she looked unsure what to do or say. I watched them for a moment before heading into Holman's. It was dark inside and smelled like old wood. I bought a beer, found an empty booth, and wrote down what I remembered about my day at work. Despite how physically demanding the job was I couldn't help but feel awestruck---I had a job in Portland, I was *really living* in Portland.

14

The next day I got to meet another of the housekeepers and I could have sworn that she was flirting with me. Sara was around thirty with reddish hair that was always pulled back. She had a great smile---and was married. S had lived in Sacramento so we chatted about our hometown. *Was* she flirting with me? It would have been amazing if she had even if nothing came of it. I found myself daydreaming about her as I vacuumed and stocked closets.

I was finding manual labor preferable to working in offices. For one thing, the returns were tangible: Bathrooms and floors were clean, the sidewalks were free of butts, and the linen closets were stocked all because of my work. In an office, the results of all your efforts remain unclear or abstract; you never see the end result that you played a small part in---it's all papers with numbers and words that mean nothing to you.

When I finished my shift I got my usual cheeseburger in the cafe. After eating, I walked up to Salmon to catch a crowded 15 bus back across the river. Thinking about Sara led me to thinking about JB and all the idiotic, moon-eyed things I had done the year before. I was ashamed of how weak and stupid I had been, falling for a married woman and allowing myself to be her last resort. One reason I had gone to Portland was to make it impossible to spend time with JB. She wasn't a bad person, just lost, and I let myself get equally lost in a foolish, unrequited crush. It was good being alone. Maybe I'd get lonely and horny, but in the end I understood that relationships were messy and got in the way of good things like writing.

Back at the house I took a shower and tried to figure out where I wanted to go for the night. After throwing my bag over my shoulder, I just started walking. The Triple Nickel on Belmont seemed as good a place as any so I went in and found a table. Even though it was a Saturday it felt like a weekday because I had to be at work early the next morning. All the other patrons were getting their debauchery on while I understood that I had to call it a night by 10:30. The bartender was cute but surly, a sexy frown of a girl in a red vest. Someone was playing dreadful rap on the jukebox including a track apparently named "Get Stupid." Maybe it's meant to be ironic but that could have been wishful thinking. There was a really pretty girl across the bar. When her friend got up to use the bathroom she immediately busied herself with her phone. Part of me was wondering why I never had the guts to walk over and talk to girls like that; another part of me realized that she was nearly young enough to be my daughter. I went back to writing in my notebook and nursing my beer.

Twenty minutes later I ordered another beer and immediately regretted the decision. Why was I sticking around that bar? The music on the jukebox had somehow gotten worse. Why was I still in the Triple Nickel? I felt old and out of touch. I finished my beer in a hurry, packed up my notebooks, and left.

Heading back down Belmont, I walked past the street I usually took to the house. There was a bodega in the mid-twenties that I had never been inside but was curious about. The clerk was in his 20s and surly, even his mustache had an attitude. I grabbed a 24 ounce beer that looked like it had a high alcohol content and paid in coins. Life was coming together, things were a lot more positive than they had been in a long time, but I was still me. My mother always told me that I couldn't escape myself no matter where I went; I always smirked and made fun of her for saying that but I understood that she was right. I am Black Irish, my own worst enemy, haunted by whatever I choose to be haunted by. Back at the house I climbed into bed with a Sam Cooke biography and my beer; it took a long time to fall asleep.

15

The next night I returned to Mulligan's. It had become one of my routines to show up on nights I knew the gorgeous Spanish-Italian bartender worked. I found her attractive but understood that I couldn't flirt with her; I didn't want to be another asshole trying to get in her pants. Looking back, I thought I was being cool and respectful but she probably saw right through me. I ordered a double Jameson and then a single Jameson as I wrote in my notebooks. Al Green was playing over the stereo followed by a singer who sounded like Fiona Apple. All around me were strangers surrounded by friends. It didn't bother me at all; solitude was serving me well. Something worthwhile inside me was emerging despite or maybe in harmony with my lecherous thoughts.

Noah was still working when I got back to the house. I tip-toed down the stairs and got on the Mac, checking out cars on Craigslist as I sipped a beer. After a few minutes, he came over and sat at the piano. I asked him how his work was going and he rolled his eyes and told me about how difficult his client was.
"Heard you playing the other morning," I said. "It sounded good."
"I was just messing around."
"It sounded really good."
He took a drink from a beer he had brought over and looked thoughtful.
"I've been thinking about a part I never could get right when I was making the album," Noah said.

"I thought it was familiar," I replied. "I never knew why you didn't record it back then, it always sounded great to me."

"There's a part in the middle, two notes that I never have gotten quite right."

I could never hear any bad notes, but I am not Noah. He could hear a few seconds of a song and ten years later play back the damned thing and probably improve on it.

"Man, my singing must have driven you nuts back in the day," I said.

He just smiled. We both knew the truth but Noah was not about to say anything unkind.

"It worked for the Eulogy," he said.

"I guess, I still cringe, though."

The Eulogy was our electronic band in the late eighties. We made a few demos, played a gig or two at shitty little clubs around San Rafael---Noah was already planning the Album. They recorded it in '93 but he had been tinkering with it for a few years. He would have stayed in the Eulogy if I had asked but I didn't; I knew he wanted to do something else. It would have been fun to be a part of the music he was writing but we both knew I wasn't a good enough singer or bassist. Noah eventually found a rhythm section that could play what he had in mind and ran into Chase at our local Safeway.

"I've been talking to a guitarist and drummer about maybe getting together," my friend said after another drink off his beer.

"That's good, you should do it."

"Yeah, it could be good," he said quietly. "I've missed playing."

Noah fiddled with the label on his beer bottle, something he did when he was trying to figure out how to articulate an idea in his head or how much of that idea he wanted to share. The door to the kitchen opened and Anne came down to ask when Noah was coming to bed. He looked over at the clock, commented on how late it had gotten, and then bade me good night. I watched them walk up the stairs and then took another drink. There was always envy in my heart, pumping away like a machine in the dark. I had been playing music erratically for thirty years, sent demos to labels and all that---it had never panned out, not at all. Noah, on the other hand, had been signed to a major label. They dropped the band when the album failed to chart or sell but for five months Noah had achieved what most of us aspiring musicians can only dream of. I envied him for it, but never resented him for achieving what he had...

Maybe I also always envied his ability to walk away from something when he understood it had run its course.

16

After a week on the job I learned how to strip rooms:
Taking out the trash, gathering up the bed linens and
towels, and removing any glasses and plates. All 67 rooms
were booked Friday and Saturday and someone had called
in sick. Short staffed, management drafted Kate and I in to
help. I didn't mind, it kept things interesting for me. It was
hard work but enjoyable; I still loved working at the Hotel
Glass and took pride in my work. March was the golden
age of my time there.

At one point I was helping Willy Gilly by stocking his
rooms. He had a lamp with a dead bulb out so I ran down to
the basement to get a replacement. When I got back he had
taken the lamp apart and was dusting it. Devoting his time
to such minutiae seemed ludicrous considering how many
rooms we had to turn over.
"People don't care," he said flatly. "I don't think this lamp
has ever been dusted right."
"We're short staffed; no one has the time."
I was getting antsy---I needed him to put the lamp back
together so I could replace the bulb and then hurry on to the
next room. Willy was in no rush, he moved slowly like the
antique elevator the hotel depended on.
"Things got too fast, man," WG drawled. "Why do we
hurry so much? Life'll be over before you know it."
"Hey, I've got to stock your other rooms, but here's the
bulb when you put the lamp back together."

I ran off before he could respond. The funny thing was that Willy Gilly kept up with the other housekeepers despite the fact he got engrossed in little things. It was a reminder that grass grows whether you can see it moving towards the sun or not.

There was a room for rent six blocks from Noah and Anne's. It was $400 a month---my absolute maximum---but in a great area. I made an appointment to see it after work and felt excited about the possibility of finding a place in a neighborhood I loved. The house was bright purple but in that part of town a calculated sort of quirkiness was the norm. Walking in, however, I knew that I would not be living there: The owner of the house was a hoarder---a hoarder who seemed to be trying (and failing) to mix six or so very different design themes. The house was a mess inside and the punch line was that the owner was unemployed. Whomever rented the room would be sharing a bath with this lady and her teenage son. Looking in, I was horrified to see that there were more than half a dozen bath towels on the racks and draped haphazardly over the shower curtain. It reminded me of all the smelly boy towels in the last house I rented a room in. I felt bad because she was a nice enough lady; when I texted her back I told her that I was house-sitting for three months. It was a cowardly ploy but I hadn't wanted to risk hurting her feelings.

I took a shower, changed my clothes, and went back to Mulligan's. The Spanish-Italian bartender was there but she stayed on the other end of the bar talking to other customers. Sometimes it's clear when people are not remotely interested in you and that bartender was definitely not interested in me. I would have been happy photographing her, but even that would have involved a conversation she probably didn't want any part of. That in mind, I was friendly but did not attempt to engage her. She seemed nice, a decent person, definitely deserving better than being hit on by people she didn't want hitting on her.

17

The next night I walked all around Sunnyside and ended up in this Mexican restaurant by mistake. I immediately realized my error but before I could walk out a friendly bartender was waving me over to the bar and I didn't want to be rude. Climbing onto one of the stools, I made the classic error of ordering a martini in a Mexican restaurant. The bartender looked barely out of his teens and was nervous about mixing drinks so I tried to gently guide him through it. A woman with garish orange hair who looked around sixty was sitting a couple of stools over. She was drunk and attempting to flirt with the young bartender. When she heard what I ordered she turned to give me the once over twice.

"Gin--that used to be my drink," she slurred. "I had to learn how to like it; they had this special at this bar near my house, two martinis for two dollars. I hated it at first, but came to like it. You know, you can mix anything with gin---except Coke..."

She went on and on about how she had turned all her friends into gin drinkers and I was beginning to wonder if she was hitting on me. Mercifully, she turned her attention back to the bartender after a couple of minutes. It was one of times it felt good to have a woman give me the cold shoulder.

The barfly was creeping me out so I walked over to Hawthorne and hopped on the 14 up to Cesar Chavez. I had no idea where I was going, all I knew was that I was seeking a bar without garish orange hair and training wheel martinis. There was Tom's Bar near Division, but it was clearly a sports bar and something about the name bothered me. Tom's---sounded like a sausage fest; Tom and his middle-aged buddies sitting around yelling at sports on an oversized television. I kept walking until I was at the Reel 'M' Inn. It was crowded, as every bar in Portland seemed to be, but I was tired of walking and found a place to sit and drink beer alone.

18

Goose Hollow is a small neighborhood tucked in a crook of Highway 405. I went there to look at a room and got lost, wandering the---(to me)---confusing warren of streets for fifteen minutes. The area reminded me of San Francisco, maybe because of the hills. Eventually I found the apartment building and texted someone named Kelsey. She buzzed me in and I made my way down a narrow hall, through a beat up door, and down a flight of stairs. The basement felt like a womb and I couldn't tell if it was a cozy womb or a claustrophobic one. Kelsey was in her mid twenties and friendly as she showed me around the dark apartment. Her boyfriend sat sullenly on the couch doing something on his laptop and didn't say a word as I looked around. He made me feel like an interloper and maybe I was: Enjoying the company of his girlfriend as I walked through the rooms they ate, watched TV, and fucked in. There were exposed pipes and my potential roommates were semi-militant vegetarians but the price is right and I could have walked to work. Kelsey was braless and I struggled not to stare at the outline of her small breasts. The room she showed me had a chalkboard on the wall and I distracted myself from her flimsy shirt by imagining all the notes and ideas and drawings I could sketch on it. I could have lost myself in that chalkboard; I could have drank whiskey and given myself over to ideas. A chalkboard wall---why had I never thought of that before? After checking out the room, Kelsey and I shook hands and she promised to call or text within a couple of days.

It was a beautiful afternoon so I walked a couple of miles across the downtown area. There was a phone booth on 17th so I took a couple of shots of it, taking time to find the best light and frame it properly. Portland still felt new to me, like I was a tourist and not a resident there; it was still unreal to me that I had a job and was looking for a room to rent after the failures of the year before. Every bus ride and walk between MAX stops felt like an adventure and I carried my camera everywhere. I took pictures of abandoned shoes on Yamhill and a bar a block east of them named the Yamhill Pub. JB and I had met there a year earlier, spending an hour drinking as we watched *Walker Texas Ranger*. Neither of us had any idea how our lives would be intertwined in the months that followed, at least I didn't. I had a deep crush on her but was prepared to keep it to myself, not let it get out of hand. How we delude ourselves.

I barely caught the next 15 over the river and ended up at the Belmont Inn. I ordered a PBR and walked around the bar looking for a promising spot to write. The window next to the sidewalk revealed apartments over the shops and bars and boutiques across the street. I found myself wondering what it'd be like to live in a flat like that, looking out on all that life and motion. I thought again about Kelsey with her thin shirts and grumpy looking boyfriend, the pros and cons of sharing such an intimate space with them. As I sat there tapping my pen on my notebook I imagined waiting to cook bacon until they were at work and then indulged in a fantasy of fucking K on the kitchen counter as their cat watched. The vibe in the Belmont was never right. I closed my eyes with the taste of beer in my mouth as I waited for inspiration. None came that night---not at the Belmont Inn, at least. After finishing my beer I walked a couple of miles and ended up at another bar with another PBR in front of me. I sketched out a new chapter of the book but wasn't happy with it.

Disappointed with the night's writing, I slung my bag over my shoulder and started walking. It was still too early to go back to the house so I just picked a direction and went in it. I passed beautifully restored houses with Subarus and Priuses in front of them. People with grown up jobs and ski racks and mortgages lived there---were they happy? Did they enjoy their newer cars and lovely homes? I couldn't even think about that sort of life, I was enjoying my freedom: Casual job, no one in my life, and no house or even apartment to look after. My life following the Crash had completely changed how I wanted to live. Prior to 2008, Teresa and I had done the things young, married couples tended to do: We looked at houses to buy, haunting the newer developments around Sacramento and eventually Phoenix. The two of us would earnestly sit on our bed with a calculator trying to figure out the maximum mortgage we could afford if our jobs didn't lay us off. We bought furniture and accumulated televisions and appliances. We paid thousands of dollars and sold them for hundreds. That money could have been used for travel or other life enriching experiences. I couldn't see that then---I like to think of myself above such foolishness but I fell for the American Dream like all the other suckers out there. The

Crash and the hardships that followed were a beautiful curse, a trying time that gave me so much. I was technically homeless and infrequently employed but it opened my mind to what was genuinely important to me. I found that I could be the happiest man in the world with everything I owned contained in a suitcase or even the two dollar camera bag I had bought at Goodwill. I had no idea minimalism could be so liberating. Honestly, it was fucking addictive. Once I had taken care of the debts that had been hounding me for several years I didn't want a car payment or a mortgage or credit card bills. Maybe I would live in a van and take jobs where the warm weather was, saving money for a little piece of land in the middle of nowhere to build a hermit shack. There I would write, have a cat, and---most definitely---a chalkboard wall.

Still happy with my vision of a rough shack out in the boonies, I crept into the house as silently as possible. The night ended as most of them did back then, reading with a drink on the nightstand. I took my clothes off, climbed under the covers, and marveled over how alive and inspired I felt. Beneath that was a melody in a minor key, the struggle of figuring out how to make my dreams and goals work out. Could I ever hold a real job? Could I ever hold my end up in a relationship? Did I even *want* another relationship? My marriage had felt claustrophobic. There were times I deeply loved Teresa and appreciated our life together but a lot of the time I felt trapped and resentful; nobody deserves that. Beyond that, '12 had been the year where I had completely given myself to a life where doing "art" was everything whether it was writing or playing music or taking photographs---how did another human being fit into that? I was nearly certain that I couldn't go back to a life where creativity was neatly contained in small blocks of time; I had allowed myself to become possessed by a wild beast that was always hungry and wanting to run. Lying in bed that night I thought about Kelsey and JB and other women I had crushes on or simply fantasized about. What did I really want from them? More importantly, what could I offer them?

19

The mornings I worked played back like a loop: Coffee.
Run for the bus. Familiar faces onboard. Staring out at the
gentle ripples on the Willamette as we crossed the bridge.
Sleepy homeless people downtown. Grabbing more coffee
in the cafe. Dumpsters. I was starting to take having a job
for granted; I could feel myself shifting from "wow" to "so
what." Was it a sign of recovery or something I should
have felt guilty about? One of the managers went from
room to room resetting the door locks; something to do
with daylight savings time. Sara needed a queen sized
spread so I took it to the room she was turning over. S
always got this look on her face when she saw me, a shy
sort of smile. I wondered if she had a thing for me but
understood that it was probably just wishful thinking. I felt
guilty for wanting a married woman but there was
something about her. It was like my situation with JB
before she separated from husband but only in my sense of
longing; JB and Sara were very different people. It was a
similar situation in that I was focusing all my longing and
desire on a woman who didn't want or need it.
I was in a new town but I was still an old fool.

An attractive couple checked in and I heard them fucking
an hour or so later. I listened to them for a while and then
spent some time in the bathroom. I thought about Sara and
other women that I knew which led to me dwelling on how
alone I really was. I wanted a woman in my life to be close
to and fuck and everything else, but I also understood that

there was a price for all those things. I also had the
suspicion that maybe I was too selfish and set in my ways
ever to be genuinely giving in a relationship.

Interlude One
(There Was a Girl)

Her name was Renee and she was in her mid-twenties. I
met her during my first attempt to live in Portland: She was
renting a room and I answered her ad. In the end, she
picked another potential roommate and I went on to my
cold room in Foster-Powell. I hadn't forgotten her, though,
and still had her phone number when I returned in '13. I
was nervous as hell when I called her. Fortunately, she was
glad to hear from me and we arranged to go out. Renee was
cute in a nerdy way and highly intelligent. We went out for
drinks a couple of times, walked around in the cold, and
then---
And then I blew it or maybe I kind of blew it and she kind
of over-reacted. I wrote about our time together in my blog.
I didn't do something overtly stupid like admit how much I
was crushing on her, my mistake was using her real first
name and that of her friend. Renee saw that as a massive
breach of trust and that was that. It was a sad end to things,
but in the end it was for the best. In the scope of days, I was
crushed and hating myself for being so stupid. In the scope
of years, I learned a valuable lesson and it left me available
for someone who would have an effect on the rest of my
life.

20

"You doing anything right now?" Noah asked
I had been heating water to make coffee when he came upstairs.
"Just making coffee."
"I need a break from work---you want to go out and get some coffee?" He asked. "My treat."
"Yeah, sounds good."
We walked down the back street that ran parallel to Hawthorne. Noah looked preoccupied so I asked if he was doing okay.
"Yeah...it's just that project is a pain in the ass."
There was something else. With Noah I knew that he would share it once he figured out the best way to put it in words. He was not a *blabber*, when he spoke it was always very measured and well thought out.
"We should work on music soon," he said. "You said you had some ideas..."
"Yeah, that'd be great."
We walked another half block before he spoke again.
"I had a weird dream last night. We were on tour; I think it was around 2000 because Chase was wearing leather pants and a shiny shirt. It was a stadium, a big one, must have been ten thousand people."
"You've been thinking about the band a lot, haven't you?"
"Ever since you were having problems last summer," he said before pausing to collect his thoughts. "You are the most insanely creative person in my life; it seemed like the only thing keeping you together last year."

"It was," I admitted.

"You know some of the shit that went on when I was growing up---you had writing and music and I had computers and music. Sometimes I think that I was wrong to quit after Chase died after the label dropped us. Usually, though, I understand that it was what I was supposed to do---does that make sense?"

"Yeah, you wouldn't have met Anne for one thing."

"That's true. I don't know...this feels right, like it's the life I'm supposed to be living. I work for some complete dipshits but my work is very satisfying. I wonder, though, the whole *what if* thing. I miss music, too."

"No reason you can't be in a band or start one, even a casual sort of fucking around in the basement band."

"I know, I just wonder if it can *be* casual. With us---"

He paused again to figure out the best words for what was in his head. I know that, technically, I was holding him back when we were in the Eulogy. Noah is probably a musical genius whereas I am a musical simpleton.

"I loved what we did in the Eulogy," he said carefully. "I always thought your lyrics were amazing, but all those times we were writing songs it made me want to do more and more complex music, music the two of us couldn't play."

He was being nice, what he meant was music *I* couldn't play---or sing.

"I saw some guy who looked like Rivers Cuomo talking about the Album," I blurted out as I tend to just blurt things out. "He said you stopped doing music because you were in love with Chase."

Noah smirked and shook his head.

"People always want things to be more interesting than they really are," he said.

"Why you quit was pretty interesting."

"That's the thing, I never quit," Noah parried gently. "I may not be writing music or playing it, but I still think about it. Why is it that even though I understand that getting out of the business was what I was supposed to do I still play the *what if* game in my head?"

Noah gestured that we were passing the coffee shop he wanted to stop at, I followed him inside.

"You're a musician who wonders what would have happened if you had been successful," I pointed out. "I think that's pretty common."

Noah looked at me like I was an asshole, but in a loving way. We had gotten to the front of the line and a sour looking girl with a nose ring was staring at us expectantly. The two of us got our coffee and started walking back to the house. What had been a serious or at least meaningful conversation gave way to talking about politics and then lapsing into cruel but highly entertaining piss takes of movie stars. That was us: Two creative guys. Very close yet tight lipped. Dipping into serious conversations but quick to see things as getting too deep too dark and reverting to jokes and impersonations. Love and understanding---truly being in sync with another human being---has many guises.

That afternoon I worked my first swing shift without a trainer. Fortunately, it was a slow night so I was able to stay on top of things. I still loved my job and felt eager to please and consequently worked hard. The head auditor made a point of introducing himself when he clocked in at eleven. Larry was black, somewhere in his fifties, and prone to offering you an easy going chuckle as his eyes performed an autopsy: *I don't know you, but I'll figure you out.* I imagined him in the eighties smoking Kools and driving one of those Cadillac Sevilles with the bustlebacks. He'd glide around town with one relaxed hand on the wheel as he studied the crazies at the bus stops and the women moving purposefully down the sidewalk. Larry seemed like a man with a regular haunt, probably a pool hall where he'd hang out with his buddies and pick up women. Between the flint and the charm I knew there was a history there, I just didn't know him well enough to ask it. I didn't know him and I have always been timid about talking to people. *You're a writer and you can't talk to people, get their stories?*

Maybe that was another thing I needed to change. Maybe now that I was in a new town I needed to create a new me.

In training it had been explained to me that the pool had to be locked up at one. At a quarter to I told the guests still in the water that we'd be closing the pool in 15 minutes. I went upstairs and Larry asked why I had told the guests that they needed to get out; L looked offended and I was worried that I had stepped on his toes, quickly explaining to him about how I had been trained. Once the words were out of my mouth I ran downstairs to let the guests know that they didn't have to leave after all. One of the women had gotten out of the pool and was walking down the hall towards me, apologizing and looking embarrassed as she did so. I tried not to stare at the girl, how wet and beautiful

she was awkwardly holding a towel around herself. I had to
fight a long war just to pull some words together.
"No, I'm sorry; Larry and I had a miscommunication; you
guys can stay in there."
She was dripping water all over the floor and I thought of
how lucky that water was getting to know her skin if only
for a few moments. The girl smiled, thanked me, and
walked back to the pool. I watched her go, put my heart
back in my chest, and went to finish up for the night.

I was thinking about that young woman in the towel as I
walked to the bus stop. Downtown seemed deserted at that
time of night; desolate, very little traffic. I was nervous,
wondering if there would be a lot of aggressive homeless
people, but it wasn't bad at all. A drunk woman asked me
the time but fortunately that was all she needed. There were
three other people at the bus stop, each of us pretending
that there was no one else in the world. After turning away
from ghosts for ten minutes we boarded the last 14 crossing
the river and going up Hawthorne. Walking back to the
house it was so quiet it was hard to believe that I was in the
middle of a city. I contemplated just walking for a while,
taking in the calm, still streets, but it was late and I was
tired.

21

I had my second meeting with a potential model and it was a disaster. I should have seen it coming but I was caught up in my own desire. Keisha was black and in her mid-twenties, pretty but not fashion magazine pretty; pretty enough to charm small time boys and men like myself but not beautiful enough to bring the world or even a city like Portland to its knees. She had a nice figure, though, and it had distracted me from all the red flags popping up. K had all this talk about other models she wanted to hook me up with and how her brother's rap act needed promo shots but it was all just talk. When it came down to our appointment for taking shots in a park, K showed up late and completely unprepared. We drove around in her beat up Lexus for fifteen minutes as I scrambled to figure out how to salvage the shoot. She stopped for gas and probably expected me to pay. I was so irritated with her and curtly asked her to drop me off at the transit stop. I must have been radiating frustration because none of the homeless people asked me for money. Looking back, Keisha was not a bad person; she was just a woman who believed that she was pretty enough to get away with being thoughtless.

.

I got on the next train heading Downtown. A young woman sitting next to me laughed to herself from time to time; she was pretty but possibly mad. A nosy woman in a seat across the aisle instructed an old lady to take the seat next to her.

"I thought on public transportation you could sit wherever you wanted," Laughing Girl said to me.

Was she crazy or should I have chatted her up? She got off the train before I could decide.

I got off the train Downtown and started walking like a fury, covering block after block as I tried to work through my disappointment. Was I asking too much of the models? Maybe. I didn't have any money to pay them so what did I expect? Feeling hungry, I started looking for a cheap place where I could sit down and take some notes. I ended up at a Quizmos on Burnside near 18th. The place was empty until a girl came in and asked to use the bathroom. The manager told her that they were for customers only. Part of me thought the manager was being a hard ass but I also knew that there were a lot of homeless people in the neighborhood who tended to camp out in bathrooms. Maybe, remembering how close to being homeless I had been, I should have bought that girl a drink so she would have been a customer. I probably owed such acts of generosity to my fellow man considering how kind people had been to me. I couldn't see that at the time, though; I was in a deep red fog moving a pen rapidly over paper.

All the rooms at the Hotel Glass were booked that night. It was my first Friday dealing with drunken people but luckily I had a lot of practice with that sort of thing growing up. I had to shush two drunken women who were jumping up and down in the elevator. The blonde was far gone and had gotten kicked out of a music venue down the street. Since that was her reason for being in town she insisted on being refunded for her room. Front Desk refrained from pointing out that she was a drunken lunatic and granted her request. FD then asked me to straighten the room out so we could sell it that night. I had never made up a room before so I missed a few things. I apologized to Front Desk but they just shrugged it off.

Halfway through my shift, I got a cheeseburger and tater tots. I ate in the empty dining room of the cafe as I looked out at the nightlife moving up and down Burnside. Around 11 I did the property walk and kept breaking from sweeping up cigarette butts to take in the sky and surrounding buildings. It was a beautiful night and I had one of those moments where I realized that I was a lot happier than I had been working in offices. In every job there are challenging things and personalities, but I was on my own a lot; as long as things got done no one bothered me. Doing one of my last floor walks I heard my first vomiting coming from one of the rooms and hoped I would be off the clock before they called the front desk.

I got the last bus across the river at two in the morning. I loved seeing the city when there was very little traffic (mostly cabs) and sporadic people (often drunk) out on the sidewalk. Seeing small groups of people laughing and talking, I thought of my friends in Sacramento; all those nights we would stumble around the downtown area after the bars had closed. Now everyone had mortgages and kids and had settled into "normal" adult lives---everyone but me. They posted pictures of their backyards and children on Facebook and I posted my weird ramblings and rants. My friends had become adults; I was still somewhere else and probably always would be. I had been married and planning on having kids but neither had come to pass. It had been sad, but it had also been a relief. I have always understood who I am and what I am supposed to be doing; you can't be that inflexible when you have a family. I was turning all that over and over in my head as the last 20 bus pulled up. It was as crowded as any commuter. When the bike racks on the front were full the driver let bicyclists take the wheelchair spaces. I got off across the street from Chopsticks and walked the mile or so back to the house. Despite how late it was, the weather was surprisingly warm. I started getting hopeful about Spring and didn't mind setting myself up for disappointment.

22

I had been a fool the year before and was still a fool. I had left JB 650 miles to the south but she had followed me to Portland. Whenever I saw a foolish man in a bar pawing at the hems of a cavalier woman's skirt it brought back memories of the two of us. I was creating a new life, hopefully a saner one, but I still had feelings for JB no matter how much I denied them. The wall I had been building between us had dissolved when I discovered that she had cancer. How could I not be there for her when she was fighting something like that? I had been looking for an excuse to be a fool again and JB's body gave it to me. I sent her postcards and photographs of cherry blossoms. She sent me risqué selfies. One was a revealing shot of her in a tank top: She was lying on the bed as she held the camera at arm's length; her nipples visible through the thin fabric. In the next picture she was topless. When I asked why she had sent the pictures JB explained that it was to show how much weight she had lost. Having no idea what to make of the situation I got a beer, went over some other business on-line, and then looked at the pictures again. Maybe she had sent them because she was going through a tough time fighting cancer and wanted to feel desired and beautiful. Or, maybe she was trying to wound me for complicating her life and loving her when she didn't feel that she deserved love. I knew it was some sort of game; I just had no idea why JB wanted to play it with me. I wasn't the man she wanted; I was just a drinking buddy, someone to watch her purse while she walked off with some guy in the hopes of getting laid. I had played the fool then and those selfies reminded me of my mastery of that role.

I forced myself to put JB out of my mind to focus on finding a room. In the space of a year rents had gone up and applying for a place had become more challenging. What I had hoped would be a simple process had ended up being frustrating as I navigated ads full of regulations that hinted at complex and finicky personalities. More than a few of the ads had clearly been pecked out by vegans teetering between pretension and insanity. Most of the places that I inquired about didn't get back to me. One that did insisted on a phone interview so I spent ten minutes walking around Fred Meyer trying to have an upbeat chat with a crazy girl. She asked all these asinine questions and used up my phone time only to shoot me down without any courtesy. I was not a wacky vegetarian with a beard and a laid back smile; I was a suspicious and cynical Californian. The more ads I answered the more I realized that as much as I loved Portland, I didn't fit in. I was Lou Reed to their Tiny Tim. The more I dealt with Craigslist ads the less I wanted to spend a few hundred a month to live in a house with people I couldn't stand and probably would feel uncomfortable living with me. Maybe it was time to reconsider an old idea and live in a van.

It was too early for karaoke so I went to Mulligan's. The Spanish/Italian looking bartender was friendly but clearly not into me. Sometimes I thought about leaving a poem or haiku under my tip but understood that it would come across as creepy. What could I add to her life? I understood that I was too self-consumed to bring any beauty into it so I just sat there sipping my beer as I wrote in my notebooks. The bartender was always talking to customers on the other end of the bar---strangers...the world was full of strangers and I had no idea how to change that or even if I wanted to. I had always been a loner, even when I was married; we had been two loners forging some weird yet tender alliance. There had been a period of a few years when I ran with a group of friends, but that was five years out of forty-five. I had no interest in running with another crowd. As fond as my memories of the people I had known in Sacramento were, I knew that sort of thing was in the past for me.

I was still thinking about that bartender as I walked to Chopsticks. The usual characters were there doing their usual songs; every karaoke junkie has songs they feel they do well and they do them to death. Some guys sat at my table during one of my songs despite the fact my bag and beer were sitting there. What can you do in those situations? Get in an argument or a fight just because some guys took your table? I pointed out that they had stolen my table but either they didn't hear me or chose to ignore me. My dark angel told me to throw a beer in the closest one's face but I wisely decided to ignore him.

23

It was another rainy evening in Portland and I was looking for a place to kill time. My black Chuck Taylors had started to leak; I could feel my socks getting wet as I walked down the wet sidewalks. Turning down Hawthorne, the rain turned into a downpour so I ducked into the Backdoor Lounge. The Bushmills I ordered was expensive but it was an interesting place: The windows were open in such a way that one wall disappeared which meant that people could smoke inside. I sat next to a heater in the hope of my socks drying out. The bar was in the back of the Baghdad Theater which I had heard was haunted. According to the stories people had told me, the basement was so creepy none of the employees would go down there.

Like an idiot I went back to the Triple Nickel for a Pabst. I had no idea why I kept going back to that place; the bartender was a cold fish, not rude, just cold and completely detached from her customers. I got sucked into an action movie playing on one of the televisions and wrote another chapter in the book. The rain never let up and the walk between bars was brutally cold; I was shivering and hugging myself as I felt water leak into my shoes. I still loved Portland then, I was still seeing the shimmering aura of an amazing place, but I was beginning to wonder if I wanted to spend my winters there.

24

The cafe attached to the Hotel Glass was a separate business and yet it wasn't; it was an ambiguous arrangement that one of the managers of the cafe took advantage of. He was under the impression that he could boss me around. The one time I pointed out that I worked for the hotel and not the cafe resulted in a reprimand---from then on I kept my mouth shut. After all, I depended on the cafe for my morning coffee and occasional meal. In return, I swept up cigarette butts from under their sidewalk tables and changed light bulbs for them. They had three or four waitresses that were attractive in different ways. Seeing them reminded me that I missed having a woman in my life, someone to be with and make feel beautiful. I craved that but was also aware of my failure as a husband. I had been good in the beginning, loving and attentive and even romantic, but then I lost interest; I became distant, drank too much, and didn't seem to care. I failed my wife and was haunted by that, wondering if the same thing would happen with the next woman I shared my life with. Maybe I was meant to be alone, some people are. Movies and TV shows drill this idea into our heads that there is someone for *everyone*, that it is possible for even the homely and self-absorbed and malodorous to find deep, fulfilling love. The more I lived, the more I saw that as bullshit. Some people are too in their own heads, in their own realities and dreams, to be capable of truly sharing their lives.

Once a week I was supposed to deep clean the showers, scrubbing them with this pink cleanser that smelled like bubblegum. I was really knocking myself out at the hotel, trying to impress everyone and make a place for myself. People seemed to accept me aside from Willy Gilly who always seemed to have a suspicious look on his face when he saw me. Many mornings that Spring it would be pissing rain as I swept up cigarette butts and other garbage. I'd lose a little more hope for humanity when I saw all those butts on the sidewalk or the gutter or flicked out in the street--- what hope is there for a people that are happy living in an ashtray? The days of gray and rain would stretch into weeks and finally months. Those occasions when the sun finally broke out I nearly lost control of my emotions; I was still overwhelmed that I was living in an amazing city that I loved. I was so glad to be out of Lodi and felt grateful for having the means to get to Portland and have a place to stay there.

After work my routine was unvarying: Catch up on my email, eat something, shower, and head out. On day twenty-four I ended up at the Hideaway sipping a Pabst and writing another chapter in the book. After an hour, I got bored with that bar and walked twenty blocks to the Horse's Brass on Belmont. It was crowded but I found a small table near the bar. I felt guilty spending money on whiskey but I was sick of drinking beer. Looking around, I realized that I was one of the few people sitting alone in that bar and of those few loners the only one scribbling in a notebook. Despite the crowds, I knew that I would return to the Horse's Brass because good whiskey was reasonably priced.

25

It was a clear night when I finished the book. I understood even then that it was a weird book, not the sort of easy-going blockbuster that people read in airports and on beaches. The book just sort of happened: It started as a way to distract myself from living in Lodi and then exploded into tens of thousands of words spread across four notebooks. It would be best described as pieces of a puzzle that had dropped from the sky and somehow landed in place. I had no idea what was next and I was fine with that. All I knew was that I wanted to get the book I had finished in good enough shape to be published. In my mind, it was the strongest thing that I had ever written---strongest novel, at least. Maybe it had turned out as good as it did because there was no premeditation: I wasn't thinking, I wasn't being a writer and keeping my distance, I was living that shit. Most projects I was always detached, just a craftsman like someone who builds chairs or custom cars. Not the book I finished that Spring, I had been on the verge of tears a number of times while writing it. I put all my hopes and heartache into that fucking thing. Maybe I was too involved in that book to be objective; years would pass before I had an answer.

The night after I finished the book I wandered around the Inner Southeast. I ended up at Goodfoot on SE Stark near 29th. It was a sausage-fest aside from one woman who was there with some slouchy guy in a Dinosaur Jr. t-shirt. I finished my beer and just started walking until I ended up at the Horse's Brass. The bar seemed busy for a Thursday night. I ordered a drink and found a little table to sit at. I felt lost because the book was finished and there was nothing to do but doodle cartoons and look at women that I was too shy to talk to.

Back at the house, I could hear piano music coming through the vent. It was good to hear Noah playing. He had gone to a couple of jam sessions and I was happy but a little jealous. There was no place for me in his new band; Noah was the final piece in their eclectic puzzle. I forced the selfish thoughts from my mind and focused on N's happiness.

26

I woke up on the twenty-sixth day to a dark sky---would the photo shoot I had planned work out? It was freezing, threatening rain; when I got up on Mount Tabor the drizzle had evolved into hail. Frustrated and doubting we would be able to take pictures, I texted J and let her know that it wasn't looking good. She suggested we give it an hour to see if the weather cleared. Around 2:45, the weather broke and I could see some sun. J showed up maybe half an hour after that but I felt off my game. I wasn't used to the light in Portland; it was a completely different animal than the light in California.

When I got back to the house, I started going through the shots I had taken of J. In the end I was only satisfied with a handful of them. At seven I took a bus back up Mount Tabor to look at a room for rent. It was an older house that needed some work but had good bones. The owner was kooky, but not in a bad way. She was squinty and somewhere in her mid-fifties with bleached hair. I realized that my potential landlord looked like Judith Light from *Who's the Boss?* but wisely kept that opinion to myself. The available room was in a basement and had its own (small) living room. It was cozy, almost claustrophobic because of the low ceiling, but seemed a good fit for me. The landlord and I talked for a bit after she showed me the room and I let her know that I was definitely interested.

27

The following morning, I took the 15 down to Grand to do more exploring. I made my way to Water Street and walked under the elevated roadways and past homeless camps. I found some good places for future photo shoots but understood that I would need to borrow or buy a car so the models would have a place to change.

I cut over to the East Esplanade which ran along the Willamette. It was a beautiful walk and I found more places to take pictures.
I was underdressed for the Esplanade, most of the other people were wearing expensive running outfits or riding expensive bikes. Maybe a hundred yards away were homeless camps situated under the freeway; the two very different worlds were about as far apart as the Germans and Allied trenches had been during the First World War. Seeing people on two thousand dollar bikes passing lean-tos made from tarps and found rope, I mused about my own weird place in the world. I had a job and a place to stay, but the latter had been temporary from the beginning. I spent too much time wondering just how far away from being homeless I really was; having a place to live and a job was something I doubted I would ever take for granted.

Crossing the river at the Steel Bridge, I heard the clank and rumble of all the cars and trucks passing overhead. Dual rail lines ran along the lower platform and graffiti was sprayed on the girders. The smell of the west side of the river reminded me of Sausalito. I got vertigo crossing the red bridge back over to the east side of the river when I looked at the river far below.

It turned gorgeous in the late afternoon. I made some coffee and then wandered through the neighborhoods south of Hawthorne. The new Depeche Mode album was playing on my iPod and the music got me thinking about my grandfather. I remembered going to see him the morning my grandmother died. He had told me that I was too late, something that has haunted me ever since---all the times that I have waited too long to tell people that I love them. Why was I having such maudlin thoughts on a beautiful afternoon? Maybe Depeche Mode was to blame.

I ended up at Mulligan's hoping the bartender I liked would be there. She was but it was surprisingly busy for a Sunday and there was zero chance of talking to her aside from ordering a beer. I weathered my slight crush in solitude. Haven't we all felt that way about someone? Haven't there been a few people like that for all of us---people that we run into on a regular basis at work or other places where people stray into our lives?
Someone we are struck by while simultaneously understanding that we can never share what we feel for them?
That's how it was with the Italian Spanish looking bartender at Mulligan's. I just went there and drank my drinks and maybe looked down the bar at her from time to time. I understood even in the moment that I was experiencing all there ever would be between us. There

would never be a time where I was holding her hand or kissing her or making love to her; we would always be strangers.

After mooning over the bartender for half an hour, I decided it was a good time for karaoke. Chopsticks was packed and people were still walking in at midnight. Noah had shown up so we listened to the other singers and drank beer. Afterwards, we walked over to the food carts twenty blocks away and sang 80s hits to the empty streets.

28

The next day I had a back to back shift, working until 11 that night and clocking on at 7:30 the following morning. As good of shape as I may have been in for being 45, I was still 45. Doing a highly physical job reminded me of that every shift; my shoulders were always sore. Nevertheless, it was a big moment when I picked up my first check that wasn't from a temp agency in nearly three years. I was making minimum wage but received a $10 meal credit during a full shift and a $20 reduction on my monthly bus pass so it all worked out.

I cleaned dried vomit off the sides of toilets and scoured dried shit out of the bowls. I wiped sundry hairs out of the inside of showers and found used condoms in the trash. Sometimes it grossed me out but mostly I was just happy not to be working in an office. People defecate and get physically ill and lose hair; it's human, just part of being alive and I could deal with it. I was okay with being a ghost around the edges, a ghost in a blue polo shirt with a walkie-talkie strapped to their waist. Prowling the corridors, I lingered near doors people were fucking behind. Iggy Pop's "The Passenger" was always playing in my head as I curled up next to the lives of strangers and picked apart their secrets.

I was knackered by the time I finished the second shift. There was a message on my phone about the basement on Mount Tabor. Squinty Judith Light said it was mine for

$435 a month if I wanted it. My only concern about the place were the nights when I missed the last bus and had to walk home. To get to Noah and Anne's it was a three and a half mile walk which I could do without a problem. The place on Mount Tabor, however, would add a couple of miles to that. Noah had offered to lend me a bike and I was thinking of taking him on even though I was kind of nervous about riding in a city, even one as bicycle friendly as Portland.

29

Portland lies. It lays out hypnotically beautiful Spring afternoons and then rips them away to reveal more gray and rain. Whenever I saw the sun, I would jump out of bed and just start walking; covering block after block and letting as much sun hit my skin as possible. On one such afternoon, I ended up underneath the I-5 bridge on the west side of the river. There in the shade I took notes and observed the sunbathers and water and bridge supports. There were lots of people out on the paths and sprawled on the grass--- people go crazy when the sun finally comes out in Portland and I had joined their ranks. I wandered around with no destination in mind as I listened to the new Depeche Mode album *Delta Machine*. Sometimes it was a struggle to contain my emotions: The feelings weren't bad, quite the contrary; I was simply overwhelmed by how good life felt after so many months of unhappiness. After nearly three years of getting by on the kindness of my family I was about to have my own place. The idea of *home* was something that I needed, an ideal. Was renting a room the right way to go? The more I thought about it the more I wanted a place where I lived alone, even a tiny studio apartment the size of a walk-in closet. I was so tired of intruding on others, of not feeling that I could just live my life and walk around in my underwear and cook at all hours. I was sick of being a pest; I wanted my own private world, my own sanctuary.

Out in the sun, I thought about when I had walked across the Hawthorne Bridge the night before. There had been a couple dozen homeless people asleep on the sidewalk and, again, I found myself dwelling on how fortunate I was. I was still unsure which option was best, though. Did I get a room in a house with a bunch of people? That would mean regular negotiations with them regarding use of the kitchen and the bathroom. It also meant crossing paths with virtual strangers when I needed to be alone or when *they* needed to be alone. Looking out at the slow moving river I found myself revisiting the idea of living in a van. It would have its drawbacks but it would be mine---*home*---flawed and with challenges, but mine and mine alone.

Walking back to the house I marveled at how lovely the day had turned out. In Phoenix the sun was a curse, something that spited you and left you pleading for mercy. In Portland, the sun was a mythical thing; a legend passed from generation to generation. It was a lover that made your skin shiver and your heart bloom before it ran out for months at a time leaving you lost, writing bad poetry, drinking too much, and all the other things people do when pining for a lost love.

I must have walked five miles that afternoon. I kept a quick pace along the Western Esplanade, weaving through slow moving crowds and keeping pace with the joggers. I went over the Steel Bridge and onto the Eastern Esplanade, crossing the floating bridge past all the homeless camps under the freeway. I was listening to that Depeche Mode album at a volume any ear doctor will tell you not to listen to Depeche Mode at. I had rarely felt more alive but my life was both light and shadow; so was Portland. At the time I felt that we belonged together; even in those bright moments I understood that feeling wouldn't last forever. Everything dies. Those moments when people and things and places are so in our blood we cannot imagine taking a breath without them eventually pass. The nature of moments is to pass and the space between them can be profound. But there are other moments out there full of light and life; you understand that and carry on. As you get older, it's easier to carry on, shrug off the pain and doubt, but you still feel the space between moments.

30

The following morning was overcast but still pleasant. I walked down to Ladd's Addition, stopping at a 7-11 on the way to get a cheap breakfast biscuit and coffee. I had overindulged the night before as I did too many nights and consequently required salty breakfast food. It was a poor meal but I ate it in a beautiful park surrounded by grass and shrubs bursting with flowers.

At five I found myself at the Watertrough drinking an inexpensive beer and taking notes on what I had done that day. Wandering the quiet streets it seemed you couldn't go half a block without coming across cherry blossoms. Looking at the ancient trees and century old houses, I found myself imagining the time when they had risen from the earth, a time before television or even radio. Those houses had been built by people who had been dead at least fifty years. Their lives were just recollections, pictures in scrapbooks---one day it would be the same with me. I was 45 then, my life at least half over. I was aware of that but I was also aware of the trees coming alive as they did every Spring, life continuing. I knew that I was going to make it as a writer in Portland; I also understood that I had to come back to Portland before it could happen. Part of me understood that maybe I was delusional, making myself believe things out of desperation, but it still felt true.

After the bar I went to an open house maybe half a mile to the west. It was an amazing place and I liked my potential roommates. The only problem was that the owner would have required that I be on the lease and consequently would run a credit check. Seeing as my credit was in the toilet, it seemed like a doomed proposition. After saying goodbye, I walked over to the Belmont Inn. The Pixies were playing on the stereo and I sat next to the window sipping Jack Daniels. I turned the economics of renting a room over and over in my head, how tight everything would be from month to month and all the stress that goes with that sort of thing. It would take a couple of years to save for a car or a van even living with extreme frugality. I decided there and then that if I didn't get that room I would buy a van to live in.

31

I think his name was Jim but he clearly lived in a place where names are irrelevant. He was somewhere between 35 and 55 with weathered skin. It wasn't the casual weathering of weekend trips to the beach; it was the skin of a man who has no shelter, no sanctuary from the elements. He wore an 1895 mustache and alcohol was seeping from his pores. I saw him stumbling up the street as he looked right at me. I tried to ignore him but he dropped onto the stoop behind me and started talking. He said a few things I didn't understand and then asked if I was getting off of work. I smiled and said yes. Jim pulled out a cigarette he had clearly picked up off the ground and toyed with it, asking me to wake him up when the bus came.
"I'm too old for this," he sighed.
It was a beautiful day and I was waiting for the bus standing next to a dying man. Some would say that we're all dying; it's just that some of us will get there first.

The sky darkened and you could smell rain in the air. I was meeting with a model up on the mountain. Once I got there it was sprinkling and I got mad at the weather. I still loved Portland, but was getting tired of waiting for it to stop being cold and wet. The sun finally emerged and we were able to get our work done.

After we parted ways, I made my way down the mountain and got a cheeseburger from Dairy Queen. I wandered the calm backstreets for half an hour or so before taking a bus back to the house to go through the 340 pictures we had taken. Once that was done, I joined Noah and Anne in the living room. We shared a bottle of wine and watched television until half past ten.

32

I worked the day shift that Wednesday. After punching out I rode a crowded bus back to the house, checked my email, showered, and headed out again. I walked maybe a mile down to 12th Avenue listening to music and looking at all the beautiful old houses and trees. I was looking for a new place to have a drink and pass the time; I would poke my head in doors only to pull it back out and keep walking.

I finally found a place that seemed quiet enough. There was a cute young woman behind the bar. She was friendly until she caught me looking and then she tightened up and her friendliness was locked behind a metal grate. I understood my mistake and focused on writing and the beer I was nursing. Once again, my awareness of being surrounded by strangers who were surrounded by friends was strong. Music I couldn't understand was coming over speakers I couldn't see. Everyone seemed to be with somebody and I was alone with my thoughts, consoling myself with the understanding that thoughts have power and in a strange way they connect us all and that loneliness is an illusion.

The sky was heavy and steel colored when twilight came over the mountains. I walked thirty blocks up Hawthorne, weaving through the hipsters and people with money who drive Audi SUVs and the homeless with days worth of urine dried into their clothes. A man in a red starter jacket waved his fist at the passing cars and snarled for a moment, but then the chemicals settled or the electrical flare died and he calmed, placidly crossing the street as people tried to pretend he wasn't there.

33

The hotel was short staffed so I stayed late to help out. I rode another crowded bus, stood under the shower for a few minutes, and headed back out. I didn't want to go out but I was all too aware that I had been a houseguest for over a month. I ended up at a nameless bar on NE 28th near Glisen. My original idea had been to go to the Horse's Brass for an inexpensive whiskey but I only had $14 on me and wanted to have enough for two beers at Chopsticks. There was a hole on the bottom of my Chuck Taylors that I had been meaning to cover with duct tape. I thought about that hole as I sat at a table near the window and wrote for a while before starting a biography on Ray Bradbury that I'd picked up at the library. There was a beautiful woman at the next table on what appeared to be a first date. It was twilight when I left to wander the streets, rain in the air but falling sparsely. I walked west marveling at all the old houses and how green everything was; even the roofs appeared to be in bloom.

It was eight o' clock when I walked into Chopsticks. I saw the same people I always saw there whether it was a Thursday or Sunday or Tuesday: There was the young woman who looked she had a half dozen cats staring at where the KJ would set up. The girl was clutching a vodka cranberry and when she realized I was standing next to her she smiled at me anxiously.
"This is the hardest part," she said.
"What's that?"

"The waiting," was her response, the smile on her face twisting with anxiety.

"I guess Tom Petty had it right," I noted.

The girl either didn't get my joke or chose to ignore it. An hour later she was singing Sex by George Michael with a disturbing degree of gusto. I imagined her practicing it at home as her cats looked on with disapproval. Another regular was a man Noah and I had nicknamed Mr. Monotone. MM was around 40 with dark hair and sang every song like Frankenstein impersonating a creaking door. His version of Tangled Up in Blue haunted me; I heard it when I was cooking and when I was at work.

34

JB posted a picture of herself and some guy, an ordinary Joe with a disarming smile. Seeing that picture I had what would be my final "fuck this" moment with regards to JB. I had experienced them in the past---quite a few of them, in fact---but that time I knew it was final. She would always be in my prayers to win all her struggles but I was done giving so much of myself to someone who saw me as a last choice when no one else was around, when no one else had her back. That picture made me anxious and jealous and hurt and I had to force myself to just cut my emotions off and say fuck it. There was nothing more to do that night but to drink beer and look at cars online and lose myself in simple pleasures.

35

When the sun emerged from its prison of heavy, dark clouds it was like that moment in a film when a horrible monster is slain. I was worried it wouldn't last but it ended up being a beautiful afternoon. People lay face down in parks like extras in a film and everything green was aglow.

I worked a short shift, took a shower, and headed out. At the High Top I had a beer and read about Van Morrison. Some god awful music was coming over the PA; an auto tuned girl going on about how she likes to get freaky and wants to be made to scream. Why did I go there? The bartender was really nice and cute as well but that shouldn't have been enough. After finishing my beer I cut across Ladd Division, stumbling down all the angled streets with the tall houses casting long shadows. There was a big park in the middle of a roundabout with places to hide and beer cans next to benches.

At Division I caught the next bus heading north. Even though it was seven there weren't any free seats. A strange Asian woman missing a front tooth boarded and stood next to me. She seemed to be reading fortunes off the pole I was leaning against and the waves of ammonia from urine soaked clothes were getting me high. I got off the bus halfway to my destination and kept walking.

Kevin was one of my trainers at Hotel Glass. He played drums in a few country and western bands but was quick to explain that it was *traditional* country and not the modern stuff like Toby Keith. We got to talking about music as he showed me how to make beds and clean mirrors. Kevin had a regular gig at the Landmark Saloon on Division and 48th and suggested that I check it out. Hearing the name I imagined horns on the walls and a collection of urban cowboys in Stetsons but it wasn't like that. The Landmark was a converted house and no one was wearing a cowboy hat, not even the band. Kevin and his bandmates were playing songs from a time before Patsy Cline crashed into a mountain or Toby Keith's parents had even met. It was like a time warp until the female singer bent down to get her beer and I could see her tramp stamp tattoo. The crowd looked like hipsters and most of them were drinking 24 ounce cans of PBRs. I left between sets, giving Kevin a wave on the way out.

36

Some people are born to be selfish. Many times in my life I have believed or even understood that I am one of those people. I have depended on the kindness of my family and only been generous with my ideas. My days were spent wandering around like a boho cliché down to the hole in my Chuck Taylors sealed with duct tape. I spent my evenings unconcerned for the welfare of others as I drank cheap beer and wrote in bars. I could have been anything, I could have been *anyone*, but I chose to be poor and artistic, living a life shaped by my impulses and wants. Was it wrong? Was it delusional to follow my calling so blindly? I could never decide. It felt right, but I was probably biased. Noah, on the other hand, was always generous and thoughtful. It seemed like every week he was marching for a good cause or giving to charity. We were like Goofus and Gallant in those old *Highlights* books. I should have been more like him but I couldn't be; my heart was elsewhere, turned inside.

It was late April; I was still in love with Portland and enjoying my job---mostly. I found myself getting more and more frustrated with the way the managers ran things. We had a meeting in the pub behind the hotel. I had been under the impression that it was going to be a round table sort of meeting where employees could raise concerns. I wanted that sort of meeting, not just for myself but for other staff members that I knew had good ideas. What we got instead was one sided: Changes in policy, being reminded to smile, and information on things within the company that didn't concern us. It was frustrating, to say the least, and I found my cynicism about the job growing

After the meeting, I drifted through my duties in the hotel. Part of it was the beer I had drank and part was that I was preoccupied with my living situation. All the vans in my price range were either in poor condition or there was something shady about their paperwork. It was frustrating and I was worried about wearing out my welcome with Noah and Anne.

37

The day after the meeting I didn't feel like leaving the house. Both Noah and Anne were home, though, and I felt the need to make myself scarce. I spent an hour just walking up and down Hawthorne Avenue. Missing my guitars, I stopped in a shop to look at all the Gibsons and Fenders and Music Mans. There was an amazing old acoustic bass at the far end of the showroom and I contemplated asking permission to play it. In the end I walked out with asking; it felt unfair, like I'd be wasting their time. Maybe I was being silly or maybe I was taking the first step down a long road.

There was an old Toyota Chinook for sale on Craigslist. Unfortunately, it had a lot of problems so I didn't bother calling. Beyond needing a truck to live in, I missed going on drives, just getting in a car and exploring. Plus, when I had a van or a camper I'd be able to go on trips and not have to pay for a motel room. I understood that living in a van wouldn't be easy---especially when it came to using the bathroom or cooking---but I believed in my heart that it was the best option for me.

Back at the house, I mindlessly followed paths on-line: Cars, naked women, and other distractions. Minutes, being social animals, fell into larger and larger groups. The garage door opened. Had Noah been out on a run? Gotten out for some coffee? No, he had taken his keyboard to another basement to play music. We said "hi" to each other and I tried to stay out of his way as he set the keyboard back on its stand next to the computer. *How was practice?* would have been a stupid question; I could tell by his face it had been a disappointment. I also understood after thirty years of friendship that he would tell me *why* it was a disappointment when he found the words. After the last cord was plugged in, he walked across the room to his desk. Noah stared at the dead computer screen as he swiveled a little in his work chair.

"You know that music is math, right?" He asked.

"You mean like beats to a measure, time signatures, and all that?"

"Yes. It's math and it's chemistry, human chemistry; I think we've had this conversation before."

"It sounds familiar," I replied.

"I hear more things than I wish I did," he shook his head, stopped swiveling. "I got a new IPA, it's really good..."

He jumped out of his chair to get us beers from upstairs. We opened the bottles, clinked, and took a swallow. N was right, it was a good IPA. It was tough drinking it, though. He bought good beer, $10 a six pack beer that I couldn't afford to replace.

"You were talking about hearing more things than you wish you did," I prompted.

He took a drink from his bottle and looked over at me.

"I heard them when you and I did music, but you and I are friends," he said. "The things I heard in the Eulogy didn't bother me as much because I enjoyed working with you. With these guys, they're just people I know---"

"Guys with earnest beards who can go on for weeks about lo-fi?"

Noah ignored my comment, and took another drink.

"Even in the stuff we did in the Eulogy, I could hear the way the music was *supposed* to sound or maybe how it *could* sound."

"The possibilities?"

"Yeah," Noah seemed to like that. "That was why I started doing my own thing, I needed to make what I was hearing in my head happen."

"I know I wasn't a good enough singer for what you want to do..."

"I wouldn't say 'not good enough,' I'd say *not right*. Not for the music I was hearing, at least. The thing is, I think the guys I played with today are skilled enough, but it wouldn't be right for me to just step in and start telling people what to play. I mean, it's *their* band."

"I understand what you're saying."

"I knew you would, I know you've been in similar situations."

"Yep."

The conversation died. Noah turned on some angular music I wasn't familiar with and got back to work. Determined not to waste anymore time, I closed the Internet browser and started writing.

38

How many times had I woken up understanding that I had
drunk too much the night before? Too many. I was thinking
about that the next morning as I lay in bed. I was 45, no
longer young; less and less resilient. Maybe I could still
maintain such a life but I knew it would come back to haunt
me in ten years or so, twenty at most. Going downstairs, I
saw that work had emailed me to ask if I wanted to work
that day. I was grateful for the hours; more money
increased the odds of getting a decent van.

As I was waiting for the bus at 30th and Hawthorne I
counted Subarus and Priuses. An old Camaro pulled into
the Plaid Pantry lot. The man driving it was so fat he
couldn't get out of the car. Frustrated, he slammed the door
closed again and peeled out of the parking lot. Two teenage
boys watched with approval. One talked about how he
would trick out the Camaro and the other countered by
saying that Camaros were pieces of shit. Both of them were
slouches with mouths, pants down past their asses and
sideways caps. The one hating on Camaros argued that a
slammed Honda was the only way to go and his companion
finally agreed.
"Yeah, a slammed Civic is fire, bro."
"JDM for life, bro."
They were talking about some high school baller named
Tyrell Dube when I got on the bus. I wondered where those
boys would be in ten years. I thought about the hippies,
how a lot of them had traded their beads for suits and

pulled their beards off like a mask that had become inconvenient. Would those boys do the same in their mid-twenties? They were still unformed, anything was possible. I was thirty years older and felt the same way about my own life.

I worked my ass off assisting housekeeping by dumping their linen carts or striping rooms for them. When I asked myself why I was bothering, why I was working so hard, the answer was that I was doing it for myself. By taking pride in what I was doing I was taking pride in my own actions. I also understand that I needed to keep proving myself to my co-workers and bosses; it was all tied in with my survival instinct. My motivation was to not be homeless or hungry or in any other bad situation. I figured that I needed six months to buy a van, outfit it, and then save enough money to have a little bit of a cushion. Once that was taken care of I figured that I would be able to save $250 a month. After six months it would still be a blow if I lost my job but if I had a van and some cash set aside it wouldn't be the end of the world.

39

The next ten days passed locked in a comfortable routine of work, bars, and searching for a van. Everything was bursting with color and life as the grayness around Portland was slowly being chipped away. Feeling inspired by the change in seasons, I put an ad for musicians on Craigslist. I got one promising response from an electronic musician and agreed to meet him at the Space Bar.

I found a Ford conversion van for sale on the east side of town. The seller was a musician with a beard and a yard as overgrown as his face. He seemed honest enough but later I would admit to myself that I had gotten impatient. The van ran well enough, but considering its flaws I paid too much. I was caught up in the desire to move my life forward and I was also anxious to give Noah and Anne their guest room back.

The Space Bar was old Portland, a dive bar that was exactly that. The lighting was pretty much non-existent and the bartender far removed from hipsters and vegan sandwiches. I was meeting someone named Dan who had told me to look for a white guy in his mid-thirties wearing a Cabaret Voltaire shirt. I told him that I'd be the guy with glasses and a stack of notebooks in front of him. Someone stopped at the table---(a blurry someone since I didn't have my glasses on)---and asked me what I was writing. I put my glasses on and saw that it was an attractive woman somewhere around 30. She looked vaguely Hispanic and was wearing a

Flashdancey sort of shirt that fell off one shoulder. I offered a rambling sort of explanation about the various crap in my notebooks, flipping a few pages for good measure. She walked away and I thought that was that but my new friend came back a couple of minutes later and sat down across from me. She introduced herself as Sofia and we chatted about local bars and how we were both recent arrivals from California. I suggested that we go to a couple of bars sometime and handed her my cell number on a scrap of paper. She studied the piece of paper for a few seconds and I was worried that she would decline my offer. Instead, Sofia put my number in her phone and texted me hers.

"Sofia with an 'f'," she clarified as I typed her name in.

"Are you gay, straight, or other?" When she asked that I noticed that her eyes were the same shade of brown as mine.

"Straight. You?"

"Other," her smile was mischievous; it had been too long since a woman had smiled at me like that

As I mentally scrambled to continue the conversation, I got a text from Dan who was sitting at the bar.

"The guy I'm supposed to meet is here," I said, reluctantly, to Sofia.

"Okay. I'm going to California for a couple of weeks but we'll talk after that."

Sofia and I shook hands and she went to the bar. I saw her sit down and start talking to another man. Who was she? A lonely woman looking for a hookup or a friend or some combination of the two? I saw her at the bar talking to an older man and it reminded me of the nights with JB when I had willingly played the fool. It was a hard memory but a fruitful one; in exchange for all the pain I accepted I got half a dozen songs and a book. That whole mess had brought something beautiful out in me, something human, something much bigger than my usual petty self-absorption. Would Sofia end up being another JB? I had no idea, but I was determined to keep my mind open and my heart guarded.

Dan was wearing dad jeans with his Cabaret Voltaire shirt. I could tell by the way he sipped his microbrew that beer was not an everyday occurrence. We talked about Depeche Mode as we slowly emptied our glasses. I told him that *Delta Machine* was a solid album but he hadn't heard it. D was a big *Violator* fan; he had listened to a couple of songs from each of the albums that followed but hadn't been impressed.

"I'll give *Delta Machine* a shot, though," he said.

His smile was genuine and open like many smiles I had seen in Portland. As a cynical Californian whose heart was basically black rubble I had no idea what to make of those smiles. Dan was a nice guy and eager to befriend me; a creep with a Craigslist ad and a habit of going over notebooks in the dark. He suggested that we go across the street to the Bar of the Gods. I agreed, but I was preoccupied with Sofia; I kept seeing her mischievous smile as I turned over and over in my head how we were both from the same part of California and had the same color eyes. There was a fierce guard up inside me, though, a scowling guy with thick arms and no neck that wasn't about to let another JB in. At Bar of the Gods, Dan bought me a beer. They were giving out PBR swag and he handed

117

some of it to me. I didn't want it but he was a nice guy who had just bought me a pint so I agreeably shoved it in my bag. I could feel the guard inside me scowling, possibly reaching in a pocket of his leather coat for brass knuckles. Dan seemed to want us to be more than just musical collaborators. Out of the blue he blurted out that he had season tickets for the Timberwolves and suggested that we go to a couple of games. I didn't know if I wanted anything more from him than backing tracks and had no idea how to respond. He was clearly a nice guy who was probably a little lonely. Listening to him as I drank the beer he had bought me I felt nothing. Dan was a kind soul, a nice guy, and I was pretty sure that I was neither.

Walking out of the bar, I experienced a few minutes of panic when I couldn't find my phone. I went to the Space Bar to look for it and noticed that Sofia was gone. Had she left alone or with that man she was talking to? Had that been my only chance to get to know her? Shaking my anxiety off, I asked the bartender if anyone had turned in a phone. She was apologetic but couldn't help me. I walked back out into the sunshine and utilized the daylight to rummage in my bag until I found my phone. A man was sleeping on the sidewalk a few feet away. Across the street from him, people were lined up outside Porque No. Most of them appeared carefree and were wearing nice clothes; they'd eat a good meal and think nothing of the $20 to $30 they'd spent. When they got home they'd go on Twitter or Facebook to share the experience:
Finally checked out Porque No on Hawthorne---delish!

They'd drink a microbrew, watch some Netflix, and then climb into their comfortable bed. The next day, they'd make coffee in the french press and ride their bicycle to the job they assumed would always be there. Outside their building and tucked away along their route to work, men and women would be living rough---no job, no hope, not even a shabby conversion van to sleep in. I was aware of both worlds and felt caught between them. As much as I bitched about my job at the hotel I understood that I was fortunate and vowed never to lose sight of that.

I texted Sofia a simple message:
Enjoyed meeting you; we should hang out in the future.
She texted back reminding me that she was going to California for her grandmother's funeral but would be up for hanging out when she returned. S ended with "talk to you later" and I understood that the conversation was closed. The guard inside me rolled his eyes:
Maybe she couldn't talk because she's with another man.
Even though I no longer had feelings for JB the wounds had yet to evolve into scars. I still felt small and foolish over that whole mess and consequently my guard not only had brass knuckles but also a pistol and a truncheon. Why had I done that to myself? Why had I felt so deeply about someone who couldn't feel the same for me? I was still haunted even if I didn't go in the haunted house anymore; I had stared too long at the windows and the ghosts had followed me home.

I grabbed a beer from the house and walked to where the van was parked. Lying on the backseat, I looked through the tinted windows at the calm, residential neighborhood that surrounded me. It was peaceful in the van and I knew that I could sleep in there and feel safe. I felt optimistic that I could make van dwelling work: Edna II would be my home and I would be alright; I would survive as I always had despite the odds I stacked up in my mind. Lying there, there was the understanding that I would have a good life; it would probably not be a conventional life, but one that made sense to me.

Finishing my beer, I tried to determine how long it would be until I was living in the van full time. My guess was three weeks: There were basic things I needed like a bed, ice chest, and places to store my belongings. I also needed a gym membership so I could shower. My goal for moving into the van was June 1, the first bloom of summer. I was excited but understood that there would be challenges. All the things we take for granted, like indoor plumbing and a normal kitchen, I would not have. Nonetheless, my instincts were telling me that everything would work out.

40

The day I had been dreading finally came, the day I fell out of love with my job and began taking it for granted. Dee was back after a two month absence and our first interaction had been her pointing out that I hadn't swept something up. She wasn't a dick about it, but it still stung. I had been busting my ass for two and a half months, trying to be a valuable employee, and I didn't feel my efforts were appreciated. My gratitude had lost its momentum and frustration had pulled ahead. Was I expecting too much from work? Why couldn't I just accept the same bullshit other people accepted or pretended to accept? I couldn't even *pretend*. Was it ego? I wasn't sure. I kept thinking about that email I had sent the acting manager three weeks earlier with all these ideas for improving the workplace--- she had never responded. Even if they were good ideas, what right did I have expressing them? I hadn't been hired to think. The problem was, I put too much value in my ideas and took pride in my ability to think; maybe my pride was the problem.

There were some cute girls in 314. I thought one of them was flirting with me but maybe it was just wishful thinking. I found myself lingering on the third floor hoping to run into them. They stayed in their room the rest of my shift, talking and laughing. In reality, I was probably too old for them. What was I doing chasing around younger women? I used to laugh at guys like that only to become one of them.

After cleaning the bathrooms I went down to the basement and hid, sitting in a chair listening to drunk people whoop it up in the pool. Needing some fresh air, I grabbed a broom and went outside to do the property walk. It was surprisingly warm for nearly midnight and the physical activity cleared my mind. Sweeping the butts into a dustpan, I understood how I could salvage my enthusiasm for the job: Write a book about it. Whenever I felt pissed off or frustrated I could reassure myself with the understanding that at least I was getting a book out of it. I stopped on the north side of the building and looked up at the stars, all of them impossibly far away and some dead. It was such a gorgeous night that I didn't want to go inside. Down Burnside, people were walking in groups and laughing just as people had been doing for over a hundred years. The young have no idea what it is like to be old, that one day decades will be behind them and they'll be too frail for anything but memories. I made a vow never to waste another day before going inside to write another chapter.

By ten past one the drunken people in the pool were getting rowdier. Looking in, I saw it was two guys and a good looking woman who I gave a second look on the sly. A few minutes later they got out of the water and went back to their rooms, their bare feet leaving wet footprints on the tile. After mopping them up I went into the storage room to turn the jets off. The smell of pot was strong back there from the waiters slipping in for a quick smoke.

There was a subtle flow to the last minutes on the night shift: Turning off the jets, grabbing my bag, locking the

gate, and walking to the bus stop. Same empty streets---
(most of the sparse traffic was made up of cabs)---and the
same Justin Timberlake poster in the shop window across
the street. From a block away the view of the hotel was like
a postcard. I always tried to imagine how it had looked a
hundred years earlier. Would the streets have been
cobblestone or dirt? In my mind I saw stones. Sometimes I
closed my eyes and tried to hear horseshoes and metal
wheels resonating on cobblestones but I never could shake
the 21st century as hard as I tried.

There were never many homeless people on the last bus;
most had already found a place to sleep or pass out. The
other riders seemed to be in the service industry like
myself, janitors and bar backs and prep cooks. The last bus
was always crowded: Everyone getting drunk or off work
understood that it was the last shot for getting home
without walking miles or waiting until morning. I had made
the three mile walk to Noah's a few times and didn't mind
it; there was peaceful beauty to the stillness once you got
past the crowds on the west side of the river.

41

The following night I worked another five to midnight
shift. Seventy percent of the rooms were full but the hotel
seemed quiet. My duties were complicated by our laundry
supplier's continuing mistakes: Everything was poorly
packaged and they kept letting us run out of key items like
pillow slips and washcloths, things I needed to keep the
linen closets stocked. It was a solitary task, quiet even
when we had high occupancy, and I enjoyed the ritual and
repetition. If I saw a customer I was obligated to give them
the elevator but fortunately a lot of them took the stairs.
Most of our guests couldn't deal with how slow the lift was;
I knew that because a lot of them commented on it. The
building had been remodeled half a dozen times but they
had kept the original elevator. It had become a curio, a
reminder of a time when life moved at a far slower pace.

By 11:45 I couldn't wait for quitting time. I was getting
sick of cleaning bathrooms and how heavily the bathroom
doors were sprung. It was tricky to get past the doors with
your supplies without getting bruised up. I lingered on the
second floor as I did one last interior property walk, hoping
to hear this gorgeous girl I had seen having sex with her
boyfriend. I had run into her earlier when they had been in
the pool. She was beautiful; willowy, with golden hair and
a sad face. On the way down to the pool her robe fell open
a little and I could see the top of her breasts. The girl
caught me looking and smiled; it was sweet, not coy, and I
felt guilty for trespassing. That didn't stop me from pausing

at their door and straining to hear the sounds of her pleasure. All I got was silence and an awareness of the darkness in my heart.

After my shift ended I walked a dozen blocks to Sixth and Main to catch the last 14 across the river. The bus stop was next to a fondue restaurant that was closed just like everything else at that time of night. The streets were empty aside from a few lone men skulking along the sidewalks and the occasional squad car slowing down to check me out. I thought of the girl with the golden hair and the sad face, I thought of Sofia and wondered where she was at that moment.

42

"Going on a walk?" Noah was sitting on the couch and doing something on his iPad.

"No. I need to get a couple of things from the store," I replied.

"I need to get some garlic---mind if I tag along?"

"Of course not."

We headed up 30th towards Salmon. A beautiful Asian woman was pushing a turquoise bicycle. She had ear buds in and I wondered what she was listening to. Noah and I talked about the weather as we walked down Salmon; I was marveling at it albeit with the understanding that we still had months of rain ahead of us.

"I can't believe how warm it is," I marvelled.

"Yeah, there wasn't any snow this winter," my friend replied.

"You think it's global warming?"

He went into a discourse on a theory of global warming that was way over my head. I half listened and half admired the cherry blossoms. The parking lot of Fred Meyer was as chaotic as a Cairo street scene. Inside, "Tin Man" by America was playing over the PA. I found myself dragged into the song as Noah picked out his garlic.

"Do America's lyric's actually mean anything?" He mused

"It was the 70s," I replied. "They were probably about feathering hair and cocaine."

"Probably."

Noah looked over at the plastic bags and then decided to just carry the two cloves in his hand.

"We've had this conversation before: You like the melodies of America but the lyrics don't make any sense," I said.

"Much like the lyrics of Seals and Croft," Noah nodded.

"Yeah, Seals and Croft also had questionable hats and mustaches."

"Tin Man" was followed by "Year of the Cat" by Al Stewart. I stopped in the middle of the coffee aisle to listen.

"If I were to ever make a movie I would use 70s soft rock in scenes where the world is ending, kind of a contrast," I said.

"You may get your chance," Noah frowned.

"Are you going to help me make a movie?" We were in the bread aisle. I grabbed some wheat English muffins, the last item on my list.

"I don't know, I just don't feel optimistic about things." He was still frowning as we got in line. "The economy is recovering, but it's only a matter of time before it crashes again, maybe for good."

"It's like I've been saying for twenty years," I said firmly. "We need to get some land out in the country."

"I know, but I'm allergic to rednecks."

"Me too," I agreed. "But I'm even more allergic to riots and chaos."

It was raining lightly when I walked to the transit stop that afternoon. The bus was running late and I kept checking the time on my phone and wondering if I was going to be tardy for work. If I was, would they say anything? If they did, what would I do? Would my resentment and frustration boil over and lead to a situation where I quit or was fired? I understood that I had to focus on the big picture, continuing to save money and use my job to get enough material for another book---I understood that but I still struggled with it.

Work ended up being okay; things were busy enough that the time flew by but not so crazy that it was stressful. At eleven, Lars took over the front desk and the two of us got to joking around. I inspected a dozen rooms for the front desk, looking out the windows as I did so. I enjoyed the view of nightlife spilling out of the other hotels and restaurants and all the interesting, old buildings in the neighborhood. As with the previous night, I walked to the bus stop at Sixth and Main and waited in front of the closed fondue restaurant. Focusing on sounds I could make out traffic in the distance, the hum of unseen insects, and an odd pinging noise coming from a nearby parking garage. I found myself thinking of New Mexico or maybe California---the desert---somewhere warm to spend the winter months. Maybe I could get another hotel gig at a resort or something and work down in the desert from October until April, returning to Portland when it was beginning to warm up. I loved Portland but it would have been great to be in a warmer place when winter came: San Diego, Palm Springs, or Tucson. The idea was getting stronger and stronger with each passing day. Maybe I was just itching to travel again or maybe I missed the desert. I didn't want to think I was bored with Portland; the town had saved my life and I owed it everything.

An okay looking girl in a really low cut shirt walked by with a Boxer on a black leash. Her cleavage was amazing and she stopped to ask if I could spare anything so she could buy her dog some food. I felt bad turning her down, but I was leery about giving people money at bus stops--- you give something to one person and then a whole lot of people come out of the shadows when they see you're an easy mark. I told the girl I only had plastic; she smiled an amazing smile and walked on.

On the bus, the guy behind me reeked of cigarettes and other passengers were talking about smoking. The river was lit by the full moon and looked beautiful and still. All the old buildings cast lonely shadows. I was hoping the liquor store at 30th and Hawthorne would still be open but discovered that it closed at midnight. I got my iPod out of my pocket and decided to drink a bottle of wine that I had seen in the house.

43

The next day, I was assigned to housekeeping for the first time. Despite the fact I was new, Front Desk gave me ten rooms. In the first room I turned over, there was hair all over the bathroom. Luckily, the Alpaca people had left me a five dollar tip. The other housekeepers finished by three. By four, Front Desk was beginning to get impatient; I finished at 6:45.

Unsure if I wanted to work with Dan, I had answered another musicians wanted ad on Craigslist. It had been put up by a drummer and a bassist looking for a singer. We agreed to meet at Lovecraft, a bar I had never been to before. Since I had finished work so late there was no time to shower or change before meeting them. I was starving by the time I got off work. The cafe and pub where I could have gotten a free meal was packed so I decided to check out Boogie Burger on the other side of the river. The young woman behind the counter was gorgeous: Long blonde hair, kind of soft focus, sweet personality. I got a simple burger and stared out at the traffic as I ate.

A block down Burnside a group of young skateboarders had taken over the sidewalk and said something derisive in my general direction as I passed. At first I was angry but then I remembered when I was young and all the shit I had said to people. We were so innocent back in the 80s, far less nihilistic.

I wouldn't want to be a teenager now; it seems like a crazy time to be a kid.

The Lovecraft was one of the few Goth haunts in Portland. There was black paint on the walls and creepy artwork. I figured out who I was supposed to meet and the three of us sat in a booth. All of us liked the same bands so the conversation flowed naturally. They were trying to talk me into doubling on guitar but I knew I was rusty and would probably end up embarrassing myself.

"Seriously, I haven't played in a year, I will suck. Besides, all my stuff is back in California."

"Just think about it, okay? I have an amp you can borrow."

"Okay."

We ordered a second round and talked another hour about all the bands we liked: Echo and the Bunnymen, Joy Division, Siouxsie and the Banshees, and the Cure. The bartender switched on the smoke machine and the original *Phantom of the Opera* was projected on a wall. Part of me wanted to stay and drink absinthe but then I remembered that I was on a budget. With some reluctance, I took my last sip of whiskey and said goodnight.

44

I woke up the next morning and re-read the texts between Sofia and I. We had only spent ten minutes together---did she even remember me? Of all the women I came across at work and out in the world, S was the one that resonated. *She has probably forgotten me. She probably went to California, got all wrapped up in her family business, and forgot me. I mean, it was just a ten minute chat in a bar; I need to just let her go.*

There wasn't time for reflection, I had many errands to run before work. I made coffee for Noah and I, figured out which buses I needed to take, and then left the house. As I walked to the bus stop I got to thinking about when *Rolling Stone* reviewed the Album; the reviewer liked it and singled out the arrangements for praise. I cut the review out and put it in a scrapbook. Noah was almost curt when I called to congratulate him, angry because the label had dropped the band. More accurately, he was upset because he finally understood that his reward for several years of work was a second tier seat in the belly of a horrible monster. I'm pretty sure Noah never wanted to be a rock star; I think he wanted to be the mastermind behind the curtain. When Chase died a few months after the label dropped them, he closed the door on all those aspirations--- that much he told me. His moving on to something else is another example of his being smarter than me. I kept having failure after failure as a writer only to keep writing; I kept approaching people only to be ignored and politely told to go away. What did I have if I couldn't make it as a writer? That sort of thinking was dangerous. I was dwelling on that as I waited for the 15 Downtown. I was counting Subarus and thinking of how close to death I had been the previous summer. One night things had gotten as bad as they've ever been; the idea of hanging myself with the extension cord in my closet nearly became too strong to resist. I guess I didn't want to die because I got a hold of Noah. I didn't tell him exactly what was on my mind but he could probably tell by my tone of voice things were dire. I got through it but I will probably carry that night the rest of my life. Waking up the next morning gave that day and all those that have followed a beauty that may have been otherwise hard to see.

I was watching the front desk around eight when two women came up looking for towels. One of them started flirting with me, introducing herself and shaking my hand. "I'm Melissa, by the way," she said.
"Nice to meet you, I'm Ike; let me know if I get you anything."
Feeling the warmth of her skin I felt a familiar helplessness. She had lots of tattoos so I complimented them. Melissa and her friend walked off and I thought that was that. An hour later I was making my rounds. Seeing the pool was full of people, I walked in to make sure no one had brought in any food or glass. Melissa was in the water by herself with a glass of wine. As gently as possible, I explained that we couldn't have glass around the pool and got her a plastic cup. She looked up at me intently.
"Thanks for looking after me," she said.

I met her gaze and we just stared at each other for a few moments. I just wanted to stay there, close to her, but I had to go back to my rounds.

Fifteen minutes later we ran into each other in the elevator. "Are you having a good time?" I felt lame for asking that, but I was so tongue tied around her no other words would form.
"I guess. I'm getting married tomorrow," she replied.
"Congratulations."
"I don't know; it's kind of creepy."
She looked so sadly beautiful it took everything inside me not to hit on her. My instincts were telling me that if I came onto her she would have let me into her room. We just stood in that old elevator looking at each other---
What would she say if I asked her to run away with me? I think she is open to our being together, at least for a couple of hours.
As much as I wanted her, I also understood that she was drunk and vulnerable. For all I knew it was just the wedding jitters and she had a good thing going with her fiancée. Also, I had nothing to offer her; I was just a guy with a dead end job who lived in a van. The elevator doors opened on her floor; Melissa gave my hand a squeeze and then walked off towards her room. I wanted to follow her as much as I had ever wanted anything in my life. Instead, I watched her walk away, fumble with her keys, and disappear into her room.

I hung out on the third floor a lot that night with the hope of running into her again. I had already passed on any chance

I had with Melissa but something in me wouldn't let it go. Luckily for both of us, our paths didn't cross again that night. Walking to the bus stop after work I understood that the next day she would wake up with a hangover and no memory of me. I had to think of things that way or I might have walked back to the hotel and knocked on her door.

45

The next morning I woke up to the smell of rain in the air. I felt both dismayed and annoyed to see the sky could still open up in late May. When would it stop? I had only lived there a total of six months but I was wise to Portland's ways. The city teases you with a few days of sun, lulling you into believing that the good weather had finally arrived, only to slam you again with gray and rain. I spent a lot of the day in the house working on various writing projects. As much as I wanted to keep working I also felt the need to get out of Noah and Anne's hair for a bit. I found my umbrella and wandered the back streets listening to *Reckoning* by R.E.M. Ending up at the High Top, I found a small table and bought a large beer. I went over my finances and determined that money would be tight until I got the van habitable. Not only did I need to buy a bed and a cooler, but the battery and a tire also needed replacing. As much as I had hoped to be out earlier, I saw my time in the guest room stretching into June.

Sitting in the High Top, I felt a familiar sense of gloom trying to settle. I forced it away, well aware that I had willingly bought into the life I led. The constant poverty was wearing on me, though: I only had one decent pair of jeans and one cheap jacket. I was working my ass off only to average around $225 per week. I was 45 and had no career prospects with regards to "normal" jobs---it was make it as a writer or die trying. There was no turning back and I knew that. Maybe it had always been that way or maybe I had only crossed the line a year earlier. On top of it all, I was hyper-aware of how alone I was. I can handle solitude better than most people, but it still got to me from time to time.

But is this life anything a woman would want a part of? Would Sofia or Melissa or any of the others I've longed for want to lead such a catch as catch can sort of life? Even if they initially agreed, would it lead to disillusion and heartache somewhere down the line?

I looked out at the rain for a minute and then pulled out a notebook and a pen. The sky was angry and metal colored. My plan was to leave Portland in the Fall. Come Summer, I would begin applying for hotel gigs in the warm deserts down south. The only *but* had to do with living in a van. Portland was pretty safe as far as cities go; I understood that I might not be as lucky in some impoverished small town in New Mexico or Arizona. There were also small town cops to consider. What if the gig didn't come with a free or cut rate room or some sort of shower facility? What if the town I was in didn't have a 24 Hour Fitness? The biggest hurdle was that I still hadn't determined if I'd be cut out for van dwelling. I had the feeling that I could hack it, but wouldn't know for sure until I had been doing it for a month or two.

I finished writing and pulled out a collection of Ray Bradbury stories. It was an enormous book that weighed five pounds if it weighed an ounce. I had been carrying it all over Portland in that $4 camera bag that I had bought at the Goodwill in Lodi. I split my attention between the book and the bartender as she went about her job. She was in her mid-twenties with a green, v-necked sweater and a pretty smile. I looked at her and reminded myself of the Vow that I made a few weeks earlier:

I will never chase another woman. I will never play the fool for anyone else ever again.

No, the security guard with no neck and leather jacket wouldn't allow such a thing. There would never be another JB---

Then why am I hung up on Sofia? Why do I keep thinking about her and looking at her texts?

That was different. I was not texting her and if we ever got the chance to hang out I would play it cool. I would not give the security guard a day off. I was determined never to love unless I was loved in return, that was the only way it could be.

I kept going over the economics of living off a minimum wage job: You spend $4 on a beer including the tip and maybe that bought you two hours out of the weather and off your feet. After walking for half an hour to an hour you went to another bar and repeated the process. I had to wonder how it would be when I was living in the van full time. The way the long-termers did it was to spend as little time as possible in their van or RV; it was just a place for them to sleep and store their stuff. Clearly my time lingering in taverns was not going to end in the near future.

Leaving the bar, I put on my headphones and started walking past century old houses and schools. The beer had made me feel mellow and the feeling didn't erode even as the blocks became miles. I crossed major streets and passed cemeteries and corner stores. I needed food, but the desire to conserve money was stronger than my hunger. Climbing the front stairs of the house where I had lived for three months, I heard the sound of the television coming through the wall; Noah and Anne were watching a movie. As tired of walking as I was, I didn't want to interrupt their movie. Turning around and walking back down the stairs, I felt miserable and sorry for myself. I didn't want to just keep walking, but felt I had to.

I used the bathroom in Safeway and bought a cheap snack. Throwing it in my bag, I walked down to Hawthorne Liquors to get a beer or two. They had Four Loco---an insanely potent alcoholic drink that I had been hearing stories about for years---so I grabbed a can. The man behind the counter was somewhere in his thirties and looked Middle Eastern.
"I keep hearing about these things and was morbidly curious," I joked.
The clerk just looked sad and didn't say anything. Seeing his expression I realized how my situation must have looked to him; he probably saw alcoholics walking in his store every day to buy their pathetic Four Locos or Old Englishs or Steel Reserves. Every day we'd show up and hand over our rumbled bills and coins in exchange for something that'd put us a little closer to death. Eventually we wouldn't show up anymore and our place would be taken by someone else. Maybe it bothered him, maybe he felt guilt, or maybe it just disgusted him.

I was sitting in the van having my pathetic first meal of salt and vinegar chips and malt liquor when a text came in. Bernie was a member of a writing group that I had considered joining. B suggested that we hit a few bars and there was enough of the Four Loco in my blood to make the idea agreeable. The two of us met on SE 20th and headed towards the Willamette. There was a place down there with a quirky name that he wanted to check out. The bar was full of beards and politically correct conversations. A band that couldn't decide if it was Sebadoh or Galaxie 500 was coming over the speakers. We got our beers and talked about writing. The conversation continued over the course of a few hours and three more bars by midnight we were quite drunk. Bernie suggested that we check out the Pirates Cove, a strip club way up Sandy. When we got there the girls weren't wearing a stitch and his jaw fell open. I was used to California where things happen slowly but within two minutes the girl we were watching was spreading her legs. It felt gross and I was ready to leave.

"I think I'm ready to call it a night," I said.

"You go ahead, Ike, I'm going to stay."

He didn't even look at me; he was just licking his lips as he stared at the girl working the pole. She had a hard face and scars on the insides of her arms; I couldn't get out of there quickly enough.

The 12 had stopped running so I walked the three miles back to Noah and Anne's. Wandering the still, residential streets, I was intoxicated enough to think nothing of pissing on trees. It was a beautiful night for being drunk and lost and primitive.

46

I woke up on top of the bed wrapped in a blanket and
wearing the previous day's clothes. Rushing through my
coffee and food I could tell that the day would be ugly---
another hungover shift. I forced myself to jog down to the
bus stop only to discover that my bus wouldn't be coming.
There was a group of college-aged women standing in a
circle nearby: Some were beautiful and all of them were
young enough to be my daughter. Other people showed up
to spread rumors that the bus had been stopped by a
marathon that was weaving through town. Deciding to try
another bus line, I called into work to let them know I'd be
late. I was still drunk from the night before and it felt like I
was falling down a hole as I walked. The dull thud of my
heart made me aware of how the liquor had turned to
poison.
*You're forty-five years old, when is this stupid shit going to
stop? How many more nights like that do you think you can
see the other end of?*
There was no answer to that; I was in a deep fog where
complete thoughts remained hidden.

Seeing the 20 in the distance, I needlessly ran the last half
block. Short of breath I took a seat only to discover that we
would be sitting on that bus another half an hour. The
passengers watched the cars beside us lose patience and
turn around to head in the opposite direction. The weather
played a light gray game to keep us guessing and I was
dying for a glass of water to kill the dehydration.

The sun was coming out a little by the time I got to the hotel. I was supposed to be the floater---helping out wherever help was needed---but one of the housekeepers had called in with a family emergency. I loaded a cart with cleaning supplies and headed up to my first room. A $10 tip had been left behind but since K had stripped the room for me I split the tip with her. I felt like crap but strangely happy and passed the time by singing to myself. I had been toying with the idea of asking one of the housekeepers out. Amy was around 22 and ridiculously small. She was a cute girl, quite sweet, and sometimes I thought she was flirting with me or maybe that was just the way she was. I wanted to find out; I also wanted to get past my natural reserve. For too long I had been shy or guarded or overly cautious and who knew how many opportunities I had missed because of that. I knew there had to be a way to ask a coworker out that wasn't creepy or needy or anything bad. I worked on coming up with a plan as I finished my first room.

Once again I was the last housekeeper to finish their rooms. My skill was coming, but I was still slow. After work I went to the pub for my free meal and ordered chili verde enchiladas. I also broke down and got a whiskey to still the pulse of my hangover. The bartender was gorgeous, curvy and covered in tattoos. I complimented her on this spiral she had on her elbow and she smiled warmly and thanked me. How do you talk to bartenders and waitresses without it being a burden? How do you chat with them and not be another creep or chump or pest? I had no idea. I felt like I

143

was terrible at reading women; I could never figure out whether they were into me or not.

Noah was messing around on the piano when I got back to the house. Not wanting to interrupt, I read in the guest room until he stopped playing. When a minute or two without piano notes had passed, I went downstairs and got on the piano. I looked over to make sure he wasn't working. "Sounded good, you keep improving on that," I said.
"Yeah, I can't get it out of my head." He swiveled the chair to face me, I looked over in turn.
"Sorry that band didn't work out," I said. "I know you were looking forward to it."
He just shrugged and turned back towards his computer. I played a couple of chords and then stopped.
"I met up with some guys a couple of days ago," I said. "Bassist and a drummer."
"Yeah? How did that go?" My friend asked.
"Okay, I was hoping just to sing but they want me to play guitar, too."
"You can use mine if you want," Noah offered.
"Thanks, the thing is, I haven't played in a long time; I'm really rusty."
"It'll come back in a couple of days."
"Maybe."
Noah started doing some work, but stopped after a couple of minutes.
"I wish it wasn't this way," he said softly.
"What?" I already kind of knew, but I could have been wrong.

"I'm not pushy, am I?" He asked. "I really hate to think I've ever been an asshole."

"You are anything but an asshole; if you were one, you would have bossed those guys around and not been bothered by it."

"Probably, but I wanted to boss them around, it was hard not to just take charge and have them play what I heard in my head. Maybe I'm not a good ensemble player."

"You're a perfectionist and you hear music in a way most people don't," I replied. "It's not an easy combination."

"I guess."

Noah went back to work. I expected him to stop after a couple minutes as he had before, but N got back in a groove and worked for several hours.

47

I didn't want to date Amy, our age difference made that a ridiculous idea. Fucking her could have been good, but she didn't seem the sort who went for casual sex; especially with a man twenty years older than her. More than anything I was curious how she would respond if I invited her out for a drink. I texted her and she wrote back saying that, while I seemed like a nice guy, she was happy being single. At first I wondered if the invitation would backfire at work---I was worried about either getting in trouble with my bosses or becoming the object of negative rumors. Despite my concerns and the risk involved, I understood that it was a good thing that I had gone through with it. In the past I would have never sent that text, I would have been too concerned about rejection, but I didn't want to be scared anymore.

One of the Maintenance staff injured their wrist and asked if I could work two back to back shifts. Needing both money and approval from the bosses, I agreed. I was told that I would work the following morning and Kate would probably come in for a couple of hours that night. They didn't want her working longer because she was about to go into overtime. Although I smiled and nodded as if I understood, I was pissed off: How did they think they could avoid overtime? I knew how much things would suffer if Maintenance wasn't fully staffed. We were in peak season with at least fifty percent occupancy every night; things needed to be stocked and cleaned. What can you say, though? If you make yourself a pest they'll find a reason to fire you or cut your hours or some other punishment. The punishment may come with a smile and a regretful tone of voice, but it's still punishment.

Someone found a blow up doll in one of the rooms, a cheap one without genitals. I nicknamed him Blow-up Beau and drew on a mustache and a gap in his teeth. People were always finding sex toys or used condoms in the rooms; you heard people fucking through the doors and smelled the sweat and the fluids soaked into the sheets when you stripped the rooms. There is a weird intimacy that you have with the guests even if you don't speak to them. At the Hotel Glass, they would leave Cheerios ground into the carpet or soiled underwear draped over the shower but they'd rarely leave a tip. When they did it was usually a couple of ones or a five. I saw a twenty once but was told that was extremely rare; even a ten dollar bill was an anomaly. Sometimes a guest would leave a couple of beers or a bottle of wine. There was a bottle of inexpensive chardonnay on the Maintenance desk when I got in on Monday. I set it in a bucket of ice so it would be cold by the time my shift ended.

As I was stocking linens I overheard a guest commenting about the "creepy paintings." I wanted to join in the conversation but that sort of thing can backfire on you. A lot of the paintings *were* creepy, especially the ones on the fourth floor landing, an area I avoided for that very reason. One was a depiction of a party from the 1940s with all these dead people with cold eyes and big smiles; it looked like a prop from *Night Gallery*. The other was set around a hundred years earlier and starred a creepy little girl. I always kept my back to them whenever I had to vacuum the landing.

There were more gorgeous women in the pool, their breasts rolling out of bikinis or straining against various fabrics. I tried to look without looking, walking around the pool as I pretended to check the water. I saw cleavage and nipples--- I also saw heavy cocks straining against spandex. I always had to stay on top of making sure that the guests weren't taking glasses down to the pool. Front Desk told them not to take glasses downstairs---there was a big sign on the door to the pool repeating the warning---but they still did it. You want to ask them if they can read or if they're just assholes. Instead, I would use a polite tone of voice and affect an awkward smile as I offered to pour their drink in a plastic cup. I had to do that a couple of times a week, but at least it was better than washing glasses. That task was one of the most frustrating parts of my job. We shared the kitchen with the cafe and used their dishwasher. Most of the time the counters surrounding it would be stacked with dirty dishes making it impossible to get the glasses washed. My routine was to check the kitchen every hour until the restaurant staff got off their asses and washed their stuff. I had a lot of antagonism towards the cafe; they were always walking across my freshly mopped floor or using the elevator or getting in my way when they dumped their trash out. When I was away from work I realized that I was being an asshole and that I got in their way as well. At work, though, I could only see their part in the whole mess.

I finished my shift at midnight, cued Bauhaus on my iPod, and walked half a mile to catch the 14. I hadn't lost my love for that time of night: Most people are asleep and all the streets are empty and you don't have to keep an eye out for cars or other pedestrians. It felt enjoyable to take in all the wide, free streets and look up at the dark windows of the buildings I passed. There were always a couple of bad or at least desperate people out there, but they were easy to avoid and never detracted from the experience.

A couple of minutes before the 14 arrived; a scowling man sauntered up to the bus stop. He had an old, unhappy face and a very obvious toupee that looked as if it had been dropped on his head as an afterthought. It was chestnut brown and looked synthetic, mussed for some reason, maybe to make it look real—as if that were possible. I got on the bus and Frank Fakehair sat across from me with the same sour look on this face. A few blocks down the road a security guard boarded, a woman somewhere in her fifties with a cane who looked like someone's grandmother. What use was a security guard like that? What was she going to do if a crime took place? It seemed like a bad joke.

Back at the house I opened the wine, caught up on my email, and read some news online. I drank the whole bottle of wine and ended up reading in bed until two. I knew I had to be up at six, but my mind refused to shut down.

48

The three and a half hours between falling asleep and the alarm going off seemed to pass in the blink of an eye. I forced myself out of bed to make coffee and pull myself together. I stood up on the 15 knowing that if I sat down I would probably fall asleep.

Michelle showed up even though she was supposed to have the day off. She wore glasses and was cute in a quirky way, tiny and often braless. I was under the impression that she was involved with someone. M always seemed nervous around me, possibly because she picked up on me checking her out.

I drank a couple of cups of coffee as I went about the job. People were fucking in 314; I stopped to listen to them for a moment and thought of Melissa the drunken bride. What had become of her? I imagined her getting fucked on her wedding night, the way her face would contort as a big dick was shoved into her. Aroused, I made a detour to the restroom for a few minutes.

Sometimes calls came through the phone in the elevator. That morning, it was a recording from a collection agency instructing whoever picked up the phone which buttons to push to get through the phone tree. The calls came through the speaker all echoey and bounced around the hard surfaces of the elevator. It was especially disembodied and surreal if you'd only had three and a half hours of sleep. I thought of the couple in 314, I imagined Melissa in there, gritting her teeth as she was fucked hard. The distraction was pleasant but I had work to do and forced it from my mind.

In my disoriented state I started panicking about that text I had sent to Amy. I created scenarios in my mind about all the ways it could blow up in my face. What if it made Suzy think less of me? I'd asked her out for a drink before and she seemed open to the idea—-what if she thought I saw her as just another woman in the hotel? I really liked Suzy. That morning we had gotten to talking when I was taking a crib out of a room she was turning over. She looked pretty and smiled one of her amazing smiles—could anything ever happen between us? Sometimes I thought something could but then I remembered my gift for misreading women. I had the feeling that Amy would tell other people that I had texted her; we all gossiped in the hotel. Amy would probably tell the other housekeepers and it would probably get back to Suzy. I couldn't blame her if she thought less of me because of that.

We were busy enough that the day passed fast. Amy told everyone she was feeling sick and pawned a couple of her rooms off. Everyone was irritated with her and felt that A wouldn't last long at the hotel; she wasn't getting faster and had a bad reputation for pawning rooms off. The housekeepers would get their list of rooms and put together a game plan for that shift. When they got a room out of the blue it would throw those plans off. Amy was a sweet kid but ditzy, immature; hopefully she'd grow out of it at some point.

Frank's voice came over the radio when I was down in the basement.

"Hey guys, it's snowing outside."

By the time I had gotten to a window the snow had turned to rain. I still loved Portland but the weather was getting to me. Why was it so fucking cold and miserable at the end of May? We had a week of warmth and sun and people lazing in parks only to have it regress to more rain and cold and I was done with it. By Halloween, I would be down South where it never got below sixty degrees.

The rain came through my umbrella as I walked to the bus stop. An old woman was leaning against a sign as the water ran off her umbrella and soaked the back of her jacket. The 15 was packed just like the 15 always seemed to be packed. A week earlier I had caught it after ten at night and even that late it was standing room only. You think and hope and wish and pray it won't get more crowded but then you pull up to the next stop and there are five or ten or eight more people lined up. Like the weather, the big city crowds were starting to get to me.

I got back to the house and made myself some rice for a simple burrito. After taking a shower I read a little of the new *Rolling Stone* and napped for a couple of hours. Sofia and I had made tentative plans for Thursday but I had to work that night. I texted her to let her know what days I had free and added that I was on my way out to do karaoke. We texted back and forth and it sounded like she was planning on meeting me at Chopsticks. I hung around until after midnight but she didn't show up. Being foolish I started over thinking things: What if Sofia showed up and we had a good time and ended up back at her place? What if she was up for having sex? What if she just wanted to be friends? I was overthinking things and getting anxious just as I always did.

49

Dee was at the front desk when I clocked in.

"Right on time as always, Ike."

"Yep. Hey, how's your father?" Dee had been out two months caring for him after his stroke.

"Some good days, some bad."

Suzy was standing in the lobby; she smiled at me when I walked in. The two of them had been talking about someone named Robert the Bear. The guest with the intimidating name had checked out earlier in the day only to slip back in his room. People had gone up and tried to roust him but he kept falling back asleep or pretending to sleep. D told me that when Michelle came back the three of us would be going up to his room for another attempt.

Why hasn't the security patrol been called?

I kept that thought to myself; I had worked enough jobs to understand that the correct response was *smile and nod.*

What if this guy has a knife or a gun?

It didn't matter: This was my job and I just had to do it.

The three of us went up to 401 which was at the end of a tight corridor. If Robert the Bear burst out of the room shooting or thrusting angrily with a knife, we'd probably just fall all over each other. Dee knocked on the door and then opened it with her pass card. Robert was under the covers and responded groggily, saying that he was leaving the room. The three of us went back to the main corridor and tried to figure out what to do. Michelle's ride was waiting so D let her go. Dee and I walked back to the room and I knocked on the door. Robert the Bear was dressed and packing a red suitcase. Every time he reached in that bag, I was watching for a gun. He was a big guy, not fat but solid, and a little over six feet tall. There were dark rings around his eyes and a weird vibe coming off him that made me uncomfortable. I tried to balance standing my ground with smiling at the guy and offering to help him get his stuff together. It seemed like twenty minutes passed before he got that damned suitcase packed up.

On the walk to the lobby, Robert the Bear told us that he had taken too much of his medication.
"That's why I slept too much," the guest explained.
He winced and I understood that was my cue to ask if anything was wrong.
"I'm having chest pains," Robert the Bear said. "Is there a bathroom around here?"
I showed him where the bathroom was and then went on with my chores. When I came back a few minutes later, he was sitting in a chair in the tiny lobby; bent over to rummage in his backpack. I really didn't want to be around him when he was rummaging in that backpack, I was *positive* a gun would come out at some point. It would be another half hour before he left; until then I was half listening for shots and screams coming from the lobby.

I always filled the mop bucket on the second floor. The kitchen was closer, but there was always pandemonium in there. On the way back to the basement, I shared the elevator with an older couple. The man made some joke about washing his feet in the mop bucket and I attempted a witty response. They both smelled like clothes they had worn in the rain but never dried right---why do old people always smell like must? Is it because they are beginning to decay? One of the musicians playing in the downstairs bar walked through when I was starting to mop. Seeing he was wearing a tie-dyed shirt I knew his music would be shitty.

Dee called me up to 405. She was wearing a long sleeve t-shirt and I could see the outline of her nipples. My cock became hard and I caught her glancing at my crotch a couple of times. We talked about Robert the Bear and then she told me about a friend of hers that had been found murdered on a tropical island.

"Islands are dangerous: Hawaii. The Bahamas. All those places in the Caribbean. People disappear and are found dead all the time; they just don't report it because it would scare the tourists off."

"Yeah?"

She took a couple of steps closer to me as I made the bed. "Being on an island changes you," she continued. "I don't remember what the condition is called, but they have a name for it."

"You know, my friends keep thinking of moving to Kawai but they worry about the same condition you're talking about," I replied.

"Islands are dangerous," Dee nodded as if I had proved her point.

She paused. I was pretty sure she wasn't wearing a bra. The way she was looking at me maybe we could have fucked on that bed there and then. *Maybe*, I also understood the consequences whether I was right or wrong. Dee seemed to pick up on what I was thinking and went to the table to rearrange the glasses.

"Hey, we had some people check into 401 but they left after twenty minutes; could you make sure the room is still ready for check-in?"

"Yeah, no problem."

Dee looked at the bulge in the front of my pants again and I stole one more glance at the front of her shirt, imagining her large, brown breasts and dark nipples. After she left I went to the bathroom for a few minutes before turning my attention to 401.

I made the bed in 401, cleaned the sink, and went out of my way to make the room sparkle in case Dee checked it. Sofia texted me as I worked: She had shown up at Chopsticks but we had just missed each other. We talked about bars and agreed to meet early the following week when things were less crazy for both of us. Turning 401 overthrew the rest of the schedule off and I had to cut corners when doing the bathrooms. I got another cheeseburger from the pub and wolfed it down as I watched the rain fall on the pavement and people hustle down the sidewalk. It was easy to tell which pedestrians were tourists; they were the ones trying to avoid the downpour. Portland natives understand that there is no point; the rain always finds you.

It was still pissing rain when I walked to the bus stop. The streetlamps were reflecting off the standing water in the road. It was beautiful but I would have rather seen it in a postcard than feel the wind coming off it.

Mum's birthday, September 27---I will be out of here by then. On May 12, Dad's birthday, I'll be back.

All the windows on the bus were fogged up so you had to guess where your stop was. I always managed to sit next to people who reeked of cigarettes. There were always a handful of smokers on the bus and one or two people coughing like they had TB. A young black guy with a prominent afro was scratching himself and making these weird faces like he had mange. Everyone else seemed to be ignoring him, I couldn't.

50

The next day I took care of the most pressing problem with the van: The battery. A week earlier, I had gone out to move it and the engine wouldn't start: No clicking, no sounds whatever. No lights. Work had been crazy so every appointment I made to get a replacement battery had to be cancelled. The morning after Robert the Bear, I walked four blocks in the rain to call roadside assistance for a jump start. The person on the other end of the line had a thick accent and apparently an equally thick skull; it took forever for her to understand what I needed.

The terminals at the end of the battery cables were badly corroded; the AAA guy had to jiggle them to get a connection. He had one of those briefcase sized jump starters and I stood back in case that crummy old battery exploded. The van fired up and ran well as it always did but I was nervous it would stall at a light and wouldn't restart. I got it to the shop without incident and read a couple of automotive magazines. The clerk was a young woman around 25, tomboyish but with a cute smile. We talked about customer service. She was wearing coveralls and looked like a girl that was more comfortable in men's clothes.

$158 later---(for the battery and the new terminals)---I drove to 50th and Powell to vacuum out the van. I had passed the car wash on the corner many times waiting for the 14. As bad as it looked from a distance, it was even seedier up close. After taking care of the battery issue I had maybe $100 left for the rest of the week. Money just seemed to disappear even after getting a decent paycheck. For a few hours I had over $500 but then I registered the van, paid my friend back half of a $200 loan, went out for drinks twice, and then replaced the battery. I knew the next check wouldn't be as fat and $200 of it would be going towards insurance and paying back the rest of the loan. After getting paid, I would have around $300 to live off and maybe buy a foam mattress and a cooler. I also needed a gym membership in order to shower and a tension rod to hang clothes; those four things were the bare minimum for living in a van. Looking in the future, I needed new rear tires and an alignment before taking any long journeys. The way things were going there wouldn't be any road trips until the end of summer or even later; maybe escaping to the desert in the winter wouldn't be plausible after all.

The rain didn't seem to be letting up. On Saturday and Sunday I was scheduled to work after the last buses ran and wondered if I'd be walking three and a half miles in the rain. I parked the van in its usual spot and studied the heavy sky through the windshield. Understanding I was fucked, I climbed out and locked the door. Did I have anything to drink after work? No. I walked to Hawthorne Liquors to get a bottle of wine. There was a knock-kneed woman with garish red hair climbing out of a newer Jaguar. She looked like a prostitute or maybe it was an ironic *faux prostitute* look not unlike the hipsters who try to look homeless. It was pouring out, just unrelenting rain, and I struggled against a dark mood building in my head.

51

That evening started with shit. The water in the toilet was up to the rim and soft pieces of shit were floating in lazy circles like paddle boats on a lake. I was standing in an inch or so of water as I contemplated the mess. After a couple of minutes, I turned off the water to the toilet and told the cafe manager that he needed to call a plumber.

Making my rounds, I saw a manager from the bar downstairs talking to Front Desk. They had a backed up another toilet and Front Desk had, once again, volunteered my services. In my mind, the bar and cafe were separate entities from the hotel and their toilets were their problem. I had gotten used to dealing with shit and toilets, but already had the bathrooms in the hotel to deal with. I just stared at Front Desk like he was a fucking asshole.
"Do you know where the plunger is, Ike?" Front desk asked.
"Unfortunately."
It sucked, in my heart it seemed like a giant injustice, but all I could do was smile and nod.

A Grateful Dead tribute band had been playing down in the basement bar all week. I had always thought the Grateful Dead were the worst band in the world but that tribute act proved me wrong; what I found in the bathroom that night perfectly complemented their set.

Down in the basement, I sorted the new linens and tried to contain the soiled sheets and towels in three over stacked carts. I made up songs as I worked about dirty hippies who were unable to use toilets properly. It ended up being a crazy night: The hotel was nearly full so I was running up and down the stairs and dodging guests and grabbing the luggage cart or helping musicians store their gear in locked rooms. On busy days the housekeepers used up all the clean linens in the closets. It was Maintenance's responsibility to restock those closets with sheets and towels and robes and soap—everything that goes into a room and needs to be replaced after a guest vacates. Restocking involved filling several laundry carts---sometimes as many as ten---and taking them through the basement where guests had stopped to marvel at the old photographs. There could be up to a five minute wait for the small elevator shared by a cafe, two bars, and a 67 room hotel. If a guest wanted on you had to smile and nod and wrestle your cart off the lift. It didn't matter if you were falling behind schedule, the guests always came first.

On one of my trips to the elevator that night there was a small group admiring all the pictures in the basement. One of the couples was in their fifties and the other in their late seventies. The older couple was tiny, manufactured in an era when people were smaller and now shrinking even more. They seemed to be enjoying the pictures of the wild history of the hotel. The couples lingered over the shots of when it was run by organized crime and frequented by people like Duke Ellington. The older folks seemed bewildered but amused by the shots of drag queens with mustaches who ran a gay bar where they were standing. The couples seemed lost in the pictures, traveling through time, and I felt bad interrupting them to get by with my cart. The younger of the two women approached me as I was looking through the window at the soaking pool.

"Is the pool original?" She asked.

"No. They installed it when they built the hotel a few years ago."

"Oh, I heard they built it when they originally built the hotel," the woman looked doubtful.

I wasn't sure how to respond to that but the woman had rejoined the rest of her party. One of the guys in the Grateful Dead tribute band walked by in a tie-dyed shirt and went into the bar.

"He was smoking pot," the older lady said derisively.

"I smelled something skunky," the woman who had been talking to me said. "Is that pot?"

"Yes," the man I guessed was her husband said.

I got back into the rhythm of stocking the closets; on nights like that it could take up to three hours. On busy nights I was always on the go, running up stairs or wrestling carts or struggling with heavily sprung doors. The only time I stopped was a fifteen minute break to grab my free meal and wolf it down. When it got warmer, I kept a mason jar of ice water with me and would drink between two and four quarts a night. One plus was that time passed quickly; I was always checking my phone to see what time it was because I knew when I had to wrap up certain tasks and start the next one.

There was this comedy act that worked in the bar from eleven to one. When they were in the basement getting some props they noticed Blow Up Beau and excitedly carried him off. Half an hour later, I saw an attractive couple walking in the basement hall. The woman was carrying Beau as she struggled to inflate him. I didn't have the heart to tell her that he had been found in one of the rooms---God knows what he had seen and been involved in. Blow Up Beau got around that night: Hanging out by the pool and going up stairs. By the end of the night he was uninflated again and sitting on top of the comedy act's stuff—-just another prop.

52

I slept in a solid block, seven hours of darkness without dreams; not a single frame where normally my mind created movies. I had been in Portland for three months at that point. It had been an adventure at first but now it was a real life complete with a full-time job and a home (the van). There was even---potentially---a woman in my life. Sofia and I hadn't been on a date but there was something about her, a weird but undeniable feeling that we were meant to play a large role in each others' lives. I drank coffee that Noah had made and did shit on the computer for an hour. I ate some food, put on some clothes, and went on a long walk before work. Camera bag swaying against my hip, I walked along the north edge of the Lone Fir Cemetery. Nearby, new condos or apartments were being wedged into neighborhoods that were over a hundred years old. Sometimes I looked at the ornate buildings from before the First World War and it felt like traveling through time or maybe being lost between times, lost between worlds. The newer buildings seemed like cold flatlines in comparison. There was nothing to untether your imagination, just soulless earth-toned boxes.

A few hours later I was in my work clothes headed for the bus stop. Even though I had a job and a place I couldn't shake the feeling that I was a breath away from being homeless. What if the van died and got impounded? Seeing people sleeping in doorways and on bridges reminded me of how close it was. Once I was out of Noah and Anne's house I was out; I wouldn't take their hospitality again. I had no idea what I'd do, but I'd figure it out.

A beautiful woman in *Looking for Mr. Goodbar* sunglasses got on the bus. She was all beige business casual, loose clothes and subtle lines. I kept stealing glances at her and wondered where she'd end up at the end of the night—alone reading and drinking wine in bed or involved in something torrid and unexpected in the back of a car or a stranger's bedroom? The woman in the sunglasses could have been a doctor or a dominatrix or a barista. I spent half the ride we shared staring out the window and the other half spinning a dozen potential stories about her. She got off the bus and took all her mysteries with her.

Michelle was at the hotel picking up some hours. She had injured a shoulder but was doing what she could with one arm. I swept and mopped and tried to be resigned when people walked across the wet floor. Outside the cement was wet and a black and a plastic wrapper in the gutter floated like a wraith until I fished it out. I felt like one of the ghosts in the hall when people passed by. A man stopped to ask me a question about one of the rooms that I couldn't answer. The pub was extremely busy so my favorite waitress didn't get my order in and was apologetic when I showed up. She was so gorgeous and friendly it was like an ache in my heart whenever I saw her. There were lots of bulky guys standing at the bar, playing pool, or chatting to women who seemed to enjoy being chatted to. Body spray dub step thumped through the speakers in the insistent but clumsy rhythm of fucking. I got my Baja tacos and headed back to the basement. I was hungry and they were good and I gobbled them up like a beast, using my fingers as I ate with abandon.

A man and a woman were in the pool and the man was saying things that I hoped were a joke or some weird form of role-playing:
"Where are you gonna go?" The man asked the woman. "You're a prostitute, no one's gonna help you."
I got called up to watch the front desk while Mike escorted some guests to a nearby hotel. A few seconds after Mike left, two people showed up to check in. I knew just enough about the system to bring up their reservation and ask the initial questions. As a couple, they seemed mismatched: A beautiful English girl and her scraggly boyfriend. Patience was something they had in common. The two of them smiled kindly after I explained what had happened. Mike slouched back into the lobby a couple of minutes later. I wanted to give him a dirty look but he wasn't a bad guy so I restrained myself. For the seventh night in the row the awful Grateful Dead tribute band was playing in the bar. For reasons beyond comprehension, it was standing room only. I thought of a meteor crashing into the planet and the sweet, fiery death we probably deserved.

I was happy to see that 209 was a stay over. I called her 209 because I couldn't remember her name. I think she gave it to me once but we were by the pool and I couldn't make out what she said over the rushing water. 209 had dark hair and was curvy, carrying a little extra weight very well; smart with a slow nicotine smile. Seeing me at the linen closet, she ran down the hall in her bikini to get a robe. I gave her two as I counted her tattoos and imagined the warmth of her skin.

"Would you like me to make them up for you?" I asked.

"Make them up? No, I can do it; I just tear the package open, right?"

"Yeah."

She thanked me and walked off back to her room. Maybe half an hour later I ran into 209 again when I was doing a pool check. She was drunk and having difficulty pulling her robe on. I considered offering to help her but worried that she would think I was hitting on her. We had a friendly chat and it was clear that she was not into me; I was just a person she felt comfortable having a conversation with. I kept hoping that would change with each encounter, that I would see a difference in how she looked at me or acted around me, but the change never happened. Nevertheless, I still found myself lingering on her floor, hoping to run into her and see a change that would remain a fantasy

People were fucking in 413. I pretended to get something out the linen closet so I could listen. I had seen them in the pool earlier, a curvy Black woman somewhere around 25 and a guy who may have been an Arab. You could see the outline of a huge cock in his shorts. I caught a couple other people in the pool---men and women---checking it out. They got out of the pool, went upstairs, and were fucking within a few minutes. The bed was creaking and the woman was very vocal. Mostly she was gasping and moaning but I heard her cry out "I'm too wet!" at one point.

I imagined him driving into her with that big dick and toyed with the idea of dipping into the bathroom.
The creaking stopped and I went back to work.

Even though my life generally felt good I still found myself quick to anger and had no idea why. Maybe I was just frustrated with my tenuous living situation or maybe it was not having a woman in my life or my failure to sell books. I couldn't narrow it down to one definite reason, there were just the usual suspects lined up against a wall. There was always darkness around the edges but I didn't mind it, it was like an old friend or at least an enemy I understood.

The comedy act that played the basement bar was leering at women in the pool. I shot them a dirty look and nearly told them to fuck off. They winked at me but when my hard stare didn't waver their smiles faded a bit and they walked away. After a few moments, I realized what a hypocrite I was, denying other people what I always took for myself. If I really looked at the situation, maybe I was just jealous of the comedy act: They were getting to perform their art in public as people gave them drinks and money while I mopped floors and cleaned toilets. Jealousy is an ugly thing, a sad beast that is a master of disguises.

When I saw lovers in the pool I wanted to stare at them, to have what they had even vicariously. After a few moments I realized that it wasn't any good and moved on. Why do we do that to ourselves? Why do we just stare at the windows of haunted houses and open doors for all the ghosts and demons?

The next thing I knew I was standing at the bus stop waiting for the last bus. Weary, I stared across the street at the music store as I did every night after work for nearly three months: Same Justin Timberlake poster. Same windows of lofts or businesses looking down at us. The last bus was always crowded and someone was always coughing or had a minor deformity or was loudly telling some story. That night it was a young line cook talking about another line cook that always showed up drunk and screwed his work up and took long breaks. Some guy sat next to me and I got as close to the window as I could. The smell of his coat made me feel claustrophobic and the blocks couldn't roll by quickly enough. I got off at 28th and Burnside and listened to Stevie Wonder as I walked. There was someone asleep in a doorway wrapped in a blue sleeping bag. Within sight of them people smoked and laughed as they lingered outside bars that had just closed.

53

The weather was good when I left the house; maybe I wouldn't have a rainy walk back after my shift. A woman in her mid-twenties boarded at the stop next to the cemetery. She had several tattoos and half of her dark brown hair was bleached platinum blonde. Moving against her skin were tight, black spandex pants and a leopard print top. Recognizing another young woman, she waved to get her friend's attention and they started talking about some bar.

"Last night was weird," the other young woman said. "I don't know--the crowd was just weird."

"Are you on your way to work?" Leopard print asked.

"Yeah."

When the girl with the two-tone hair got off, a man shaded by a white straw Panama hat boarded. He was wearing a dark blue suit made of very light fabric, and white loafers. *His name is Willie Styles and he ain't got time for your jive. All he got time for is tha ladies.*

A few blocks down the road he took a call on a mobile phone that matched his shoes. I imagined a shelf in his closet for different colored phones. Willie Styles looked like Snoop Dogg in late middle age or maybe Snoop's uncle. I couldn't hear his phone conversation but he looked disappointed.

*Why that boy gotta change his name to Snoop **Lion**? Why he gotta start doing that reggae music? The reefer is okay, but those Rastas don't know how to dress.*

Getting to work, I discovered that the Grateful Dead cover band was carried over for an eighth night. I asked Front Desk about it when I was grabbing my walkie talkie.

"So--another night of shitty music?" I asked.

"It's part of Jerry Garcia's birthday celebrations. You don't like the Dead?" John looked sad at the possibility.

"No. I think they're the worst band ever."

He looked around nervously and then pointed up at a camera in the corner.

"The owners love the Dead. You know they named two rooms in the hotel after their songs, right?"

"How could I forget," I sighed.

Radio in hand, I went over my list of assignments. Downstairs, one of the dirty hippies was testing his amp; all I could do was grit my teeth and hope they didn't destroy the toilet again.

I was sad to see that 209 was no longer in the hotel and a small family had taken over her room. I fell into my routine of looking for burned out bulbs and seeing how we were on linens and other supplies. Someone had smoked marijuana in the first bathroom I checked. Why hadn't they just smoked in their room? Front Desk came on the radio and asked me to take an iron and ironing board to one of the rooms. The woman who answered the door was cute with glasses and a tight, white tank top. I was hoping she'd need something else as the night progressed.

After I checked the bathrooms I started stocking the linen closets. Called down to the lobby, I was asked to store a banjo in the pit. The guest it belonged to was wearing a suit and tie and looked vaguely like Ethan Hawke. I took the banjo down to the locked room where we store luggage and bicycles. After closing the door I messed around on that banjo for a couple of minutes. I wanted to keep playing it but there was work to do.

As I stocked the linen closet a couple in robes--- presumably on their way down to the pool---walked by talking about how men's fashion had changed.
"If you look at pictures of men's pants from the fifties, they went a lot higher."
"Yes, that's because the waist is up high; right now pants just come up to the hips."
The pool was busy all night. The beautiful English girl and her boyfriend were there for hours. For some reason, I was especially acerbic. The comedy act had been given carte blanche to store their props in our tight basement and it was pissing me off even more than usual. I heard stories about their drunken shenanigans and they sounded like jerks. They were waiting outside the bar, listening for the MC's cue, and I didn't want to get in the way of their entrance.
"Uh, I don't want to be in your way if you're about to be called on," I explained.
"No, no, it's fine, there's just no room in there," they were very nice, very gracious.
"Okay, well, I don't want to be in the way of Portland's version of *Everybody Loves Raymond*," I added.
They said nothing and I instantly realized that I had been an asshole. I think God made a point to show me that I was in the wrong because right after that I had a problem with a toilet and lost my keys for a few minutes.

Yeah, message received, I really need to keep that side of myself in check.

I tried to redeem myself by helping the comedy act store their chairs after they finished their set.

There was a cute lesbian couple on one end of the pool, an employee of the pub and the girl she was seeing. When the girlfriend went to the bathroom I knelt down to talk to the employee.

"Nice girlfriend you have there," I said.

"She's not my girlfriend," the employee smiled. "Not yet, but I'm hopeful."

She had a glass so I reminded her that we didn't allow glass in the pool. I ran upstairs to get a plastic cup and poured her beer into it.

"Thanks, dear," she said.

They were both in their mid-twenties and looked like 21st century hippies. When they climbed out of the pool a few minutes later they were clutching their clothes and hoping to change in the basement restroom.

"We're kind of drunk," the employee said.

"No worries, it's Friday," I smiled.

"I thought it was Saturday."

"Oh, yeah; I've been working for seven days straight; I get the days mixed up myself."

"Someone is still in the bathroom," the potential girlfriend said.

"I can let you into another bathroom upstairs," I offered.

We got in the elevator. They both looked at me and whispered something to each other about how I reminded them of someone. They were so cute and sexy I just wanted to go home with them and fuck them or watch them fuck or something.

The halls were quiet for the most part when I did my final property walk. I could hear people partying in a couple of rooms but mostly the rooms were silent and still. Wrapping things up I figured out what music I wanted to listen to on the walk back and was dismayed to see that it was raining. I was dreading walking three miles in a downpour but what can you do?

A drunken guy with his shirt open ran across a side street; a girl and another guy were laughing as they watched him. All the bars were letting out so the sidewalks were crowded on the west side of the bridge. I closed my umbrella and just dealt with the rain as I weaved down the crowded sidewalk. There were a lot of cop cars out; one had even blocked a left turn lane on Burnside. People standing outside Dante's Bar were staring at something but I couldn't see what.

No one was sleeping on the bridge. The river was moving delicately and the light on the water was beautiful and peaceful. It was a gorgeous night and I forgot about the rain and how long the walk was. All those people in their cars and the people on the earlier buses had missed that view--- it felt as if it were mine alone. Halfway across the bridge two girls were embracing a guy, it was more loving than sexual and it touched me for some reason. More bars were letting out on the other side of the bridge. I didn't slow my pace; I kept walking fast, not even stopping for red lights. It was still raining lightly but I was warm and even sweating a little as sparse drops fell and created subtle rhythms in the gutters.

54

I was wide awake after the long walk in the rain. The van was parked two blocks from the house so I made a detour to stop and look at it---my future home. Was it a bad idea? I had been preparing to live in a van for a year and now it was going to happen. On paper it seemed like the right thing but there were still realities about that sort of life that made me nervous. I walked in the house as quietly as possible but every footstep seemed to echo on the wood floors. After setting my bag down, I opened a bottle of wine and crept into the bathroom to take a shower. I ate and drank as I messed around on the computer and the minutes became hours. Around three, I took the last glass of wine to bed and fell asleep reading Ray Bradbury.

The alarm woke me at a quarter to eleven. I found a cheap dresser on Craigslist and made an appointment to pick it up. Edna started on the first try and I drove slowly and carefully down the narrow streets. The sun was out---I had to take my jacket off as I drove---and I felt thankful for the good weather. No one was home when I got back so I went downstairs to play piano. After fifteen minutes of messing around with chords, I typed up the notes I had taken at work the night before. There was no motivation inside me to look for literary agents or do anything that would further my writing career. Nothing I had been doing had worked; everything I had been trying seemed a waste of energy and time.

I went to work late in the afternoon. For the first time I noticed a creepy face that had been painted on one of the pipes on the third floor. Every time I passed it I would mutter "Hi, scary pipe face." All the rooms were booked and you could feel an undercurrent of activity in the hotel. Doing the bathroom check I discovered a toilet that was full of brown liquid. My horror diminished somewhat when I realized it was beer.

The floor in the kitchen was greasy and I struggled not to slip while moving twenty pound racks of glasses. I found myself getting drowsy as I cleaned the bathrooms a little before midnight. Walking in one of the bathrooms, I noticed that a guest had left a garbage can from their room in there. I started dumping it in the regular trash can and---
Wait. Is that? Oh...
The guest had shit in the trash can; they had defecated in the bin and left it in the shared bathroom. It looked like rocky road ice cream. I just stared at the mess for a minute or so knowing that I would have to deal with it one way or another. Part of me wanted to just toss it in a dumpster but then one room would be short a trash can and there would be questions and maybe I would get in trouble.
So I started scooping it out.
I tried to determine which guest had left it and decided it was a girl in the Misfits t-shirt I had seen earlier.
I had complimented her shirt and she had left a trash can full of shit in one of my bathrooms.
I kept changing my plastic gloves when they became smeared with feces. I got the can cleaned out pretty good

but it still smelled awful so I filled it with disinfectant and left it in the mop closet.

One of my responsibilities was restocking glasses in the supply closets on each floor. I usually did it at the end of the shift so the glasses had a chance to dry. The thing was, restocking involved rolling a squeaky dish rack down the halls. I always worried about waking the guests. Also, whoever was in the room next to the closet couldn't leave while I was stocking the glasses. At two I did my last property walk. One of the Hispanic janitors was getting his equipment together for his shift and I greeted him in Spanish---big mistake. He started talking a mile a minute and I was instantly in over my head. I'd say "Lo siento pero no comprende" but he didn't care. He kept going on and on—I think he was asking me about women in the hotel because he was leering a bit: *Me gusta chicas*. I was smiling and nodding and trying to slip away but the conversation wouldn't die.

55

I woke up at nine after another night of staying up until four. I had a Housekeeping shift that day so I guessed that I'd be done around six. Sofia and I had our first date at 8:30 that night. I had to be at work at 7:30 the following morning but I was willing to risk another drowsy shift. I had been thinking about her all month, nagged by the feeling that there had been *something* between us during our one conversation.

It was another cold morning of walking down the hill and waiting for the bus.
Portland—where late May looks like early March.
Portland—where it is green and beautiful and full of amazing old buildings and character.
Portland—where you live your life with a deep ache for that mythical thing known as the sun and your clothes start smelling like old rain.

Clocking in at work, I checked all my rooms to see what shape they were in and if I had any tips. It was a good morning; I found that I had $40 in tips. Seeing a $20 in one room I nearly started crying out of gratitude. K was helping me with my rooms so I gave her $5 and explained that the guests had been generous. The funny thing was that it is always the cheaper rooms where you found the biggest tips.

There were five housekeepers on staff that Monday. I got three of the nine rooms with their own bathrooms and was confused about that seeing as I was the slowest housekeeper. Some of the rooms I worked in looked down on the sex shop across from the hotel that had put a bunch of big signs reading "Sale!" in the windows.

Kevin put the glasses he pulled out of rooms in a pillow case that he stored in a mop closet. When I went in to get more gloves, I clumsily kicked the glasses and broke a couple. Taking the pillowcase down to the basement to salvage what I could and dispose of the broken glass threw me off my schedule. I kept watching the clock and saw that time was racing by; it felt like it was taking forever to make up each room. I was excited about my date and wanted work to be over with. Even though I had worked enough to get a free meal I decided to save time by grabbing a frozen burrito from Plaid Pantry.

Sofia lived about half a mile away so I walked over wondering what the night had in store. I was turning over and over in my mind all those things you think about when heading to a first date: Would she be into me? Would I be into her? Would it be comfortable and easy or awkward? Is this a stupid outfit? S hugged me at the door which was a pleasant surprise. She was finishing baking a pie so we talked in the kitchen. I sat in the living room while she put her makeup on. We went out to her car and I felt self-conscious when I saw how nice it was; a newer hybrid that was a beautiful shade of blue.

Sofia drove us to the Sandy Hut, a purple cobblestone bar without any windows. The bartender was a tattooed blonde with generous cleavage. I got the first round, S had a vodka tonic and I got a gin and tonic. We talked easily with little awkwardness. After finishing our drinks, Sofia suggested a bar over on Hawthorne that catered to the goth/industrial crowd.

When we got to Analog there was a girl in a bikini performing acrobatics on a hoop. Across the room, a shirtless guy was doing acrobatics on some ropes hanging from the ceiling. Sofia and I took our drinks upstairs and watched a burlesque show. We sat closer and closer to each other and eventually our hands entwined. I put my arm around her at one point but it felt wrong so I went back to holding her hand. It felt good to be close to someone that I wanted to be close to. Bored with the bar we walked outside. The night was cooling but not uncomfortably so. I kissed Sofia in the car and she kissed me back passionately. We ended up in her kitchen making out as the fridge watched. Sofia said that I could spend the night if I wanted and I said that I did. Nothing happened and I was fine with that, happy that we fell asleep in each others' arms in her bed. I woke up in the middle of the night needing the bathroom but didn't want to break the embrace. I had the feeling that when I got back from the bathroom she would be curled up with her back to me and our embrace would be a memory.

56

In the morning, Sofia went upstairs to use the shower. I sat
on her bed and tried to put all my thoughts and feelings into
a poem. I did a decent job considering how my mind was
reeling—had that really happened? Was I really watching
Sofia getting dressed as I sat on her bed and kept her
company?

Getting back to Noah and Anne's I ate and threw on my
clothes in a daze. The rain was drizzling as I rode the bus in
to work; I was thinking about Sofia and wondering if she
was thinking about me. I drifted through my shift like that:
Thinking of the way her hair framed her face as she leaned
down to kiss me, her telling me about how she knew how
to pick locks and make costume jewelry...what it felt like to
feel her in my arms. I sent her a text thanking her for the
good night and then regretted it.
*What if it's too soon? What if it comes across as needy or
clinging?*
A few minutes later I got a text back suggesting we meet up
that evening.

I got back to the house, ate a little, and showered. I couldn't
wait to see Sofia again and was tempted to run over to her
house: Everything was new and exciting and unreal. As I
covered the blocks between us, all the colors seemed to be
jumping out at me. I recognized what I was feeling as
giddyness and that realization frightened me a little. I
understood that it would be very easy to fall for Sofia; I

could already feel it happening even if I denied it and fought it. She had made it sound like she wanted to keep things casual---could I? Of course, what if things went the other way? I was very comfortable with my life--did I want it to change? It was nice having someone to hold and be with but were those things worth sacrificing my freedom? I hadn't really dated since Teresa and I had separated. There was the situation with JB which had resulted in one night of drunken sex, and there was one date with Cindy; Cindy and I had clicked, had even made out, but then she had ended it. Had that been a blessing in disguise? Was I ready for something serious? On the other hand, could we keep it casual and still remain close? Would I get jealous thinking about her with other men and women? Would *she* get jealous of the women I crushed on and photographed? I thought about all that as I walked between houses. I saw the door opening slowly to some form of love; I saw chinks developing in the walls Sofia and I surrounded ourselves with---what if those walls fell? How would we react to what we found on the other side? How would it change our lives?

Sofia and I walked over to East Burn and sat in a cozy booth in the basement drinking beer. The feeling between us was comfortable and easy. We went back to her basement room but after a couple of hours she drove me home in the rain. I didn't want to leave her, I wanted us to sleep in each other's arms again; I also didn't want to come across as clingy. Both of us had to work in the morning and that was a convenient excuse for both of us not to get too close too fast. Back at the house, I poured a glass of wine and read Ray Bradbury. My mind was half on the story I was reading and half on a beautiful woman maybe half a mile away.

57

The following morning was gray and drizzly. Everything was fuzzy around the edges from a lack of sleep and set to the rhythm of a stranger's ringtone. I had missed my bus and the odds were good that I'd be late for work. That didn't concern me; the fact that I was probably falling for someone overshadowed everything in a beautiful yet terrifying way. I knew, even after two dates, that there could be something big and real between Sofia and myself. I also understood that I was on the way to getting lost and all I could hope was that she would get lost with me. There was worry about what she wanted and the fact that I hadn't dated since separating from my wife—could I just jump into another monogamous relationship? Or, would I get into another situation where both of us would end up unhappy? Could she be satisfied sharing her life with a guy with a dead end job who was focused on becoming a writer? Was I really willing to give up my freedom? Was I the man she needed and deserved? So many questions, none I could answer.

We had a meeting after work that only made me even more frustrated with my job: Temporary chairs. A printout of the agenda. Someone standing at the front of the room with a big smile and big voice. Talking points, new and exciting things, introductions with cues for the audience to clap. I was so done with all of that. It wasn't just me; my co-workers had ideas as well but management wasn't listening to any of us. Did I really want to make the workplace better or was it just my ego? If I really shined a light on it I couldn't say for sure.

I struggled all day not to text Sofia. I felt the need to keep my distance, let her miss me---let *her* be the one to reach out. I had been too "easy" in the past, too available, and I understood that I needed to not be that way with Sofia. Still, I couldn't stop thinking about her and wondering if she was thinking about me. I spent all day stopping in the middle of chores to kneel on the floor and scrawl out the lyrics to falling in love sort of songs. Were we fucking or making love or some combination of the two? I was getting more overwhelmed, more over my head, and the experience was as terrifying as it was exciting.

Checking my email back at the house I saw an invitation for dinner from Sofia. I stared at the screen and vacillated between accepting it and playing hard to get. I really wanted to see her, wanted to hold her and ask her about her day and kiss her and find out more about her and let her find out more about me, but also there was the concern of coming across as too eager. Should I have made up someplace I had to be? In the end, I accepted her invitation.

Sofia was still in her work clothes when I got there. It had been a hard day for her beginning with a mudslide that slowed her commute. I kept her company in the kitchen as she made fajitas. She had tracked me down on Facebook and I was nervous that she would find something that she didn't like; I hated the idea of losing her before we had a chance to become a real couple. She had a lot of things to do and so did I but we also enjoyed each other's company. It was difficult for me to leave her that night but I tried not to make too big a thing of it.

58

I had spent months and years fantasizing about having a woman to share my life with. Now that I did, I was fucking terrified. I was nervous that Sofia would decide to bail; maybe I was insecure or maybe my fears were logical. S had made it sound like she was looking to meet lots of people. I couldn't fault her for that considering that I fantasized about a number of women. A friend offered to set Sofia up with a "handsome older guy" and S turned the blind date down with the explanation that she was seeing someone—me; we were on our way to being boyfriend and girlfriend despite my fears and anxiety.

Back at the house, I had been feeling more and more like an intruder with each passing week. Noah and Anne were nothing but kind and understanding but I still felt lousy that I had been there so long. Needing to get out, I grabbed my camera bag and started walking. Ten minutes later I found myself sitting in the Sandy Hut nursing a beer and listening to classic rock. As I sipped my beer my worries kept me company. There was a Portland guy with a duckbill cap and a beard asking if the music on the jukebox was the Allman Brothers. He walked out of the bar and into the last rays of sunlight as a Led Zeppelin ballad came on.

It got to be 7:45 and I was itching to start walking again. Sofia and I had agreed to meet at her house around 9:30 so I had some time to kill. Another evening fell open like a book, words and plots taking on new colors when exposed to the light.

59

The next day I drove the van over Mount Tabor to buy
supplies at Target and Home Depot. For the first time I
noticed that the oil pressure gauge was kind of low and
fretted over it. Would it break down on the other side of the
hill? What would I do if it did? Anxiety, I was letting too
much anxiety into my life. I spent about $200 getting stuff
for the van. It was sunny when I got back to the
neighborhood and I went about building the platform for
the bed. I had never built anything in my life but felt that
my plan was solid. My work was clumsy and there were
bent nails and things that didn't line up; the platform was
solid but far from perfect.

Noah and I had planned to go see the new Star Trek so he
drove us to the theatre late in the afternoon. Halfway there,
my shitty phone finally gave me a message from an hour
earlier: Sofia had a flat and needed a ride. The message
went on to say that her phone was almost dead. I hemmed
and hawed on that one; she had probably caught a bus by
that point or called one of her other Portland friends. A few
more blocks passed and then I got to thinking about how
Sofia---like myself---didn't really know anyone in town and
might really need me. I also thought about N; how I didn't
want to just ditch him after we had been talking about
seeing the movie for weeks. We pulled into the movie
parking lot and I had sorted out my priorities by that point:
I wanted to spend time with Noah and see that movie, but

Sofia needed my help. I apologized to N and started walking.

I had no idea when the buses were running, my plan was to just head in the direction of the van and then figure out where Sofia was stranded. I walked a couple of miles back to her house. She wasn't home. The voicemail was nearly unintelligible; I had to listen to it four times before making any sense of it. I walked the rest of the way back to Noah's house. Once there, I poured myself a glass of wine and looked over maps in an attempt to determine where Sofia was. S came on Facebook and sent me a message to let me know that she had gotten home safe.

A few minutes later, I got an email from Mom: She was in a bind and needed to borrow some money. Even though I only had $200 to last two weeks, I agreed to send her the $100 I could spare and borrow an additional $200 from Noah. That sent me over the edge and I started drinking in earnest. I left the house in a foul mood needing pizza. New York Pizza had a line out the door so I spun on my heel and turned up a side street. I had a sort of tantrum that lasted half a block. I kept walking, ending up at another pizza joint where I got a pepperoni slice. At Hawthorne Beer and Wine I grabbed a couple of 24 ounce cans of Old English malt liquor. Ending up at the van, I sat on the platform and ate my pizza and drank my beer. I was thinking about my relationship with my mother and then I thought about my life in general and what was happening between Sofia and I. All these intense emotions were churning through me but the beer seemed to be keeping me calm.

It was dark when I climbed out of the van. I was drinking beer as I walked down the street but not caring if it led to trouble, texting Sofia while prowling the neighborhood; we had a good text conversation. I left beer cans on the sidewalk but someone would pick them up before the following morning.

60

I finished another day shift and walked over to Sofia's. We lay on her bed and made plans for things to do together. I wanted to believe that we'd have time to do them all; I also understood that neither of us had any idea how long things would last. People are weird. People are fickle. I had two lines in my head from an old song that had never been written:
I feel like I'm falling for her like she's falling for me. But you never know; no, you never know.

There had been a parade the day before and the bus to work had been hemmed in by traffic. Knowing I could walk faster, I jumped off and walked the last ten blocks. It was beautiful out and I was listening to Stevie Wonder and thinking of Sofia as the blocks fell behind me.

The hotel was hosting a scavenger hunt at the hotel. Consequently, it was even harder than usual to mop or vacuum the halls. The weather was so nice that I didn't mind sweeping up cigarette butts. I wanted to believe that the warm weather would stay until the Fall. Everyone told me there would be more rain before summer really started but I didn't want to believe it. When I was making my second attempt to mop a nerdy couple were discussing a Captain Picard i-Phone case. They were so cute and awkward I wanted them to star in one of the many sitcoms in my head.

Another Saturday another overwhelmed toilet. Once again, the bar downstairs asked us to deal with a stopped up toilet. The water was so murky and there was so much paper floating in the filth that it was impossible to guide the plunger. I couldn't decide what was worse; the stuff in the toilet or the earnest singer in the next room. He had a beard and an acoustic guitar and the proper hipster clothes. All his songs sounded the same and I understood at that moment that I was paying for every bad thing I had ever done.

There was a black waiter I had named Gentleman Doakes. He was always dapper and appraising me with what appeared to be suspicion or disdain or some combination of the two. GD was always leading guided tours through the basement when I was trying to mop or through the upstairs halls when I was trying to stock the closets. I had no idea if it was part of his job or if he just got bored and corralled people off the street. I hopped on an elevator to avoid one of his tours and shared the ride with a man and a woman. The guy was flaming with bracelets on both wrists and peach colored shorts.
"He won the crazy lottery!" Peach shorts ejaculated all over the elevator.
That's all you get in elevators, snippets of people's lives and the people in their lives. People in peach colored shorts or dapper black men giving you a catchphrase or a suspicious look then vanishing forever.

The front desk had made a reservation without assigning a room to it. That meant that I had to go upstairs and make up a room which threw my entire schedule off. After I made the bed I went down to check the pool and some guy asked if I could turn the temperature down.

61

The following day I worked the floater position backing up the housekeepers and anyone else who needed help. I stripped and stocked rooms, dumped the soiled laundry from the carts, and picked up the glasses that had been left in the mop closets. Near the end of the shift, Amy asked if I could help her make up a room because her neck and back hurt. As I helped her make up the room she got to talking about becoming a Scientologist. According to her it was having a positive effect on her life and bringing her happiness. Part of me was happy for her but half of me was concerned that she was being sucked into a cult. We cleared the air about when I had asked her on a date and even joked about it.

After eating my meal at the pub I took the bus back to the house. Sofia and I got to chatting and agreed to meet downtown. I got on the 15 again and headed back to the hotel where Sofia was having a drink. It took awhile to find her but she looked beautiful in a sundress with an elastic top. Half a burger was on her plate and half a beer was in her glass. Just looking at her I could have fallen in love in that instant and struggled to contain my emotions. She was done with her food so went across the street to check out the sex shop. I had been curious about it because we were always finding things that had been bought there in the hotel. The sex shop was bigger on the inside than it looked on the outside, kind of like Snoopy's dog house but with cock rings and vibrators. We looked around a bit and then headed over to Powell's. Walking out of the bookstore we decided to head back to our side of the river and waited for the 20. The two of us held hands as we crossed the Hawthorne Bridge and looked out in opposite directions. There were three cop cars on the bridge and we wondered aloud if they had cornered a jumper.

With the setting sun a chill settled on the town. We walked down to the Goodfoot on Stark near 28th and ordered cucumber infused gin and tonics. S didn't care for it but I thought it was good. There were artists at the next table drawing on pizza boxes as they ate pizza and drank beer. I got to talking about the future--(not us, just the future in general)--and it bummed Sofia out. After finishing our drinks we walked back to her place in the cold. S was talking but I didn't hear her, my mind was elsewhere and yet right there.

Are we making love or fucking or some combination of the two? I can scarcely contain what I feel for you sometimes—often, in fact—and I am concerned I am seriously falling for you.

Sofia put on a zombie movie and we got maybe ten minutes into it before kissing passionately and forgetting about the movie altogether. We woke up in the middle of the night for a few minutes. Sofia appeared agitated so I asked what was wrong.

"I am never going to see you again," she said.

That rattled me and I asked what she meant. She said that she didn't want to talk about it and eventually we fell back asleep.

62

I loved waking up in Sofia's bed, in her room, and loved looking over at her still asleep. I didn't want to go back to sleep, I wanted to keep my eyes open and savor that time. Her car was still in the shop so I walked her to the bus stop. We kissed and I walked on, struggling to ignore the cold.
I am never going to see you again.
What had she meant by that? I had a shoot with a model that afternoon—was Sofia seeing a future where something happened to me? Was it something else? It freaked me out more and more each time I thought about it.

They called me in to do housekeeping and I worked from 11 to around 5:30. The first couple of rooms were fine, I even got $11 in tips, but then I lost my momentum and pretty much hated it by my last couple of rooms. A housekeeper had called in sick so I had seven rooms. One room was trashed: Big box of Voodoo Doughnuts with pieces of Ritz crackers mixed in with the crumbled doughnuts. There were even crackers in the drawer of the nightstand and the kicker was that they hadn't even left a tip.
I am never going to see you again.
I knew I wasn't in the right frame of mind to take pictures. Something had changed---being with Sofia had changed things---so I cancelled the shoot with the model, making something up about dropping my camera and shattering it.

After work I headed out to the nameless bar on 28th between Burnside and Glisen. I was getting more and more neurotic about what Sofia had said and the fact she hadn't sent me a message all day didn't help. She had told me that she loved me but didn't want us to define our relationship by referring to each other as boyfriend and girlfriend.

I am never going to see you again.

What did that mean? Was she ready to stomp on the brakes and then jump out of the speeding car I was pinned in? Was the enormity of telling me that she loved me last night like cold water in her face making her realize this whole affair had gone further than she intended? As stressed out as I was, I knew that I couldn't share my feelings with her; that would be clingy and needy and neurotic and she definitely didn't want that. So, I sat in that bar wrestling things on my own as I thought about her, hopeless yet hopeful.

After leaving the bar I walked east on the side streets. I had been all over those streets, looking for likely places to overnight in the van---*the van*. Freedom, my life. There I was stressing about a woman when maybe a girlfriend didn't fit in my life. I enjoyed my life, the freedom was amazing---did I really want for that to end?

I got back to the house and Sofia had sent me a Facebook message so I walked over to see her. I had felt a sense of relief that she had messaged me; maybe everything wasn't lost after all. We got beer from the corner store and sat on her front porch to watch the traffic going up and down Stark. The two of us were planning to go to a Goth club later. Around nine, I watched her dress as we drank more beer and then tucked a couple of beers in our coat pockets. It was amazing, like a scene from a movie you can't help but watch over and over: Lovers walking early summer streets drinking and talking, bathed in the streetlights, watching for cops, and stealing a kiss every few blocks.

At the club there was this beautiful Amazon with blonde dreadlocks that I eventually realized was a man. Some guy in his early 30s was trying to pick up on he/she, clearly smitten, buying the Amazon drinks. At some point they went off to talk and the amazon came back alone a few minutes later. I wondered what they talked about: In my imagination I saw the Amazon cutting through all the ambiguity by whipping her penis out.

63

I sat in the very back row of another crowded 15 bus. It looked like someone had coughed up a chunk of salmon on the floor. The sun seemed to be coming out but I didn't want to get my hopes up.

Sometimes it felt like the scavenger hunt would never end. The participants were there in the morning and they were still in the halls when guests were trying to sleep. They took pictures of pictures as they noisily tracked down clues. A couple of 'bros' with beards were laughing and goofing around as they did the scavenger hunt. I watched them for a moment before moving on to the next room I had to strip and stock for housekeeping. It was a king suite and it had been trashed; not rock band trashed where furniture had been destroyed---that might have been more interesting---it had been trashed by a family with a small child. There were cracker crumbs all over the carpet, open yogurt and drink containers, and dirty diapers in the trash. Your garbage tells many stories: What you like to drink, whether you practice safe sex, what sort of things you like to buy--or that you're raising a spoiled brat.

I moved between housekeeping and maintenance. In one of the shared bathrooms there was a wadded up towel with rust colored stains on it. That went right in the trash, no debate allowed. I had learned my lesson after trying to clean out that shitty garbage can a week earlier. The utility lift was out still which meant we couldn't get the garbage or recycling out to the curb for pick-up. You never realize how much trash you create until you're trapped with it like ghosts on a submarine.

The rest of work was a blur. One moment I was surrounded by garbage and trying to breathe through my mouth and the next thing I knew I was on the 15 trying to breathe through my mouth. On the first stop after crossing the river a friendly looking black man boarded. He was wearing a t-shirt reading "Police, please do not shoot me."

Getting back to the house I messed around on-line and then took a shower. Sofia invited me over for ribs and reminded me about going out to a Goth club later in the evening. Sofia's car was in the shop and I hated parking the van down by the clubs so we walked from her house. Beers in hand, we walked the back streets and kept an eye out for cops. It was a beautiful night and the conversation flowed easily. The feeling was like a scene in a movie where everything is vibrant and good and people are falling in love and the future seems promising.

The club was packed. We sat off to the side in a booth and watched the night unfold. The DJ looked bored and was wearing sunglasses. He had a doughy face and lank, blonde hair. The beat was relentless, mechanical, and I didn't feel like dancing. I got S a Grey Goose and tonic and myself a gin and tonic, spending too much on drinks again. Part of me fretted about it but part of me understood that life is short and sometimes you just have to enjoy it and be foolish sometimes.

64

I was sick for a few days. It was bad enough that I missed a day of work. I needed the money and hated letting people down but I knew I'd end up in the hospital if I tried to work; my job was too physical and took stamina. I used my down time to re-do my resume and look for a new job. I didn't want to work in an office again but I wanted a regular schedule so Sofia and I could make plans. More money would be good, too, so I could afford a room if I decided to spend another winter in Portland. People spent winters in vans there but it sounded miserable.

On Saturday night there was a naked bike ride through Portland. Both Sofia and I were sick but determined to see it. We went down to Water Street, got a beer and a snack, and marveled at all the hippies passing by the window. The bicyclists were still clothed as they approached the Hawthorne Bridge. Once they were on the span, however, they stripped off their clothes. It seemed cold for a naked bike ride but they were in good spirits.

The day after the naked bike ride I had another floater shift. It was a busy but uneventful seven hours. I found an unused condom in one room and left it for the housekeeper in case they had any use for it. Floater was my favorite position at the hotel and one I had kind of made my own. The housekeepers kept telling me that I helped them out a lot and it felt good, good in a way few jobs had ever felt.

One of the assistant managers gave me two rooms of my own to work. I was still feeling under the weather, possibly from drinking too much, but I needed the practice turning rooms over. One of them was 208, a room everyone agreed was haunted. All you can do is be respectful; whatever was in there was benign and we all wanted to keep it that way. I never saw anything. I sometimes expected to see something in the mirror but it never happened. There was definitely some sort of presence in there, though.

Pushing a laundry cart down the hall I saw the AM opening and closing a door and looking dismayed.
"They shaved this door yesterday; it shouldn't still be sticking," she said.
"Wonder why it's still doing that?"
She toyed with the doorknob and then looked at me.
"It means the hotel is sinking faster," the AM explained.

I pushed the cart into the elevator and imagined the hotel bobbing in the middle of a calm but deep sea, inching further below the surface while the staff worked at turning over rooms and the guests had their drinks and laughed in the pool. The windows would take on the blue-green tint of the sea, the air would get cooler, and the sky would darken as we slipped yards and then miles under the surface of the water.

Getting my free meal was always a priority of mine. Luckily I got just over six hours on Sunday and headed over to the pub for a cheeseburger and fries after clocking out. The 15 was really late, I must have waited half an hour. When I got back to the house, I got a message from Sofia inviting me over for salmon and vegetables. She took a nap after we ate and I cleaned up the kitchen. When I was done I crawled under the covers with her and we slept until a quarter past eleven. There was this Goth event we had talked about checking out so we got dressed and Sofia drove us over. As we parked there was some sort of homeless drama going on down the block. The Star Theatre was in Chinatown down by all the missions and shelters so you had a lot of people sleeping in doorways and on sidewalks. Sometimes they fought; slur yelling about dirt caked grudges.

They were playing an old Cabaret Voltaire song in the club which I thought was promising. There were old movies and smoke machines like any other Goth club. Everyone was wearing black and a lot of make-up, there was even a young woman with a cane. The bartender had a beard but still could have been a woman. We didn't stay long; opting to drive over to the Lovecraft and see what was going on there. Walking in we saw a shirtless guy who looked like a skinhead clearing the dance floor. There seemed to be a lot of older people but the energy was good. Sofia and I sipped our drinks and watched other people. I was pleased to hear the DJ playing music from the 80s and not that Industrial crap.

65

Work started off bad and didn't get any better. I don't remember what set me off, it could have been that the basement was a disaster or maybe it was because we didn't have the following week's schedule yet. It was just one of those shifts where I was ready to walk off the job. The never ended scavenger hunt didn't help my frame of mind. People---not guests---were blocking the corridors and staring at the pictures or generally being pests. Two women in their early twenties were clearly lost---
"Google Little Richard so we can see what he looks like," one whined.

Country and Western Kevin was getting his housekeeping cart together when I went back to the basement. He had a bald spot the size of a silver dollar on the top of his head and it was hard not to stare at it. We got to talking about the rooms and what you find in them housekeeping and this led to a discussion about the sounds of fucking coming through the doors.
"Willy Gilly is always talking about that," Kevin shook his head and made a face. "He seems to like it."
I kept a straight face and said nothing.

After work I walked over to Sofia's house. She made us dinner and we had a couple of beers. Every so often she would smoke a Pall Mall and I would take a drag or two off it. When it got cold we went into the living room and sat on the couch facing each other.

"True confession time," she said. "It really upset me when you were going to meet up with that model. I hate that it does, but it does..."

I explained to her why I had cancelled on the last model and by the end of our conversation the air felt cleared. It was easy giving up taking pictures of women when I weighed them against what Sofia and I had. I felt more at home in her place than I had in years. We had still had the big house to ourselves since all of her roommates were out of town.

66

It was still raining in Portland in the middle of June. Portland doesn't care if it's technically summer, it will turn the sky dark and bring the rain. Summer? What's that? Not in Portland. Maybe there will be a few nice days here and there, just a taste for the starving man, and then the rain will drift back in. Even on the nice days Portland would bring on the wind. You'd see the wind in the branches, just a breeze, too meek to rip the leaves off but still a sign that the next day would be ugly. Twenty four hours later the gray and drizzle would return and people would be walking hunched over to try and stay warm.

The next day at work was better. We got the schedule and I saw that a meeting was scheduled for the following week. As I was organizing the latest delivery Frank walked over to where I was working.
"Still got that cold?" He asked.
"Yep."
"You should do what I do: When I start getting sick I make Theraflu and I suck on a cough lozenge as I drink it."

D took me aside a couple of hours later on the 4th floor.
"Tell me I'm crazy---" She started.
"Okay, you're crazy."
"I was talking to one of the managers in the cafe and they said Ike can't plunge a toilet. They said they were busy and asked you to plunge one of their toilets and you couldn't do it."

"I can plunge a toilet---"
"That's what I told them. Just so you know you aren't responsible for their toilets, they said they don't want customers seeing waiters plunging toilets but I don't buy that."
"Thank you," I replied.
"No problem," she smiled.
I shot a glance at her breasts and she shot one at my crotch before we parted ways.

Sofia was having a bad day and wasn't sure if she wanted company. I drove the van over to her street and sent her a text saying that I was drinking in my van and that she was welcome to join me. Locking the doors so I could walk to the Penny Market, I realized that I had left my keys in the van. I called roadside assistance and that was a painfully drawn out experience. Sofia had responded to my text; from down the street I saw her approaching the van and waved. I followed her back to the house as I talked to the operator. S got a couple of things from the kitchen so she could attempt to jimmy a door. She worked at a couple of locks on the van but didn't have any luck. Roadside assistance showed up maybe half an hour later and got my van open---the keys were in the ignition. Sofia was feeling stir crazy so she drove us over to the industrial part of town where we could look at all the warehouses and strip clubs. Back on our side of town we just rode around aimlessly looking at all the old houses and shops. When the mood broke, we stopped at Hot Lips for some pizza. We ate in silence just looking at each other. The world felt magical, like anything was possible, and on top of that we had this beautiful, possibly mad love crackling between us in fevered blue lines.

67

The weather had been spring-like for a few days. People had been telling me that we wouldn't get out of June without more rain but I was hopeful. Knowing I needed more things for the van, I tagged along with Sofia on a trip to Goodwill. It seemed nice for a Goodwill, didn't smell weird or anything. They had some decent looking sleeping bags but I was short on cash and settled for a frying pan and a stainless steel spoon. We spent a long time looking at shoes and joking about some of the clothes. I kept the words out of my mouth light and easy but there was this lunatic bird in my chest---
She's here, this person who actually loves me and wants to be with me who I want to be with.
On top of that it was sunny...in Portland. It felt good to be alive and that feeling scared me. Movies of the past couple of years still played in my head: Grim people making prisons out of rooms. Fools chasing people who laughed when they saw who was on their heels. I couldn't turn those films off, maybe I wasn't supposed to.

I needed a camping stove and S told me that she knew of a sporting goods store downtown. Neither of us could find it at first; we must have driven around in circles for fifteen minutes. We ended up in a store that sold saddles and western boots instead of stoves and tents. There was nothing we needed there but we still had fun looking around. Back outside, we walked down to a food cart we had seen while parking the car. As we split a Peruvian sandwich, the two of us watched an Asian family attempting to park their minivan. I waved at them and they stared back.

"Maybe we knew these people," I said. "Maybe we were in two tribes that went to war and there was murder and revenge between our groups, and a few hundred years later it's this---a sandwich and a minivan and a semi-cute nerdy Asian woman."

"What?" Sofia had been looking down the street at a hobo pulling at the back of his pants.

"This is a really fucking good sandwich."

68

Things were still fresh between Sofia and I. We were at the
stage where we wanted to spend every day together,
experiencing that intense beautiful bloom of love. We both
understood that, after more time passed, the things that we
found adorable or at least easy to ignore would become
annoying or dull or irritating; we would grow accustomed
to each other and probably take each other for granted. I
hoped not, maybe that was usually the way it went but
maybe we would be different.

I took Sofia on a long walk to see the goats on Belmont.
There were eight of them grazing in a large, vacant lot.
Afterward, we picked up a pizza and watched a TV show
on her computer as we lay on the bed. It wasn't a passionate
night, it was more comfortable but I loved those sort of
nights as much as the fevered ones. Some hours later I
walked two blocks to the van and lay in bed listening to the
faint sound of traffic. I turned the sounds of motors revving
and relaxing into a string octet and let the music I found lull
me to sleep.

Although I was still grateful to have a job I was getting
more and more frustrated with the hotel. It was pretty clear
that things wouldn't be changing, even the little things that
would have been easy for management to fix. I worked my
ass off for minimum wage but it wasn't the money that
bothered me as much as other things. I could feel it getting
closer to the time when I would need to move on but in

what way? Before there had been a grand plan to head south, but that was in the days before I met Sofia. I had no idea what I would do. In my heart it felt like I had almost everything in the world, but that was one of five things missing.

69

Sofia knocked on the door of the van in the middle of the night. I let her in and we fell right back asleep.

I was looking after Noah and Anne's cat and needed to check on it the following morning. Sofia walked with me back as it was just getting light. It was crisp, but not really cold. She stopped to look at various plants and trees and I pointed out all the houses I liked. We kissed and embraced at the corner of 29th and Salmon and then parted ways.

The night before I hadn't wanted to be the one suggesting to get together as I tended to be. I still worried about being too eager and coming across as clingy. I had vowed to myself never to chase another woman but it seemed like Sofia and I were chasing each other. That night there had been a lot of vagueness which got kind of weird and it took awhile for the two of us to get back on track. Twilight found us as it often did then, sitting on her front porch drinking Back in Black beer and smoking Pall Malls.

70

It was a typical crazy weekend day at work. I scrambled to get my maintenance stuff done while keeping the housekeepers stocked up and helping them strip rooms and dump soiled linen. The time went fast and it only seemed like a couple of hours passed before I was back to the house trying to figure out what to wear that night. When I went to polish my boots I discovered a big crack in the sole. Walking to the bus stop, I saw a man in a white suit and a straw hat grumpily looking up and down the train tracks. He had a moon face that looked red and sweaty even from a hundred feet away and a large belly. He looked out of place in Portland; like an old John Bull poster come to life. *His name is Cofab Teel and he has been watching the world run circles round itself for a hundred-fifty years...* Someone was superimposing a novel onto reality. The magic of everything had overloaded my mind, but it wasn't anything I couldn't handle. A busker was playing "The Drugs Don't Work" and I nearly joined in before remembering that I'm an introvert. Shaking my head at the close call, I walked on.

Sofia and I had our first argument that afternoon. It wasn't as much an argument as a general sort of sourness and airing of hurt feelings. We were supposed to go to this bondage club that opened at eight. She always told me to "just show up" so I did but it was a bad night for that; she was not happy to see me and said as much. My feelings were hurt so I sat on the front porch smoking and drinking a beer and hating the situation. Things didn't smooth out for a couple of hours.

The bondage club seemed pretty tame. A nerdy looking girl in a net shirt with electrical tape over her nipples was spanking this androgynous looking man in time to some industrial music. He had scratches all over his back and whimpered like a puppy from time to time. An old man stripped naked for a paddling, his balls hanging disturbingly low. No one was being degraded or really whipped and Sofia guessed that it was because the club served food. Downstairs was where all the whipping was going on. Upstairs there were a series of acts on stage: A young woman pouring candle wax on herself, a man running an electric zapper over a naked woman, and a man using a knife sensually on this blonde. Sofia had a couple of vodka tonics and I was drinking gin and tonics. A couple of times we went out front so S could smoke a clove. Riding back to her house I thought about how tense things had been earlier in the evening. The fight had been the first time reality had stuck her ugly, broken nails in. Maybe we were just like every other couple and there would be petty ripples and squabbles. Maybe, but I still loved her like I had loved few people in my life and was pretty sure it was the same with her. I took Sofia's hand as we turned on 20th and saw her smile into the rear view mirror.

71

Sofia had the day off so we went exploring and then I tagged along as she ran errands. The bank where she got a document notarized had American flags everywhere and I just wanted to sigh and run out. In the car outside of the bank she told me that her husband and daughter were coming up on Friday.

"We won't be seeing much of each other for the next few days," she said quietly.

"That's okay, I get it."

Two lovers sitting in a bank parking lot, invisible to the world and glad for it. When she dropped me off it was hard saying goodbye, both of us could feel it. I sent this stupid text from work about how when we had been looking at a houseboat that afternoon it made me think about a time in the future when we could be looking at a place for real. She didn't respond for hours and I got more and more anxious that I had said too much too soon and screwed things up. Eventually, she texted back:

I was thinking that, too. Love you lots bby.

I felt all the relief in the world at that moment.

Next time keep your loose lips pinned together, Ike.

72

I had lost all motivation to do my job. A couple of months earlier I had been all hustle and enthusiasm; that time was long gone. I still enjoyed organizing and stocking the linen closets for some reason---if you had judged my work by those closets alone you'd be impressed---but when it came to my other responsibilities I was skating by and doing as little as possible. I was sick of cleaning the shared bathrooms. My trick was to make the toilet and the sink look good which took about five minutes. I could get all twelve shared bathrooms done in an hour.

Our reality was that we made the same amount per hour as an 18 year old starting at McDonalds. I didn't feel money was the real issue; it just seemed unreasonable considering all the things we had to do---I worked hard and didn't make enough to even rent a studio apartment. Equally discouraging was the growing understanding that things would never change at the hotel. Sometimes I got my enthusiasm back and hustled to get things done and did them well; those times were getting shorter in duration and further and further apart. I felt like an alien around at least half of my co-workers. I saw an early 90s Mercedes wagon parked out front and started going on and on about it, just geeking out, and there was this silence. I slinked away, back to the basement where I could hide. It was a cool Mercedes, though; I could have talked about it for hours.

Those days I rarely got as much done as I would have liked to. After a night shift I got up around 11 in the morning and it always took at least an hour to wake up whether I had been drinking the night before or not.

After getting paid I walked to Fred Meyer and got a small rug for the van as part of the bed. I had been spending most nights at Sofia's but there had been a few in the van parked on the street. Those evenings had been comfortable, but I knew I was still a tourist---could I hack it when the days became weeks becoming months? Sometimes I looked forward to it like any new adventure and sometimes I had my doubts about pulling it off. I didn't enjoy driving it and always worried about a breakdown or taking out a bicyclist because of the missing passenger side mirror. Maybe I was just out of practice driving; it had been over four months since I had driven on a regular basis. Usually I rode the bus or walked or Sofia drove us around. We were spending more and more nights together at her place, even the ones where I worked until 1:45. I went back to her room because we didn't want to sleep apart. It was one of those sweet moments, two people still falling in love with each other. She had so much going on with her rental property in the Midwest and everything with her husband and her kids that I wondered if there would be a long term place for me. I hoped so. And what about my life, wherever it led me--- could I fit her in? Again, I hoped so; I really wanted that but the certainty was still small, still struggling to grow.

We finally had a decent meeting at work. They had it in this little bar that was part of the cafe. Beer and pizza was brought up for us. I was happy that all of us got to bring up our ideas and concerns and ask questions. I had a review scheduled for a week after that and hoped it would go well but I always fretted that they would have a list of things that I didn't get to or the times that I hadn't bothered to hide when I was pissed off.

73

Sofia had applied for a job down in Napa, California. I was
taken aback but tried to be supportive. I knew that if she
got the job I would follow her if she was up for it. Wisely,
I didn't say as much, keeping my cards close, smiling
across the table but with my guard up. I could see my
guardian's formidable scowl and smell his cologne. I
understood that I would leave Portland if she did for any
reason, especially if we broke up. I'd just be tripping on the
shards and ripping my skin with them, driving myself mad
by dwelling on how they reflected the light.

I was looking in at the pool when this young guy walked up
to me. He had a crew cut mohawk and was somewhere in
his early 20s.
"Can girls get topless in the pool?" He asked.
"No, sorry."
"That's too bad; they're really good looking girls."
He walked off and I wondered about what sort of girls he
was thinking he could lure down to the pool.

I was stocking linens, half lost in my thoughts and half
listening to the sounds coming out of the rooms and
watching people walking up and down the hall.
"I'm coming home, so I'm the prodigal," a man said.
"Wait--isn't the prodigal the father?" His companion asked.
"No, that's the paternal."
I heard fucking in one of the rooms and lingered near the
mop closet. When they emerged half an hour later I was

repulsed to see it was a sloppy looking couple in their fifties. The woman winked at me and I shuddered inside.

74

Another bar, another cheap beer, another day lapsing into night. I had drunk three-quarters of a bottle of wine before heading out and had no interest in slowing down. The idea was not to drink to oblivion but rather to the point where the edges were smoothed and everything felt warm and sensual and fun. I wanted to escape from the weariness I felt for my job and all the challenges I faced in my life. One of those challenges was the possibility of Sofia moving away. What would I do if she got that job back in California? I couldn't imagine staying in Portland without her around—at least that part of Portland—but was our relationship ready for me following her? Also, what would I be following her to? The job market in California was still bad and the struggles looking for work were still fresh in my memory. Despite those worries there was the understanding that we loved each other; I loved her enough that, if that job happened and she wasn't ready for me to follow her to California, I would have let her go---made the whole thing as easy for her as possible.

And then I would leave Portland. The way I felt, I understood that every street and building and bar would be a painful reminder of our time together.

There was a general lack of motivation but I made myself edit the first book and query some agents. Another agent sent an email rejection and I took it best as I could. Sofia sent me a text and I wrote the phrase *mein liebe* in a notebook and then circled it as a strange bird called outside the window.

My yoga mat came in the post that afternoon eliminating any excuses I had for not sleeping in the van. Sofia had her husband and daughter visiting from California and we agreed not to sleep together while they were in town. Chatting on Facebook in the afternoon we agreed to "probably meet up" at some point in the evening. Around six I drove the van to a filling station and got $20 worth of gas. There was still a quarter tank but I knew that gas had to be old.

I parked the van a few blocks from Noah and Anne's. A smoker was watching me from the back porch of a house down the block and it made me feel uneasy. I walked to Noah's house, poured a glass of wine, and checked to see if Sofia had sent me a Facebook message. I kept thinking about that guy checking me out. I knew that house, an anomaly in a neighborhood full of rich people. At any time there were half a dozen people living in it for cheap. I wasn't worried about being rousted, I was more concerned that the man would figure out that I was a van dweller and assume that I had valuables in the truck. N came downstairs and said he was going to Ole Ole and asked if I wanted a burrito. When I said I did he refused to take my money as was his habit. After he left I went to move the van before drinking anymore. It was a beautiful late afternoon; I drove Edna four blocks to another spot I had scouted out and then walked back to the house.

After eating my burrito and drinking another glass of wine I put my pajamas in my bag and headed out. I listened to Depeche Mode and Afghan Whigs followed by Steely Dan as I walked. My plan was to stop at the nameless bar on 28th but I was enjoying the walk and the music so I continued down Everett. Seeing a 1965 Barracuda I took a picture of it for Sofia.

Seeing the purple mass of paving stones that was the Sandy Hut, I walked in and sat at the bar. Rainer on tap was the cheapest thing they had so it was what I ordered. I sipped my beer and soaked in the conversations as I watched a television with the sound off. A couple of punks were getting drunk and griping about the music when they weren't talking about sluts they knew.
"I hope his dick got tested."
"His dick probably fell off."
When most people have drinks they open up and talk freely; I had once been that way but with age had become more of a listener. Half listening to those kids I checked out women even if there was only one woman I wanted. The bartender was cute, carrying some extra weight but still attractive. She was wearing a white tank top with a black bra underneath and had a lot of cleavage to admire. I imagined photographing her in that tank top without the bra and then thought about Sofia and felt guilty---I missed her and wondered what she was up to. S had told me that she would probably be divorcing her husband. From my own experiences I understood how stressful that could be.

With each song the punks got more vocal about their displeasure. When they started moaning about "What's Going On" I had to speak up.

"Ah, come on—it's Marvin Gaye," I said.

"It sure is gay!" One of them laughed.

I took a drink of my beer. The punk played with his mohawk and looked thoughtful.

"Nothing against Marvin Gaye," he continued. "Marvin Gaye is great when I'm getting busy with a girl, but sitting in a bar getting drunk? No way."

They were nice enough kids and I knew they had meant no offense. I wanted to order another beer and start talking about Marvin Gaye, how he juggled brilliance with darkness, but understood that no one probably wanted to hear that sort of thing and packed my bag up.

I finished my beer, cued Stevie Wonder on my iPod, and headed out. It was half past eight and there was still light in the sky. Because of the bad weather in Portland it was easy to miss when the days got longer. I wandered around until I found myself in Sofia's neighborhood. I kept walking until I reached the Safeway on Hawthorne so I could use the restroom. Still feeling more intoxicated than drunk, I decided to head over to Holman's for a whiskey. Sofia texted me as I approached 30th and Belmont asking what I was up to. When I told her where I was headed she suggested that we meet up at Holman's. I wondered but did not ask if she would be bringing her husband or if she was slipping out to meet me on the sly.

I got a booth and went over the whiskey list. After maybe fifteen minutes Sofia showed up and slid into the booth next to me. Milfred sat across from us; he appeared to be around forty and kind of stocky with a receded hairline and glasses. He was stubbly and looked his age and I felt good about that. I was worried that there would be some *so you're the guy fucking my wife* awkwardness but it wasn't too bad. All three of us ordered whiskey. Sofia and I held hands under the table and I worried that it was obvious. I didn't want to be a dick to Milfred, understanding that the situation had to be difficult and weird for him. Nevertheless I also wanted to hold Sofia's hand and kiss her, though we were respectful and did not kiss or even hug while Milfred was there. We were sitting close enough that I could feel her leg against mine and it made me want her. We sipped our drinks and talked and everything felt okay until S went out to smoke and then it was awkward; Milfred and I sitting across from each other, two men in love with the same woman...both of us hoping that in the end Sofia would choose us over the other guy. Sofia came back and we parted ways a few minutes after she slid into my side of the booth. As Milfred led the way out of the bar S paused to turn back and give me one of her beautiful smiles.

I walked to the Plaid Pantry and got two Schlitz 24s. I probably only needed one to lull me to sleep but I wanted to be prepared in case I was feeling restless. Fishing my keys out, I slipped in the driver's door and crawled into the back to lay on the platform. It was peaceful in the van lying on my side and with the sleeping bag wrapped around me. Sipping my beer, I felt nervous about the headlights of passing cars and all the windows looking down on the street. Sofia and I texted for a couple of minutes and then I finished my beer and drifted off.

At two the need to urinate woke me up. I walked maybe a block and a half, looked up and down the street, and pissed on a tree. It was a beautiful night and I was voiding my bladder in the middle of a city---it felt good, primal in a strange way. It had gotten cold so I climbed in the sleeping bag after relieving myself. The yoga pad was insufficient so I didn't sleep that well but it still felt right spending the night in the van; I felt strangely proud to be sleeping on something I built. I woke up a little before eight, moved Edna, and headed into Noah's house to make coffee and write.

75

Enjoy fucking my wife.
I was sitting on a bed feeling wound up as a husband and wife argued a few feet away.
The night had taken a bad turn.
Enjoy fucking my wife.
I felt like an eavesdropper but I couldn't leave; if things got more heated, got physical, I would have to step in.
The husband was crying, making accusations but barely fifteen minutes earlier we had been sitting in the living room having a good time—how had things gotten so bad so fast?

The day had started out well. The weather had been perfect so I had walked to Fred Meyer to get a foam pad and a couple of other things for the van. N and A had been packing for a trip up to the Olympic Peninsula so I made sure they had the house to themselves. I did it for them and I did it for myself, to be prepared for when I was living in the van full time. Later in the week I would get my gym membership and would begin scouting parks with picnic tables where I could use my propane stove.

Around one, I threw my four dollar camera bag over my shoulder and headed out. N had put U2's *War* on my iPod so I listened to that as I walked west. I ended up in Buckman Park looking for a shady spot to write. As I walked around looking for a bench that wasn't in the sun the first lines of a story were forming in my head. The previous night in the bar they had been playing Guns and Roses and out of the blue an idea had come to me. I wrote most of the story sitting next to a playground in Buckman Park. Children were laughing, people were playing soccer or napping, and I was writing about a famous rock star chaining people up in his basement and slowly murdering them. It was a beautiful day, a man with a wife and small child went down a long slide. Sofia texted me to let me know that she was bringing her daughter over to see me. The man who was there with his wife and small child asked me what I was writing. He seemed impressed with the idea and we got to talking about writing. S and her daughter Lily showed up. I nodded to them and explained to the guy I was talking to that I had to go. He asked my name and I told him.

"I can say I met you before you were published," he smiled. It was a nice moment and an admitted ego boost.

I can say I met you before you were published.

There were times that I struggled with my doubts; there were days where it felt like the odds against getting published were staggering. Nevertheless, there was something big in the air---a big change coming for me--- and I was pretty sure that it was positive and not something like death.

Things were happening, important life changing things; I just couldn't see what they were.

Sofia, L, and I went to the cemetery. Lily seemed--(and Sofia confirmed this)--an old soul at 13. She was still a teenager, though, and her face was buried in her phone as she griped about internet service. She wandered off and

Sofia and I found a spot to lie on the grass, drinking beer as we talked. Milfred called so the two of them had to go home. Sofia and I embraced before walking off in opposite directions.

Needing to use a bathroom I headed over the hill to Safeway. After using the restroom I bought a chicken sandwich and walked over to a park just south of Hawthorne. I finished the story that I had been working on and then jotted down notes about everything that had happened that day. It was a gorgeous afternoon and a handful of summer scenes played out around me: Lovers on a blanket nearby. A family at a picnic table with a red, plastic tablecloth. Kids playing in the distance. People walking their dogs. I took it all in as I tried to come up with a game plan for that evening.

Sofia and I texted back and forth. She was thinking of heading to Lovecraft later in the evening and we agreed to meet at her house around 10. I showered, brushed my teeth, and drove the van over with the idea that I would sleep in the back. Milfred was friendly when I got there, offering me a slice of pizza that I accepted. We chatted as Sofia got ready and things seemed okay. The three of us spent an hour driving around looking for a place to have a couple of drinks and listen to music but nothing came of it. We ended up back at the house drinking and chatting. Things were okay until Sofia suggested that Milfred go next door to bed. She walked him over and ten to fifteen minutes passed. Lily was doing something online so I went down to Sofia's bedroom to pass the time reading. I heard angry footsteps and voices and a few seconds later Milfred came downstairs with S right behind him. At the foot of the stairs he stopped to glare at me.

"Enjoy fucking my wife!" He yelled.

Before I could say anything he continued into the next room and I could hear him crying and having a heated discussion with my girlfriend. After a few minutes Sofia came in to suggest that I leave. I asked if she'd be okay and she said she would be. We hugged and separated for the rest of the night.

76

The following afternoon I trained a new employee on the
Floater position. It went relatively smoothly and he got to
experience a bed with both a cum stain and what I think
was watery shit. Training on Sundays was always tough;
too much work to stop and explain things well, too much
impatience in the air. My impatience was clicking its teeth,
every muscle taut, and I struggled to kick it away.

After six hours of showing Kyle the ropes, I walked up
12th to catch the 15. A guy who looked like Lee Harvey
Oswald walked by but no one seemed to notice.

After darkness claimed the sky I went over to Sofia's and
Milfred let me in; the awkwardness was palpable. I felt for
the guy---he still loved Sofia and wanted her to come home
with him---but he needed to come to terms that their
marriage was over. I kept thinking about what happened the
night before and couldn't look at him---
Enjoy fucking my wife.
S came downstairs and I made an effort to be breezy and
not add to what she was dealing with. The three of us had
drinks in the kitchen and then Sofia drove us down to the
Star Theatre. The DJ was playing this thumpy sort of Goth
Industrial music that Sofia loved and I feel an indifference
towards; snarling Germans going on about pain and slavery
and other happy stuff. Film clips of war and leering men
and other disturbing things played silently in the
background like a drug induced nightmare. S went up to

the bar to buy us drinks and when she was gone I felt the awkwardness return, thinking about the night before with Milfred crying and acting generally tormented. Every time I held Sofia's hand or found us sitting close I knew he saw it and that it was eating at him. I could imagine how I would feel going out with a woman I still loved and her new boyfriend, it would drive me nuts, I would be running to the bathroom to puke.

David J from Bauhaus was the headliner that night. I had been suspicious of the whole affair due to the whole dodgy nature of celebrity DJs in general but I was pleasantly surprised by David J's set. He wasn't DJing nor was he playing a normal musical instrument, it was somewhere in-between. Sofia and I both enjoyed it a lot, especially the way he prowled the stage like a scientist, seeming to study the reactions of the crowd. Sofia ordered a vivid blue drink and left it at the table when she went off to smoke. Sitting there with her husband I wanted to chew my leg off. Fifteen minutes passed and then I saw Milfred go off to the dance floor where S was dancing. I was caught up in all the charged emotions and got emotional myself, feeling ditched. In my stupid frame of mind I walked out on the dance floor and told Sofia that I was leaving. She looked surprised and followed me to the bar. We talked a bit and then went out to the patio. David J was out there trying to pick up a woman young enough to be his daughter and drinking something amber with ice cubes floating in it. In the soft lights of the patio he looked younger than 56. I congratulated him on his set; he didn't hear me at first but when he did he offered a gentle thank you. Sofia and I watched him picking up on the young woman and made a few jokes about it.

We went back to her house. Not wanting to create more tension I said goodnight and went off to sleep in the van which was parked a block away. Sofia said she'd text after Milfred had gone to sleep but I didn't hear from her until the following day.

77

I woke up around 6 and drove the van back to Noah's neighborhood. I had a housekeeping shift and it started off benign up to the point when I was asked to tidy up a stay over.

"Just to let you know this is a special guest, so give it the VIP touch."

"Special guest?" I asked.

"Yeah, he was in Bauhaus."

"David J??"

"That's the guy."

I rushed through the rest of the things I had to do in the room I was in and then jogged to 306 where David J. was staying. The blinds were drawn and the clock was on the floor facing the wall. One of the nightstand lamps was on the floor and his toiletries were in the sink. A leather jacket was over the back of a chair and I just stood there and took it all in. I wrote down details like the cologne he uses and the pain reliever I saw on the nightstand but it seemed disrespectful so I threw out what I wrote. A hotel room is supposed to be a sanctuary, especially for people who are well known or semi-well known like the bassist from Bauhaus and Love and Rockets. I saw some used towels on the floor and started to pick them up only to discover that they were covering up homemade CDs. The one on top was labeled "David J Photography." I left the towels where they were. David had requested the bed be made up so I started on that. The room he was in was the smallest in the hotel and all his stuff was on one side of the bed so I had to struggle not to step on his belongings. I was having a case of the nerves so I calmed myself by singing Doors songs in a dim room surrounded by the possessions of a man whose work I had admired for thirty years. A hotel room is an intimate place. In a stayover where their possessions remain scattered around you see what toothpaste they use and what cologne they wear, you see the things they throw out and what they had for dinner. Your lives intersect a little bit for the fifteen minutes or so it takes to tidy up. Intellectually, I understood that he was just an ordinary man who happened to have a really cool job, but my blood was moving a bit faster than normal.

78

It was another gray morning, another reminder that Portland didn't care if it was nearly July. Sofia had driven me back to Noah's house. I hadn't wanted to wake her but she had to get up to get ready for work. As I got ready for my own day of toil I drank black coffee and tried to collect my thoughts. I was looking after the cat and felt sorry for him because he was following me around and clearly missing his people.

Riding the bus the streets looked wet but nothing was coming from the sky. I was still not awake, not sure I wanted to be, just drowsily looking out at the shops and the old buildings and the rippling river as I headed in for another day at the Hotel Glass.

The night before had been typical for that week, the little things I did when I had the house to myself: Play piano. Do some cooking. Spend time on Facebook to see where the people in my life were standing. Sofia invited me over to have dinner with her and L. I tagged along when they went to Fred Meyer to get some shopping done; it was an odd experience seeing as it was the first time I had gone shopping with anyone in several months. It made me remember a long dead life, Teresa and I pushing a cart up aisles. Everything had been beautiful once, was my life with Sofia equally doomed?
No, I refuse to think like that.

We tried to find a liquor store but they had all closed at seven. S made cabbage soup and toast to go with it and we drank some red wine. Milfred called from back in California and Sofia handed me an apologetic note that she said he had written. It seemed to be colored with sarcasm but maybe I was just seeing my own. S and I sat on her bed watching a movie on her computer. She fell asleep lying against me so I turned the movie off.

79

The following night Sofia, L, and I walked down to Babydolls to get some pizza. There was graffiti on the bathroom chalkboard and customers were invited to add their own. S and I drank beer while we waited for our food. There was a young, attractive couple outside. He was a black guy with scarification and she was a white girl with a nerdy look complete with glasses who informed us that she was a stripper. The girl kept telling me that she had seen me around. Sofia invited them back to the house where we ate pizza and drank but I was feeling weird because I saw how good looking the guy was and had no idea what was going to happen. The two of them kept butting in on Lily's skyping with her friends and saying really adult stuff. I almost told them to stop a few times but wasn't sure if it was my place or not; it wasn't my kid and it wasn't my house. The four of us were in the kitchen talking about sex and it was making me nervous because I didn't want to share S with another guy, especially such an attractive one. We went over to Chopsticks for karaoke. Every once in a while the guy would touch Sofia flirtatiously and I wanted to slap his hand away. Sofia and I did a couple of songs and then we drove the couple back to Alberta where one of them lived.

It was nearly two before we got to sleep. The alarm blared at six and we climbed out of bed to face another morning with less than required sleep and bleariness from too much alcohol. I kept thinking about how weird the night before had been and how I didn't like the fact that Sofia had given the guy her number even if he had asked for it. It bothered me, but I also understood that Sofia wanted to meet new people and she had assured me that I was the only guy she wanted to be with.

The morning was rainy despite the fact we were only four days from July; I was getting more and more convinced that it never stopped raining in Portland. I was preoccupied by the previous night during my shift at work, kept turning over and over in my mind how attractive that guy was and that he had Sofia's number.

80

The following day Sofia, Lily, and I went to the Japanese Gardens. The day had started off overcast and humid but then the clouds broke and the weather was ideal.

I took the bus out to the 205 Mall so I could check out the 24 Hour Fitness. I was getting a gym membership so I have a place to shower and a bathroom for emergencies. The girl behind the counter called someone over the intercom to give me a guided tour. A minute later a tall woman somewhere around thirty with a dramatic blond streak appeared. She had the kind of tan that looks orange--she was very nice but very orange---I felt as if I were getting my daily supply of Vitamin C staring at her. Miss Orange asked what I was looking to do and explained the machines to me, recommending a personal trainer so I could get the most out of the gym. I just smiled and nodded, understanding that I couldn't tell her the truth.
You see, I won't really be lifting weights or spending time on a treadmill or anything people usually do in gyms; all I need are your showers because I will be living in a van.
At the end of the tour she sat me down for a special offer that was only good that day but Sofia and I had been touching on the idea of my living with her which would make a gym membership unnecessary. She had brought it up the night before, wondering aloud how much extra the rent would be if I moved in. It wouldn't have been that big of a step; I was sleeping there most nights and eating dinner there a few nights a week.

I felt utterly unmotivated at work and my mood soured when I discovered that they didn't have any coffee in the cafe. As I was stocking a linen closet I spotted an older woman walking down the hall with her laptop. I saw the puzzled look on her face and how it changed to a hopeful expression when she saw me. The guest asked about the internet connection and I reluctantly walked over to the closet where I knew the router was kept. I had no idea when the little lights signified but they were green so I told the lady the connection appeared okay. She did something with her computer and looked up at me with that puzzled expression I had first seen her wearing.

"Are you tech savvy?" She asked.

I said no and inside I was getting more and more pissed off; how dare she ask someone who makes minimum wage if they could fix her computer? When I cooled down I understood that there was no way she could have known how much I made or how ridiculous it was to expect a janitor to sort out a laptop. The real problem was my anger and I knew that something had to change.

81

It was Mom's birthday so I sent her an email. I wished that
I had a touching; heartfelt message in me but the words
weren't there. Guilt turned the moments from light to dark
because I knew that such a message would have meant the
world to her. I also owed Dad a call and always struggled
with my distaste for talking on the phone, understanding
that I was being selfish with both of my parents.

Sofia had jokingly asked if I was cheap a few nights before
and I said no, explaining that I was simply careful with
money. Maybe the previous three years had made me weird
about money, all the times I'd be down to my last $20 stuck
in Lodi and wondering if I was going to run out of cash.
There had been many instances of Mom having to pawn
more silver jewelry just to pay bills and buy groceries that I
was eating. Even though I had loathed being there I
understood that I owed her everything. Without her, I
would have been homeless. Without her, there would have
been a lot less love and compassion in my life.

I spent the night at Sofia's. In the morning, she drove me
back to Noah's house and came in for a cup of coffee. We
sipped from our cups, looked out at the garden, and had a
good talk. After she drove off I started some laundry and
packed up more stuff to put in the van. Picking up my
check I saw that it was only $406 after the cashing fee;
things would continue to be tight for some time. I took the
money back to the house and thought about how the

following day I would officially be living in my van. I needed to finish cleaning out the guest room; I really wanted it to look good after they had put up with me staying there for so long.

Feeling pressed for time I hustled to the store for ice so I could pack my food in the ice chest. It felt like summer for the first time but I was hesitant to believe there wouldn't be any more rain. People were sweating on the bus into work. They let another shirtless guy on board and he was all leathery and flaccid looking and getting his back sweat on the fabric; I saw his armpit hair and felt my stomach roll.

It was another night of feeling completely unmotivated to do my job: More linen stocking. More bathrooms. More drunk people laughing in the pool. More futile attempts to communicate using the radio. More waits for a hundred year old elevator---I was even bored with the sex noises coming through the walls. I struggled to focus on the good things in my life: A woman who loved me. Making a life in a beautiful city. Having a job after scraping by with temp assignments for three years--
I was aware of all the things I had to be grateful for but pettiness had its claws in.

Picking up a ham and pineapple pizza from the pub, I sat in a corner booth and watched all the people on the sidewalk. There was a black guy in his early twenties with a full beard sitting in an older Chevy Cavalier. He was bumping the beats and jumped out of the car wearing a big smile and no shirt to chat with a middle aged white guy. The older man was sitting at a table next to the window I was looking out. Hearing a rap lyric in my head, I wrote it on the pizza box.

It was a warm night and I was sweating as I went through the motions of doing my job. Everytime I had to check the jacuzzi I nearly swooned from the heat. I had my first hall puker outside one of the shared bathrooms on the second floor; the mess looked like a patch of dying snow. A woman stepped over it to use the bathroom and I was waiting for her to get out so I could go in and get some paper towels. Another woman in a robe was watching me from down the hall.
"A woman threw up there," she said expectantly.
"I'm about to take care of it."
This seemed to please her enough that when her robe opened to reveal a breast she didn't seem to notice. She walked away and I went into the bathroom and locked the door.

82

It was noon and I still hadn't had my coffee. Sofia had lent me her house key so I could go to Fred Meyer and make a duplicate. Even though I didn't have to work I got up when she did so I could get a start on my day. I watched her dress and put on her make-up and then walked her out to her car. After getting dressed, I went back to Noah's house to take care of the cat and water some plants. Afterward, I walked to the van and took a nap.

On the 15 east there was a guy on the seat in front of me with a t-shirt reading "Open Source Citizen." Mall 205 struck me as a weird place but then again I found most malls to be weird in a way that felt like the essence of America: Faded hopes. A third of the shops were abandoned with faded signs on the windows. You open a shop with all these dreams and a vision but then the economy tanks or maybe you're selling the wrong thing at the wrong time. Star Shots and nearby was the Blue Star which was supposed to look like an "old fashioned burger joint." Surreally enough, the Oregon Department of Child Support was upstairs. In the middle of it all were these old people close to death taking their exercise in a half dead mall.

On the bus back there was this woman sitting behind me with a pug named Precious. The stupid beast kept barking shrilly as if the girl in the well was trying to escape again. I was feeling good about day one of living out of the van. I bought a bunch of supplies and non-perishable food for when I didn't have the means to cook. After stocking up I drove over to Sofia's to cook dinner for her and Lily.

83

It was a beautiful morning and Sofia made us breakfast.
After cleaning up, she went out on the front porch for a
beer and a cigarette. I was worried about her having a drink
so early but understood that it would be hypocritical of me
to say anything. Nevertheless, I worried, especially about
the cigarettes. She told me that she hadn't been smoking in
California but in Portland she was smoking Pall Malls on a
regular basis.

The night before I had cooked dinner for the three of us. It
went the way our nights usually go: Food, closeness, and
drinking gin then beer and finally red wine. We both liked
drinking. I thought about that as we sat on the porch and
shared her cigarette. The beer was probably no big deal,
that period of indulgence would pass for both of us.

I had the floater position and was hoping to be done by
four. Someone had called in sick so I was pulled in to turn
over rooms and didn't clock out until well past five. The
Assistant Manager had me training a young, black guy
named Issac who had tattoos and didn't say much. His
silence was unnerving because his eyes were blank and
hard like a doll's. He was just a kid, maybe 18 or 19, with a
peach fuzz mustache and Converse All Stars. His language
seemed to be a series of mumbles strung together by a
complete lack of interest.

It was a tough day for training and I had to keep an eye on Issac. We learned that the hard way after I turned him loose to strip some rooms on his own and he screwed up. It was my fault, not his, but I still resented how it added to my workload.

Several hours later I fell asleep on Sofia and she understandably felt neglected. We talked about it the following morning and eventually made up. She drove us to Safeway so I could get ice for the cooler in the van and she could pick up some groceries. I bought us both coffee and acted loving but I was thinking about conversations that could be seen as arguments. S had gotten upset with me because I was tired after a hard day of work---how was that my fault? I resented how I had felt obligated to apologize for being human. I was still thinking about that as we sipped out coffee and later when Sofia was making the three of us breakfast. It brought back memories of the dark side of relationships:

*This is part of it, not just the warmth and closeness and laughing at in-jokes. You need to ask if you will be better off--if **both** of you--will be better off together, if it's still a positive thing for both of you?*

And then she smiled at me from across the kitchen. It was just another smile, she probably didn't think about it afterward, but it reminded me of all the love between us and everything else seemed unimportant.

The weather was finally warm and I knew to savor every day before Portland brought the gray and the chill again. Another thing I knew was that I couldn't blame Sofia's kids if they resented me; I was playing a role in the destruction of their family. I was pretty sure it would have happened with or without me, but I understood that they had to see me as playing a role in the whole mess.

We drove out to Tillamook to tour the cheese factory. The three of us walked around the crowded factory for maybe fifteen minutes and then went down to the shop to get ice cream and pepperoni. Sofia then drove us up the coast, it was beautiful out and surprisingly warm for being next to the sea. A slow train that appeared to be 150 years old was creeping up the coast so we stopped to watch it pass. Lily put a penny on the tracks and then fell but caught herself. US 101 slithered through all these tourist towns with sea related names for most of the bars, motels, and restaurants.

Back at the house we had a nice, low key evening. I hadn't seen *Top Gun* so Sofia had made a point of tracking it down for me. After watching the movie the two of us sat close and talked about what we wanted in the future. Both of us wanted to travel and have a little house somewhere. S told me about the thirty foot trailer that she owned and planned to restore. The more we talked the more shared desires we found that we had; the only question was how to make those dreams or goals happen. How long would it be until I got an agent and sold a book? I had no idea; it could be months or it could be years. I could see the life I wanted to share with Sofia very clearly, I just had no idea how long it would take to make it happen. She had asked a couple of times if I wanted to have children but I didn't see a kid fitting in with the life we both wanted. Maybe it would work several years down the road but it would probably be too late by then.

84

The next morning it was warm by eight. A guest wearing a robe and sunglasses was smoking as she went over something on her tablet. She asked where Forest Grove was because a lodge out there was hiring a massage therapist. I shared what I knew about getting to Forest Grove before continuing on the property walk. There were scores of cigarette butts around the building. Watching the traffic for gaps to sweep them out of the gutter, I felt myself losing a little more hope for the human race.

I had worked in hotter cities but my jobs had always been behind a desk or standing in an air conditioned shop. Even though it never broke a hundred degrees in Portland, my job was physical enough that I felt what little heat there was. Aside from the rooms, the air conditioning was weak in the hotel. Willy Gilly looked stunned when he saw me drinking coffee that morning. I felt the heat but loved it; I was in my element.

I was beyond sick of the walkie-talkies by that point, sick of how they stretched out my pants when they were clipped to my belt and how they kept falling off or snagging on stuff. No one knew how to use them and most of the housekeepers would leave them in their carts parked in the hallways. I was also fed up with the guests who didn't tip the people who cleaned their rooms or carried their bags and bicycles. Sometimes I caught myself, looked at my deep sense of disgust, and wondered what had happened to all the optimism I had felt a couple of months earlier.

By the end of my shift I was beat. The service lift had stopped working so we had to manually load out the dirty laundry using the linen carts. Getting off work all I wanted to do was drink a beer and unwind. I sent Sofia a long, complaining text and she told me that I could go in the basement and relax. Walking up to the house, I saw two roommates on the front porch. They saw me and got weird looks on their faces so I just kept walking. Luckily it wasn't that hot in the van so I opened a beer and sat in the passenger seat. I kept thinking about the way the roommates looked and felt guilty; I didn't want to screw up Sofia's living situation by pissing off the people she lived with. We had talked about living together but I wasn't sold on five people sharing a single bath. Beyond that, her roommates had to "approve" me before I officially moved in and two of them were out of town.

After Sofia got home the three of us went to a bar for Taco Tuesday and then S showed her daughter where she worked. It was another quiet night, but a good one.

85

It was another gorgeous morning, shirt sleeve weather. I left Sofia's to walk to the Plaid Pantry for milk. Walking down Morrison I struggled to wake up, longing for a cup of coffee.

The Assistant Manager texted me to let me know that I had July 9th through the 11 off. The plan was to drop Lily off in Santa Rosa and then pick up the rest of my stuff in Lodi. I was nervous about Mom meeting Sofia and the two of us spending the night in her house; I knew that Mom would be judging Sofia and not just because she smoked.

Back at work, Issac walked up to me and mumbled something about training with me. I went to the Assistant Manager and it turned out that Issac had misunderstood and would be training with the same housekeeper (Kevin) that had trained me. I knew that K would not be happy to hear that just as I would not have been surprised if he quit in the near future. Kevin had it good; he could survive off the money he made as a musician. It made me envious and happy for him---imagine being able to survive off doing what you loved?

86

I continued to worry about Sofia's kids resenting me for playing a role in the end of their family. To them it wouldn't matter that their mother was already on the way to getting a divorce; I was the guy she was dating after their step-father. I liked Lily and wanted her to like me and hoped that was possible.

There was a large wedding party in the hotel, someone told me they were from Canada and had booked half the rooms. The bride-to-be called the front desk and asked to have her bed made up. I went up to her room with an armful of sheets and pillow slips a little after eight. There was a lot of luggage in the room; despite the fact it was the largest suite in the hotel it was still a challenge to make the bed and not stand on a suitcase or a box. Members of her wedding party kept sauntering in and getting in my way or just gawking at me as they drank beer. A couple of men went on the balcony and I half watched them as I fluffed the pillows to make sure they weren't smoking. The kicker was that they didn't tip me; I didn't know if it was because they were from Canada or simply because they didn't have any class.

It was a deeply frustrating night. There was lots of foot traffic where I was trying to work and a couple episodes of dealing with broken glass. People would call on the radio only to not follow through when I responded. The elevator reeked of vodka and you could feel craziness radiating from some of the rooms. I had to wonder how many housekeepers would have to clean up vomit the following day.

87

I need a break---you want to go on a walk and get coffee?
Noah texted me around 10, I met him in front of the house
an hour later. We talked about some country Obama was
bombing which somehow led into a discussion about *Hail
to the Thief* by Radiohead.
"Jason keeps asking me if I want to get together," my friend
said.
"Jason?"
"That band I played with a few weeks ago."
"I know you were having problems with that," I offered.
"Yeah, but I don't want it to be like that, you know? It's like
you; I know it's hard for you to be in crowds, but you try
and work through it."
"Those are life coping skills, though, things you have to
deal with."
"True, but music is important to me, I really want to play
with other people again. Is that an Andy Gibb CD in that
box?"
The two of us poked around in a free box on the corner of
Taylor and 34th---sure enough, it *was* an Andy Gibb CD.
"I'm tempted to take this," I said, turning it over in my
hands.
"I know you love 'I Just Want to Be Your Everything'."
"Totally under-rated song. Anyway, about the band..." I
trailed off meaningfully.
"I think I'm going to give it another shot. I want it to
work...there is something in my head holding me up,

blocking me, and I don't want it anymore. Does that make
sense?"

"Yeah..."

"So, I'm going to text Jason back, see what days they're
practicing."

"I'm glad, man."

Noah looked over at me and smiled.

"Me, too."

It was the first time the 15 had not been crowded in the late
afternoon. The driver had a mustache and looked like a 80s
porn star twenty years later after his star had descended.
The guy in front of me was wearing a jeans vest and
hacking away like a TB patient. I made a point to not touch
anything he had touched when I was getting off the bus.

People had to have been picking up on my attitude at work;
I knew they'd eventually talk to me about it so I tried to
figure out what to say when the time came. Honesty was
dangerous but lying was transparent. I had spent some time
that afternoon looking for a job but hadn't found anything.
A big problem was that it was too soon; I was still burned
out from three years of job hunting.

I was woefully unproductive in the hours leading up to
leaving for work. I got stuff done but not nearly as much as
I would have liked. Sometimes I went to Noah's to get on
line, looking at cars, drinking wine, and playing piano.
Sofia and I got to spend maybe half an hour together
between her getting back to the house and my catching the
bus across the river.

I had a crack in the sole of my boot and was living out of an 18 year old van. On the other hand, I felt fortunate to have a very understanding girlfriend who loved me and let me sleep in her room. I may have been working for minimum wage but I was well aware of all the people out of work and knew that I had no right to complain. Sometimes I read what I had written earlier that year and thought it was really good. Sometimes, though, I wondered if I was deluding myself. That was a scary thought; I knew that I couldn't keep up with those grunt jobs forever, either mentally or physically. The year before had changed me; I was no longer as on top of day to day stuff as I had been in the past, day to day stuff like papers or jobs---my life was a threadbare improvisation. I was used to it, maybe I was even comfortable with it, but how could I expect Sofia to want to be a part of it long term? In the end of it all I understood that I couldn't live my life any other way---even at the risk of losing the woman I loved---I had tried in the past and it was a complete disaster.

I got off work at 11 P.M. Parties were spilling out of rooms and people were wandering the halls drink in hand in the midst of a warm haze of intoxication. I dropped my radio and keys off at the front desk and walked outside to wait for Sofia. Someone has thrown up on the sidewalk but it wasn't my problem.

88

I had emailed Mom a few days earlier to tell her that Sofia
and I would be coming down to pick up some of my stuff.
Her response was weird; something was up with her and
my instincts were telling me that things would be awkward
when we got to Lodi. Mom was losing the house and I
needed to get my stuff out but wouldn't be able to take
much in Sofia's Prius---I knew that would cause trouble.

My shift ended badly. Front desk asked me to close the
pool at 1 a.m., so at 12:45 I went down there to give
everyone a fifteen minute warning. I had to raise my voice
to be heard over the pool jets, everyone seemed to hear me
and nodded and there didn't seem to be a problem. At five
minutes to one this guy weaseled into the pool and I didn't
want to get into a fuss with him so I let him in with the
caveat that the pool would be closing five minutes later. A
girl slipped in behind him. I stuck my head in the door and
gave everyone a five minute warning and asked them to
start getting out as it usually took guests five to ten minutes
to climb out of the water and put their robes on for some
reason. The people in the pool just looked at me. I gave it a
couple of minutes, turned the jets off, and then walked back
into the room to address the people still in the pool.
"It's now two minutes to one, please start getting out, thank
you for your cooperation."
This guy around sixty with a hairy chest and man boobs
looked over at me sharply.
"What is your name?"

"Ike."

"You cannot come in here and raise your voice like a cop!" He said sternly. "I am a guest!"

I tried to explain about how I had to raise my voice to be heard above the jets and conversations but he rolled right over that.

"I want you to get out!" He continued.

"You don't have that authority, sir." I said as calmly as possible.

"I want you to get out!"

Everyone was staring at me and a couple of people were actually applauding the old man; I had become the bad guy. Getting nowhere, I walked up to the front desk. The two of us walked back down to the pool and Hans flicked the lights on and off before then talking to the old man, I stood outside and did not hear the conversation. We walked back to the front desk and watched the pool through the camera. Everyone was getting out, a couple of people were shaking hands with the old man and I'm sure he'd be telling his wrinkle buddies about how he led the "great pool rebellion of '13."

At least the night ended well: I walked a few blocks to Jack London's to meet Sofia. She bought me a Jameson and we sat in a booth holding hands and watching people dance.

89

I woke up in the middle of night thinking about the confrontation with that old man. I couldn't imagine getting in serious trouble for that but you never knew. Maybe the Great Pool Rebellion of '13 would be added to the list of things that I had been doing wrong or badly at the hotel.

The next morning I went to 24 Hour Fitness but didn't take a towel thinking that one would be provided. I took the bus out to Mall 205 and spent maybe five minutes wandering around the gym looking for towels. There was an employee sitting at a desk and texting. He looked bored and I knew the conversation would be a frustrating one. When I asked him about towels you would have guessed from his expression that I suggested a bestiality site to look up on his mobile phone. No towels, I was informed. *No shower*, I realized; I would be having my first baby wipe bath in the van.

I walked over to Target and got some coffee before doing my shopping. There was a guy around thirty with a backwards baseball cap and a t-shirt emblazoned with "Fatal Crew." I thought about this woman who wrote about the bees dying and that when they did the human race would soon follow. I saw that man in the Fatal Crew t-shirt and thought of all the cigarette butts people just crush into the cement and heard the death of bees as beautiful music.

It was one of those days when I felt burned out not having a home. It seemed like I was always scrambling to figure out where I was going to bathe and where I was going to the bathroom. When Sofia was there her house felt like home to me. When she wasn't there I felt like an interloper just as I had felt at the place I had stayed my first four months in Portland.

I could have used the restroom in either 24 Hour Fitness or Target but I wanted to get back to my part of town. What had happened the night before in the pool kept bothering me; I was worried about blow back---if that old guy complained to the right person who would then discipline me. The customer is always right...even when they're a dick and you're just being firm with them because you need them to follow the rules.

I had been getting in the bad habit of drinking before work. It wasn't much, just a glass of wine or a beer, but I knew it wasn't a good thing. Sofia and Lily had an argument the night before and I suspect some of L's anger was about what was happening to her family. I couldn't blame her; I had been angry when I was a kid and my family fell apart. I had been angry at my step-father for many years, of course part of that was because he was an asshole. The truth was that my parents' marriage had an expiration date whether or not Norman had come into the picture. I'm pretty sure it was the same for Sofia and Milfred.

Out walking around, I got into a phone conversation with Noah:

"Your friend Dan wants me to call into his podcast," he said.

"Yeah, he's asked me a couple of times; I have been hesitating about passing on the messages."

"It's weird but it's cool, you know? It feels good to think people are still into the album but I have to ask why..."

"No, you don't; you know as well as I do that album is awesome."

"I am proud of it, which is ironically why I hesitate to do another one."

"Are you going to do the podcast?" I asked.

"I think so, I always enjoy it, I just worry, you know? Last time I did an interview they asked all these weird questions about Chase."

"I know. I can talk to Dan, if you like."

"I'm not worried; he doesn't seem like a dick."

"He isn't."

"Cool. Everyone alright with you? How is living in the van going?"

"Mostly good, just getting in the swing of things."

"Yeah, I imagine that's tough. Hey, I gotta go, I have a conference call in five minutes."

"No worries, talk to you soon."

I got back to the van and ate some peanuts and drank some water. Had the neighbors figured out what I was doing? Needing the bathroom, I walked over to Safeway. It felt good being able to survive like that, even figuring out simple stuff like where the best bathrooms were. Listening to cheesy 70s lite rock I wandered the tree lined neighborhoods and life felt good. At Safeway both stalls were full so I lingered in the corridor next to this wire rack full of clearance stuff like Spicy V8 and carrot cake mix with a gross picture on the cover. A middle aged man with a prominent salt and pepper mustache walked out of the bathroom and I knew the stall he had used would be foul. He had the weary expression of a man who has seen a lot of disappointment and had acquired the skill of making a bathroom smell bad. Sure enough, the smell in the stall was hideous and there was residue on the seat. I tried to cover it up with one of those paper seat covers but it was so flimsy I had little luck. I made a mental note to buy some bleach wipes for situations like that.

I walked back to the van and got the last Sierra Nevada from the cooler. The cemetery was four blocks from Sofia's so I strolled over to get lost in there, drink a beer, and maybe do some writing. I opened the bottle standing next to a tree that had sprouted from a couple of graves. I could see people in old fashioned clothes planting a sapling and after some time it took root and sent tendrils into the coffins and entwined with the remains. It was kind of macabre but kind of beautiful, the whole cliché of something beautiful and alive coming from death.

That night at work created vivid memories despite the fact that nothing out of the ordinary happened: I watched the pool, stocked the linens, and cleaned the bathrooms. I stood behind the front desk when Hans went to get his dinner from the pub. Sofia texted me; she was drunk and had gone out to play pool with a female friend. I sat in the basement for the last hour of my shift and did nothing but text back and forth with her. When I was leaving some guy was yelling up at the windows of the sleazy hotel across the street. I said goodnight to Hans, cued Depeche Mode on my iPod, and started walking. A few blocks down Hawthorne I smelled shit and saw that there was butterscotch colored diarrhea all over the ground in one of the bus shelters. Someone was changing the letters in front of Dante's and people were taking advantage of the warm weather to sleep on the bridge. In the middle of the Burnside Bridge I looked down at the reflection of the lights on the dark water and imagined the bridge collapsing, falling into the depths surrounded by a rain of concrete. On the other side of the river I could smell bread being baked and worked to keep up my pace as I headed up the hill. It was a beautiful night, I was in love, and anything seemed possible.

Written between February 17, 2013 and 30 April, 2016
Music listened to: Rolling Stones ("Heartbreaker"); Elliott Smith; Depeche Mode (*Delta Machine*), Bruce Springsteen ("Hungry Heart") Richard Ashcroft ("Check the Meaning"), The Verve (various)

Jackie Bonner

the woods seem cold and dark tonight, but the stars are bright; and you don't want to go back to a place that doesn't feel like home. I think we're lost, no idea where we are. It's three a.m and you're crying and there's nothing I can do. I know it doesn't matter, I'd fall off the edge of the world for you.

A novel

the moon lights your driveway like a stage. And I don't want to leave you but I do anyway. I think we're lost, no idea where we are. We're both bare and broken hearts and you're as beautiful as the stars.

By "Ike James"

Forward

I went back and forth many times whether or not to include *Jackie Bonner* with *The Passenger*. On one hand, it is not as "good" as the story it is included with (or *Memory* or *What Peace Means to Us,* for that matter). On the other, I thought it might be interesting to read as a "curio," the book "Ike James" is writing as he moves from bar to bar in Portland.

I started *Jackie Bonner* in Lodi, California in the summer of 2012. To be blunt, I had allowed myself to become miserable enough that suicide seemed a valid option. California was still suffering the Great Recession so I was getting little work through the temp agencies; my plan was to save up to buy a van to move out of my mother's spare room and become a workamper but I wasn't bringing in enough money. If that situation wasn't frustrating enough, I also had this massive crush on my friend Cat aka Jackie Bonner: Man…I was so into her. Removed from my feelings by several years, I can say Cat is an awesome woman: Smart. Funny. She could come off normal but there was something delightfully askew about her observations and interpretations of those observations. She was beautiful to me but to the casual observer her face could appear coarse. We will always have a history---for several months we were like two whips sometimes cracking the same air. To her, I was a close friend—and the dude she'd settle for if she was unable to hook up with anyone else when we went bar hopping. It was stupid, it was pathetic; even then I understood that. Honestly, I am embarrassed at what a schmuck I was nine years ago but I own my past and the mistakes that went with it. Not that Cat wasn't deserving of someone being off the rails for her, I was simply not the right one to be derailed by her charms; she was looking for more of a firefighter or off duty policeman type. In fact, one night she drunkenly ran into the street in old town Jackson waving down an attractive man in an SUV. He was an off duty cop and warned us that Cat would be arrested if she kept making a scene. It's funny now but at the time I was worried for her, I worried about her a lot back then. Beyond everything I cared about her very deeply, I still do even if I haven't spoken with her in eight years.

In between feeling trapped and hopeless and dealing with my crush on "Jackie Bonner" I was desperate for an escape, to create an alternative universe where I got over Cat and had some success as a writer—that was what led me to write *Jackie Bonner*. It started as a few blog entries, a wee diversion, but it became much bigger and all encompassing than what I had intended. It got me through tough times, you know, so in a way I owe the story *Jackie Bonner* a debt of gratitude, life. I started working on it in July of 2012 and finished it the following April. As I said, I have gone back and forth whether or not to include it with *The Passenger*; in the end, I leave it up to you whether it is worthy for inclusion or not.

The lyric on the title page is to Stars, a song I wrote after one particularly memorable night with "Jackie Bonner."

March 29, 2016

Today marks four years since I fell for Jackie Bonner. I experienced that derangement most easily described as *love* and wrote feverishly about it in an attempt to both celebrate and exorcise my feelings. I wrote about the lives I imagined the two of us would be living a few years in the future; nothing turned out like I imagined it would. Back in late 2012 that story was my every waking moment but it became just another file on my external drive---until coming across that story last night; I opened the file out of curiosity and then it was three in the morning. I am so disconnected from the feelings that led me to write what I wrote that it read like fiction---it read like fiction but I understand that time in my life made me who I am. Impulsively, I emailed it to the only address I had for Jackie Bonner.

I did not exist four years ago, I vanished off the face of the earth and a ravenous yet pathetic beast took my place. I probably would have killed for Jackie Bonner, certainly almost killed myself. After such an extreme, how is it that I feel nothing for her now? Did I just need her to inspire me? That's the party line I sell these days; no one wants to admit they've been weak, especially men. We are shamed by weakness. Ask me about Jackie Bonner and I'll shrug and say I got all these songs and a novel in an attempt to make it seem like I got the upper hand. I didn't get the upper hand; I am just another fool at the end of strings controlled by ghosts.

During the day I promote my latest novel and at night I play songs about Jackie Bonner in small nightclubs. If you have been following this blog you know that I have been the opening act for an Italian boy band the past week and a half. Their average age is 30 and most of them are obnoxious. It has to be weird for them: Fifteen years ago they were huge in Europe and now they are playing dingy little clubs where you bump your head on the ceiling. Back then photographers were jumping out of bushes to capture them and now their manager has to beg tiny webzines to write them up. Their stage costumes look good from out on the floor but close up you see the clumsy attempts to patch them up and the discoloration from years of sweat. The suits they wear look dated and were designed for teenagers, not men in their early thirties with expanding paunches. They used to have private dressing rooms but now they have to fight to get a small area to set up the threadbare curtain they carry from venue to venue. Each night I see them jostling for space behind it as they chatter in Italian. I feel for them, but they're still pricks. The only one in the band I get on with is Malo. We had a couple of drinks the other night but I couldn't keep up. He was drinking tequila and I remember that striking me as funny because I thought Italians drank wine.

Tonight I will take a glass of heavy red wine on stage with me. I will set it on the rented keyboard and stare into the lights as I work my way through my set and pretend that I am being embraced by angels as I sing to them in the hope of finally earning my freedom.

March 30, 2016

I must be careful what I share. One of you is angry with me for emailing Jackie Bonner. What's done is done, let's just move on. Please.

April 12, 2016

They asked me if I killed her; I could not answer for nearly
a minute.
They asked more firmly: *Did you kill her?*
I was in my room. I did not remember walking there. There
were two policemen in there with me.
I couldn't believe it was happening again.

The gig with the Italians ended in Budapest and I became
the opening act for a singer-songwriter named Marija. I had
never heard of her before but became a fan the first night
we played together. What struck me wasn't her talent---
(though she had a lot of it and I liked her songs)---nor was
it that I found her beautiful---(though she was sexy in a
grimy tomboy way). No, I was struck by how she seemed
to be wrestling with something much larger than herself.
Inspiration? Something that happened in the past or was
still happening? Emotions? Mental illness? I didn't know
her so it wasn't my place to ask. I started reading
everything I could find online; there was lots of speculation
but no real answers.

After my set I watched her play from the edge of the stage.
I bought all of her music and loaded it on my netbook. The
rest of her band were equally grim and Nordic in
appearance: A bassist, a keyboardist, and a drummer.
Marija played guitar with a slowly unfolding derangement,
more imagination and emotion than skill. The way she
played reminded me of Lou Reed, the Edge, and Daniel
Ash from Bauhaus all rolled in one. I was transfixed. My
attempt to talk to her was hampered by her poor English
and my non-existent Danish. I could sense that she didn't
really want to talk to me, anyway. Maybe she saw me as
another older guy who wanted to fuck her; maybe she saw

me as a peer out to steal her ideas or maybe she was just rude. I did not find out that night.

We would part ways after playing two nights in Hamburg. I had dreamt about that city since I was a teenager because the Beatles became the Beatles there. I wasn't thinking about John, Paul, and George at that point, I was thinking of Marija. I rang Maggie to see if I could get more opening slots and stay with the tour another week but it wasn't possible. Another band had been selected, I was told; *she liked your music, though.* She did?! I asked if I could change my tour arrangements and stay in Europe another week. There was a long pause and then my manager reminded me that I was running out of money and there was no way I could afford it.

They asked me if I killed her...
Sitting on my bed, my eyes red, in shock.
How could this happen again?
I told the police what I remembered. Wandering the halls of the hotel as I tend to do when I can't sleep. Seeing an open door, peeking in, and seeing a young woman in a transparent slip sitting on the edge of the bed. She looked hypnotized and was taking rapid, shallow breaths. I could see her breasts through the fabric and below them the handle of a knife. I walked in and just stared at her for what felt like a couple of minutes. It was Marija; she was still alive but she did not seem to notice my presence...
And then I was calling the front desk; I could feel the words coming out of me but it sounded like someone else speaking. Hanging up I knelt down in front of her and took one of her hands. It was warm and there was surprisingly little blood. Maybe the wound wasn't so bad; maybe it hadn't hit any major organs or blood vessels.
No, I just *knew* the blade was in her heart.

279

I was still kneeling there when I heard voices and then felt people moving me aside so they could treat her. They told me I was crying when they got there. I don't remember that but I guess it makes sense. It was no longer Marija sitting on that bed dying---it was someone else---someone I never had the chance to say goodbye to.
They asked me if I killed her.

The American Embassy was called but the police already knew that I wasn't the killer. It was a suspected suicide; Marija had attempted suicide in the past and had a long history of self-injury. I was free to go and yet I wasn't. After the police left I just sat on the edge of my bed for what may have been a couple of hours. I had a boat to catch later in the day but I had no idea how I was going to get up. I posted a short blog entry about it and a few minutes later a female friend instant messaged me; the same female friend who chastised me about sending a story to Jackie Bonner a couple of weeks ago.
"Are you okay, Ike?" My friend asked.
"No. Not really."
You see, I changed things a bit when I wrote that blog on March 29th. My friend wasn't angry that I had shared something with JB; she was worried that I was going to regress to the state I was in three years ago. I am healed but the fact remains that I can never forgive myself: Maybe if Jackie hadn't been pissed off at me she would have called me when she needed help. When I am thinking clearly I know that she would have never asked for help, but even now I rarely think about her in a fashion that is remotely *clear*. Our last conversation was a series of acrimonious texts---that was how our friendship ended. A few days later, Jackie Bonner disappeared and has not been seen in three years or so. A week or so after that the cops interviewed me; I was a suspect for a while due to my unrequited love for JB.

They asked me if I had killed her.

All I could do was shake my head.

We'll never know what happened. Maybe she got drunk in a bar and let the wrong guy pick her up or maybe one of her boyfriends got jealous, killed her, and disposed of her somehow. Believe me, I have come up with every possible scenario and I had nightmares about all of them. Her being shot in the head, being strangled, or being stabbed like Marija was.

"You still there, Ike?"

"Kind of. Don't worry; I am just in shock a bit. Oh, you should check out Marija's stuff, I think you'd like it. It's a cut above the rest."

And I laughed this forced crazy sounding laugh that fortunately my friend couldn't hear.

"I was worried when you wrote about Jackie two weeks ago," she wrote.

"I know; I'm sorry."

"Don't be, I know how much you loved her."

"I still do."

"I remember how you explained to me how your writing all that Jackie Bonner stuff was to deal with her disappearing."

"Yeah, I couldn't deal with her being gone. I kind of lost it for a bit…"

But we are a peculiar animal bent on surviving even when ninety-nine percent of us just wants to lay down and die. I focused on getting an agent and then getting a publisher. I lost myself in playing music; eventually I met other women that I would fall in love with to varying degrees. They would read my blog and ask about Jackie Bonner and I would lie and say that she was a fictional character. Often they would tell me it was my finest work, that it seemed so *alive*.

I never have a response to that.

April 13, 2016

"You've got to stop killing people—this has become a bad habit with you."

I am sitting in my cabin on the freighter that will take me back to the United States. We have yet to leave the dock. Part of me wanted to watch us disembark like I had done when we left New York but it was unseasonably cold on deck. Opening my bag and pulling out my netbook, I saw that there was a message from Maggie. Seeing she was available, I wrote her back, an inquiry about how things were with my manager.

"How is this singer going to deal with finding out you murdered her in a story?" Maggie wrote.

"I didn't murder her—"

"You know what I mean; her dying. People are not going to want to tour with you if you keep killing them off, Ike."

"I changed her name. Besides, she doesn't really speak English."

"And how is your friend going to respond to the latest installment of *Jackie Bonner*? You killed her off, too."

"No, I just said she disappeared."

"But you said you imagined her being murdered. People don't usually take that sort of thing very well."

"I doubt she is even following it."

"I thought you were friends again."

"We're always friends, I just don't think she follows it."

"Because it's partially about her?"

"No, I think she's flattered by that, but I think it's more that she can't deal with my feelings for her in the past."

"Did the two of you actually date like you wrote a few days ago?"

"No, that was fiction. I kept getting all these notes and messages from people, mostly men, who hoped we had been a couple."

"You're a whore, Ike."

And then she mercifully allowed the conversation to take a different tact: *You're running out of money*. Yes, poverty, thank God; anything but talking about the inspiration for *Jackie Bonner*.

Last night I finally had a conversation with Marija. We were talking about George Harrison and couldn't decide if he was under-rated or overrated. She was impressed that he had died on my birthday and we agreed that he was our favorite Beatle. A bandmate of hers was drinking vodka and translating when we got stuck; he seemed bored with both of us. I tried to flirt with Marija but she was not having it. I could smell her sweat and see her nipples through the fabric of her shirt. The more I had to drink the more I wanted to touch them: She probably fucks like she plays guitar, like the world is ending and there is nothing left to lose.

We've been putting installments of *Jackie Bonner* on the website for a few weeks now and people seem to like it. People always ask if I have ever gotten a response from the real Jackie Bonner and I can truthfully say no. I suspect that she reads it but I can't say for sure. I almost talked her into traveling with me across the country a few weeks ago when I drove to New York to catch the freighter---almost. Right before departure she opted out, explaining that her boyfriend wouldn't have been comfortable with it. Looking back maybe it would have been a bad idea. Maybe it would have been like four years ago with me sitting at one end of a bar feeling miserable as she flirted with other men. Of course, from that misery came creative inspiration. Back then my female friends thought I was an idiot and saw Jackie as a horrible, manipulative, compulsive liar. They pointed out that she was a villainess who was capricious with the feelings of the one man who

284

probably loved her more than any other man in her life ever would. Perhaps some of the accusations were true, but there was a lot more to her....

I have written too much about that already, have defended her enough in the past to feel like an apologist. In the end I prefer to accept my own part of the blame; Jackie never asked me to have feelings for her, if I could have shut my heart to her somehow none of this would have ever happened. On the other hand, the pain and confusion inspired me, and inspiration is everything to me.

February 23, 2016

A year and a half earlier---
It is nearly dawn and we are speeding down a dirt road
somewhere in Mexico. Jackie Bonner is in the passenger
seat of my van, semi-conscious, frowning at the sun. As is
usually the case she remembers nothing or says she
remembers nothing from the night before: The bar, scoring
cocaine, her nearly being assaulted in the parking lot and—
I look between the seats at my gun. Two of the chambers
are empty.
*Hey, since you're going to be in San Diego why don't we
go into Mexico?*
I knew the answer to that before I agreed to have an
adventure with Jackie Bonner across the border. Now the
sun is rising and I have no idea where I am going. I hear
sirens in the distance that are getting closer by the minute.
This is going to be a really bad day.

I am lying in my bed sipping coffee and thinking about the
Summer of '14 when I visited J in San Diego. We had a
few drinks and talked about going to Mexico but it was
more of a joke; something that sounds like a good idea at
four in the morning.
"Sounds fun, we can take my van."
In the present, I text Jackie to wish her a happy birthday
and she sends an apologetic response a few minutes later
informing me she won't be able to join me on my cross
country drive after all. I knew the chances were slim; JB is
dating someone and he seems the possessive type. I can
never express this concern, even as a friend, because Jackie
knows I have thought of her as more than a friend. It was
stupid of me to invite her in the first place; the odds would
be high of us ending up in a bar and replaying one of those

crazy nights from the past that left me feeling disrespected and jealous.

I am picking up a car to deliver to Cleveland at the end of the month and figure it will take four days unless I hit some bad weather. From Cleveland I take the Amtrak to New York where I will catch a freighter for Europe. I'm excited enough that I have not been really sleeping. Both Maggie and my agent have given me a lot of grief about the fact I don't fly, they do not seem to appreciate how uncomfortable I am on planes. Everyone keeps pointing out how little money we have for this tour---*can't you just take some sleeping pills?* No, I will sleep on floors in Europe or stay in hostels but I won't fly. In the end, we were able to get the money together. Some of it came from this series idea I got a development deal for. I can't say anything beyond that; it may never get made, that's the way these things work. At least I got the money which means I don't have to fly.

I am subletting my room to Allison for the month of March for half the rent. That way she can get away from her roommates and I can keep my rented room. A was pissed off when I asked Jackie Bonner to travel with me across the country; she said she almost broke up with me which I thought was kind of strange seeing as she is always telling me that she isn't my girlfriend. Many times she has pointed out that things are casual between us and in fact has been seeing this mutual female friend of ours. How does she have the right to be pissed off about J and I going on a trip together? I guess I should have expected Allison to be uncomfortable with the idea considering I told A about my history with JB. Allison is not looking at the fact Jackie has a boyfriend and never has thought of me as anything more than a buddy—she's looking at my admitted feelings for JB. I would have asked *her* but neither of us have the money for her plane ticket back. I would have loved to take A to Europe with me but there was no way we could have made it work.

After Jackie texts I pour myself another cup of coffee and go to the window to check on the van. There is a small hole in the side. Whenever I see that hole I think of a small town in Mexico and a rough bar on the edge of that gritty, little *pueblo*. We drove all day from Jackie's apartment in San Diego and crossed deep into Mexico on the mainland. Men automatically surrounded J in the bar, drawn to her; JB held court and accepted their flirtations as I sat nearby chiding myself for getting into that situation again. A few hours later Jackie was whispering in my ear about scoring some coke. We went into this storage room where this evil looking old woman was ready to make a deal. A couple of hours later we were out in the parking lot and these greasy looking fucks were all over JB and the situation was quickly getting out of control. They were so close I could smell their cheap aftershave and eager sweat and feel lust coming off them in waves... I could see Jackie starting to look scared through the drunkenness and the patchy euphoria of the cocaine. In my heart I knew what was going to happen and I was scared but once again I was the more sober one and understood it was up to me to look out for us. I fished in my pockets for my keys; I had to get something out of a locked box in the van.

March 3, 2016

"Did you shoot someone in Mexico?"
Those are the first words during a phone call from Maggie;
she *never* calls. I had been dead asleep—*where the fuck am
I?*
Seconds pass before I remember: *Mississippi. Super 8.*
"Ike?"
She wants to know what happened in the Summer of 2014--
what happened the weekend I visited Jackie Bonner in San
Diego…

I know my blog has been boring the past couple of days
and contemplated adding some fiction about fucking a
chambermaid or something equally lurid but the reality is it
has just been a lot of driving and trying to avoid bad road
food and ending each day in anonymous motels. The South
is strange; my family is from here and it still feels like
another planet: The stores are different, the accents are
different--the way people look at life is different. It really is
a different country.

I am driving a 2013 Ford Expedition and it guzzles gas. I
drive 65 and everyone passes me and it still only gets
around sixteen miles per gallon. I feel safe, though; in a
sick way I get why people buy these things, this feeling of
invulnerability.

It has felt as if I have been living in someone else's life
these four days, driving an SUV and eating fast food. I love
fast food but I normally never eat it. The rules are different
on the road; you can eat shitty food and it's okay.
McDonalds and Burger King and a couple of other places--
-cheap food in a bun you can eat as you drive another few
hundred miles down the interstate.

Allison called me when I was back in the room last night. She told me she loved me and was crying when she said it. The cynic in me wants to think it's because she had a fight with her girlfriend but a larger part of me wants to believe she really loves me—

Like you loved or love Jackie Bonner.

We have told each other we love each other in the past but it is always a matter of fact: *I love you. I need coffee. I love you. I need to do laundry.* Last night was different and honestly it broke my heart a little. I have been conflicted about my feelings for A since we met; it was supposed to casual, *fuck buddies* is the crass term that comes to mind, but we fell for each other. She is always the first one to say "we need to keep this casual" but she is also always the first one to say "I love you." It hurt so much to hear her crying last night; I wish I had the money to buy her a plane ticket to Cleveland and take her with me to Europe and do all that romantic shit people do over there, but neither of us have the means to make it happen. The really fucked up thing is that tomorrow she will probably re-erect the wall and be anti-commitment again. It's not an easy relationship, not for either of us, but since when is love easy? Real love, volatile-losing sleep-occasionally obsessive love.

I will be jealous of any man you ever fall in love with.

I think back to late '12 when I was so hung up on Jackie Bonner and all my female friends were giving me shit about it. What did they expect from me? Did they think I could just flip a switch and suddenly feel nothing? Life moved on like it always moves on. Jackie started dating guys and I eventually started going on a few dates myself. We'd be buddies but every so often things would go past that and then there would be this awkwardness between us and we wouldn't speak for months and then we'd be friends again. That is the way it is to date. We will probably be friends the rest of our lives and there will probably be something weird between us the rest of our lives—

"Are you still there, Ike?"

"Yeah. Sorry."

"I am really liking this story, but I am worried."

"Worried?"

"Yeah. What happened in Mexico two years ago?"

I look over at the clock on the dresser. It is a cheap, rectangular alarm clock with square, red numbers. In three hours I need to be out of bed and drinking coffee in preparation for driving to Cleveland.

There is a voice on the other end of the line but I have no idea how to answer it.

April 3, 2016

I believe he is going to fuck her. Malo, at the bar; chatting with a blonde who is somewhere around 30. She looked German but then she spoke and I understood that she was Italian or at least extremely fluent in Italian. She had been watching him during the whole set, rapt like a bird circling a yard when it spies something it wants.

My martini glass had been dry for half an hour so I left the bar. Malo interrupted his courtship to offer me another drink but I thanked him, said goodnight, and consequently exhausted all of my Italian. He already had an erection; it looked like someone had shoved a beer can down the front of his pants, a tall boy. I thought about him and the blonde fucking as I walked the streets of another unfamiliar yet beautiful city.

Several hours from now I will be boarding a train for Vienna where I will be the opening act for another band. My blood has conquered the gin and the chill in the air has become distinct. Budapest is an old city, full of ghosts. They play like out of focus movies on the streets and on the side of buildings that are centuries old. We don't have anything this old in America. I travel to all these cities and realize how young we are; children don't have ghosts, just imaginary friends.

Elvis and his wife have been very kind, giving me a room to crash in and insisting I share meals with them. If that weren't enough they even took my bag and my guitar back to their house after the gig. I have no idea what their real names are; if you have been following this blog you understand I am terrible with names. I call him Elvis because he is obsessed with the singer, almost like a

Hungarian version of the Dad from *The Commitments*. He asked about Memphis and I dredged up some memories of when I spent a couple of days there last year searching for the ghosts of Alex Chilton, Chris Bell, and the King. Elvis kept trying to ply me with liquor last night and I felt the demon coming back. I crippled the demon, but he is still strong because he is a demon and because I never finished him off. I like Elvis and try and explain to him about when I took the demon into the wilderness with the intension of murder.

"I thought you were a drinker, Ike." He looked confused.

"I was--I guess in my heart I still am, but I don't really drink anymore."

"I am sorry I did not know you were sick. How did you stop?"

And I told him the story: The Summer of '13, driving the van to this remote part of California named the Yolla Bolly Middle Eel Wilderness. I had been planning the trip for months, had been intending to save my life for some time but it wasn't until that summer that I could make it happen. I had a break between assignments and enough money for the gas so I drove out there for four of the most intense days of my life. It was like an acid trip without the LSD, all this stuff just came to the surface and I spent hours crying. It is a remote enough place you can scream your lungs out and not bother anyone so I just screamed and cried and during the day I'd run up these trails until I felt like my heart was going to explode.

Since the trip to Yolla Bolly I only drink on special occasions or—(in Elvis' case)—if someone pulls out an absurdly good bottle of whiskey and it seems an insult not to join them. Living in the van you can't get drunk, you have to keep your wits about you in case a cop comes or if dodgy people start hanging around outside. I had curbed my drinking by the Spring of '13, but I was still having relapses. I was still hung up on Jackie Bonner, dwelling on how she was dating these guys and not me. It was too easy to be in that rut because I was broke and living with my mother and didn't have the means to date anyone or I was in Portland and didn't know anyone. Even when I started dating people late that Spring I still thought about Jackie as I suppose I always will. If you have been following this blog you understand I love her like I have loved few people in my life. That will never change though I suppose the definition of that love has.

I am back in the spare room writing this. I should be asleep but this will probably be another instance of my staying up all night. Elvis has gone to bed and his wife let me in. She is really cute and I think she was flirting with me. I feel bad because I flirted back; I am not such a nice guy if you really examine the facts. I have the feeling that she will show up in this room before the night is over and I also have the bad feeling I will not turn her away. I have shared this side with you before, how I have not killed or even maimed *all* of my demons. I have slept with other men's wives; I have been involved with girlfriends and fiancés. I couldn't stand killing all my demons, I guess; maybe I'm frightened there will be nothing left of me if I do.

April 4, 2016

I believe I will be murdering a German this evening.
More accurately, I will be murdering an Austrian.
The amp they sent to the gig was not functioning so I had
to borrow one from Marija (the singer I am opening for).
To be fair, the equipment supplier has done an amazing job
up to this point making sure I have a keyboard and an amp.
Every time they bring the gear it's on the back of a scooter.
Every time, be it in Paris or London or Budapest---Europe
is awesome like that.

Allison and I had a text conversation on the train from
Budapest. It was a lot like the conversation we had when I
was in Mississippi; her telling me how much she loves me
and misses me; I really want to believe it, but I *know* her.
If we were in the same town things would be different, she
would be keeping her distance. I guess that is part of the
reason why I love her: I also keep my distance.
"I drove your van this morning," she wrote.
"That's fine, it needs to be driven."
"There's a little hole in the side, I didn't do it, I have been
really careful—"
"No worries, it's an old hole."
"It looks like a bullet hole."
I skillfully divert the conversation as I always divert the
conversation when the hole in the side of my van comes up.

"Did you fuck Elvis' wife?" Another woman, another
conversation.
"Yes; while he watched from the closet."
"I'm serious, Ike."
"So am I."
I am in the lobby of the hostel I am staying in working on
this blog. Maggie has interrupted me as she tends to do.
"You are supposed to be working on *Purgatory*."

"Soon, mon amie, soon."

"You are not going to tell me the truth about Elvis' wife, are you?"

"No," I admit.

"You're an asshole. Try and get some sleep for once in your life."

Tomorrow we travel down to Rome for two days. I think it's funny that all that time I was with the Italian boy band and we never went to Italy. My nights will be spent on a stranger's couch, some friend or relative of someone who works for the European distributor. Maybe I should change the title of this blog to *Please don't murder me in my sleep*.

I will probably head back to the dormitory and fall asleep soon. Didn't sleep much at Elvis' house nor did I sleep on the train and once I got to town it was straight to the book signing. It was such a small bookstore we had to set the table up in the alley behind the shop. I shared the stage with some cats who were putting on a show using garbage cans for props; this is the glamorous life of a traveling writer. I thought this beautiful forty-something woman was hitting on me so I flirted back and she looked horrified. One of the cats was looking on as if enjoying my predicament, I flipped it off and it ran away.

Marija is a sullen Danish woman. She is one of those sullen people you can't help but be drawn to. Talented. I have no idea why she isn't a bigger star just as I always wonder why so many people choose Kurt Cobain over Elliott Smith. M looks more Russian than Danish, dirty brunette hair barely down to her shoulders and dark green eyes. I am guessing she is in her late twenties. Braless in a black thermal shirt. Chain smoking. I tried to talk to her but either her English is nearly as bad as my Danish or she just couldn't be bothered. She plays the guitar as if she hates it;

her hands seem repulsed by the feel of the frets and either skitter over them or wring the neck. I spent two entire songs just watching her hands last night. She wears the guitar up high so everyone probably thought I was staring at her breasts.

Most Europeans have been courteous about my butchery or complete ignorance of their languages. I try to learn at least a couple of phrases in each one but am visiting so many countries it'd be impossible to have a real grasp on all the languages. Most people speak English and understand what ignorant schmucks us Americans are. Last night, though, this fat Austrian guy in a hideous sweater was giving me an Oktoberfest of grief. At first I thought he was joking and so I smiled at him and my smile infuriated him which made me want to smile more. His blobby face got all red and these flecks of angry spittle started flying out and it was so fucking ridiculous I started laughing. Chubs Von Jumper then shoved me and I was about to fucking level him.
 "Come on, motherfucker, I'll make you eat that sweater!" But then people were grabbing us and separating us and the moment passed.

Everyone who talks to me asks about Jackie Bonner. They don't ask about the book I am here to promote, they want to know about Jackie. Strangers who don't know either of us tell me they think she's a stupid bitch for not wanting to be my girlfriend or they tell me I'm a sorry asshole for being into someone who is not into me. They ask who we shot in Mexico or if I ever was involved in a three way with Jackie and one of her boyfriends. I am tempted to sometimes incorporate some of the emails and texts I get into this blog, weave them into the story. I have written the real Jackie Bonner about the things people say to me but she never responds. I hadn't seen her much in the months preceding coming to Europe. I have gotten to the point where I can hang out with her and whomever she is dating but her latest boyfriend doesn't like me and the feeling is mutual. He seems like a blowhard but he treats Jackie well and I guess that's what really matters. The four of us (including Allison) went out for drinks last Fall when Jackie started seeing this guy. That meeting was a minor disaster because both A and Jackie's boyfriend were acting jealous and then they started sniping at each other because the boyfriend was a blowhard and Allison gets combative with people like that in her own highly intelligent, subtle fashion. I hadn't seen Jackie in a couple of months and wanted to hang out with her but we had to end things early. A was angry at me because she didn't think I had stood up for her which is funny because she is such a strong, independent person and always pointing that out.

I went back to my room alone and Jackie texted me a little after midnight. Stupidly there was a period of wondering if she and the blowhard had fucked that night but that thought was forced out of my mind as I have forced similar thoughts out of my mind countless times over the years. Jackie and I agreed that we'd have to hang out---just the two of us---in the near future. When the conversation was over I went over to what A calls my "shrine." In the middle of it are pictures of my grandparents and other people I love that have passed. Surrounding the pictures are a few of their belongings and on the outer ring are things belonging to loved ones that I feel could use guardian angels. There is a lighter there, a green disposable one, which is the one thing I have ever lied to Allison about when I told her it belongs to friend in Sacramento who committed suicide. No, it was Jackie's; I pocketed it the fifth night we spent in a bar together. My perception was that we had agreed it was just going to be "Ike and Jackie" hanging out but sure enough she started flirting with guys at the bar. When she went out for a cigarette I just exploded and started pouring my guts out and she just watched me while smoking her cigarette with an unreadable expression. She snubbed her cigarette and what she said to me perfectly sums up our relationship.

"If you ever tell me you love me again, I will stop speaking to you."

November 29, 2015

It was a tough decision renting a room but I came to the realization that I didn't want to spend another winter in the van. Honestly, the decision was kind of made for me. A friend of a friend is having money problems and decided to rent their master bedroom out. It has a separate entrance, a tub with jets, and the owner doesn't mind if I do some cooking in there; it's technically a room but with some of the perks of an apartment. It's in a great part of town for $400 per month; not Downtown which is where I saw myself living but good for going on walks and safe even in the middle of the night.

The book has been out for two months now. As all of us predicted it is doing a lot better in Europe than here in the States. By doing a lot better I mean it is selling by the hundreds instead of the tens. Sales should pick up since I have been doing interviews on skype and over the phone and on email. I have already written about how it was always my plan to tour behind the book but there just isn't the money for gas let alone motels. This is a tough time of the year, both for selling a book and getting temp work. The last gig I had was on November 17th down in Burlingame: Four days. Data entry. Allison had mentioned several times in the past that she wanted to go with me, that my overnights in the van sounded like an adventure---I believe she has been cured of that misconception. She's not a girly girl but one night of having to use Target bathrooms and sleeping on a strange street did it for her---using the bucket in the middle of the night sealed the deal. If you read this blog you know all about "the bucket." Poor girl; I make fun of her about it but I felt bad for her. Her misery actually woke me up.

"You okay?" I asked.

"I have to go."

"Do you want me to drive us to a restaurant? I know you don't like the bathrooms in Target."

"Then I will have to get dressed," Allison sighed.

"There is another option—"

"I don't want to pee in front of you."

So I put on my overcoat and stood outside the van while she handled her business. A was embarrassed about it for days. The next time I told her she was beautiful she turned up her nose.

"How can you find me beautiful? I peed in a bucket."

April 22, 2016

Unseasonal snow and *moving truck* are two phrases I would prefer not sharing the same sentence---I experienced both today. I am saving the money I would have spent on gas for the drive away car by helping a "fan" move from Portland ME to Austin TX. In exchange they are buying my meals, hotel rooms, and an Amtrak ticket home. It's about 2000 miles so we were planning on five days but now with this snow it could be a week. Hopefully the weather will be clear when we go over the Appalachians.

The good news is that my new friend and his wife are minimalists and everything fits in a sixteen foot truck and their Honda CRV. It started snowing a few hours into the trip. It was just a light snow but enough to make me nervous: Being from California; I can count the number of times I have driven in snow on one hand. What can you do? I just slowed down and took it really easy on the off ramps and curves.

Lindsey and Pete do something with advertising design. If you have been reading this blog you know that I rarely have a clue what the people in my life do for a living. They are friends with a couple of people who work for my publisher and that's how we got introduced. Pete was leant my book by a buddy; he enjoyed it and passed it on to Lindsey who enjoyed it somewhat less but still liked it. Their friends in publishing thought it would be a good idea for all of us to get together before I left for Europe. So, there I was...having dinner with two couples in a romantic restaurant.
"We could have introduced you to someone Ike but we thought you had a girlfriend," Lindsey apologized.
"I do, kind of, but we see other people."
"We come here all the time; it's a really romantic place."

"I can tell," I replied. "That was *my* leg, by the way, Pete."
They found out I am in the habit of helping people drive
moving trucks so they asked if I'd be up for an adventure
when I was back in the States. Silly question.

That brings us to the present. I am sitting in a bar in Eastern
Pennsylvania nursing a Dewers and listening to people talk
as I write this. Chuggers--the name of the bar is Chuggers.
The waitress is around ten years younger than me. I could
have sworn she was flirting with me but it was probably
wishful thinking.
Yeah, it *was* wishful thinking; I just tried to flirt with her
and she nimbly ducked my advances.
Pity. She reminds me of Jackie Bonner, like a slightly older
cousin or something. Same figure, same hair, similar
smile.
"Your accent—where are you from?" The waitress asks.
"California."
She asks me what I do and I tell her. I have come up with a
pretty good way of saying I'm a writer without it sounding
like I am full of myself.
"Do you make a living off it?" The waitress looked
doubtful as she inquired.
"Not yet, but I got to see Europe so I'm happy."
She asks some questions about Europe and then I redirect
the questions to her life. A couple of guys come in and she
goes to serve them and I assume that is the end of our chat.
"Another Dewers?" The waitress asks as I put my notebook
back in my bag.
"I'm good, thanks though."
"Hey, I get off at eleven if you'd like to get something to
eat."
"Now that you mention it I am kind of hungry."
I am playing it cool but I am completely taken aback.
Didn't see that coming at all.

April 23, 2016

"You are going to be okay to drive right, Ike?" Lindsey asked.

"Yeah, I slept three or four hours. Three."

Mary had just driven off and Lindsey and Pete and I were talking in the parking lot. They were very nice to her, even offered to buy her breakfast, but they were worried she had kept me up all night. M had offered to leave my room a couple of times but we both enjoyed the company. I haven't shared a bed with anyone since Budapest; there is something comforting about it. Something warm and not just body heat.

"Are you going to be picking up bartenders in every town?" Lindsey was smiling playfully.

"The odds are against it."

I doubt I have a seduction in me today: I am thinking about Jason as I drive down the freeway. Today marks ten years since he committed suicide. I still remember that phone call so clearly, my friend Amy breaking down in tears after telling me Jason was gone. We all met at Amy's house and just hung out and drank beer. I was one of the few people who didn't cry, I think I was in shock. After my wife and I got home I finally broke down and it would be months before I could think about Jason without crying.

We are now in the mountains but fortunately it has stopped snowing. Another Super 8, another busy polyester bedspread. I forced myself to eat a salad for most of my dinner but it was iceberg lettuce so I guess it was a wasted effort. I almost called Mary by Jackie Bonner's real name last night. Like I said, they share a lot of physical characteristics. They even have a similar facial expression after kissing them. Of all the moments I enjoy that is near the top of the list, just looking at someone's face after kissing them. That warmth.

Got bored and walked maybe two hundred feet down the road to a bar. In honor of Jason I ordered a double Jameson. *Are you going to be picking up bartenders in every town?* Seeing as this one is a guy in his sixties with an eye patch the odds are low.

Fuck me in my socket, sonny!

Everyone else is a local. They keep feeding the jukebox and I've been hearing a lot of .38 Special and Merle Haggard. They keep looking over at me--men and women-- but those looks seem more curious than threatening. I am guessing not a lot of strangers drop in to Mikes' Anvil. I started playing with my phone and ended up writing a text to Jackie Bonner.

Last night I did something that would probably surprise you; I picked up someone in a bar. Mary looks like you, even smiles the same, which is probably why I invited her back to my hotel room. You know I love you, we had a long conversation about this three years ago and since then I made a point to tell you I am over wanting to share my life with you as a couple. You know, the times I say that are the only times I lie to you. The truth is, I am still in love with you. I have never gotten over you and I doubt I ever will.

I stare at the message for nearly a minute, push the "erase" button, and take another sip of my drink.

May 2, 2016

I may have to call into the temp agencies tomorrow; I really don't want to but I am nearly out of money.

The train got into town last night and Allison picked me up at the station. Her car isn't running so she was driving the van and nearly rear ended a Lexus. I was too tired to be more than mildly upset.

Neither of us have the money to get Allison's car fixed so I will be taking her to and from work when I can. Our lives are further intertwined due to the fact she is at odds with at least one of her roommates and is consequently staying with me. Seeing as she has been living here the entire time I was gone maybe it is more accurate to say I am staying with *her*. With Allison's stuff here this room feels really small; I may need to go out in the van for a few days. Just got back after being on the road for two months and I am ready to go back out.

I dreamed about Mexico last night, the two of us speeding down a bad road in my van as the sun rose. How far to the border? Everything happened so fast I am not really sure what really happened and what is pure imagination. I think I was scared enough that I simply blocked most of it out.

This morning has been tense. Allison follows this blog so she knows about Mary and muttered something about "going out and finding a bartender of her own." In the next breath she pointed out about how she had told me that she loves me and wants us to be a real couple while I was on the road. I have no idea how to respond to that. The key phrase is "on the road." Now that I am back she will probably start feeling "confined" and back off like she always does—as one of us always does.

Allison's car is parked in the driveway. Matt is not pleased with this just as he was not entirely pleased with my subletting the room. We have a conversation I really don't want to have in the driveway. He is wearing some really ugly sandals and I just want to run away from him. I guess I said the right things to placate him because he finally walked back inside.

Earlier I asked A what the car did when she tried to start it. It sounds like a fuel issue, hopefully something cheap like a filter. Turning the key I realized the battery was dead and I felt my insides clenching from the stress: I need to get her car running, I need to resolve this problem so she can be independent and consequently I can be independent. I went back to the room and Allison was sprawled on the bed reading. She brought one of Matt's dressers in to store her clothes since my dresser is full. Something about the dresser bothers me just as something about his sandals bothers me. I hate the dresser; it's like a pressboard tourist, an invader--a violation to my personal space. But, A needs it and she is not happy with her roommates; how can I say I care for her if I won't offer her a place to crash? I need to get her car running. I need to sort that mess out somehow. I felt a headache coming on. I rarely get headaches.

I have roadside assistance through my insurance company so I called the 800 number and spent ten minutes trapped in a conversation that made me certain I was losing my mind. Then it was time to cool my heels on the sidewalk and feel Matt's eyes on me as he watched from the living room. The guy with the tow truck tried to jump the car but the motor wouldn't turn over and made a horrible clacking sound I know too well: Starter. Matt had come out in his unspeakable sandals. At first he looked hopeful but then he heard the same sound I did and I saw his face fall. Allison was out there, too, all three of us bonded in misery. I know Matt wanted me to tell the tow driver to tow the car somewhere, *anywhere,* but where? To where A normally lives and can't stand anymore? To a garage where neither of us can afford to get it fixed? Allison is smart, she knows Matt hates having her crappy old Mazda in his driveway and I could see she was hoping I would stand up to Matt or at least talk to him man and man about letting us keep the Mazda in the driveway a little while longer. The tow truck driver was watching us expectantly, picking up on the tension; I could see that he was getting a little uncomfortable; at least in a few minutes *he'd* be driving away.

"One second, okay—Jim, was it?" I asked

"Jason."

"Right-- just a moment, Jason. Matt, can I talk to you for a second?"

And I led him back into the house and when I stopped walking he just stared at me earnestly. He is such an earnest guy, a good guy, but very earnest. I'm looking in his face and down at those sandals and I just want to run: Run to Europe, run back to that town in Eastern Pennsylvania, run back to a time before I agreed to rent that room. Somehow I force myself to have a conversation, force myself to smile and open my mouth and ask my landlord to give us two weeks. Two weeks and the Mazda is gone. Matt does not like that but like me he is non-confrontational and nodded his agreement. I could tell he was unhappy even as he patted me on the shoulder before walking off. I watched him walk off in those sandals and I was thankful the conversation was over but I still felt like shit. He deserves better than this, deserves better than being dragged into my crazy life.

May 9, 2016

"So, you still are in love with (Jackie Bonner's real name)?" Allison asks.
"What makes you say that?"
"Your blog; the night you were in the mountains in that bar."
I am driving her to work; the Mazda will be in the shop another couple of days.
"You know a lot of what I write is fiction, right?"
"You can see why I wonder about *that*."
"Yeah."
"Are you really over her?"
"I have been for three years."
"How did it happen?"
"What?"
I knew what she was asking; I just didn't feel like having the conversation when we were only a few blocks from where she works.
"How did you get over her?"
"Someone told me I was acting pathetic."
"And that was it? Someone told you that you were acting pathetic and you instantly got over her?"
"No. You know that *pathetic* is one of my red flag words; it made me really examine what I was doing to myself and how stupid I was being."
"How long did it take after someone called you pathetic?"
"Months. I had to date someone myself—"
"And write *Jackie Bonner*."
"Yes."
We're in the parking lot—*thank God*.
"We should move in together," she says.
You're bringing this up as I pull into your work?
"Where did that come from?"

"I'm just being practical, Ike. I hate my place and Matt is done with you."

"I'm done with his sandals."

"What?"

"Never mind."

"We could get a two bedroom so you could have your *brooding artiste room*; maybe a duplex since both of us like having a yard."

"Can we talk about this tonight?"

"Yes. But I'm taking us out to dinner."

"Are you going to have the money?"

"I am going to pay you back for my car, Ike, don't worry. You know, when you sell some big TV series I am going to write a book about you and there's going to be a whole chapter about you and money."

"Oh, I know there will be, my love."

The van is running good; for being well over twenty years old it's a great van—

I could probably drive anywhere: Alaska, back East, down into Mexico. It's nearly summer, I could live in it again; maybe boondock in a national forest...

I pull out of the parking lot and just start driving down a street. I am so lost in thought I have no idea what street I am on.

We should move in together.

And I am thinking about how messy Allison can be and how I love being around her and how she lets pots sit in the sink overnight sometimes and how much I care about her and want to share my life with her.

And I think about Matt's sandals.

And I think about again being in a situation where someone always wants to know where I am going and what I have been doing. I have been free of that for three years now. Am I ready to be in that situation again? I have to be certain, you know? The funny thing is I am not worried about committing to A; I am more concerned about committing to this town. Of course, when I am making more money I could support both of us and we could live anywhere--a city here in America or Europe or New Zealand. Anywhere.

I go back to the room and work on the script I was sent last week. It's a really bad script; the structure and plot are good, but a lot of the dialogue and scenes are hackneyed. Maggie--playing the role of concerned manager--texts me seemingly every couple of hours to check on my progress. "I'm liberally applying gold spray paint to a turd, mon amie," I write.
"Don't be like that, Ike; without this job you'd be doing temp work again."
"I know, Maggie. You know I am grateful for this job, it's just a bear, you know?"
"You can wrestle a bear, Ike; I have faith in you."
The pep talk has weariness around the edges so I wisely stop my complaining.
"Have you heard about whether or not they like the latest sections of *Purgatory*?"
"Yeah," Maggie brightens a bit and her tone of voice relieves me. "It is looking possible to release it at the end of next year."
"Maybe even on my fiftieth birthday."
"Maybe."
"OK, I'm going to work on this script some more."
But I didn't work on the script anymore today, I had too much on my mind and Matt was home for some reason and listening to Hootie and the Blowfish—
Who the fuck still listens to Hootie and the Blowfish in 2016?

February 29, 2016

I am standing out in the middle of the desert having mad thoughts. Part of me wants to set the car ablaze, stomp my phone and netbook into uselessness, and just see what happens. How far back is Interstate 10? Twenty miles? I just turned off on some nowhere exit and bounced down this road for half an hour. I didn't even bother pulling onto the shoulder; I just skidded to a stop in the middle of the road and got out. A dinging is coming from the open door, an insistent maddening rhythm; it is maybe an hour from sundown. Half of me is almost ready to allow the moment to die, to cautiously turn around and head back to the interstate and follow the planned course of the next seven days which will conclude with me boarding a freighter in New York City.

Half of me wants to figure out how to set this drive-away SUV ablaze and just head out into the open desert.

I have no idea why this has come over me.

This should be the best time in my life, right? I published a book six months ago—something I had been working at for over 25 years—and now I am heading to Europe to promote it and play music in nightclubs. I am on my way after years and years of working jobs I couldn't stand and the past few years of hardship.

But here I am in the desert, ready to follow a course of action that would be suicide.

"I think I had a sort of nervous breakdown."

I explain to A about driving out into the middle of nowhere and contemplating blowing the car up.

"Well, you always have hated SUVs."

She is joking but I can hear the worry on the edge of her voice and it is absurdly touching to me.

"You know what's weird? I almost think the relief caused me to snap."

"Maybe you felt confused because you have utterly no reason to be miserable."

"You may have a point there; you know what a miserable bastard I am."

"I moved one of Matt's extra dressers into your room; there was no space in your grandfather's dresser for my stuff."

Although I don't like the idea of filling up my room anymore than it is, I know Allison needs a place to put her stuff. She has stayed with me there in the past for a few days; both of us know it is a trial run at living together some day but neither of us are ready to acknowledge that yet.

"I can tell he doesn't want me here and yet he has been checking me out."

Does she want me to act protective? Maybe jealous? Sometimes she likes that sort of thing--(*you're* **my** *woman*)--but sometimes that sort of thing alienates her; I never can tell with her. Maybe I need more time; maybe I am still too selfish to pay attention to what she needs.

"He's a man; even when a man doesn't want you around, he does."

"Is that how it is with you?"

Run away! Danger! It's a trap!

I am scrambling for a safe answer, a few moments later I hear her laugh.

"He was listening to Hootie and the Blowfish—who listens to Hootie and the Blowfish in 2016?"

Hearing her laugh, this beautiful yet terrifying love washes through me.

Is there anything more frightening than falling deeply in love with someone?

We say goodbye a few minutes later, I can see the possibility of us never saying goodbye until I die. It's an

313

incredible thought; it makes me feel alive and yet small and scared at the enormity of it.

I make it to Blythe which is still the same burned out, desperate town it was when I visited there twenty years ago. Finding the Super 8 I check in and go up to my room to take pictures as I do with every hotel food. The bedspread is heavy, a rococo explosion of textures and colors. I pull back the blankets and check the sheets. In my bag I can hear my netbook beeping. It's a reassuring sound, a familiar heartbeat in another lonely hotel room. I go to the window and pull back the mustard colored drapes. There is nothing within walking distance aside from fast food and I am trying to avoid that when I stop for the night. Trying. I bring up *Purgatory* with the idea of getting some work done before dinner but I am too preoccupied. Something was up with Allison. Was it just the way she said "I love you" when we ended our call? We always say "I love you" but it is usually more matter of fact like some people say "Talk to you soon." This time there was something in her voice, something different. The past three months we haven't seen much of each other; she has been spending more time with her girlfriend and the two of them have seemed pretty serious. Their being together is more logical, I guess; both of them are around 30 and have a lot in common. A and I both like the same films and books and we both have a black sense of humor, but I am 17 years older than her. She graduated from high school after 9-11 and has never operated a VHS player—the world she grew up in was completely different than the world I experienced as a kid. We both care about each other, love each other even, certainly enjoy spending time together, but sometimes the age difference is very apparent. My theory is that a big reason we work well together is because both of us need a lot of space. Her girlfriend is kind of clingy and is clearly looking for a serious commitment; that could be their undoing. I feel bad for them but still savor every bit of bad news about their relationship.

The guy behind the front desk is so squeaky clean looking he has to either be a Mormon or a serial killer: Ruler straight part. Wrinkle free white shirt. Big smile. Somewhere around 25--as inoffensive looking as a human being can be. I bug him for a restaurant recommendation and he happily tells me about a cheap Mexican place down the road. The place he sent me to wasn't that busy and I got a good table near the window. I felt nervous about the safety of the drive away car and I almost laughed at the irony of that. I struggled with the menu, wondering if I should get a beer. How could I have Mexican food without a beer? My general rule is I do not drink wherever I live or where I am staying--that is how I keep my drinking in check. I also have kept my tendency to make excuses in check--keep my weakness on a leash because it likes to run. In the end I order a Negro Modella with my chicken enchiladas. Nearby, an attractive woman somewhere around forty is eating what I am guessing is a taco salad and reading a book. She has dark hair and is wearing a sleeveless white peasant blouse. I don't see a jacket on her chair and absurdly wonder if she'll be cold when she leaves the restaurant.

At this moment, everything becomes weird.

You see; the book she is reading is *mine*.

How random is that?

If you have been following this blog, you know how I am about women. One of my female friends has called me a "likeable letch" and I don't think she meant it as a compliment.

And here is this attractive woman reading my book.

What would happen if I "smoothly" walked over and introduced myself? My picture is not on the jacket but obviously I know the book well enough it would be clear I wrote it.

Are you really going to go there? Hi, I wrote that book you're reading—wanna come back to my hotel room?
Why not? What if I introduced myself and wasn't a dick about it? What if I introduced myself and didn't overtly come onto her? What would happen? I have always been so fucking introverted and awkward with people---when am I going to change that?

With each sip of my beer I was feeling more brazen.

Life is short. Maybe I wasn't having a breakdown, maybe God was reminding me how precious life is or something. Maybe God was showing me that I need to celebrate being alive and not be such a chicken shit.

I took another drink of my beer. I was going to do it; I was going to walk over to that woman reading my book and introduce myself—

And then I started thinking about the way A said "I love you" at the end of our phone conversation.

And there I was two hours later about to try and pick someone up?

I took another drink of my beer knowing I would stay in that chair, focus on my meal, and then go back to my motel room alone.

God really has a sick sense of humor sometimes...

December 31, 2014/January 1, 2015

(Blog started around 3:45 New Years morning)
Another New Year's another night crashing outside a dying party in the van. It is almost four. I'm not really drunk, not even intoxicated, but I don't want to risk the roads right now.

The party was fun, a few people I knew and a few I didn't in this great house in an older part of town. I nursed four beers and alternated between socializing and going off by myself. The host got too drunk to run her iPod so I took over as DJ around eleven o' clock. If you follow this blog you know it has been two months since Emily and I broke up. Part of the reason for going to the party was out of the hope I would meet someone, even for a short term thing. By eleven I had given up and decided to just have fun and playing DJ struck my fancy.
"Is this music from your day? Did you have the first copy on wax cylinder?"
Those words came out of a young woman in her late twenties, thirty at the very oldest. A little Hispanic a little Asian looking with brown hair and maybe two or three inches shorter than myself. Was she beautiful? Was she ugly? Somewhere in between? You know, the first thing I noticed was her smile; it was a sarcastic twist to her mouth.
"This is where you subtly check out my boobs," she added.
Who the hell are you?
"Maybe I already did. Maybe I was so subtle you didn't notice—"
"You're fumbling."
"What?"
"Your attempt at witty banter was derailed by you verbally fumbling. I see you're drinking beer, I thought someone your age would be drinking prune juice."

"Not until after my nurse gives me my enema."

"Much better," she nodded, toasting me with her glass. Her name is Alison and I almost asked if she was named after the Elvis Costello song but feared one of her fearsome comebacks. She kept me company and actually complimented some of my song choices. A had come with a girlfriend but they had a fight and the girlfriend had driven home. That made me relax somewhat because there was no point trying to try and "win her over," right? She was clearly gay or at least that's what I was thinking as midnight approached. We talked about her office job and how great her roommates are and I did everything to avoid telling her I pretty much live in a '91 Dodge van. Even though she was into girls I was hoping we could be friends and potential friends have become awkward around me when they find out I am technically homeless.

"You're a drifter," she shrugged when I told her. "Cool. Grow out the skullet and get some stone washed jeans."

"Those are two of my New Year's resolutions."

"Well, now it's 2015 so I'm counting on you to make it happen."

We talked for maybe half an hour more and then she went off to check out the rest of the party. I went looking for her half an hour after that, couldn't find her, and assumed she had made her way home. Oh well, maybe someone would know who she was and I could message her on Facebook or something. No, a few people knew her girlfriend, but no one seemed to know Alison.

(Seven hours later; a few minutes before 10 in the morning) I am writing this at a Denny's as I eat the requisite greasy New Years hangover food. Right in the middle of typing up my New Year's blog there was a knock on the door of the van. It was Alison and she was brandishing a bottle of cheap vodka that was two-thirds full. I let her in. The bed

318

was already folded out so I suggested we sit in the front seats. She saw "the bucket" and smiled that amazing, sardonic smile of hers.

"Do you keep human heads in that bucket?"

"Yes, and I'm glad you showed up because it's currently empty."

A climbed into the passenger seat.

"Seat covers," she intoned.

"Pardon?"

"If you and I are ever going to go on a road trip I require seat covers, at least one on my seat."

"Right."

She took a long swallow of vodka and handed it over. I took a long drink and handed it back. It was a beautiful night, cold but surprisingly clear. We talked and I found out that she had just been walking around with no destination in mind and ended up back at the party. It was, of course, pretty much dead by that point. Seeing the light on in my van she had been hoping I'd be up for a conversation.

"Here's the deal, in exchange for sharing this nasty vodka I am going to crash in your bed. But if you try anything I'll file one of those Meagan's Law things or however they punish lecherous old men."

I chuckled and shrugged but inside I was going in a thousand different directions.

Who the hell are you?

June 2, 2016

"I know you're scared, but it will be okay."
Allison is holding my hand as we stand on the sidewalk.
"It's a big step."
"I know, but you'll survive it, you'll be okay."
I look in the display window of the second hand furniture store.
"A couch."
My voice is so soft I am not sure she can hear me.
"Yes, a couch; so we can have people over, so we are not hermits like, you know, weird old men who live in vans."
"You're living with a weird, old man who lives in a van."
"No, I am living with a weird old man who lives in a house—who has agreed we can have a couch."
A couch: You know, couches are nice. They are comfortable, but then you need a coffee table to put in front of the couch. And wait—the living room is so nicely furnished we need to get a dining table, too! And so it goes; the next thing you know there is so much shit in your house you can't breathe.

If you're been following this blog you know that A and I moved into a small house two days ago. It's a few blocks from a pretty bad neighborhood but the price was right and it has a lot of charm. We have a decent sized bedroom and a smaller bedroom that I will use as my office.
I will admit I am still concerned. I have admitted this to A:
I am concerned.
We had to sign a six-month lease. The landlord wanted a year but for a higher deposit he accepted six months. Six months—what if in that time Allison loses her job? What if I don't get any writing work? I am supposed to get my advance for *Purgatory* in September but a lot can happen in three months. This little house is $900 per month, nothing

for a house, but it is still a lot of money to come up with every month. I used up the entire advance from the first book on the trip to Europe. Sales have been picking up and I could cover the rent on my own, but what about everything else? Allison hates her job and I worry about her getting fired. I don't know; most of us have money worries, don't we? I am okay writing about this stuff because I know you can relate. The advance could be in September or even later. Right now Maggie and my lit agent and the publisher are in negotiations. M and my agent want to double my first advance but the publisher is arguing that sales have not been strong enough to justify it. Maggie and I are also hoping one of my development deals comes to something. The small advance I got from those also went into the trip to Europe (and paying rent on the room I rented from Matt). Money--it's always a *thing*, isn't it?

Allison has a bed but it is only full sized and I am pretty sure the next thing we buy will be a queen sized bed or maybe a king. More stuff: A bed, a couch, the dining table, a big TV—these kinds of things take on a life of their own. Next thing you know you have forty cats and your house is full of old magazines and newspapers. At least I have my room; at least I can keep *that* clean; no couch, no bed, nothing but my little table and my bookcase. I moved some of my stuff from my dresser into my closet. My dresser—I guess it's *our* dresser now. I am sharing a dresser for the first time in five years. It's a huge step. How can such a simple thing feel so enormous?

I know it isn't easy for Allison. She never says anything but she has been smoking more. Usually it's just the occasional cigarette here and there but she is now going through a couple of packs a week. Sometimes she leaves on long walks or drives off somewhere without a word. We're both loners; everyone craves not to be alone, but for some of us loneliness is less painful than dealing with other people.

"What do you think about this one?" She asks.

"I like it."

"Are you saying 'I like it' like a man who is just trying to get something over with?"

"No, I like orange couches."

I tell her the story about how my ex and I coveted this orange IKEA loveseat.

"You guys browsed IKEA? Wow, you really *were* married."

And it hits me and I feel a whole lot of stupid emotions coming to the surface. Yes, I was married and when it ended it was the best thing for both of us but it still hurt. We shared a life together for seven years and it fell apart and it will always be this huge, sad mess. That's the fucked up thing about loving people, you are bound to lose them at some point and then there's just this hole.

"Are you about to cry, Ike?"

She squeezes my hand and I squeeze back though part of me just wants to run out of the store, get in my van, and just go *anywhere*....just get the fuck out before my heart is too wrapped up in this—whatever *this* is.

"Maybe I just really like orange couches."

March 20, 2016

Whoever booked this gig should be shot. No--they should be given ten thousand paper cuts and then dropped in a swimming pool full of rubbing alcohol. What a toilet. Literally--and the rest of the pub is equally nasty. The walls are covered with old sports posters and it reeks of stale beer, dead cigarettes, and body odor. When you think of London you may think of the Big Ben and Westminster Abbey and the Queen waving--all that fun tourist stuff. You don't think of the nastier, dangerous parts of the city because the English are smart enough not to include those in the travel brochures. This part of town looks as bad as West Oakland. Not as bad as Stockton---nothing is as sketchy as Stockton---but definitely as rough as Oakland. I even saw a couple of burned out cars.

"Can you play a bit of guitar during their set?"

Liam has appeared at my side reeking of cigarettes and bored alcohol fleeing his pores. He is the manager of the Italian boy band I am opening for; a Brit managing a has-been Italian boy band---so much for the European Union. Liam looks like Benny Hill after a three year coke bender.

"I don't know any of their songs," I reply.

He looks over at the stage and makes a face.

"I thought it might toughen up their sound a bit."

"Nothing is going to help them with this crowd."

The truth is I don't want to go back out there; I barely got through my set. During the softer parts the regulars snarled some choice remarks in my general direction--they hated me. At one table--a *small* table--is what appears to be boys' entire London fan base. They are the only women in this nasty pub and they look as nervous as I feel. I go to the bar for my second drink and order a pint of stout.

"Where ya from?" The bartender asks.

"California, western United States—"

"I know where California is."

The bartender actually snarls at me, his teeth as yellow as malaria.

"Whatcha doin' with these dago fags?"

"I thought fags were cigarettes here," I reply without thinking.

"Are you fucking with me?"

"Oi, this weedy little fuck bothering you, Jimmy?"

A landmass wearing a dirty looking cap has invaded my space.

"Nah."

The bartender laughs but shoots me a deadly look. Chewing tobacco; he has to chew tobacco to get that deep a brown color between his teeth. I grab my pint and head over to where the guys are testing their mics. I just met them this morning but they seem to be a bunch of pricks except the oldest one who I want to call Malo for some reason.

"I have no idea why Liam has booked us here; they don't even have tequila," he says with a frown.

"Maybe for the charming atmosphere."

Malo looks confused and I am not sure if it is due to a lack of English or if my sarcasm has thrown him.

I really don't want to see how this crowd reacts to a "bunch of dago fags" but I also don't want to be wandering around this part of town by myself. This gig is making me think this European trip is jinxed. The bad luck started when I got to Bremerhaven Germany two days ago. The twelve days on the freighter were great, I got a lot of writing done— (and I know I wrote about this already but some of you tend to skip around)--met a couple of cool people; it was a good experience.

But then I got to Bremerhaven and things went south.

No one was there to greet me at the dock. I know I sound like a pussy whining about that but I really felt alone and vulnerable. It was the first time I had ever been to a foreign country (I don't count Canada and Mexico) and I was a little overwhelmed. I rang up Maggie to get the address of the hostel I was staying at. It was mid afternoon so I figured I'd check in, lock my stuff up, and get a meal before turning in. Maggie didn't answer at first—(normally she is completely reliable)—so I wandered around the city for a couple of hours. When M finally called she was extremely apologetic and gave me the address of the hostel. By then I had about an hour of daylight left. I manned up and lugged my bag and my guitar maybe half a mile to the hostel but they had screwed up the reservation and no space was available.

I had to calm myself down before calling Maggie back. I was already in a bad mood and I knew it wasn't her fault; the hostel had screwed up. When I called her she was apologetic and said she'd see what she could come up with. I went into a bar and got a large beer and a small snack. Nobody spoke English so I had to point at the menu and felt like an ignorant schmuck. In German I can say please and thank you and that's it.
"Ike, great news."
"I could use some."
"The German offices of the distributor know of the hostel you were supposed to be at, suspected there would be a problem, and made other arrangements for you."
"Excellent—"
"It's just crashing on a couch in a small apartment—"
"I have no problem with that, I'm tired, I'd be grateful for a couch at this point."
"I thought you'd be. Her name is Bettina, I will tell her where you are and she'll pick you up."

Half an hour later, this gorgeous woman somewhere in her early twenties walks into the bar. Everyone stares at her, men, women, a dog near the bar—*everyone.*

"Please let this be Bettina," I mutter.

She walks right up to me and smiles this beguiling smile. Now every living thing in the bar is watching me with jealousy including the dog. I am imagining B wandering around her apartment in a towel or less; you know how Europeans are about nudity.

"Ike, right?"

"Yes, nice to meet you. I apologize for not speaking German."

"It is not a problem; I am pretty good at speaking English."

She takes my shoulder bag instead of my guitar.

"I know how musicians are about their instruments."

Beautiful and thoughtful, too, I believe this trip has been salvaged.

Bettina led me out to a ten year old VW Polo and we put my stuff in the back. On the drive to her flat she started talking about her life and how she had been a bit lonely since breaking up with her boyfriend the previous week.

Dear Penthouse Forum...

She lit what I thought was a joint in her car. Automatically I glanced around for cops but I had no doubt Bettina could talk her way out of a ticket. B handed the joint over and I thought "why not." It didn't taste like pot. No, it tasted like pot but it also tasted like something else was blended into it.

"This is more than marijuana, isn't it?"

"Ah, yes. I am trying to think of what you call it in English..."

She brightened and smacked the dash really hard.

"Angel dust!"

"I just smoked...angel dust."

"Don't worry, it's pretty mild."

By the time we got to her apartment I was pretty high. I'm not sure if it was all in my head, but I was feeling confused and seeing static on the edge of my field of vision. I made it up the stairs to Bettina's apartment and resigned myself not to wild sex with a beautiful German but lying on a couch and trying not to lose my mind. It wasn't a bad high, kind of euphoric really, but I was still terrified because of everything I have heard about PCP over the years. I lay on the couch and Bettina was pacing the entire apartment and talking about a mile a minute about a thousand different things. She had a cat and I swear that cat talked to me at some point. Finally, I passed out or fell asleep or a combination of the two.

I woke up to Bettina shaking me. She looked terrified and a familiar white powder rimmed both nostrils. B was just wearing a thin t-shirt but I didn't notice her nipples through the fabric as much as I noticed the huge gun in her right hand—
Dear Interpol.
"Sorry to wake you, Ike, but you need to wake up. You really need to get up."
"What happened?"
She got up and started pacing.
"Bad things. Noises. I think people will come in, I think they will break the door in."
She was swinging the gun around as she said that.
"I have a couple of lines for you; I need you to sniff them so you can wake up."
"Uh, I don't do hard drugs, Bettina."
And then she turned on me and I could see the paranoia radiating off her, it was coming off in waves and making this beautiful sort of haze as it blended with the static I saw.
"Don't you trust me, Ike? I need you to do this, okay?"
And so I snorted two lines of coke. My first day in Europe and I had done PCP and coke. It did wake me up and after I did it Bettina seemed to relax. Kind of. The next few hours she talked and talked about all the people in her life who didn't like her and had fucked her over. B told me about how every man in her life wanted to fuck her and

eavesdroppers and people watching from cars and any sort of paranoid talk you can imagine. She was so clearly out of her mind I had no idea how much of it was real. The sun started coming up. Bettina let me lie down on the couch and I fell asleep a second time.

I woke up a few hours later to my second Bettina shaking. This time she was fully dressed and wearing sunglasses. "We overslept; I need to get you to the station." I threw on my clothes and she raced through the streets to the train station. "I feel like shit," she rasped. "Yeah, we were up pretty late." "It's always hard, entertaining people." *Oh, and that was certainly entertaining, my beautiful, crazy friend.*

"Maggie--I am going to tell you something and you have to promise me you will not tell anyone because I don't want Bettina to get fired." I told her about the night's adventure. "I can't believe how much I screwed up yesterday." "How could you have known? Listen, I survived and it is going to be an amusing blog entry." "No one's going to believe you, Ike." You know, she may be right...

June 30, 2014

"I may have some good news, Ike..."
Good news is good. I really hate my latest temp
assignment. Hate. Don't get me wrong, I am grateful for
the work after two weeks of nothing, but this is the sort of
gig you take out of desperation. This assignment is
supposed to end on the 2nd or the 3rd but now they're
talking about needing me next week. You never know.
Kimberly--(my agent)--sounds upbeat, upbeat is good.
"We think things are a go with—(name of publishing
house, don't want to jinx it by saying their name). They
like a few of the stories a lot."
"A few?"
"Well, we always discussed how a publisher would
probably want to change out a couple."
"Yeah, I'm just glad they're into it."
"They are. What are you up to?"
"Temping down in Fresno."
"That's in the Central Valley, right?"
"Yeah, about 200 miles north of Los Angeles."
"OK. Hey, gotta run but I'll keep you in the loop—good
news, huh?"
"Yeah, thank you, this means a lot to me."
"I know, Ike; that's one reason I've been really working on
this one."

My friend Emily up in Sacramento may be more than my
friend. I don't want to jinx it but I have been thinking about
it a lot. I've known her for about a year, met her through
some music friends, but she was dating someone back then.
When I was up in Sacramento last week we met up for an
inexpensive dinner and things ended up happening. I
wasn't sure whether it was a one-time thing or not but we
have been texting and talking on the phone the past few
days. Maybe something will come of it, maybe not.

I wrote the first part of this during my lunch break. It was hot out but I managed to park the van under a tree and had the side doors open while I ate. I saw a co-worker on her way over to snoop. I was thinking about Emily and had my guard down so by the time Sally or Suzy was waddling over it was too late to close the doors without looking more suspicious. I make a point to keep my "mobile home" a secret from co-workers. If they ask why I have a van I tell them it's because I'm in a band, which is kind of true.

"Didn't feel like having lunch in the break room?" Sally or Suzy asked.

"I like coming outside to get some fresh air."

"But it's hot out here!"

"It's not bad."

And she was trying to subtly check out the inside of the van and I knew she could see the bed and all the other stuff including "the bucket."

"Looks homey in there."

I have no idea if she was being friendly or a snoop who will go back and gossip about the "weird temp who lives in a van." It's a shame but you always have to keep your guard up.

I went into my usual spiel about how I love going camping and started rambling about places I have only seen on a map but know enough about to fake it. Big smile. Enthusiastic tone of voice. *I love camping; just believe that is why I have all this stuff in my van. You feel no need to gossip about me.* I have no idea if my Jedi mind tricks will work. Sally or Suzy seemed to be playing along but you never know.

I got a message from one of you: *Bro, so many people are out of work, you can't really bitch especially when it sounds like you have a publisher.*

I agree. I just have been at this gig three days now— (actually *was* camping in the mountains over the weekend)—and I guess it has been wearing on me. A big part of it is that they are Christians and it is important to them to show any non-Christians "the light" or "the path" or whatever it is. I considered lying and saying I was Unitarian or something, I wear a cross after all, but worried about the consequences of being caught in a lie. These are bold Christians, they didn't beat around the burning bush; they asked me if I belonged to a church. When I said I didn't they seemed concerned and then started working on leading me down the path of salvation or whatever. It's not constant, but it comes up every couple of hours. This is not the only challenging aspect of this job. My supervisor is often out of the office and is really hard to reach. So, I get stuck and when he finally contacts me he gets pissed off I haven't gotten more done. It's frustrating but, like one of you pointed out, I am fortunate to have work. I had a two-week dry spell before this so I definitely understand that.

Cooking some chicken in a park. I scoped this park out on my first day in Fresno; it seemed safe and had grills so I am taking advantage of it. I got ice when I bought the chicken; when it starts getting hot I have to drain the cooler every three days. After a year of living in a van everything becomes second nature. Minding the ice in the cooler, finding safe places to park, and keeping your mouth shut around co-workers or having a believable lie ready.
Found a decent residential area to park in for tonight. On Friday night I drove into the mountains but on Thursday— my first night here—I parked in a Target parking lot. Not too far away I saw an old Dodge RV that someone was clearly living out of. I had the vents open because it was hot and it still took awhile to get to sleep. Around three I heard a commotion; the security guy was rousting whomever was in the Dodge RV. The owner came out and

331

was arguing about how he wasn't hurting anyone. Wrong: Never argue. You always appeal to their better nature and if that fails then you start whining and acting pathetic and throw yourself on their mercy; make them feel powerful, appeal to their better nature or some combination of the two.

Or you just drive off before they call the cops.

Dodge RV drove off, revving his engine and speeding away like a lunatic with a portable toilet. I just sat there wondering if I was going to get rousted. No—the security car drove off and didn't come back.

September 9, 2016

You know those mornings when you wake up and can't remember the night before?

When you wake up and you don't know where the hell you are?

When you're in bed with a couple?

That was this morning. I wanted to make a quick and silent getaway but I was in such a world of misery I also didn't want to move. The woman was between us and embracing the man. Kelly? Carrie? I wanted to say her name was something like that. I hadn't the foggiest what her boyfriend's name was.

Husband. She moved her arm and I saw the ring.

We were all naked and the room was not exactly daisy fresh—what the hell happened?

It took me a month to roll over and the world spun in celebration.

You are almost 49, asshole—what the hell are you doing??

My clothes were a collection of sad rumples on the floor. It was agony to pull on my underwear and pants and I nearly screamed when I felt hands on my back; it was the woman, Kelly Carrie Casey whatever her name is. Looking back I saw she was smiling at me sweetly as she pulled me towards her. She wanted to kiss me and I didn't resist but I was wondering what would happen if her husband woke up.

"Taking off?" She asked.

"Yeah, it was…fun. Great to meet you guys."

She looked at me funny.

"You must be really hung over."

"I am."

Is she pissed? Who is she? Why should I know her name? Damn it brain, I know I drowned you in poison last night but I really need you!

333

"Kimberly. I'm your literary agent."
And then she laughed and I struggled to smile as if I was just joking.
"Shit, I knew that, sweetheart."
"No, you didn't, but I still love you."
And she leaned forward to kiss me again. I saw her husband stirring, muttering, and struggling to get up. The sheet fell back and I saw his nakedness.
*Jesus, I hope I didn't do anything with **that** last night--I'm afraid of snakes.*
Kimberly's husband looked over and smiled hazily, clearly as hung over as I was.
"Hey, guys," he said in a rough morning voice. "Shit, we need greasy breakfast food."
Sitting up, he started rubbing Kimberly's back.
Part of me wanted to run, just find the van and figure out what city I was in and just start driving.
Part of me was thinking "I could really go for some bacon right now."

Kimberly, Alec, and I walked to a hip little restaurant both of them couldn't stop chattering about. Through my drunkenness I realized we were in the Hawthorne District in Portland. None of us were talking about the previous night although Kimberly was walking between us and holding our hands as we stumbled to the restaurant.
"Gin, Ike. Gin is not your friend," she said in a singsong voice. "Look, the warning rhymes, that makes it more logical."
"Yeah, I do not remember last night at all."
Alec giggled a bit. There was a "school-girly" quality to the giggle that made me ill-at-ease.
"You drove up to Portland to see your friend Mark. I emailed you an update about the publication and invited you to dinner when you told me you were coming up."

Dinner, right. Pizza—really good pizza. I remembered the pizza and mentioned it.

"You had a fight with your girlfriend..."

Yes, now it was coming back: Allison said she couldn't share the house with me anymore, I watched her leaving—was there another man involved? A woman? She didn't say. She packed a bag and left in her crappy old Mazda. A couple of days after that I couldn't bear being around that orange couch and the bedroom we had shared and her things and got in the van and drove north to Portland. Mark was in the middle of a project so I called Kimberly. The three us met for some really good pizza and then went to a bar and then—

Who knows.

"You look stressed, Ike."

Kimberly stopped me on the sidewalk. Alec looked back then said he was going on to get a table.

"I am, Kimberly; I hate forgetting things. I have drunk a lot in the past, but I usually retain my memory."

"You drank a lot last night. You had a couple of martinis then started drinking beer."

"Jesus."

Kimberly laughed; she is a beautiful woman maybe seven or eight years younger than I am. Alec is even younger, maybe late thirties.

"It's no big deal, Ike. Really."

And then Kimberly kissed me on the lips but it was not a sexual kiss; it is more reassuring and the amazing thing is that it actually did reassure me.

Everything will be okay—

I think.

September 27, 2015/September 27, 2013

The book was officially released this morning---nothing
has changed. On Monday I start the third week of an
assignment in San Jose. If you have been following this
blog I have mentioned it's a good gig; nice people, work is
up my alley, and they bring us lunch a couple of times a
week. I even have a really good place to park the van
though the situation still makes me leery. A co-worker
spotted me getting something from the back and the side
doors were open allowing her to see inside. She pointed out
all the stuff and tried to come across as joking but I am
naturally suspicious and wary when it comes to co-workers
knowing where and how I live. I went into my spiel about
"loving camping" and Katie listened but I saw in her eyes
that she knew I was bullshiting her. When I wrapped up my
threadbare pitch she casually told me about how one of her
brothers lived out of a van. What can you do in that
situation? Lie and say you'd never live out of a van? Does
that mean you're putting down her brother? So, I admitted
I was. Katie has been letting me stay in front of the house
she shares with her husband and three children. They said I
could use their shower but I demurred, not wanting to be a
burden. They seem fascinated with my lifestyle and I
wonder if the "brother" really exists. I mean, couldn't *he*
have answered all these questions? I keep waiting for
blowback, for Katie to gossip about the "weird temp who
lives in a van" but it hasn't happened yet. *Yet.*

I found some notes I took two years ago (September 27,
'13) that I never put into this blog. I had taken the van in to
get new tires and got to talking with a fellow in the waiting
room. I'm sure you've experienced those waiting rooms:
Strong smell of tires, posters extolling the safety of new
tires and shocks, car magazines. Rims and rubber on
display. The guy I got to talking with was around 35 and

completely ordinary looking; he could have been in one of those posters, the every man: Brown hair, white skin, trimmed goatee, Cincinnati Bengels starter jacket, dad jeans. Name was either Bill or Bob.

"Is that your van out there?" Bill or Bob asked.

"Yes."

"What is it, a 1995?"

"1991."

"V8?"

"Yep, 318."

"Why did they ever stop making the 318? I have a Suburban with one of those newer motors; it was a sad day when they stopped making the 350…"

And we talked for a few minutes about old school engines not all gummed up with computers and other technology and how it's harder and harder to work on cars yourself. It was a good talk—and then he made some comment about how he had been putting off tires because of higher taxes.

"Obummer strikes again!"

He laughed, but it was a bitter laugh and I could feel the conversation going someplace I really didn't want it to go. I really didn't want to get into a heated political debate in that waiting room that smelled strongly of tires and all those posters full of smiles and half-truths.

"Seriously, man is going to ruin this country," Bill or Bob continued.

"It's been going downhill for awhile."

Could we now just change the subject—please?

"Guy needs to be impeached or shot or something."

"Ike! Your van is ready!"

Thank God for timing.

"Well, that's me, nice talking to you!"

I have never been happier to hand over $795 in my life.

Back in 2015. I typed up those notes in the back of the van and was interrupted by a tapping on the side doors. It was

Katie's husband Kent. Katie and Kent. Very nice people. Christian, but they seem to accept I am not one and leave me to it. Kent knocked on the door and invited me to dinner. As I have been turning them down for a few days I thought I should accept. They have two girls and a boy that are between four and nine. Relatively well behaved. We sat at the table and had a nice meal.

"I hope this isn't rude, Ike, but why do you live in a van?" And I explained about my experience with employers and wanting to eliminate stress from my life and so on.

"Please tell me to butt out if I am being too nosey, but what are your long term plans?"

Oh boy: I am not worried about explaining about my goals as a writer, but if I tell them I just published a book they will want to know what it's about.

You see, there's this online group that engineers workplace shootings so they can become famous. Oh, and there's another story about this online group that fetishizes feces. You know, poop.

I could just see Katie and Kent dropping their forks and staring at me as if I'm the Devil.

"I am taking online courses through the University of Phoenix in business administration," I said.

Katie, who had asked the question, just stared at me.

"Why do you feel the need to lie to us, Ike?"

And how did you know it was a lie?

"Because the truth is I just published a book today and seeing as you guys are Christians I didn't know if what I write about would be unsettling. Even if you weren't Christians I'd be leery."

"If it's things you're ashamed of, why do you write them?" Kent asked.

"I'm not ashamed of them, I'm actually proud of them, but I know they are out there. It's what I write, I have no idea why I get these ideas but I see inspiration as a God given gift."

"Then you have nothing to be ashamed of, do you?" Katie smiled.

And we all went back to eating.

Kent walked out with me to the van. He had smuggled out a couple of beers because Katie only wanted him having one a night and he had *that* beer with supper. It reminded me of Teresa always grabbing my tail if I drank too much. She was grabbing my tail a lot, and I regret putting her in the position she felt she had to. Life with an alcoholic; *good times*. My host walked over to the van and poked at the side.

"What happened here? Looks like a bullet hole."

I started to come up with a story of how I had bought the van with the hole in it—

Why do you feel the need to lie to us, Ike?

I ended up telling Kent the real story of the hole in the side of the van. His eyes widened and I was worried he'd drop his beer. That would have been a shame; wasting beer is a sin.

Next Friday A and I are having dinner with Jackie Bonner and her new boyfriend. His name is either Rick or Ryan or maybe Rich.

"Are you sure you're okay with meeting him, Ike?" Allison asked.

"You're going to always give me shit about that, aren't you?"

"Yep. It hasn't even been three years; you're going to be hearing about this for a long time."

Allison knows about my past with Jackie Bonner and always acts a little jealous. I always remind her that all that was a long time ago; I tell her and maybe I also remind myself.

September 20, 2013

I have needed to get tires for maybe a month now. I am thinking when I get my next paycheck I'll get that done. I have a little over $500 saved and need maybe $300 more. I have had the van for barely three months and have put over 6000 miles on it.

If you have been following this blog you know I have had a literary agent for about two months. Tom seems like a nice guy, seems really in my corner, but his partner Kimberly is hard to read. Sometimes I think she doesn't like me. K is based in Portland; maybe next time I am up there visiting Mark I will have to take her out to dinner and make friends or something.

I may have a gig next week up in Rocklin—(a small town maybe 25 miles outside of Sacramento). Indenture-Temps is not entirely clear on what it will entail or how much it pays, all they know is the company makes sofa cushions. So, it could be an office job or a line job; I will just be glad to get some work as it has been three weeks between assignments.

I try not to complain about the van life after all those months of boring you with my efforts to buy a van. Nevertheless, it can be hot in the summer. Last week I escaped the heat by driving up to the coast and camping not far from Gualala where Jackie Bonner and I spent a couple of days last year. I was tempted to send her a playful text telling her where I was but we have just gotten back on good terms after a few months of estrangement. There were some really cute college aged girls camping, maybe five of them, and I caught myself checking them out—

Okay, you're 45 and old enough to be their dad. Do you see how creepy this is, yet?

I nearly broke down and bought some beer--a six-pack. It has now been almost two months since I went up to Yolla Bolly and I haven't had a drink where I live or stay since then. Had a couple of drinks in a bar or two, but otherwise I have been sober. It isn't always easy...I try not to go on and on about this sort of thing but I lead a pretty lonely life. No, more a *solitary* life. I don't have an apartment, I live in a van. I rarely have much money. I have dated a couple of women in '13 but it has been pretty casual. Most nights find me in the van alone and trying to stay cool. In Gualala I kept going back and forth; part of me felt like a dirty old man for checking out women in their early 20s but part of me was thinking *why not*? I mean, I am 45; I am not pushing a walker around with leathery skin and a colostomy bag. I got to thinking that I should just go and talk to them or something. How much of my life have I spent in this van or a room just making all these plans to go out and meet people only to do nothing? When do I change?

Maybe tomorrow.

September 16, 2016

When I got back to the house Allison was home, sitting on the orange couch I had been reluctant to buy and I couldn't stand to look at it after she left. The kitchen was a mess and I could tell she had been smoking inside and I was reminded how deeply I love her. She looked over at me from her book with a smile but did not get up to hug me; that has never been her way. I sat next to her; she took one of my hands in hers and we sat in silence for a couple of minutes. A started crying and I held her hand tighter.

She didn't hook up with anyone while we were separated. I didn't want to lie and told her about waking up with Kimberly and her husband. Allison was hurt by that but either believed or is making herself believe they drugged me or something. I love her so much but know I shouldn't express that, not now after what happened in Portland. I love her like I have loved few people; I understand we cannot live together. But there are three months left on the lease and neither of us can afford to pay our share of the rent and rent on another place. At least I still have the van. Three years and now closing on 200000 miles. Sometimes I feel like that stupid old van is my best friend.

It's hard to believe it has been almost a year since the book was published. I remember getting that check—($4581.09 after the agent's cut and taxes)—and just turning it over and over in my hands, scared I would get a call or a text telling me a mistake had been made and it wasn't mine. My life didn't really change. I helped out my mom some with that money and did a couple of small things but saved the rest. I was already planning on a trip to Europe or at least around the United States. It was around that time that Teresa's book was getting a buzz--*lionized* was an expression they used in the old days. It had come out a few months before mine and by September of '15 it was being called one of the most important books of the year.

And somehow they found out her ex-husband was also publishing a book.

Part of me was worried people would think I got published because of Teresa.

Part of me wanted to milk the attention I was getting, maybe even drop some hints I had written part of her book or something along those lines even if our writing styles are completely different—

And I am not that type of asshole. Not quite.

Teresa is working on a second novel for publication. Understandably she is scared and a bit overwhelmed; there is so much build up after everyone telling her she was one of the best writers of '15--how do you follow that? I never envied her. People think I do, but I don't. I have a long time education in pop culture and have read countless horror stories of the things best selling writers and musicians face. No, thank you. Sometimes I look at that old van or the fact I am stuck in a lease or I realize how cash poor I am and I think *maybe it would be good to have a lot more money*, but those thoughts are few and far between. No one has outlandish expectations of me, I am just Ike: I write weird stories. I add my eccentric mojo to scripts they send me. I come up with ideas for odd net series. Ike. Cult artist. Broke ass motherfucker---

And I wouldn't want to be anyone else.

343

November 1, 2014

Halloween is a day with a lot of meaning for me. Back in '75 it was the day my parents separated or at least the day they understood their marriage was dead. In 2003 I met Teresa at a Halloween party. Eleven years later I have broken up with someone else. Emily and I were supposed to go to a Halloween party last night. I knew things were weird because she hadn't called or texted or just come by in a couple of days and when I texted her she seemed—weird. You know how it is when you can tell something is wrong and you don't really want to know what it is because it could be something *big*? It was.

She showed up a couple of hours before we were supposed to leave for the party. I have been parked in front of a friend's house for a few days so she knew where to find me. Emily knocked on the side door and I let her in. She had been crying. Seeing the redness around her eyes I thought back to those text messages and I understood what was about to happen.

If you've been reading this blog you know I had been dating Emily for about three months; we reached our expiration date yesterday. It was the first time I had ever broken up with someone in the van; the van gained a bit of poignancy yesterday. It was sad, she cried and I almost did but learned long again women hate it when you cry in front of them. I have a lot of love for Emily. Was I *in* love with her? Was she in love with me? Who knows. Honestly, since what happened with Jackie Bonner two years ago I am a lot more guarded with my emotions. Maybe I will meet someone who gets me past that in the future but for now I always hold back a bit. It was that way with Emily. I could sense how much of herself she was investing in our being a serious couple and I just couldn't go there. Part of me wanted to, but I was scared. Part of me lives in fear of having my heart broken again to coin a cliché. Part of me understands that Emily and I want different things in life. That was how she sold the break-up to me. I'm the art guy with no money who lives in a van and Emily wants to own a house and have kids (she's 37; still has time). She talked about that, she talked about the differences in our goals and wants and nearly sold it. Nearly---I could tell it was bullshit. We had a conversation a week or so ago, another talk where she cried and I would have done anything to take her hurt away. Em expressed how she was falling for me and she didn't think I was falling for her. What could I say seeing as she was right? I have deep feelings for her, I have love for her, but I couldn't fall for her. I wish I could. I feel shitty having made her cry at least twice. I never cheated on her, I have been monogamous with her these past couple of months, but I have the feeling cheating on her would have hurt less.

We lay on the bed for the last time, fully clothed, saying nothing for a long time, looking up at the ceiling. She knows about the situation with Jackie Bonner and understands why it is so hard for me to just give into my feelings for her—doesn't make it any easier. After a while we got up and she climbed out of the van. I gave her one last hug and didn't want to let her go because I had the feeling I might never see her again. I wanted to just keep holding her and smelling her hair and tell her I loved her. But I knew I was just being selfish and maybe even cruel and eventually let her go.

December 3, 2016

I have been at Slab City for two days now. I resisted temptation until this afternoon when I drove into town and bought a bottle of Bushmills. So, here I am in the desert giving into my alcoholism once again. If you have been reading this blog you probably saw this coming.

Two days ago Allison and I did the final cleaning of the house, had the landlord inspect it, and then turned the keys in. The orange couch was sitting in the driveway and I wanted to empty my gun into it. It's like everything I feel over that whole mess was perfectly summed up by that fucking couch. It wasn't me that gave up on us living together; it was hard, but I was ready to stop being chicken shit, you know? Allison is an amazing person; I was really going to work at it, it was *her* that wasn't ready. And, you know, I get it: She's still young, she still deserves time to live her life and be with different people. Doesn't make it hurt any less, but that's what I get for dating someone in their early thirties. Maybe what happened with Kimberly and Alec played a part in it, but I think she had made her decision weeks before that.

I am getting kind of drunk. I have had a third of the bottle and the sun only set an hour ago. I really need to just stow it away or smash it but it tastes really good and I am feeling okay for the first time since we gave up the house. Maybe since I got back from Portland. The past three months either I have been staying somewhere in the van or she has crashed somewhere else. One time she came back to the house with a hickey on her breast. I only saw it when she bent down to pick something up. Didn't ask about it; didn't want to know what had happened. Still obsess about it.

God, the desert is beautiful. Still warm in the beginning of December though the nights are chilly; I feel at home here. Of course, I feel at home in Portland, too. I am going to do a fourth "Big Adventure" soon but haven't decided where; I am always open to suggestions so send me an email or leave me a comment if you have any ideas.

"Are you drunk, Ike?"
"How can you tell when I'm *typing*?"
"You have told me how incredible I am three times in the course of this conversation and we've only been chatting for two minutes."
Maggie. Chatting about when *Purgatory* will be released (September 9, 2017).
"I have some good news," she writes.
"You're sending a twenty year old Japanese hooker to my van?"
"What?"
"Just ignore me."
"God, I really try to sometimes. Anyway, you got a green light on (name of another project I have a development deal on that I have to keep secret for now)."
"Wow, amazing; you are incredible, Maggie."
"So you tell me."

With this deal comes a much needed infusion of money. I won't be "monocle and gold bidet" rich or anything like that, but things won't be as tight as they were. I can send my mother some money, for example.
I can get my diesel van, for another thing.
I actually walked aways off and out of sight of the van to write this. I feel guilty; Edna II has been such a great mobile home the past three plus years but things are starting to pop up. She has started to shift differently and the rear end has started to whine a bit.

I am thinking of leasing a little studio apartment, maybe in Portland but I'm not sure. I would miss everyone I know around Sacramento including Allison. A guy came around with a pickup truck to pick up the orange couch and the TV we bought but I said she could have. They seemed more than friends, the way they looked at each other, but I guess it doesn't matter now. We're not broken up, but maybe we never really looked at our relationship as boyfriend/girlfriend. Maybe we were just playing house and grew bored with the game. Honestly, it is too close to my heart to really see it clearly yet.

Did the dude helping her move put that hickey on her breast?

January 23/24/31, 2017

This is a sad day, but it is a good day. Sharing a beer with Dennis Wilson in the Arizona desert. The sky was overcast and we were leaning against the van; the same van I had owned three and a half years. If you have been reading this blog you know that every year I attend the Rubber Tramp Rendezvous down here, a gathering for people who live in vans or—(as in Dennis' case)—in tents. Dennis is an Afghanistan vet and has some PTSD. He's been living out of a beat up Hyundai Accent and an equally thrashed tent for a few years. D was a mechanic in the Army which is probably the only reason that old Hyundai still runs. I was introduced to him because the community knows I have been looking for someone to give my old van to. We finished our beers. I had already signed over the paperwork and taken five dollars as a token payment from Dennis. I handed him the keys and walked off before my emotions could come to the surface. Still holding the empty beer can I headed off deeper into the desert.

I was going to do something simple like buy a diesel step van but I have always wanted an old VW bus. They are very temperamental, though, and a challenge on hills. I also wanted another diesel. Long story not quite as long, I bought a '75 VW Bus with a high top that had an early 80s VW diesel engine with a turbo installed in it. It had been someone's pet project but abandoned when they lost their job or something like that. I spent about three times as much as I would have on a step van—in other words, I used up a big chunk of the money I got last month. E3 is a thing of beauty, though; smaller inside than the old Dodge van but at least you can stand up in it. The engine makes a little under 100 horsepower so it's slow, quite a bit slower than the van, but a lot better than a regular VW bus and you don't have to adjust the valves all the time.

"You spent $20000—on a 42 year old VW bus..." Maggie, of course.

"But it's an awesome 42 year old VW bus."

"Ike—what am going to do with you?"

"Hopefully help me get some more work or another pitch meeting or something."

"I want to talk to you about the next book."

"I thought we were going to omnibus the first three *Big Adventures* after *Purgatory*."

"The publisher is going to want a fiction project lined up if they're going to agree to publishing non-fiction."

"There isn't anything, Maggie."

"I thought you said you have three or four stories that just need to be finished or reworked."

"I do, kind of, but I just...I haven't been into working on them."

"How did you ever finish a novel, Ike?"

"I have no idea."

The conversation with Maggie was a disappointment but not a surprise. I was hoping to put out *The Big Adventure* next summer but the publisher is hesitant to put out something a lot of you have already read for free. The thing is, I have been editing it and making changes so it would be different; not completely different but—

Maybe I see their point but I still have idea what to do. As Maggie pointed out I have maybe four stories that are either novel length and need a lot of work or need to be taken to novel length. I just don't want another *Purgatory* situation; *Purgatory* lived up to its name—four years of struggling and reworking that damn story over and over. It turned out really good, I think you will enjoy it, but it was a largely unpleasant experience.

The VW is not perfect. It needs to be repainted and the interior is worn; looks a little beat up, actually. All of the money the last owner spent was on mechanical stuff. After I picked it up I drove to a secluded area down by a polluted river, broke a bottle of cheap champagne on the back bumper and wrote "Edna III" on one of the fenders in black nail polish..

It's now the day after giving up the Dodge and I am parked on the ocean just north of Ventura. After handing the keys over to Dennis I walked back to E3 and sat in the open sliding door staring out in the distance. I could see my old Dodge van, it looked the size of a die but I could make it out anywhere. Three and a half years. I needed another beer. No, I needed something harder.
No—I would stick to water as I have been since my night on the Slabs in December.

This morning I got up before the sun and left Quartzite. I drove west on I-40, keeping at 60 and being passed by nearly everything. The VW is noisier than the van but thanks to the five speed transmission gets 25 mpg if I stay at 60. E3 ran like a champ and was able to maintain 40 mph through the mountains. I even passed another old VW bus. The only downside is the pass was really cold and old VWs don't have much in the way of heaters. Not much in the way of heat and no air conditioning. I still do not regret my decision.

I am parked in a lot overlooking the beach. It's about an hour after sunset and I am debating whether to keep driving or park here for the night and risk getting rousted. I heated the kettle and am having some tea, sitting in the passenger seat and looking out in the direction of the sea. It's cold out but I have the window cracked so I can hear the sound of the ocean.

Maybe it was stupid spending all this money on E3; I can't really afford to rent a studio apartment now. Should I sell it and get something cheaper? Maybe an older diesel truck with a big camper or something? I don't know. The conversation with Maggie has made me worried about money. My show got greenlit and I get points of the sales etc. but it could be months or longer before seeing any of that money. My publisher is going to see how *Purgatory* performs before throwing more advance money and I haven't been getting much "script doctor" work.

(One week later)
That was hard: Man, I loved that bus. All eleven hundred miles I drove in it were a kick, but this wasn't the right time to have my VW Bus. We found a buyer with $18000 cash which means I lost a couple thousand but that's the way it goes with cars. I've had three of my dream cars: An International Travelall, a Mercedes diesel, and a VW bus. I loved them all, but I had to give them all up; at least I had them for awhile.

For $7000 I found a '98 Ford diesel van with a high top and relatively low miles (165000). It is not nearly as cool or nor does it have the personality of the VW but it is a much more practical choice. The question is *where* do I want to live? Sacramento? Portland? Somewhere else? I have no idea. I have a chat coming in so I guess this is a good place to wrap this up. It's Kimberly the lit agent—I'll write more later.

December 23, 2015

Matt is playing Hootie and the Blowfish again. Little does he know all the ways a writer knows how to kill; I could coat his sandals with arsenic or hide a deadly snake in his hemp shoulder bag.
Don't fuck with writers; we are creative and more than a little crazy.

"Thanks for getting this back to me so fast."
"No worries, I am looking forward to working with you, Maggie."
I finally have a manager. It has been over a year of hustling and wooing and having a few firms seem to be in the bag only to opt out at the last moment. Maggie isn't part of a "big name" firm, but they are "known" in the mythical land of Lost Angeles and should be able to get me a pitch meeting. I have never met Maggie or even spoken to her on the phone; our conversations have been strictly computer chat. Perhaps she is my Charlie and I am all three Angels rolled into one.

Allison is back with her ex-girlfriend. Is it serious or is it just for fun? Who knows. She has always been honest with me, has never gone behind my back; she just told me a couple of days ago that she can't deal with being in a serious relationship right now. Of course, maybe I'm not ready for that myself. I find it easier to fall deeper for A than I did with Emily but the times she stays here more than a couple of days I just want to be alone for a week.
You know, we are going to end up completely breaking each other's' hearts.
She said that to me that first morning when we had New Year's breakfast at Denny's. We had known each other twelve hours but it felt like much longer than that. With

some people it feels that you've been chasing each other from life to life; it has always been like that with Allison. Lying with her in the van fully clothed, staring at the ceiling and listening to yelling and gunshots in the distance. Unconsciously linking hands as we talked about anything, everything, and nothing. Falling asleep, still fully clothed, as the sun rose.

You know, we are going to end up completely breaking each other's' hearts.

And I just smiled and shook my head and sipped my coffee when she said that, but I knew she was right. I knew it then and I definitely know it now.

If you have been reading this blog you know I have a drinking problem. The general rule is I do not drink where I live or I am staying which means I don't drink in the van (New Years was the last time I did that). Tonight I just want to get fucked up---sitting in this room listening to Matt warbling along to Hootie and thinking of Allison making love to someone else. I can see them in my mind; it plays like a movie, amateur porn. But it's not sexy or I don't see it that way, it's just gut wrenching; just as gut wrenching as early '13 when I wrestled with my feelings for Jackie Bonner---

Someone was pounding on my door. I keep my gun in my room; what if I went to the door and leveled it at whomever is intruding on me? Would they piss themselves? Yeah, I get in dark moods sometimes and this is one of them. In the end, I left the gun under the mattress and threw open the door with a glare five degrees darker than murder. It was Matt and he was drunk.

"Ike, I'm sorry to bother you, bro, but, uh, would you like some beer?"

This is a test, right? I love ya, God, but this is pretty harsh.

"Yeah, sure."

I followed Matt into the kitchen. There were already half a dozen dead soldiers on the counter. Micro-brews; dead soldiers in dress uniforms. I opened one and drank half of it in one swallow as Matt looked on appreciatively.

"Wow, you sure can drink, Ike."

"Yeah, it's kind of one of my fatal flaws."

He looked forlorn and I knew he wanted me to drag out whatever was bothering him.

"So…what's up? I rarely see beer bottles in the recycling."

"It's Britt, I think we broke up this afternoon."

Oh man, is he going to cry? He knows the guy code about not crying in front of other dudes unless it's about sports, right? Even though he has that shoulder bag and those sandals he must know the guy code.

"Relationships suck, don't they?"

I drawled that and shrugged a bit but inside me something is twisting. I think of Allison and her girlfriend, lying next to each other, laughing—

"Did you finish that beer already? It has only been about two minutes."

"I guess."

He got me another beer and I fought to drink it slower than the first one.

"So, why are you and Britt having problems?"

"She found out that I cheated on her."

Beer nearly came out of my nose: Maybe he woos the ladies with his sandals and Hootie and the Blowfish CDs.

"Yeah, people don't usually react well to that."

"Why did I do something so stupid?"

Oh God, please don't cry, please don't…

"Because you're human, Matt, and human beings fuck up and hurt the people we care about the most."

"Did you finish that second beer already?"

Shit, I had. I shook the bottle a little, shrugged, and gave him a sheepish smile. He tried to slam the last third of his beer but gagged on it. Must have taken him all afternoon to get through the ones on the counter.

"The thing is, Ike; I don't think I really care for her. I mean, I care for her, but not like you do for Allison."

"Clearly, if you cheated on her."

"Then why am I so torn up about this?"

"Because, even if you weren't so into her you don't want anyone else to have her."

"No, that's not it."

"I tried."

I hung out with Matt a couple more hours. He insisted on putting on a Creed CD and I resisted the urge to beat him with a bottle. He started babbling about his feelings for this Britt and I guess I earned my Nice Guy of the Week points by listening and nodding and trying to be a good ear. Finally he was drunk enough to think that calling Britt seemed like a good idea. With most of my guy friends I'd talk them down, but I really wanted out of that room with the bad music and questionable sandals so I left him with his half finished beer and his iPhone...

March 19, 2015

"Are we going to die, Ike? I know you hate ruining surprises, but I was just wondering."
We are on a road that is little more than two wheel tracks bouncing through the high desert.
"Remember on New Years when you asked if I keep heads in that bucket?"
I say that in a pretty good Hannibal Lecter impersonation.
"Wow, old *and* creepy, what a catch. I am truly a lucky girl."
According to the forecasts we have a couple of days of decent weather so I have taken Allison up to a magical land I call NVORCA; the high desert where California, Oregon, and Nevada meet. It is as solitary a place as you can imagine.
"You know I trust you, right? I mean, quite a bit for only knowing you for only three months."
"Yeah?"
"What if we break down or we get stuck?"
"I have an emergency signal, extra battery, and enough water for a couple of weeks."
"I am not getting a signal on my phone."
Her voice is small and strangely vulnerable. It is times like this I am reminded of our age difference. I could toss my phone out the window and say good riddance; Allison would be lost without hers.

I think Allison is asleep. Sometimes she snores but it's still new enough to be endearing. I can't sleep. I am a little drunk and turning something over and over in my mind. We found a good place to camp, gathered some wood, and started a fire. I made us dinner and A surprised me with two bottles of wine she had brought.

"I know you're a complete drunk and if you have a sip you'll probably rip your clothes off and start howling at the moon," she said. "But the *Sacramento Bee* called this a delightful little Pinot Noir."

We sat by the fire and drank our wine. As is her tendency Allison spent half the conversation making jokes about my alcoholism or my age or the seediness of my living in a van. It's all part of why I feel so deeply for her; why I have the undeniable feeling we have known each other before--- that maybe we have been chasing each other from life to life.

You know, we are going to end up completely breaking each other's hearts.

She said that as we ate our New Year's breakfast. Even though we had only known each other about twelve hours I knew it was true and that we had probably done so countless times over the eons. Back in the present, A took another drink of wine and started in on my receding hairline and how, in my case, it is clearly not linked to a healthy testosterone build-up.

"I may be a balding asshole, but you're the one spending time with a balding asshole."

"Only because I'm just a little bit madly in love with you."

Why did you have to say that? What can I say in response— even if I have been starting to feel the same way even if I try to deny it?

"I'm just messing with you, Ike."

Her voice had changed and I sensed she was backing away from something I didn't want her to back away from.

"Every day I struggle against falling more deeply in love with you because I didn't think you wanted anything serious," I said.

"Why does it have to be serious? Can't we be in love and not have it be this big, serious thing? If I am in love with you and you love me, why do things have to change?"

A few hours later I am lying next to her, turning that exchange over and over in my mind. I want to get out, maybe climb on top of the van and lie on the roof to look up at the stars like I have done so many times but I am not alone; it would wake Allison up and she'd be pissed off at me. So, I am just lying here and rapidly losing a battle I have been fighting for three months...

"This is a shitty hotel, Ike."

"But this is Jim Morrison's room; this is literally the room Jim Morrison slept in."

"That makes sense because only a complete drunk would stay here."

Allison is sitting on the edge of the bed; she could be pouting or she could just be winding me up, I still can't tell sometimes.

"We should have taken my car; we could have saved money on gas."

"The van is more reliable."

"We just got the starter fixed."

"But your car has lots of things that could go wrong at any time."

"Then why did you tell me to spend all that money on it?!"

We have a serious discussion that could be mistaken for an argument about her car for a few minutes. The walls are covered with graffiti, tributes to the singer of the Doors. It is a weird place and I realize I was self-indulgent booking this room.

"This room still sucks. And I'm not going to be your Pam."

"And I won't fuck you up the ass."

"What?"

I explain to her about Jim Morrison's *preferences*.

"I think he had a closet to pop out of," Allison frowned.

If you have been reading this blog you know we are in Los Angeles because I have a pitch meeting tomorrow. Allison has decided to become my fashion advisor and insisted I buy some new clothes for the meeting. She has been spending hours researching pitch meetings and probably knows more than I do. A drills me, making me practice my pitches over and over; shaking her head and telling me I suck and making me love her just a little bit more.

(Next morning)
I am nervous as hell and didn't sleep very much. Kept having nightmares of a drunk Jim Morrison trying to bugger me, his Mr. Mojo clearly Risin' in the front of his leather trousers as he chased me down the corridors of the hotel from *The Shining*. Jimbo was bellowing drunkenly about how he was going to fuck me up the ass until I cried like a little girl.

Allison found a place to get breakfast and I drove over to what looked like an anonymous industrial park.
"I thought it would be in a high rise or a nice hotel or something."
"Another myth shattered."
Partially out of embarrassment and partially because I don't remember a lot of it. I am not going through a blow by blow of my pitch---I was nervous as hell but I think I did a good job.

When I went back to the van Allison asked about the meeting and then went into something that had been on her mind.
"Do we have to stay in the dead drunk guy room again?"
"No, we stay where you want to stay tonight."
"Can we afford to go to San Diego?"
"Yeah, we can't go five star, but we can get a decent place. The ocean is really nice down here."
"We could go to Mexico!"
"Don't you have to be back at work on Monday?"
"That's three days away. I think one day in Mexico would be more than enough."

Mexico: Makes me think of two years ago---Jackie Bonner. It's Friday the 13th, the traffic is terrible and yet for some odd reason I feel deeply and truly happy…

March 20, 2017

Yesterday was Allison's birthday. I sent her a short message and she responded with this long, emotional email. She found another roommate situation but I guess it has gone sour and now she is looking for something else. As it transpires she *was* seeing the guy who helped her move but he started getting possessive and jealous so she told him to fuck off. I wrote her back and she popped up on IM and we chatted for a couple of hours. In the end, Allison asked if we could meet up today and since I was in Sacramento I agreed. I miss her. I have lost faith that she is ready for anything serious, but I care for her and miss being around her.

"You should have kept the VW, I bet it was dope."
"You don't like Edna IV?"
"Seems like a decent van, but that VW sounds bad ass."
"It was, but it was the wrong time."
We were heading down Business 80 after deciding on getting Willies for lunch.
"So, how is it living on the coast?"
"Good. My place is really small, a trailer the size of a bedroom, but I am only ten minutes from the ocean."
"Sounds really nice."
"You should come out and visit."
Was it too soon for that sort of invitation? Would it ever be appropriate to offer such invitations again?
"I'd love that, Ike."
I could tell by her tone of voice she was being sincere. I got off on P Street.
"Well, if you think your car could handle it, you're always welcome."
Allison nodded and looked over at the aquarium store at 30th and T. It was a few blocks before she spoke again.

"You said someone might be adapting one of your stories into a movie?"

"Yeah. It's a semi-famous filmmaker but I am not allowed to talk about it."

"Even with me?"

I told her about the filmmaker and she seemed nearly as awed as when I explained to her the cause of the small hole in the side of Edna II.

"That'd be incredible if it could work out."

"It would be; we'll see what happens."

We got our food and took it to Land Park to have a picnic. Neither of us wanted to part ways so I drove us into the hills and ended up at the end of a country road. It was nearly dark by then. I folded out the bed and—(as we had a little over two years ago)—lay on it fully clothed.

"There's something that has bothered me for awhile, Ike."

"Yeah?"

"You remember when you were driving to New York last year and I called you and was all emotional?"

"Yeah, that was when I was in Mississippi."

"I did something really terrible the day before. I have no idea why I did it, but it happened."

Here's where she tells me she had sex with someone else.

"Well, if you hooked up with someone else we didn't have an agreement to be exclusive."

"I know, and I know you were with people on your trip, but this was just extra shitty and stupid."

"How so?"

"It was Matt."

"*Matt*? Sandals and earnest face, Matt?!"

"He does have some redeeming qualities."

"I really don't want to know about them."

We lay in silence for a few minutes. Allison took my hand and I didn't resist. She squeezed it and I squeezed back. I wanted to invite her to come and live with me in my tiny rental cabin but also didn't want to give too much of myself too soon.

"I had to tell you about it; I think you know why."

"I do."

It had been a few months since we had been that close---the last couple of months in the rental house we shared had been tense. I kept seeing the hickey on her breast that time she bent down to pick up something.

"How many centuries have we been doing this, Ike?"

I started massaging her hand with my fingers a bit feeling this weight on my heart.

"I'd guess more than a few."

I drove her back to the house she lived in near Watt and Marconi and I took a short detour to point out the house my aunt and uncle have lived in since the early 70s.

"You have no idea how much I want to come back to the coast with you."

"You're welcome to if you want."

Too much? It felt okay since she had opened the door, as it were.

"You can't support both of us and if I miss work tomorrow I will probably get fired."

And look what happened when we tried to live together last year...

Allison undid her safety belt, leaned over, and kissed me. It was a great kiss, but I could taste the sadness in it...

March 25, 2017

More nude people kept getting in the hot tub. When it was just Lynda and I it was fine---she's really cute---but then Hippy Guy dropped in followed by Diver Guy with his big, oddly shaped penis and Old Lady. It's not that big of a hot tub. Our feet kept touching and it was kind of freaking me out. Lynda and I were having a nice chat and maybe I was getting a little hopeful but then Smelly Drunk Lady with Amoeba Shaped Areola slid in and I knew it was time to make my exit.

I have been living here in Mendocino for about three weeks now. I tell people I live in a small cabin but the truth is it is a travel trailer. A small one. At $400 per month the price is right. We are a few miles east of town on a decent sized piece of property; the owners have their house and parked a couple of trailers to pick up some rent money. I miss having a bathtub but there is the hot tub—even if the neighbors keep stopping by for a naked dip. It's never the people you *want* to see naked, is it?

I am now back in the trailer thinking about Lynda in the hot tub with her bathing suit molded to her body. She looks like I imagine Allison looking in ten years if A starts exercising and stops smoking. Honestly, every woman I look at makes me think about Allison and lying in a van with her again and holding her hand and kissing her. It was hard leaving her at that house, it has been hard these past few days not texting or calling or emailing. I think about her all the time but I know I can't make myself too available. I learned that lesson four years ago with Jackie Bonner. Knowing my tendency to obsess, I busied myself with going over potential novels when Maggie came up on chat.

"I am curious about one thing, Ike."

"What's that?"

"What were the first couple of months of 2013 like? I know you were writing *Jackie Bonner* and trying to find an agent."

"They were, to be inelegant, quite fucking awful. If you go back far enough in the blog I wrote about them a little."

And I went on to explain about not getting any work and being stuck at my mother's house and dealing with my feelings for the woman you readers know as Jackie Bonner.

"How did you get out of it?" She asked.

"What do you mean?"

"It sounds like you were miserable and despondent, how did you get through it?"

"A combination of my own self belief and writing *Jackie Bonner*. And my friend Mark let me stay with him which got me back to Portland where I got a job and eventually a van."

"It's too bad they're looking for a novel, I bet that could be interesting to read."

"Some of it was good. There was a lot of my wandering around, discovering the town, and hanging out in bars. I'll find it and send it to you if you like."

"Do you have a name for this book?"

"*The Passenger*," I said, getting the Iggy Pop song in my head.

"The Passenger?"

"Yeah, it's a song off Iggy Pop's first album."

"Oh."

We chatted about the release date for *Purgatory*. She asked about my money situation and I told her I was good until May and then things would get dicey.

"I am curious about that part of Northern California; I may have to come up."

"You mean I may get to see your face?"

"Only as a reward for a fiction project we can sell your publisher."

When we ended the chat session I saw that Allison had sent me an email. Emails are rare from her; like most people her ages she usually texts. It was a poem. I read it over and over and struggled with my emotions. I am alone, I do not mind crying when I am alone, but this is much bigger than that…

June 1, 2017

If you have been reading this blog you know that last week I sold the van and rented a small studio in Portland. Year lease at $850 per month. For the first time in four years I don't have a van (or a car for that matter).

My apartment is in an older building on the edge of the Hawthorne. It's quite small, the main room is about twelve by fourteen with a kitchen on one end, but I have little furniture so it works--my grandfather's dresser, a bookcase, a queen sized futon folded in half, and a low table in the corner I use for eating and work. I love it. It's a great area for going on walks. It is strange, though, not having a car, not being able to take a spontaneous road trip. Despite that I have been turning over and over in my mind how I will be turning 50 at the end of the year and how it'd be nice to have a real home again.

Even after selling the van I figure I have six months before I run out of money. They've been casting the show they greenlit last December. The hope is that they will be in production by the end of the Summer; that would still mean at least a year before they start selling the first season. Hopefully I will get some more script doctor work or maybe I can get another development deal. If not I will be completely broke right around my birthday and this time without a van to live in.

Have not had an online chat with Maggie for two months now, since she came up to visit me in Mendocino. I suppose it is to be expected; things got kind of crazy. I get oblique text messages along the lines of "Soon" or "Reconfiguring things" or "Friends forever." Friends forever? Sounds like something you write in a high school yearbook. But it makes sense in a Maggie way; I understand her now, a lot more than I did before she came to Mendocino.

Jackie Bonner and I just missed each other; she was in town maybe three weeks ago to visit her cousin. Haven't seen her in a few months and I am guessing it will be another few months before we run into each other again seeing as she is in California.

January 27, 2014

This is a very welcome break from winter and waking up in the van shivering like I do in Oregon or Northern California. I am in San Diego where it always seems to be somewhere in the mid-seventies—or so I have been told. This is my first time in this city. If I didn't have a long-term assignment lined up starting Thursday I wouldn't have dared spent the money on gas to get down here.

My agent has not approached any publishers yet. They have asked me to take out stories and then rejected the replacements. The stories they have accepted have been torn apart and rewritten; we spent two days on a *sentence* last week and I cannot complain---I want this to be right; I want to blow away anyone who reads this book. They had me add a couple of stories so we can have the word count be above 60000 (and yet it's still called *9*, go figure). I am making the latest corrections and rewrites parked at the ocean, looking out at the sea in the passenger's seat with the window down to hear the sound of the waves. That said, how could I even begin to complain?

San Diego reminds me of Marin in its affluence. Parking for the night will be a challenge but I have been doing this for six months now so I am up for the game. Last night I parked in the lot of a 24 hour grocery store. When I got up a note had been left under a wiper: *If you spend the night here again, I will contact the police. Thank you.* Thank you; at least they were polite—at least they gave me one night. So, after a bit more editing I will scout for other places to spend the night.

Last week was miserable. I had my first assignment in two months; it paid well but it was a bastard. Lots of phones. I am just thankful for the money. Last Fall I was watching every nickel because I knew I'd have a dry spell and thank God I did. Honestly, it was frivolous to take such a long trip, to burn up 1100 miles, but I needed this.

Southern California really is another state; people seem different down here. It isn't bad or good, just different. I came down Interstate 15 to avoid the Los Angeles traffic but everywhere in Southern California is faster paced. The weather is really nice, though. Wearing a short sleeve shirt in January is strange but welcome. It's completely different from last year around this time when I was in Portland.

I am really excited about having a literary agent; I'm excited but I'm nervous--how long will they work to find a publisher for me? How many attempts until they send me their regrets? They have been working so hard to get the book in good shape, but being by nature pragmatic or maybe pessimistic I know there will be a point where they decide to cut their losses. Sometimes I think that, but mostly I feel in my heart this is meant to be and they will find a publisher and things will move forward. I cannot explain why I believe this, but I do...

January 30, 2014

I am drunk in San Luis Obispo. I just flirted disastrously with a 23 year old waitress and now am leaning against the van smoking a cigarette. Some guy just walked by and gave me a dirty look. I glared back, daring him to make something of it. I don't want to hit someone as much as I want to be hit.

It has been three days since I have worked on this blog or *anything* for that matter. I have six emails from my agent but haven't had it in me to respond. Am I fucking up my career before it has even started? I seem to be embracing every disaster I am capable of throwing my arms around.

I finished my cigarette and am now writing in the van. It is parked behind a bar and I can hear people laughing and talking with that loudness drunks get. They sound so carefree and happy I want to machine gun the lot of them. I had never seen this bar before a few hours ago but now I know all the waitresses and I'm sure I have made a bad impression on the regulars. If they try and roust me I will explain I am too drunk to drive and that will not be a lie. Tequila—I have been drinking tequila. The money I was going to spend on food while waiting for my next check was spent on good tequila. What am I doing? I thought I was past doing stupid shit like this.

I lost track of where I was the last time I wrote. I had to actually go back through this blog to remember that I was sitting on a beach in San Diego. It was a beautiful day and the sound of the waves coming through the window was musical. I was sitting in the passenger seat and needed to stretch my legs so I hid the netbook and locked up the van.

The beach had quite a few people for a Monday but I found a solitary stretch and stared out at the waves. A few minutes passed and the feeling in the air changed as I became aware of someone standing nearby. Glancing over I saw a woman who was looking out in the same direction as me; she looked like a thinner Yoko Ono but with much better hair. It fell past her shoulders and was blue black, drawing the light in and then absorbing it. She caught me looking, smiled, and nodded. I walked over and introduced myself.

"Yes, you were sitting in the van. I saw you. You do not belong here, but not in a bad way."

"I don't belong here?"

"No, you belong somewhere else. But so do I, maybe that is why we are talking."

She introduced herself as Tiyo and we chatted for maybe fifteen minutes and then she said she was hungry and asked if I would like to accompany her to a restaurant. I did, but money is tight and I was trying to think of a gracious way to bow out—

"I wouldn't offer unless I was buying. You are living in a van, it is safe to assume you are broke, right?"

"Usually, yes."

She shrugged. I think Tiyo had the most amazing shrug I had ever seen.

T had taken a taxi to the beach so I drove us to an Indian restaurant she likes. On the drive over she mentioned that she was 56 and recently separated. We did the usual talking about books and movies and found that we like a lot of the same stuff but my tastes tend to be a bit darker.

After dinner we walked out and I offered to drive her home. She accepted with the suggestion that I park in her driveway that night.

"But first we should get a good bottle of tequila. Do you like tequila, Ike?"
Well, actually Tiyo, I am not usually into tequila but you see I am an alcoholic and if you put a bottle of cleaning fluid in front of me there is always a chance I will drink it.
She seemed to read my thoughts but it didn't bother me; I wanted her to know me.

Tiyo bought a really nice bottle of tequila, the kind that BevMo keeps in locked cases. We went back to her home in one of the better parts of San Diego and I felt conspicuous in my old van.
"I feel like a hillbilly in my old van."
She had opened the bottle and had taken a sip from it.
"No one cares, Ike. Everyone is like you, everyone is so wrapped up in their own life they don't give a shit."

We drank the tequila and talked. She explained that she was in remission from cancer. Her husband was staying at a condo across town, unable to deal with the situation. I shook my head and offered the opinion he was shallow but T cut me off.
"My husband has lost many people to cancer: Aunts, his mother, even a sister. How many times can you face that? Believe me, I've been angry about it, but what good does it do? I love him; I know there will be a time when he comes back. Maybe I will take him in and maybe I won't, but I know he'll come back at some point."

From there, things get a bit less clear. We finished off the good bottle of tequila and moved onto a bottle of Cuervo she used for mixing—

The next morning I woke up on the couch suffering a severe insult to the brain. Tiyo walked out like misplaced royalty and stopped a few feet short of where I was lying.

375

"I bought your drinks last night, the least you can do is make coffee."

I made us coffee and cooked breakfast. It was a beautiful kitchen in the middle of a beautiful house. My brain was a disaster and my hands were shaking. Tiyo was wearing this amazing kimono. She didn't seem to care how open it was or that I could see most of her breasts. We sat at the kitchen counter and ate.

"Have you been to Mexico before, Ike?"

"No."

"Then maybe we should go. Is your van reliable?"

"Yeah, I just got tires three months ago."

She looked at me like I was crazy and then drank more of her coffee.

"I nearly died a couple of times so you will find me almost painfully honest. Is that a cliché?"

"Yes, but not a bad one."

"You are a weird combination of selfish and kind, Ike."

"Yeah?"

"Some people are born to be selfish, but good things come from their selfishness. Where they fail as people, they excel in other ways, so it all works out. I can tell how much you like hearing me talk about you and yet I find you very dear."

For the first time I was not nervous about going down to Mexico and I have no way of explaining that. Tiyo reminded me of those Civil War generals who would stand up in the midst of withering rifle fire and inspire their men because they didn't get a scratch—
Of course, most of those men were shot down.

We drove east on Interstate 8 to avoid the busy checkpoint at Tijuana. I turned down onto State Route 94 with the intention of crossing the border at Tecate.

"Do you feel safe living in this van?"

"Sure. I mean, I'm not stupid, I am careful where I park. Plus, I have a gun."

Her eyes widened a bit and she smiled.

"A gun? What kind?"

"A Smith and Wesson .41 Magnum."

"Isn't that the gun Dirty Harry has?"

"No, that's a .44 Magnum. I only got this one because it was a really good deal."

"You don't like it?"

"I like it, I just always dreamed of a .357 magnum."

"Can we shoot it?"

"Sure."

"There's an exit coming up; let's see if it takes us to some cactus we can shoot."

Ten minutes later we were walking out into the desert. I had put the gun in a tote bag and Tiyo made fun of me.

"You're white and I'm a 56 year old Japanese woman; what do you think a sheriff is going to do? I'll show him the scars from my surgery and explain I am a cancer survivor. Don't make that face when I know you want to smile."

We came upon this cactus that must have been twenty feet high. It felt a shame to shoot it. I pulled the gun out and gingerly handed it to Tiyo with the barrel pointed at the ground.

"It is really loud and has a strong kick."

She took the gun facing the other direction, looking down the sight and trying a practice stance—and it went off. I should have been watching her finger on the trigger. Tiyo had shot in the direction of the van and I half expected the round to hit the gas tank and see a fireball in the distance. She didn't look worried; instead she turned around and blasted in the general direction of the cactus. One shot. Two shots. Three shots. It was comical because she was such a tiny woman the recoil would send her two steps back. Finally, she handed me the gun and shook her head.

"That's enough for me."

"Cactus not as fun as shooting a van?"

"Could you shoot someone, Ike?"

"Yeah, I'm pretty sure I could if I had to."

She looked into my eyes.

"I see that. You have that coldness in you. I know it because I see it in myself; it's why I am still alive."

We walked back to the van which was fortunately not a smoldering ruin or sitting on a destroyed tire. Tiyo rubbed a spot behind the side doors.

"Here it is."

I went inside to see if the bullet had gone through—no. It had gone through a cooking pot and later I would find the bullet on the floor under the sleeping platform. Tiyo lay down on the bed and looked up at the ceiling.

"Are we still going to Mexico?"

"I don't know."

I thought about the way her kimono had fallen open that morning and lay down on the bed next to her.

We drove back to San Diego. I was starting to get past my hangover when Tiyo suggested we get another bottle of the good tequila and go back to her house. That night was a replay of the first one but I remember most of it.

Yesterday, we had a fight---I don't remember how it started, but it was stupid and bad enough that I left full of anger and started driving east towards the desert. I hated leaving like that; she was an awesome person and it just seemed wrong. So, I texted her this long, apologetic message and she didn't write back for a couple hours.

"The next time you hear my name, I will be dead."

After all her Zen talk and what could be mistaken for wisdom it seemed such bullshit. So, I called her on her

melodrama and maybe I was a bit harsh because she has
not written back; I have the feeling she never will.

This brings us to the present: Me parked behind this bar
being an asshole with my alcohol and my cigarettes.
And my van has a hole in the side.
Maybe I'll make up a tall tale about how Jackie Bonner and
I went to Mexico and I had to scare some men off outside a
bar with a gun to keep them from raping her.

Tomorrow is going to be ugly, hours of tasting ash and my
head throbbing—I think I saw a diner down the road;
greasy breakfast food may be my salvation. In the
meantime I will try and find some peace and attempt to
distance myself from the drunken joy of crowds and the
memory of certain women...

April 12-13, 2017

It is early in the morning, early enough that the sun isn't up. I've been up since three obsessing about the next book—whatever that is. Maggie will be getting up here this afternoon; she is expecting me to have *something* but I have nothing. I keep going over novels I have partially finished and they're not good enough. I look at them, the amount of work they'd require, and I shudder. If you have been reading this blog you know how much work I put into *Purgatory* to get it in shape. I really don't want to do that again. If I don't, though, how will I live? Even if a show gets made out of one of my ideas it will be over a year before I see that money; Maggie keeps reminding me what a slow process screen work is. She keeps doling out these nightmare tales of writers sitting on their hands and selling more of their impulse purchases as they wait years and years for something to happen. I need to send her away with something she can sell to a publisher working in tandem with Kimberly. That's another touchy situation; Maggie is trying to take over the literary agent role and for obvious reasons Kimberly isn't happy with that—and I am caught in the middle.

A couple of hours have passed and I have finally decided on what book idea I will go with. It is maybe a third finished and I am not so happy with what I've written so far but the concept is strong. It's early afternoon now and I feel like I could sleep but I need to go into town in half an hour to meet Maggie. There is some sort of hippy argument going on outside. Hippies argue in slow motion; I love watching it, it's fucking hysterical, but if they catch me laughing I will have angry hippies on my hands and no one wants that.

Maggie is staying in town at some sort of bed and breakfast place I had never heard of until she told me about it. M flew into San Francisco, rented a car, and has been driving up the coast all morning. The funny thing is I have no idea where she lives but I want to say New York. What shirt should I wear? What pants? I want to make a good impression but if I wear something too nice then it will be obvious and she'll think I am out to seduce her or something. What if she's really attractive?

Don't go there, Ike. Let's not sabotage the relationship that is keeping you from temping.

What if she finds *me* attractive? What if I feel the ol' hand on the leg under the dinner table routine?

Why do I have to overthink *everything*?

(The Next Day)

It is 24 hours later and I have not slept. Maggie is on the road, heading south. I asked if she was okay to drive and she just nodded, not really looking at me. Didn't say anything else, just got in the Chevy rent a car and drove off. Some fat Italian looking guy in his sixties was watching us.

"Lady troubles, huh?"

I wanted to make a mean inquiry about the last time he had seen his feet but knew he hadn't meant anything by his question.

Maggie looks like Olivia Newton John. Not Olivia when she was having the hits in the early 80s but how I imagine her looking several years later. More professional with the hair and clothes of a successful business woman around 40. I extended my hand in greeting but she just laughed and hugged me.

"We've talked too much to settle for a handshake, Ike."

It was a real hug; I could feel her breasts and got paranoid I'd get an erection.

Nice to finally meet you, hope you like pup tents.
She was hungry so we went into a restaurant that I knew
was good. I rarely eat out, but on my first day in
Mendocino I was too tired for grocery shopping or cooking
so I splurged.
"I know you try not to drink, Ike; would it bother you if I
got something?"
"No, in fact I'll probably join you."
Maggie ordered a bottle of wine even though I said I would
be getting a local beer. Had she not heard me? Was she
expecting me to drink the wine? Would it be a faux pas if I
didn't have a glass? As it transpired she was not expecting
to share that wine with me.
We talked about her home (Chicago it turns out) and then
she asked the dreaded question about the next novel. I was
smooth—if you read this blog you know that usually I am
far from smooth but yesterday I was like oiled glass. I
didn't mumble or stammer; I sold that book like my life
depended on that pitch and maybe it did. She liked the idea
and you cannot imagine the relief I felt.

M finished the bottle and ordered a second. I was nursing
my beer but sped up a little so we'd be able to
communicate and also so she wouldn't be embarrassed by
being the "drunk one"—
*And, let's face it; I am an alcoholic and any excuse to
drink, well…*
"I'm sorry we couldn't make Europe happen this year,
Ike."
"No worries, maybe next Spring. Let's think that way;
Purgatory will do well and I will be able to go to Europe
next year."
"I have a confession to make; I have always liked your
music better than your writing. I like your writing a lot, but
you always have your guard up. You are a lot more human
in the songs you do."

382

"I'm glad you like it—"

"I shouldn't have said that. I'm your manager, I shouldn't prefer either, that was crass of me."

"No, it's okay."

"Let's walk down to the beach. Would you be up for that?"

"Sure."

With a long swallow she finished off the second bottle of wine. *Could* she walk? As it transpires she wasn't really drunk, not yet.

There was a cold wind coming off the sea and Maggie didn't have a real coat with her. I grabbed an extra one from the van.

"I like the way you smell," she said.

"Thanks. I use this soap from a store called Lush."

I like the way you smell? She is drinking and commenting on how I smell, this could go in a bad direction. A fun direction, but a career destroying one. Great, I feel an erection starting…

We walked on the beach; it was maybe an hour before Sunset. Maggie was intoxicated but not drunk. She checked into her bed and breakfast and it was a tatty place that smelled of cats. I could tell Maggie wasn't happy with it so I pulled her aside.

"Listen, I can sleep in the van tonight and you can have my bed in the trailer. I changed the sheets this morning."

Maggie gave me a funny look.

"Why did you change the sheets, Ike?"

What? No, wait, no, don't think that…and don't join in pup tent from Hell!

"I'm surprisingly clean for a man."

"I'll take your invitation on one condition; if you let me be the one to sleep in the van."

"Okay."

I stopped in the restaurant and explained that Maggie had drunk too much to drive and luckily they were cool with her leaving her car there overnight. I loaded her bags in the van and we headed out of town.

"I finally get to ride in the Van."

"This is one of them, my fourth van, actually."

"Not the one with the bullet hole, though?"

"No. Dennis Wilson has that one."

"I thought Dennis Wilson was dead."

"He is if that van is still a target for large caliber bullets."

Maggie had brought a bottle of Johnnie Walker Red. I usually don't drink where I live, but I didn't want to be a bad host—

And, again, I am an alcoholic.

At the trailer I got us two glasses. I had mine neat and she had hers on the rocks. The sun set and mercifully the hippies had taken their argument and their bad music indoors. Why do hippies listen to such bad music? You think they'd listen to Santana and Jimi Hendrix and on rare occasions they do but mostly it's jam bands: A bunch of unwashed guys with beards insisting on playing a ten minute solo in every fucking song. We sat outside with our drinks and looked up at the stars.

"Tell me about Jackie Bonner, Ike. Something you have never written about."

I started telling her a story and even though it had happened four years ago I felt my emotions coming to the surface in the middle of that stupid story and barely got through it.

"That's why I really like your music; it's not clever and calculated like your writing, you seem human. And I can see how much you loved (JB's real name). She was kind of shitty to you, wasn't she?"

"All my female friends feel that. The truth is, I fell in love with a woman I had no business falling in love with and what happened happened. She was a mess then, not herself at all, but that was four years ago."

She refreshed her drink pouring maybe four shots worth in. After a couple of sips Maggie opened up to me and told me things for obvious reasons I am not including in this blog even though I am blocking Maggie so she can't read it. I have no idea why she opened up like that, maybe she felt safe because she had been exposed to my songs or maybe it was because she was drunk or some other reason completely removed from those two things. It touched me deeply, though, she was just sitting there telling me of all this woe and how life had hurt her and I wanted to cry myself. I knelt next to her chair and put my arm around her and she started sobbing, just bawling and shaking. Maggie was really drunk by that point; I helped her into the trailer and tucked her in bed.

"I wanted to sleep in the van."

"It's too cold in the van at night and you're too drunk to use the heater safely."

"I'm sorry, Ike, I don't know why I did this; got drunk, told you those stupid stories."

"Nothing that ever breaks your heart is stupid, Maggie." But she had passed out. I found another blanket and put it at her feet in case she got cold in the night.

I poured another drink and took it outside so I could look up at the stars. Seeing her pain made me aware of my own. I thought of Allison, that poem she sent me, all the times I have looked at her and felt this deep, helpless love that has always terrified me. I am 49, my life is more than half over and sometimes the way the months race by scares me. I wonder if I will spend the rest of my life alone and I understand if that happens it is nobody's fault but my own. I see my friends with children and sometimes the fact I will never be a Dad tears at me in ways I cannot describe. Like Maggie pointed out, that side of me is never in my books and maybe it is why I am just a good writer and not a great one.

It was nearly midnight when I climbed into the van. I was hoping to get some sleep, but I just lay there staring at the ceiling like I have done so many times. I heard the trailer door open and close. I heard and saw the van door opening. Maggie climbed under the covers with me and asked me to spoon her. I did. We were both fully clothed, I couldn't have imagined having sex with her last night and maybe I will never be able to again. I didn't sleep; I just held her and said a prayer for her happiness.

I drifted off a little but it wasn't real sleep. I got up to go to the bathroom a couple of times and when I got back I lay on my side of the bed only to have Maggie snuggle up to me again. When she woke up she was obviously in a lot of misery. I drove us into town to the same restaurant where she had drunk all that wine. M seemed embarrassed, had trouble looking me in the face, and spoke very little.
"Maggie, you know I have lost track of the number of times I got drunk around people."
"I fucked up, Ike; let's just leave it at that."
We spoke very little during the meal and then she got in that rental car and drove off. I am not worried about my career. Granted what happened could affect our working relationship, but I am more concerned with Maggie. I have felt the pain she clearly feels and I have drunk the way she drank to numb it. I have been there, I still go there from time to time, and to think of another human being suffering like that breaks my heart. It really does. I wanted to follow Maggie home and take care of her and try and protect her from unhappiness. You and I know that is impossible. We can't save the ones we love from their own misery; we can just let them know we love them and keep them in our prayers.

June 28, 2017

Things have gotten weird recently. If you have been reading this blog you know things are usually weird with me, but they have gotten weirder. I think Maggie has gotten past what happened in Mendocino; things seem back to normal between us. A couple of days ago she made me aware of a cult---a small one but one that touches my heart---that is obsessed with my writing. All fourteen of them are apparently besotted with my book and the other stuff like this blog. It's an amazing feeling and it makes me think about My Bloody Valentine and Guns 'n' Roses. Yes, those are bands, but people waited decades for them to release new material. The Las. Brian Wilson's *Smile* project---God forbid I compare myself to Brian Wilson but maybe you see what I am getting at. What if I can turn *Book Three* into this enormous, mythological *thing*: Truman Capote's *Unanswered Prayers*. Another J.D. Salinger novel. What if we were really clever and built this third book into this huge event; just built the excitement and made it out to be this big thing. I would never have to fucking write it! I could milk this the rest of my life. I could turn out an amazing chapter or two every few years and tease, you know? What if I could string my publisher along, get them to advance me more money to finish the thing until they had advanced me so much it was too late to stop and in the meantime I was wasting my days with opium and 20 year old Japanese hookers instead of writing, dying fat and debauched and with the novel nowhere complete.
Do you think I could pull it off??

June 28, 2015

The situation in Lodi has been worsening. My mother had a kidney infection and between the medication and missing work she lost several hundred dollars. Luckily I still had most of my advance and could help her but if it happens again we will not be so fortunate. This is a worry. I worry about that situation a lot.

I drove down to Lodi and things were as they always tend to be: Lots of dogs, my mother making it clear she always knows best, and a not so gentle reminder of the truism that once you see something for how it really is you can never see it how you used to see it. I love my mother and I worry about her a lot but it is hard to be around her. It's better now than when I lived with her but still challenging. If you have been reading this blog you understand that we are very different people.

Mom is proud of the fact I am publishing a book and has already pre-ordered a copy off Amazon. It was a touching gesture even if I told her I could give her a copy for free. This is how it is; my mother is always loving and supportive but there are lots of strings tied to that and it's too easy to get tangled up in them and feel choked.

She asked me to stay a couple of days but I needed to get out of there. I lied and said Allison and I had plans but in reality I just needed to get out of that house and out of Lodi. It overwhelms me, all these conflicting emotions. I love my mother and I worry about her but our relationship is a haunted house. Either a haunted house or like being a couple of miles under the ocean with all the crushing pressure, I haven't decided.

I have to get a manager; I *have* to get money coming in somehow. Not just enough for me; I can tell the time when my mother can work is coming to an end. When it does, she will not be able to pay rent or go to the doctor—(that is already beyond her means)—or take care of the dogs which are now eight to nine years old. Being the only child it is my responsibility to pick up the burden and right now I can't; I am barely scraping by living out of my van. I have some of the advance money left, but I want to spend that on publicity. I see the door opening and am pushing against it with all my might. I have to; I need to have enough money to be able to support my mother. It's scary--believe me I have lost many nights of sleep over that.

April 28, 2016

Texas: *Wow.* This is my second trip through Texas and the South in general and I am still slack-jawed. It really is like another country. My mother's family is from the South, they came to California in the early 60s, but this trip has reminded me how far removed I am from my Southern heritage. I made the mistake of telling Pete and Lindsey about my roots last night and they have been ragging me to no end. If I told them I have fantasized about my cousin I'm sure it would just be fuel on the fire.

"So, where are you right now?" Maggie writes
I message her back sitting in the parking lot of a Taco Bell.
"We're a couple of hours away from Austin."
"Something's bugging me for a few days…"
"Yeah?"
"Why is this story called *Jackie Bonner*? I mean the further along it goes there is less and less of this woman you were in love with."
"That was the purpose of the story."
"To write her out of your life?"
"No, to write my feelings for her out of my life. We couldn't be friends until I did that."
"It sounds like she wasn't always a good friend herself."
"She wasn't, she went through a year or so of chaos and flux and so did I. Eventually we worked things out; last Fall."
"Has she ever read the story about her?"
"I have no idea. Sometimes I think she has, sometimes I think she hasn't. Honestly, I have no idea."

I had a bad dream last night: Getting back home and finding Allison with another man. The crazy thing was that guy she was fucking was my/our landlord Matt. I woke up upset and had no right to feel that way. We agreed that we are not exclusive; I have been with other women on the tour. It frightens me because I understand I have dreams like that because I have fallen for Allison. I'm pretty sure she has fallen for me as well, but I also know she is flighty. Maybe I see that because I possess that quality myself.

August 15, 2017

Sorry I haven't really written in the past couple of weeks, my mind has been elsewhere. It's four in the morning and I am drunk. In four hours I will need to be back in my cubicle doing—whatever it is I do. In that office.

I have not written on this blog since the 3rd. That was the day I got the call; my mother lost her job. More accurately, due to a neck injury she couldn't fulfill her job requirements anymore so they "had to let her go." My aunt wrote to me about this because my mother didn't want me to worry. Like that ever fucking stops. Like that has ever really stopped since 1976. Mom has had neck issues for years but not the health insurance to deal with it. I guess this year it has been getting worse and worse to the point in early July when she simply couldn't do her job anymore. Losing that job cuts her out $700 per month. Losing $700 per month means she doesn't have a roof over her head. My aunt and uncle are just getting by and can't really help her. They've offered to take her in but what about my mother's four dogs? What happens to them? After hearing from my aunt I sent my mother $1000 which means we're good through the end of August for her rent but it also means I won't be able to pay my own rent past Halloween. If you have been reading this blog—when I bother working on it—you know I have no money coming in for months. This is why I decided I had no choice but to get a job.

I went round to the temp agencies I have used in the past. I even bothered to put a tie on, polish my shoes, and shave my facial hair off. That was a mistake: I keep staring into the mirror and seeing a man older than I am prepared to be. Here I was, 49 and hustling to get some job I didn't want, the sort of job I thought I had left behind. I hated my mother for all her mistakes for a few moments. Moreso I hated myself for all of mine—and that never really stops. This is just the norm: People get old and their kids take care of them; it is only a problem in our case because I had to lead this artistic bohemian sort of life living in vans and playing music for Europeans and drunken managers. I stared at my face too long in the mirror and just got sadder and more frustrated than I had any right to be.

It happened amazingly fast as if God had some cruel sort of plan. No, this job saved my ass. I hate it but I am grateful for it like I have been for all the office jobs I have gotten in my life. It has just been weird going back.

My mother keeps writing to me and she is probably the last person I want to communicate with right now. I have expressed this on certain social networking pages and people have sent me private messages basically telling me I'm an asshole. They have no idea what the past 40 plus years have been like but I don't really feel like going into that now. This is already coming across bitter enough.

So, the past week I have been working in this office.
So, this past week I have been drinking again.
So, I have utterly no fucking idea what to do when the book comes out next month.
I need to throw myself into doing publicity and making sure people know about it—
How do I fit that in when I am working eight to four-thirty five days a week? This is a good paying job and they've promised health insurance when my probation is over in November—
And it just feels deeply wrong like every cubicle job I have ever had…
God, I fucking hate going on and on about this but I really thought I was free of this shit. I thought that since I have

sold two books and have my development deal I would never have to deal with straight jobs again but now I am back in that mess and it is genuinely fucking with me. I find myself alone in this studio drinking and reading Allison's poem over and over.

It's now half past five. I have been drinking water the past hour and a half in an attempt to dilute the alcohol. I called Allison, actually phoned her. She was asleep; I didn't ask if she was alone because honestly I didn't want to know. A was confused and then worried. I just broke down and told her how I have been reading that poem she sent me over and over the past few months—
I don't know, maybe I'll write about that conversation at a later date, right now I need to try and get an hour or two of sleep before the alarm.

I just looked out the window; it's a beautiful summer night. Part of me wants to go outside and just walk, just roam the streets and be in motion when the sky lights up the city. Stop for coffee and flirt disastrously; maybe take a notebook along and try and flesh out a few ideas. But I can't, I have to be at work in a couple of hours so I am turning off the computer and reluctantly crawling into bed.

November 10/11, 2013

I am writing this at the Flame Club in Downtown
Sacramento. The Flame Club plays an important role in the
whole Jackie Bonnie story. It was the end of March 2012
and JB and I had driven down from Chico. Our plan had
been to drink in Chico and find a sleazy motel to spend the
night in but that was not meant to be. We ended up at the
Flame Club, a place she knew and liked. We drank spicy
Bloody Marys. She bought us lunch. We had our first
kisses over there by the bar. You know how when you kiss
someone and then pull away to gauge their reaction?
I still see the look on Jackie's face.
I had to kiss her again.

I will not be kissing anyone for a while. If you have been
reading this blog you know I broke up with my Portland
girlfriend last month after six months of dating. If you
don't care to weed through old entries I met her at
Burgerville in early March. To keep out of Mark and
Laura's hair I'd be out late every night, wandering the
streets and writing in various cafes and cheap restaurants. I
could nurse a coffee and a cheeseburger for three hours.
Four bucks including tip. That was how I got to know
Chiandi, she worked nights at the Burgerville on
Hawthorne as an assistant manager. C was 22 and a couple
of years into a master's program. I know this may sound
like some wishful thinking on the part of this nearly 46 year
old writer, but it wasn't like that. Portland is full of weird
but somehow interesting people but I guess I stood out.
Andy—as I nicknamed her—didn't see me as boyfriend
material or anything like that, she just felt compelled to talk
to me. Eventually she allowed me to get refills of coffee.
Not long after that, she started slipping me an extra
cheeseburger because she knew how poor I was. A bit after

that we hung out away from Burgerville when she wasn't wearing a uniform and then we became involved. She rented a room in a large house in Beaverton. Her family had wanted her to continue living with them but she insisted on living away with roommates. Seeing as she is Indian I was surprised at both her standing up to them and them agreeing to let her move away. I was staying with Mark and Laura and I wouldn't have thought to bring anyone back to their house so I began spending more and more time in Beaverton. This was never a "dear Penthouse forum" sort of situation; I think Andy was looking for some fun and there was no risk in falling in love with me because I was so much older. I went into it looking as a way to excise my feelings for Jackie Bonner and I did to some degree; Andy and I used each other and were happy with the situation. In September she started seeing an old boyfriend and I kind of allowed myself to drop out of the picture.

You are probably still wrapping your head around a 22 year old wanting to be involved with someone my age, just a couple of years younger than her parents. I have no definite answer, only suspicions.

March 4, 2016

"A 22 year old?? Ike, no one is going to buy this bullshit!"
Maggie is laughing; she sounds a bit drunk but very happy
and it is contagious.
"You read November 10 and 11, 2013 I take it."
"Uh, yeah. You know, where you clearly write some nice
fiction about fucking a cute, Indian girl in her early
twenties."
I am sitting in my room in one of the Knoxville Super 8s. I
wonder if all the motels in Tennessee are this sketchy.
"I knew people would call bullshit on that one."
"Not to be harsh, Ike, because you are almost attractive in
your own curmudgeonly way, but you were 46 and white. It
is totally not believable that any 22 year old woman would
want to hook up with you."
"Thanks, I love you, too."
"I'm just being honest because I'm your manager. How is
this story believable? Let me guess, she had perfect tits and
looked like a Bollywood star."
"No. I mean, her tits were very nice, but she wasn't a
model. Very petite, glasses, very faint mustache, definitely
nerdy, but I found her beautiful."
"Still, this *character* was 22, Ike; make me believe it."
"We didn't break up because of an old boyfriend, though
that was going on and I didn't make a fuss because I didn't
give a shit."
"Hold on, you are *claiming* you actually were involved
with this 22 year old?"
"Yes, for five months or so. Not all the time because she
was so busy with school and work."
"Okay, as a woman, I have to say this sounds like the
fantasy of a sexually frustrated middle aged man."

397

"I know it sounds far-fetched but it happened, Maggie. I think I just met Andy at the right time and I think I offered her something she never had experienced before—"

"Oh, please!"

"Nothing like that; I think she was going through some sort of rebellion and I was a way to tell her parents 'fuck you'. You should have seen their reaction when she took me home for dinner. That was a lifetime's worth of awkwardness in a couple of hours. The thing is, Maggie, I have no idea if Andy was actually even into me. I may have just been a way to pass the time, a way to piss off her parents; maybe she was bored with the life she had experienced and here was this middle-aged white guy who was into her and treated her differently than guys in their twenties. I don't care, to be honest. I think we just used each other for our own reasons and it was fun but now it is in the past."

(Maggie does not type for over a minute).

"When I was 18 I dated a 35 year old. Well, dating is a polite way to put it, but there were definitely merits to being with an older man so, okay, maybe it is a bit more plausible—"

"Okay, if you lived it then when would you doubt me?"

"Because you were ten years past 35. And she is Indian. And the whole story about meeting her at Burgerville—was that how it happened?"

"No."

"I knew it!"

"I was *working* at Burgerville and she was my boss. I don't write about that because the whole 'writing in strange places' thing is a bit more romantic than paper hats and flipping burgers."

"You worked at Burgerville in Portland?"

"Nights. And during the day I eventually had office work. That's the real story of how I was able to save up for a van."

"Why did you stop working at Burgerville?"

"The manager caught Andy and I fucking in the storeroom…"

"Oh, fuck off, Ike!"

"If you knew Andy you would believe it. You see, she grew up in this conservative environment. It's a terrible cliché, but she toed the line and followed the rules and did as her family expected her to—she was a virgin until she was 21. That was when she just got sick of it and kind of went crazy. She started smoking pot and letting her grades drop and hooking up with middle aged men. What happened in the storeroom, I think she planned that; I think it was both a fuck you to the manager and a way to get me out of the restaurant."

"But she was your boss, she would be fired—"

"Unless she was fucking the manager, who was married."

"Wow."

"Yeah, Andy kind of went off the deep end, she would make a great movie character. And this is why we broke up. That summer she started in on coke and was on the verge of dropping out of school, she was even carrying a gun."

"I can see why you broke up, she sounds like a lunatic."

"No, I could handle that, and it was fun hooking up with her; her family threatened to hurt me."

"Aren't all Indians like Gandhi?"

"Apparently not. What happened was pretty gangsta. A well-dressed black guy approached me in a bar I went to on a regular basis. He was very polite, could charm the birds out of the trees, but he mentioned the family name and basically told me that my relationship with Andy was not in my best interest. I told her about it, she seemed bored with the whole conversation and said 'whatever'."

"Why is *that* not in the blog, Ike? That is amazing."

"Because I thought people would believe that even less than what I put up."

"OK, and you meet up with Jackie Bonner at the Flame Club—what happened there? Did you guys hook up? Did she end up throwing a drink in your face? Did you throw a drink in her face?"

"That is all in a blog I will be putting up soon."

March 5, 2016

"I hate you, Ike."

Those four words after my phone beeps; Maggie.

"But in a weird way you love me—"

"There weren't any female employees with an Indian last name at that Burgerville in 2013. In *any* month of 2013."

"How do you know that?"

"That is not important, Ike. So, what is the real story? Did you work there or did you write there or neither? Did you walk by it once and get ideas about a story—"

"All three. When I got to Portland I would write there a couple of nights a week. The assistant manager started talking to me, suggested I fill out an application, and by the end of the month I had a job."

"Was it even a woman?"

"No."

"You know I am going to find it nearly impossible to believe you in the future."

"I won't lie about anything important."

"Important is a subjective term."

I am halfway between Knoxville and Philadelphia and parked at a rest stop in the mountains. It is freezing cold but I am making myself hike around this scenic area as I text Maggie.

"So, you did not date a crazy Indian girl with a peach fuzz mustache—"

"Not even peach fuzz, even fainter than that—it was like a peach fuzz mustache had been walking by a wall when the bombs landed in Hiroshima."

"I hate writers. Okay, did you date *anyone* in Portland? And if you say you had a tryst with an Iranian woman with a fondness for playing the tambourine I will kill you."

"Hey, that's pretty good."

"Maybe you and your pathological lies are rubbing off on me."

"Sounds like sexual harassment, but in a good way."

"Just…continue, Ike."

"When I was working in a hotel a couple of months later I hooked up with a co-worker a few times, a manager actually."

"How old was she?"

"Not 22."

"Go on."

"It's cold out here, my fingers are getting numb. I'll email you later just trust me when I say it was a boring story; fun, but boring. Typical. Co-workers in an office, hanging out after work and so on."

"Hey, when are you going to write about Jackie Bonner and that night in the Flame Club in late 2013?"

"Oh, hey, we're breaking up, I am losing my signal."

"I hate you, Ike."

September 5, 2017

I was good last night, I am going to try and be good again
tonight. I got really drunk Friday night and spent Saturday
in a daze which made me concerned that I was losing
control of my drinking again. I *am* a little scared I am
losing control of my drinking again so I did not drink
yesterday or Sunday. Monday was busy at work---frenetic
really---but I was determined not to drink and somehow I
kept that promise to myself.

Ever since we started communicating again, Maggie insists
that we use cameras for some reason. I'm just glad things
seem to be back to normal; after what happened in
Mendocino I was worried they wouldn't be the same.
Tonight she greeted me with a big smile. Maggie looked
really pretty, beautiful even; suspiciously made up for
being on the camera with one of her writers. I sometimes
wonder if she's into me then dismiss the idea as arrogant or
vain or just dangerous.
"You look really good, Mags."
"You look tired, Ike."
"I love you, too."
"Still working in that office?"
"No choice; I told you about how my mother can't work
anymore."
We spent a couple of minutes talking about my mother and
then Maggie got to why she called.
"You ready for Saturday, Ike?"
"Oh yeah, after all the work we put in this book that past
four years I am totally ready. Hey, how have talks
regarding the third book been going? I haven't heard from
Kimberly."
Maggie looked a bit uncomfortable—maybe she was
regretting the whole camera idea.

"The US publisher has decided not to pursue a third book. The good news is, the European publisher is interested…but they need a commitment."

"What, like *have the book done within a year* sorta commitment?" *Fuck me.*

"Partially that and partially they want you to do publicity in Europe this fall like you did last year."

"What's the point? Why can't we film things and do email and phone interviews?"

"They were impressed last year how you used part of your advance to go over there and hit all those tiny bookstores and local net shows and everything else. The problem is, they *expect* that now and if you opt out of going over they will think you are not fully committed."

"This is a problem for two reasons: One, I do not have the money to go to Europe and two I have to hold onto this job to keep paying my mother's rent."

Maggie was looking down; I couldn't see her face and the fact she was hiding her face made me really nervous.

"They are willing to advance the money to travel to Europe, but beyond that it is up to you."

"But I'll lose my apartment and I won't be able to pay my mother's rent."

I was really hoping not to drink tonight…

"I really need money, Maggie—is there any work or any way I could land another development deal or something?"

"I'll see what I can do, Ike. I can't promise anything, but I'll try and help you out."

"OK, and I'll try and sort things out on my end."

That was seven hours ago. No, I have not had a drink but I am wound up and can't sleep. If I don't go to Europe they will not sign on for the third book. We could find another publisher, but I will have this huge black mark on my "resume." I could sublet this apartment for the rest of the term but what about my mother's rent? I have maybe

$2000 right now—if I give it all to my mother she'll be good through the end of November—and what will I do when I get back from Europe? If they are giving me an advance to travel over there—(which would probably be $3-4000 I am guessing)—I'll be paying that back for a long time which, again, means I won't have any money coming in so who knows how I will live.

I have no idea what to do.

December 10, 2015

I am beginning to regret renting this room. It's not full on regret, that will come later, this is more like those first moments when you see your regret off in the distance: *I knew I'd run into you again.* It's about my landlord Matt. He's nice, maybe even annoyingly nice; so earnest it's like a motorcycle wreck of good intentions. When I checked out the room three weeks ago and reported my feelings to some friends they accused me of being a "misanthrope with an unhealthy suspicion of nice people."
I should never share my suspicions with people who know me so well.

I decided to give Matt the benefit of the doubt—little did I know about the sandals. When he showed me the room he was wearing normal footwear, they even had laces. Plus he had been suffering at work so he was cranky and consequently we were nearly on the same wavelength. The iPod was not hooked up to the speakers in the living room so I was not made privy to his seeming obsession with Hootie and the Blowfish.
Who the fuck still listens to Hootie and the Blowfish in 2015?
If you have been reading this blog you are already aware that I am an asshole. You also know I try and mention something positive each time I write so here goes: I had a really good on-line chat with Maggie this morning; I think she is going to sign on as my manager. That would be *huge* because she can get me pitch meetings and maybe I can get some screen work. I messaged my literary agent to share my good news—(including that Maggie could also help set up the European tour for next spring)—and Kimberly murdered my good mood.
"Don't rush into anything, Ike."

"She's very respected. Plus, she can get me those pitch meetings I have been going on and on about for two years."
"I know about her. She will try and become your overall manager."
"Are you worried she won't respect the fact you're my lit agent?"
"Not worried, I know it. Give it a year or two and she will try and take over our responsibilities."
"I hope you understand I wouldn't just jettison you guys…"
"I know you wouldn't, Ike; but Maggie could put you in a situation where either you go with her or it seriously damages your career."
I didn't like where the conversation was going so I turned it to book sales and whether or not she had a chance to go over the manuscript I sent over (*Purgatory*). The call ended on a good note but my good wishes were not entirely sincere; I have worked so long and so hard to get a good manager and now I have one lined up and Kimberly doesn't want me to go with her.
No, I'm going with Maggie if she wants to work with me; Kimberly is just being territorial.

Allison and I are casual again I guess. She made this big deal out of my birthday and turned it into this big proclamation of love. It was great, I really wanted to give into it and did a bit, but a few days ago she got freaked out and now I suspect she is back with her girlfriend. Allison runs off yelling about how she needs time alone but then she gets lonely and runs back to her girlfriend. Or, as has happened in the past, A is running from her girlfriend and ends up with me. I know she loves us both, I suspect she would marry either of us, she just has the misfortune of being an acutely solitary person who is also acutely in need of affection.

September 6, 2017

I do not remember work today. I have no idea how much I screwed up or did right for that matter. I remember lunch; I remember sitting outside, picking at my sandwich, and leaving two-thirds of it. It was a beautiful afternoon. There were these strange birds watching me as I tried to eat. My sandwich was left on the picnic table for them.

Called Kimberly at lunch to see if she was busy for dinner. She said that her and Alec already had plans but that she could tell by the tone of my voice something was wrong. I explained about the situation with the European publisher and my mother and it was all I could do to not get choked up.
"I hate to say it, but you brought it on yourself, Ike."
"What do you mean?"
"Maggie. I told you almost two years ago she would be a problem."
"I needed a manager, Kimberly. She did get me two development deals and arranged for the European tour last year; she has been a huge asset."
"I warned you about her, Ike. It has finally come to the point where you have to choose who you are going to work with."
"That is not fair at all. I can see about getting her to back out of working with the publishers—"
"The thing is, you have already chosen. Or, more accurately, you have allowed her to choose for you. We've been talking and have decided that we want to end our contract with you, Ike."
I was getting angry. I know a lot of it was the stress I was under, but it also felt like Kimberly was being petty and shitty.

"OK, fine, whatever. I am gonna let you go now, send me whatever you need to send me and I'll sign it."

"Are you okay, Ike?"

"Not really."

I hung up on her and I immediately felt shitty for hanging up on her. I *had* allowed Maggie to walk all over Kimberly and her partners. I *had* been in a rush to sign a manager. Kimberly was right, I just couldn't admit it.

"Well, you are officially the manager for my writing now."

"What happened?"

I told Maggie about my conversation with Kimberly, leaving out all the warnings K had issued about Maggie. She didn't have the camera on this time and it made me uneasy.

"It was bound to happen, you outgrew them."

"Outgrew them? I am still broke. I can lose my apartment in a couple of months and I have no idea how I am going to help my mother."

"I can help you, but we need to renegotiate your contract with the studio."

"What do you mean?"

"(Name of a currently hot actress) is interested in getting involved. I happen to be acquainted with her brother and can get in with her. When I get her on our side, we can re-do the terms of your contract."

"I didn't know you could do that."

"Usually you can't, but I can. There's one thing, Ike."

"Yeah?"

"I can get you maybe a point more, but I want half of your points on the show. You'll only come out half a point behind what you're getting now."

I had no idea how to react to that—had Maggie engineered this whole situation to fuck me? Was it really a good deal? Would it be that, now that she was up for getting some of the money, M would move things forward? The truth is I have been feeling more desperate and it has been a struggle not to let that desperation make my decisions for me. I kept thinking of Maggie when she visited me in Mendocino, all the things that happened that I have never included in this blog. I had no idea what to do, but I wasn't about to let her see that.

"Maybe that could work, but I am going to need money if I am going to Europe and to survive when I get back."

"How much?"

"Ten thousand. If you give a ten thousand dollar advance personally, I will agree to your terms."

"I think I can make that happen, let me think about this a bit and I'll get back to you."

I started pacing around the apartment, really wanting to drink. There is a corner store a block and a half away; I could have been back in my apartment in ten minutes with a bottle. Was giving up that half of my points for $10000 idiotic? Maybe. What if the show became huge? What if those points became worth hundreds of thousands of dollars or even just $25000? Part of me was chiding myself for being greedy, part of me really didn't want to be a sucker. The bottom line was that I was desperate and felt I had very few options.

February 13, 2014

Lots of people were worried about me a year ago when I moved back to Portland. The thing is, for the most part I was doing good; I was back in a city I love and felt a sense of excitement and purpose in life. I was alone a lot which allowed me to really sort things out in my mind. The only thing that troubled me were my feelings for Jackie Bonner. I was so wrapped up in her then and couldn't stop thinking about her. I was an idiot just wasting my time and my energy on some woman who could care less about me. I know that now--I knew it then, but I still had to work through it and it took into that Spring. I threw myself into many different things—volunteering at a crisis hotline, taking photographs, working with other musicians, and eventually getting a job. Don't get me wrong, I still thought about her; I thought of her kissing other guys and falling in love with them and all sorts of other things I had no business thinking about. There was a period of time when we couldn't even be friends; my feelings for her were too much for either of us to bear. That only really changed last Fall.

I am down in Phoenix for a few weeks doing a temp assignment. Four of us from the agency are setting up a new store in a mall. It's a funny gig but it's good to have work and to be someplace where it's relatively warm. Plus I know lots of people here and have been doing a lot of visiting.

It's tricky living in a van here in Phoenix as it has become a kind of a police state. I've already been rousted twice; one time the cop actually started yelling about how he could arrest me. It was ugly. If you have been reading this blog you know I am very careful with cops. I always keep my hands in sight, always smile, never argue or even raise my voice—and this pig still got all 5150 and red in the face like the stupid pig he was. Phoenix—something about all that sun just cooks the cops' brains, I guess.

February 16, 2019

The snow began falling as I lay in the bathtub, I sipped my glass of whiskey as I watched it fall. It was coming down feathery and soft, drifting a little in the wind. The chill in the air was sucking the warmth out of the bath water as I lay on my back and looked up at the stars through the glass roof. I was not worried about when I'd be able to get back down the road, I was lost in the moment; enjoying the stars and the solitude and the contrast between the warmth of the water and the chill of the snowy night.

I lasted maybe twenty minutes in the tub before the late winter's night drew all the warmth out. Putting on my sandals and robe, I trudged back to the bus and let myself in. Allison was still asleep in the back, her fever about to finally break. I am sitting in the driver's seat writing this, looking out into a night made nearly day by the bright blanket of snow. The road has disappeared. We are all alone out here. It is peaceful and still and the stars are flickering overhead...

November 10, 2013 (more on)

I had not seen her in nearly a year. Seeing her smiling and looking glad to see me brought all those stupid feelings back to the surface---feelings I had been trying to kill the past year. I had been hopeful I was past them but seeing Jackie Bonner in that bar looking happy to see me reminded me they had simply been dormant; hibernating like some huge, vicious beast that can kill with one swipe of its paw. I got up and she came over to hug me. I wish she hadn't nearly as much as I wished that hug would have never ended. I could feel her warmth, smell her, hear her breathing and in my mind the enormous murderous yet somehow pathetic beast was rearing up, ready to kill; the smell of my blood driving it towards a peculiar sort of madness. I wanted to cry, wanted to fuck her, wanted to push her down a flight of stairs, wanted to profess my love with intensity and passion and conviction and foolishness-- foolishness above all else. The bartender came over and took her drink order; in my idiotic jealous mind I was certain she was flirting with him. I knew I had to make my excuses and flee at the first opportunity but that was my brain speaking and compared to my heart my brain's voice is small and meek whereas my heart can scream loud enough to drown out the thunder or a gunshot or---most definitely---reason.

Jackie and I caught up for maybe ten minutes and with each moment I could feel my love for her regenerating itself like some poisonous tree that you chop down and desperately tear the stump from the earth only to have a stubborn root pop out of the ground and create a new tree that rises from the soil like a curse. I managed to make an excuse after maybe twenty minutes. Jackie just looked at me for a few seconds, probably understanding why I felt the need to leave--I have no idea, I just liked her looking at me, being close enough to see that she needed to trim her fingernails and that she had rushed putting her lipstick on. I didn't want to go; I wanted to share another drink, maybe suggest we share the rest of our lives but I got up and gave her a hug goodbye. She kissed me on the cheek and it took everything inside me not to turn my head so I could kiss her lips. It is burned in my memory what it is like to kiss her lips and the way her eyes look after she has been kissed and enjoyed it. I held her tightly and thought of how much I loved her and maybe some tiny but insistent part of me was hoping she'd pick up on what I was feeling and beg me to stay, suggest we go back to her apartment and do stupid amazing loving hateful savage tender things to each other. She said nothing, I said nothing, and I walked out of that bar like I have walked out of countless bars. But this was nothing like any other time I had ever walked out of a bar in the past, this was something else, a feeling so intense it is beyond tears, beyond any sort of expression.

Standing on the sidewalk I willed myself not to turn around and walk back in there, to a woman I love so deeply, so stupidly. My feelings for Jackie Bonner are just a beautiful mess, the glory of self destruction, a vast fiery pathetic celebration of wasted energy and emotion. It's funny how our deepest incarnations of idiocy bring out the beauty in us, the poetry.

I walked out to the van still fighting the urge to walk back in that bar, back to something that has dug my heart out, stomped it, and set fire to the ruins too many times to count. I could feel my keys in my hand but wasn't allowing myself to remember how to use them. I could see Jackie Bonner's Jetta parked next to the van and thought of all the times I had ridden in it, sharing a beer with her as she drove. I knew it'd be in my best interest if I never saw that car again, never saw her again, but I have never embraced or even acknowledged my best interests with respect to Jackie Bonner. It took what felt like an hour to unlock the door, climb behind the wheel, start the engine, and drive away...

November 29, 2017

"I considered a career in the arts but I am allergic to poverty."

Some smartass on the ship back from Europe said that to me. I guess it was better than the endless complaining he did about Europeans and how "everyone smoked" and that the food was weird and that there wasn't enough of it. I was trapped with that asshole for a week and a half. For some reason he thought I liked him or maybe he liked me and didn't care if I liked him or not because he always tracked me down. Believe me, I tried to hide from him but he always managed to find me and his soft, red face would light up.

Nowhere to run in the middle of the Atlantic, buddy.

The sea got rough halfway across and that gave Bob or Buddy or whatever his name was something new to bitch about. He was also constantly throwing up and smelled like puke for half of the trip. To make matters worse Buddy or Bob or Bill was a close talker. He was always crunching on breath mints but they weren't strong enough to mask the vomit smell so it was like this constant wave of Altoids and puke. I used to love Altoids but I can't even look at them now.

What can you do? I didn't want to be an asshole and I hate confrontations so I just put up with his vomit breath and hateful rants about Europe and catty comments about artists and how we're all poor or drunk or both. That should have issued me a license to tell him to fuck off but I couldn't. Maybe I felt sorry for him and his petty little view of the world. Imagine being trapped in Bill or Bob or Buddy's head for ten minutes let alone a lifetime? I would be scrambling for a rope and looking for a stout branch after five minutes.

Today I turned fifty. Allison surprised me by coming up to Portland for my birthday. I have stopped going on and on about that poem she sent me last spring; I have said too much and I know that because the awkward silences have gotten longer and longer every time I bring the poem up to her. I can't help it, I am still blown away; no one has ever written me a poem before let alone one so beautiful. But, I'll just keep it to myself from now on.

A showed up with this strange brown duffel bag---she has always been the sort of woman who finds bags like that and adopts them. We have been having a really good reunion, the sort where you pick up where you left off and it feels like it's only been several hours and not several months. I hadn't realized how much I missed her until I opened my front door and saw her standing there with a gorgeous smile and an ugly, brown bag.

Today I have allowed myself to remain in a sort of drunken haze. Allison got the ball rolling by suggesting we have Bloody Marys with lunch because we woke up too late for breakfast. I took her to Foster Burger and I have a couple of cheap Mexican restaurants in mind for dinner. It's funny to be riding on all the TriMet buses I ride on all the time with Allison. It's odd, but it feels good, really good. Comfortable. Part of me wants to be impulsive and invite her to move in with me. I have been having these impulses every half an hour since she got here; believe it or not one actually woke me up this morning and I sat up in bed and looked at her for a couple of minutes as I debated waking her up. I think it's good I have been keeping these feelings to myself--why spoil a good visit? Why risk wreaking things when most likely Allison is not up for that sort of thing? Am I? Who knows; I think so but I am not certain.

Maggie is excited about the show so I am trying to overcome my natural pessimism whenever we chat. If you have been reading this blog you understand my natural pessimism is a big thing to fight. The producer in charge of the show is a famous guy. The cliché that keeps coming to mind is "midas touch" because every project he gets involved with blows up and becomes a big deal. Could that happen with my concept? I have been leading this tiny, threadbare life for so long it is impossible to fathom. I mean, I totally believe in and love my work (usually) but I have always seen my career as "on the fringes" where I would be "some cult guy" and usually poor and scrambling for money. I have never seen myself as a name in the New York Book Review that your friends know, I would be the sort of writer that when you mention my name to your buddies they'd think you were purposefully reading obscure shit to be hip like so many people in Portland do. This producer is not obscure. I know when I mentioned his name in the past I got a lot of impressed sounding comments from you guys. What if this became some huge show? What if I never had to scramble and hustle and fret over money ever again? What if I could help my mother and all the other people in my life who are struggling financially? That ten grand I got from Maggie is more than three-quarters gone--the tour, paying my rent and my mother's. Luckily I got some good press in Europe so sales have picked up. A lot of it is for the electronic version which means less money but I'll take what I can get, you know?

OK, Allison is out of the shower now, time for us to catch a bus and get some Mexican food...

January 3, 2018

Maggie has deflated like a cheap balloon. The show airs in sixteen days and it could be dead before anyone sees it. The problem is that the Producer--according to the rumors Maggie hears--has been pissing a lot of people off in the industry. Some people blame drugs, some blame ego, some claim he has gone off his meds. The end result is the same: He has gone from a prince to poison in the space of a few months. The fucked up thing---(or even *more* fucked up thing)---is that from everything we've heard the three episodes they have shot so far are amazing. It fascinates me, taking a semi-cool little idea I had a few years ago and blowing it up into this *event*.

Maggie heard the bad rumors yesterday and clearly is shaken by them. Every time we chat I can tell from all her typos that she is drunk. She never uses the camera anymore. We finally talked about what happened in Mendocino last night; it seemed a terrible time to bring it up but she wanted to hash it out. Even though I couldn't see her face and she certainly would never admit it I knew she was crying. Part of it was probably what happened in the van and part was what happened with the show---I know she had plans for that show. M wants to build her own reputation and not having reached her goals by her early forties has made her feel like a failure. She has me and a couple of other cult artists but she wants to manage a big act or at least a medium sized one. I want her to have that, too; I love Maggie as I am sure she loves me. Our love for each other is as strange as it is meaningful.

Who knows if she will ever get her ten thousand back out of our deal. My "third book scam" is already coming back around to bite me on the ass. I thought I could milk it, thought I could create some mystery, a real happening--- craft and grow expectations and blow it up into an event over a decade or two but the Publisher is not having it. A

lot of my heroes, writers and rock bands, they knew how to work the "scam," getting more money and support from their labels or publishers, building up all this hype—
That hasn't been happening for me.
The Publisher has been curt, has been taking exactly zero bullshit/no quarter from yours truly. They are emailing or texting or requesting to chat every day: *What have you completed? Can I send it over? Do you have the basic plot completed? What about that chapter you were talking about last week---have you finished it?*
Fucking Germans: They are so anal and precise and on top of things. If the Publisher was based in France or Spain maybe I could have pulled this scam off but the Germans are clearly not having it. They make the trains run on time and they will make sure this book will be out by the Fall of '19---a book I have done very little work on and feel no inspiration to complete; even completing a chapter is beyond me. I write all the time, if you have been reading this blog you know that, but I have done squat on the third book. They only advanced me $10k and I am seriously doubting I will get a Deusche Mark more. They are not happy. I feel like I am sinking deeper and deeper into a fucked up situation I can only blame myself for---
And the potential for the show is crumbling before my very eyes.
And if I don't make this Publisher happy my reputation will probably be fucked.
Everything just feels toxic, fucked up, a series of disasters.
I am beginning to feel scared, to be honest...

May 22-23, 2013

The past few weeks have been a blur. I got a second job; it's only fifteen hours per week but it makes the possibility of buying a van more likely. With my regular job I make around $900 each month. My rent is $350 and a bus pass is $100 so if I live frugally I get by alright. I have been able to survive in Portland. I may see if I can get a loan from someone to buy the van sooner---as much as I love this town it'd be good to get away for awhile. Of course, I already borrowed money to buy my netbook and to bring some stuff up from California but the more I think about the van the more it sounds like a good idea. The thing is that I don't want to just give up on the rest of the world by being close minded and saying "Okay, I'll stay in Portland the rest of my life." I know there are other amazing cities out there to discover and explore and get lost in and fall in love with. I should be exploring and going on adventures while I am still young enough to do it. This is why I am leaning towards buying the van and vacating my rented room. On the other hand I have a really good job for the first time in three years. I don't make very much money but it's still a good job. The only drawback is Dalhia; she isn't as much a drawback as a complication. I find her attractive which normally wouldn't be a problem as the majority of women I find attractive are not attracted to me. Dalhia, on the other hand, flirts with me sometimes---she does that casual touching thing and when our eyes meet I am always the first one to blink. My boss has made it clear that she doesn't want me dating Dalhia. I have no idea why she would have a problem with it just as I can't fathom how she thinks it's any of her business but it still creates a problem. Dalhia is really cute. Not like a model or anything like that, she isn't even beautiful in a conventional fashion, but I find her really attractive. She is in her early thirties and carrying a little extra weight; devastating eyes and a great smile. She told me where she is hanging out tonight and I am really tempted to go there and see what happens.

(Fourteen Hours Later)
It's a little after seven and I just got home. Walked maybe three miles, didn't feel like taking a bus, just wanted to walk. It's a beautiful late Spring morning; it feels like Portland is finally warming up. I didn't even need my jacket after the first mile. It's a beautiful day. I may be in a lot of trouble. Portland is gorgeous right now and I may have done something that will force me to leave it again.

I didn't sleep last night for various reasons. I spent a lot of time lying in a strange bed in the dark staring at the ceiling; I was feeling really good and at the same time understanding that my tendency for self-destruction may have reared its ugly head again...

October 23, 2015

I think I just got my first death threat but with Miguel it is
hard to know for sure. Miguel lives in either Barcelona or
Madrid and is enamored with my book. Enamored? No,
he is *obsessed* with it. The book is only 190 pages long and
M has already sent me over two hundred pages of his crazy
letters. He mails them to the Publisher who forwards them
to me. Who the fuck even writes letters anymore? I mean,
normally I love writing letters and usually I like getting
them but it is an anachronism, isn't it? The paper smells
like flowery perfume, the sort old ladies use because it got
them laid back in 1913 and those were good memories and
don't we like to surround ourselves with good memories? I
get the bad feeling Miguel is naked when he writes those
damned letters, naked and possibly sobbing. In my
overactive imagination I see him naked and blubbering as
he sprites cheap perfume he probably stole from his
grandmother on the weird, peach colored paper he always
writes on with a black ball point pen. On one hand it is
really cool to have someone who is really into your work---
on the other hand Miguel is a spooky, little fuck.
The world would miss you if you disappeared but life is
unpredictable isn't it, Ike?
How the hell would *you* take that? I don't think I'll write
back. I mean, I haven't responded to the last three letters he
sent and have felt guilty about it but this time there won't
be any guilt.

I made the mistake of telling Kimberly about Miguel. I can
tell it was a mistake because I can tell she is scared for me,
a lot more concerned than I am. I am a little unsettled and
maybe a bit creeped out but I have always known people
like Miguel are part of the deal. I am a student of pop
culture; some people would go as far to say I am as

obsessed about it as Miguel is obsessed about my book. I know what happens when "your art enters the big bad world"---there is always at least one Miguel. They send creepy letters reeking of old lady perfume or pubic hair or freaky little songs they wrote about you or razors colored with their dried blood. They tell you about how Mr. Drizzle---(the goblin that lives in their coffee grinder)---has told them that you are *the one*. It's part of the package. Whenever I am in Spain I will have eyes in the back of my head for Miguel but I am not overly concerned.

If I ignore him he will move onto another obsession.

February 23, 2018

It's official: We're fucked.
Five episodes shot, four aired, and that's it.
Maggie is so upset she can't even talk to me about it.
Thanks to my natural pessimism I am doing better than her
but I am still pretty upset. If you have been reading this
blog you know I was depending on that show to bring in
some money---especially since the Publisher has expressed
a desire to tear up the contract for the third book and
request my advance back. Fucking Germans. I mean, I
could just knock out a piece of shit in order to fulfill my
contract but I may as well take my reputation and my pride
out in a field and shoot it in the fucking head. It would also
be a dick move. Not to be full of myself but I have readers
out there who will buy the book the day it comes out even
if they don't have the money to spend on it. I know what
that's like and I know how it feels when an artist you're
into betrays you by phoning it in or just tossing some
deathless piece of shit out so they can get a payday. It's a
lousy move and I really don't want to do that but I am
scrambling to find other options. The show has died, my
second development deal is a long way from getting a
green light, and I have no inspiration regarding the third
book. One of Mom's dogs needed surgery and that was two
grand so my money problems are getting more dire.

I need to get Kimberly back in. Maybe she could sell my
non-fiction stuff and Maggie could be in charge of the
fiction. I have some really strong non-fiction but Maggie
has not been having luck finding a publisher for it. Could I
get Kimberly in on that deal? Could I get Maggie to agree?
Man, she is not even communicating right now; I'd have
better luck teaching an otter how to play hockey.

I have become friends with a photographer in Madison, Wisconsin. She tells me it's a cool city and there's a strong art community. More importantly, rent is really cheap. The question is if I could deal with the cold. Those Midwest winters are no joke---people die. Even the winters in Portland still get to me and I've been toying with the idea of buying another van and following the weather. That'd be cheaper than rent. Seeing as I am 50 I wonder how long I could do that. *Why* would I want to do that again? I've gotten spoiled having indoor plumbing.

February 23, 2014

I really shouldn't be drinking this much. I shouldn't be
drinking this much or spending this much money. I am
operating on the excuse that I am creative in bars, that I get
a lot of work done in places like this, but that could just be
an alcoholic making excuses. If you have been reading this
blog you know I am in Phoenix on a long term assignment.
I know people in this town but it's such a big city and my
friends are few enough that it is an impossible ratio. So, I
bounce from bar to bar, nursing a cheap beer for an hour or
so before moving on unless I have made a strong
connection and am getting a lot of work done/am
inspired/whatever. It's not like in Portland. When I was in
Portland it was easy to walk everywhere and the buses ran
late and the town generally felt safer.

I rarely feel lonely but I am aware of how alone I am.
Sitting in a bar full of strangers laughing and having a good
time with their friends makes that understanding clear.
Being alone works for me, however, so I am not bothered.
A year ago in Portland I was walking miles every night,
just wandering around and sitting in bars by myself writing
or doing my stupid cartoons or flirting with bartenders. I
was unemployed and broke and staying in Mark and
Laura's guest room but it was still a good time. I felt really
alive for the first time in a year and life made sense in a
weird way. It's a cheesy thing to say but it felt good to be
alive. I mean, it still feels good to be alive, even in Phoenix,
but it's not the same as it was in Portland, there's not that
same connection, that feeling of "home."

I made a life in Portland and then I fucked it up. I was
renting a room in a cool house and I had a good job in a
city I love and I had to just throw a wrench in things by
hooking up with Dalhia. I *knew* that would lead to disaster

429

but I tend to embrace disaster which is probably why I tracked her down at that bar and then went home with her. I honestly have no idea why I do these things. Is it boredom? Is it that I don't feel I deserve a decent life? I have no fucking idea. My boss was on the verge of tears when she fired me. She kept asking *why* and it was clear to me she felt deeply betrayed and I felt like the biggest asshole in town. I *had* betrayed her; I had also betrayed myself. Why? I have been turning this over and over in my head the past several months and I have no idea why I had to sabotage things.

Everyone has music in their lives: Some people need beautiful, simple melodies and some people need driving rhythms and some people need dissonance.
Some people have impatience and boredom hounding them like ghosts.
Some people like crying because they feel like they need to pay for whatever laughter they have in their lives.
Maybe some people are just sick: The idea of being happy, of everything being easy makes their skin crawl. Man, all I wanted in life was to be a creative genius. That may sound like a lot but it's really nothing. In fact, it's pretty fucking meaningless when you really think about it. Yeah, maybe I can write well and am pretty good at music but there are so many things---most things, really---that I am completely useless at. There are so many defeats to a handful of victories and I'm pretty sure you feel the same way. But those victories mean a lot, don't they? It's like how anything that's scarce becomes very precious. For all I know I may ensure my victories are few and far between so they remain precious. Maybe success in any shape or form scares me because I'm afraid if I get it someone will just snatch it away, I have no fucking idea...

April 3, 2018

"We're getting an amazing following for the show."
Maggie. She sounds happy for the first time in months.
"I thought it was cancelled."
"Over a month ago and luckily for us a lot of people are pissed off about it."
"Tell them to get in line..."
"This could be an amazing development, Ike; we could be sitting on another *Carnivale* or *Firefly*."
"Neither show was ever renewed."
"Come on, Ike; let me be happy."
"Sorry, it *is* amazing, just bittersweet."
"I know, but you go on and on about needing money and this could help."
"Can they package four episodes?"
"Five plus outtakes and behind the scenes footage. Maybe they could film an interview with you or something."
"I'd be up for that. Hey, since you're in a good mood, Mags..."
I brought up the idea of bringing Kimberly back in to handle the non-fiction. Though I had been dreading Maggie's response she took it quite well.
"I know you need money to help your mother and, yeah, I haven't had any luck finding a home for your non-fiction so I am open to the idea."
"Thanks for understanding."
"Do you think Kimberly will up for it?"
"I have no idea."
I really didn't.

"I don't think that'd be a good idea, Ike."
Just the reaction I was dreading from Kimberly. I guess it would have been unreasonable to expect a good reaction for both of them.
"It will be different this time; a strict division of control."
"Whose side will you be on in a conflict, Ike?"

"Mine. And my side is keeping the peace so all three of us can sell books."

"That was a surprisingly good answer, but I am really leery of this..."

"Please just think about it, okay? I really love working with you."

A long enough pause to make me anxious.

"Give me a couple of days, okay?"

"Thank you."

After we ended the chat session I thought about that morning I woke up next to Kimberly. Should we be working together after that? Did the fact I didn't remember any of it make it okay? I wonder if Maggie asked herself similar questions after Mendocino?

March 26, 2016

I don't like this restaurant. The food looks terrible and overpriced and the staff is rude. I really don't want to leave. No--I want to stay here all night---let me sleep all night in your Spain kitchen. Turn me out and I'll wander and find Miguel on every corner.

If you have been reading this blog you know about Miguel, my Spanish stalker from last year. He sent a whole bunch of creepy letters that mercifully petered out in early November. My instincts told me that was too easy, that I would be hearing from Miguel again. Maybe it would be in the form of more creepy letters that reeked of old lady perfume or maybe it would be a personal appearance when I toured Spain. The thing is, I threw out his letters and couldn't remember if he was from Madrid or Barcelona and I was the one who decided what town in Spain we visited. Lots of people recommended Madrid over Barcelona so I went with that. It probably didn't matter; I'm sure creepy Miguel would have shown up in any city west of the Pyrenees. I was leery of him doing something violent if his adoration went sour when it became clear I was not a willing recipient of his nasty smelling letters as full of deranged fawning as they were typos. I had no idea what he looked like. I get pictures from men and women all the time, some of them nude—(sadly mostly guys)---but none from Miguel. What did he look like? Wild eyed like an assassin or a timeshare salesman? Wearing a mask of normality? I hadn't a clue. All I could do was be aware of my surroundings and not let anyone's hands get within stabbing range. I didn't see Miguel as a shooter: Shooting you can do from a distance, it's very impersonal, kind of a rude way to kill someone if you stop to think about it. No, Miguel would be a stabber. He'd want to be up close and drive that knife in, break the resistance of flesh, just fuck you with the blade.

He'd want to be close enough to be sprayed with your blood and feel your breathing change as you became a dying man.

The bookstore was tiny and in an old part of town that reeked of olives---black olives. I speak some Spanish but it's Mexican Spanish and not *Espana* Spanish and the owner of the store was being snooty and making jokes with his chums about that. All of them were fat and had bad skin and the lot of those pitted lard asses were having a good old time pointing and laughing at the American who couldn't speak their language correctly. I really try to learn a few phrases in the language of each country I visit but there is no way I could have gotten competent in ten languages. I was not happy with my performance. The whole time I was trying to go over well and get people into my writing I was preoccupied by those Spanish Jabba the Huts chortling like fat, pox scarred parrots and the fact that any man in that room could have been Miguel. I should have known it'd be obvious the moment he walked through the door even though the door was not in my direct line of sight. I could feel the weird energy *before* he walked in which made sense because he spent a couple of minutes just staring at me through the window before coming in. Miguel is somewhere around thirty, small in stature, clean shaven, and very calm. He radiates calm. The only thing not calm about him are his eyes---his eyes are intense, unblinking, seeing right through you, so alive and yet as cold as the deepest reaches of space. He walked in and placidly got in line. M had my book under his arm but he had made a custom cover for it adorned with various sketches and small paintings of hyenas because he knows I am fascinated by hyenas. I know this because ten pages of one of his first letters was about hyenas; facts about hyenas, jokes about hyenas, links to information about hyenas, even an oddly sexual poem about hyenas that made me want to wash my hands for the rest of my life. Miguel stared at me the whole time he was in line. He was clearly looking down a tunnel; there was no bookstore or other people, just me and him. I can see his eyes as I type this and it is still making me uneasy. There he was, looking for some face time, looking for the connection all the voices had promised him when they weren't instructing him to kill kill kill. His English was flawless, probably better than mine, but his voice was a flat line devoid of any emotion or life or any human characteristics. When it was his turn his jaw just unhinged and he started going on and on about how much he loved my book and how great I was and on and on---I just felt shitty. People can't help being obsessive, being crazy, falling in love or whatever. Here was this dear lunatic who clearly loved my work and I had been making jokes about him and dreading ever meeting him. I was scrambling to think of what sort of inscription to write. His book was dog-eared and stained and highlighted and underlined and had clearly been read dozens of times. I have books like that, books I have moved many times and re-read at least once a year. I *know* about having that sort of a relationship with a book, I totally get that. But I also knew I couldn't encourage Miguel, both for my sake and his. But I also knew if I dashed off some cheap inscription it might offend him and who knows what road that would lead us down. In the end I wrote something along the lines of my appreciation for his love of my book. He didn't stop talking even as I handed the book back.

Book is signed, boyo, time to move out of line so I can help the next person.

But he didn't move out of line, didn't break his gaze; he just kept on staring with those spooky eyes and the talk that said everything and yet said absolutely nothing. It was the owner who stepped in and started yelling at Miguel in

435

Spanish. M reached in his jacket and I wondered if he was going to pull a knife or something. His hand stayed in his jacket for what felt like thirty seconds and I was *certain* something bad was going to happen. Finally the hand reappeared and he walked out of the bookstore like a robot.

After the appearance we had a gig and I was sure Miguel was going to show up and punish me for not standing up for him. He didn't make an appearance but, dragging my shit back to the hostel, I kept thinking I saw him down the street, down *every* street I turned down which is why I ducked in this restaurant. It is really late. Restaurants in this town stay open past midnight, but the waiters are beginning to shoo people out---
Man, I don't want to go out there; I *know* I will see Miguel and I really don't want him to know where I am sleeping. The hostel is not very secure. When I bought it up the manager just laughed and shrugged and told me it's a safe part of town.
No, it is not, not as long as Miguel is around...

February 27, 2013

I am disastrously hung over and emotionally overwhelmed right now. The woman I interviewed with last week called back last night and I missed the call. What if she was on the fence about hiring me and the fact she couldn't reach me made her decide to go with someone else? I can't go back to Lodi. I have two months at Mark's house, eight weeks, one of which has been used up. What do I do if I am not working at the end of those two months? What the fuck do I do? Go back to California? Stay in Oregon and be homeless? Some days I feel optimistic and alive while other days I am scared shitless. This is one of those days. It doesn't help that I continued the slow murder of my brain last night: Beer. Vodka.Tequila. Gin. I am totally out of it. I have literally pissed away another day. I know I talk about this a lot but I need to invoke what I call the Liam rule and never drink where I am living. Never. Can I do it? Once I have a drink I don't want to stop until I am going to bed. I love drinking as I read myself to sleep, it is one of life's simple pleasures, but I am killing my brain among other things.

I learned last week that Jackie Bonner has cancer. How am I supposed to stop loving someone who needs all the love in the world at this moment? A lot of my female friends think she is a total bitch for the way she has treated me just as they think I am an idiot for being in love with her. Maybe both observations are true, honestly I am too close to have any perspective, but it all seems so petty and small and meaningless when you realize that Jackie Bonner could die. She is young, just turned 32, but people younger than that have died from cancer. I want to send message after message telling her how much I love her---not as a woman but as a close friend---but I know she doesn't want that from me. She told me she didn't want a fuss made over it and it is taking everything to just be strong and keep my mouth shut.

Honestly, I am tired of being strong at this moment. I am tired of always having to be strong and keep fighting and keep up a brave face. The past three years have just been a battle followed by uncertainty followed by a war followed by a disaster. And on top of it right now I am ashamed of myself. I am ashamed of letting my alcoholism get out of control yet again. I hate feeling stupid and uncoordinated like this. I feel like an idiot for risking my health. I feel like an ingrate for damaging the greatest gift that God gave me: My mind.

I am so desperate for some comfort in my life. I have no idea if I will ever find it or if I even deserve it and right now that realization is really getting to me...

May 12, 2018

Optimism scares me. Feeling that things are "looking up" scares me. But things *are* looking up. *Good times for a change*, as that Smiths song goes. There has been a huge shake up at the publishing house. All the people responsible for my book have been fired. My first thought is that it is like when you run up a huge tab at a bar and then the bar burns down. Yesterday Maggie got me in a chat to tell me the good news. I guess a bunch of Chinese investors bought the publishing house and they are totally fine with me working on book three at my own pace. It's like a dream--- after months of those Germans riding my ass I can finally relax. Maybe I *can* milk it for a couple of decades or something.

"Don't count on it, Ike. They have already asked me how you're doing on the book. They are a lot more relaxed than the other editors but they will still be expecting you to deliver the manuscript within two years at the latest."

"I have no enthusiasm for this story, Maggie; I haven't worked on it in months."

"I thought you said you did some work on it recently."

"A few pages maybe a month ago; they were totally forced and uninspired."

"I don't know what to say, Ike. Our contract is for that story so you'd better pick it out of the air or whatever you do."

"Maybe if I moved to another city the change would inspire me."

"But you love Portland; you always tell me how it inspires you."

"It does, but not when it comes to writing this book."

"Not every story is going to come as easy as *Jackie Bonner*---you need to just find it."

"Just find it? You can't Mapquest inspiration."

The rest of our conversation just went in circles and both of us were still frustrated when it ended....

May 12, 2014

This is the story of the fifth "Jackie and Ike" night out. It is a story of gullibility and drinking and frustration.

Yesterday I was in Lodi visiting my mother. It was the first time we'd seen each other in several months but nothing had changed. Do things *ever* change with how we relate to our parents? It never does with my mom and dad. I get on with my mother a lot better now that I rarely see her. It may be a shitty thing to say but maybe you can relate.

Jackie Bonner and I got to chatting on Facebook and she suggested I stop by her apartment so I did yesterday afternoon. The first part of our visit was really good; our friendship just fell back into place.
"We should go get a drink, Ike."
And there it was. I had no idea how to handle her suggestion. Even if I am not as madly in love with her as I was a year and half ago I still didn't want to be twiddling my thumbs in another bar while she ignored me to flirt with other men. On the other hand I knew she'd get defensive if I brought that up. Every time in the past when I've been blunt about the shit that bothers me Jackie has gotten pissed off. I knew, however, that I had to say something or I'd be stuck in a bar hanging out by myself while she flirted with whatever men were there. Jackie was busying herself in the kitchen as I told her my concerns. She promised me it'd be different, it'd be just Jackie and Ike hanging out and having some drinks and catching up.
"OK, let's hit the bars then."

We walked down to the Pine Cove and the first hour was good. We drank and had a good talk about the past year and a half of our lives. J talked about how fighting cancer had

441

changed her, made her look at the world and people differently. We were sitting pretty close and, God help me, as we caught up and rekindled our closeness something else was coming back into focus---that I love her. Not *loved*, not past tense, *love*.

And then I got really stupid and started wondering if maybe this time around we could be a couple.

I am such a fucking idiot.

A couple of guys came into the bar. I had been talking, telling Jackie about something big in my life, and I felt her attention leaving me as her eyes followed those guys from the door to the bar. They laughed with the bartender as they ordered their drinks. J was half listening to me and half checking out one of them. One of them felt her eyes on him and turned to see who was checking him out. As a man I could tell he liked what he saw. He walked over and Jackie said "hi." The guy looked from her to me and back to her. "We're not a couple, he's just my friend."

And there it was. Those eight words I have heard many times in bars when hanging out with Jackie Bonner; those eight words that never fail to make me feel small. The guy pulled up a chair and started chatting with Jackie. His name was Mike---a nice solid name for a nice, solid looking guy that Jackie clearly wanted to fuck. I was no longer there. Mike said he needed to get back to his friend and Jackie said she needed another drink and followed him to the bar. When I have written about this in the past I have made it more dramatic, like I poured my heart out to her when we went out for a cigarette or something like that. I didn't pour my heart out last night, there was no point. Jackie Bonner didn't give a fuck; she was lost in the idea of hooking up with Mike and was just staring down a tunnel of lust. I didn't pour my heart out; I just got up and walked out of that bar. J didn't see me go, she had her hand on his shoulder and was telling him about a boat she didn't own or a career she didn't have or any of the other stories she spins in bars and will continue to do the rest of her life. I looked at them for a few seconds before walking out of that bar. I love her and in some way I always will. I love Jackie like I have loved few women. There have been times I would have died for her or would have given up anything to have grown old with her. She has inspired me to write songs and stories and has brought up feelings in me both profound and intense.

I love Jackie Bonner...

The thing is, she doesn't love me.

September 9, 2014

In my more cynical moments I believe we are born to break
at least one person's heart. I may be on the way to doing
that. Emily seems to be falling in love with me; it's things
she says, it's the way she looks at me with equal parts
adoration and frustration, it's how she gets really emotional
over stupid stuff. I mean, some of the things she gets all
terse about I have no idea how or why they could set her
off. Of course I don't; I am a man and men are pretty much
clueless about women. Most of the time we have no idea
what is going on with them. Sometimes we *think* we do,
but we are just fooling ourselves and pissing them off even
more. Women are so much more complex than us and
motivated by completely different things they may as well
be a different species. This is why I say that Emily seems to
have fallen in love with me. We agreed to keep it casual
and I knew that is why she hasn't said anything. Not to
sound full of myself, but I can tell she is about to explode,
that she is overwhelmed and has to acknowledge and
release everything she feels or she will go mad. I know this
because I felt the same way about Jackie Bonner. If you
have been reading this blog you know my breaking point
with JB came four months ago; I will always care for her
but I am not in love with her anymore, not after she ditched
me for another stranger in a bar. Before that, though, I was
mad about her. I was just stupidly in love with that woman.
So, I can tell when I see that sort of hopeless yearning in
someone else and I am pretty sure I see it in Emily.

Emily is an amazing woman. Maybe if I met her a year
from now or even three months from now I could give her
the love that she deserves, the kind of love she pretends she
could take or leave but all of us want. We all want to be
adored and cared for, desired and appreciated. The thing is,

we are *choosy*. Jackie Bonner didn't want that from me and even if I wanted it from Emily I cannot return it at this time. I have been aware of her feelings for a few days and I have been losing sleep over it. Why haven't I fallen in love with her? We'd be an amazing couple; we get on really well in every way couples need to get along. I can speculate about the reasons I can't completely open my heart to Emily but whatever the reason is it is meaningless. I have toyed with the idea of pretending I am in love with her in the hope that those feelings will come for real in a few months. What if they never did? At least one of us would be completely miserable. Love is a fucking mess. Relationships are a disaster but they are also two things that make it worth the effort to go from one week to the next. But they're still a pain in the ass.

Some days I genuinely hate having emotions, I loathe having feelings.

Sometimes it's good, happiness can be amazing when it creeps up on you and bashes you on the skull. Love, when it is mutual, is incredible, but most emotions I'd like to tie to a brick and drop in the Marianas Trench. Why do we get so messed up over trivial shit? Why do we have our Jackie Bonners? Why does it hurt so much to lose someone even though losing people is nature at its most basic? If you've been reading this blog you know me quite well---maybe you are able to read between the lines and know me better than I know myself.

I am so frustrated right now---frustrated with Emily for falling for me and more frustrated with myself for not being able to fall idiotically and hopelessly in love with her. I wish that, at this moment, I was turning my phone over and over in my hands and agonizing because she hasn't texted me in twenty minutes. I wish I was obsessively checking her status online, wondering where she is and what she's doing and who she's around. I wish I found myself lying in bed in the middle of the night seeing her face and that smile she has right after I kiss her. I wish all those things, but that is just not how it is.

June 28, 2018

The day started with me wishing my mother happy birthday down the phone. I felt bad for her because one of the dogs has been really sick---that money from the show got here just in time because Teddy's vet bill took it all. That was a hard phone call; not just the heartache my mother is going through but also because my mother kept asking when I was coming back to California. Part of me wanted to point out that because I had just laid out $2700 for Teddy's vet travel is not really in the cards right now. The books are selling okay in Europe, enough so I can pay our rent and my expenses, but I still have to be careful with money. Very careful. Still, how could I complain? I mean, I make a living---however sparse---off writing which few people do. I mean, I don't have a car and I live in a studio apartment but I am doing okay.

(Three hours later)
OK, that message from Kimberly has turned things around. She probably has a publisher lined up for the stuff I wrote when I have been traveling or living in a van. She has been working on these guys for several months, back to the time when she was not technically my agent.
"I had the feeling we'd be working together again so I kept shopping your stuff."
With someone on my side like Kimberly how could I ever complain about anything? I mean, that is pretty fucking awesome---and it makes me feel kind of shitty for when we fell out last year. K was really hurt by that and I have no one to blame but myself; I really should have stood up to Maggie but I was worried about alienating her and having it affect my career—
I really can be a selfish piece of shit sometimes.

If you have been reading this blog you are probably nodding and smirking to yourself:
Yeah, Ike; your head is roughly ten miles up your ass.
Believe me, I see that as well as you do but saying I'm sorry is meaningless and cheap. I have apologized to Kimberly and over and she always tells me to forget it but I can't. I don't want to. I want to be reminded of all the selfish shit I've done in the faint hope I'll never do it again. I am genuinely haunted by the memory of how I hurt Kimberly and Emily and a few other people. We want to be remembered for the good things we've done but we're defined by the weak fucked up pathetic thoughtless things we've done.

(Two hours after that)
And this day keeps getting weirder...
Allison got me on chat just after I finished writing that last paragraph and I got off line with her maybe five minutes ago. It was one of those long intense "How long are we going to keep doing this?" conversations. So far it has been three and a half years. How many times have I nearly sent her an email or a text suggesting we live together again? Would it be different than a year and a half ago? Both of us are scared it wouldn't be; we're both scared that if living together is a disaster the second time it will drive us apart for good. We're afraid it will hurt so much we won't want to be around each other ever again and we love each other enough that the risk of that is unthinkable. How fucked up is that? We love each other so much we don't want to live together. We care for each other so much we're scared to even live in the same town. I read that poem she sent me once a week—I never get tired of it. I can never tell Allison this but in my will I have instructions for it to be read at my wake. We both understand we are meant to be together until the end of my life but we don't know when. Allison

had been turning that over and over in her head for a couple
of days before finally getting me on chat. Halfway through
the conversation I had to be the one to take the leap--
So I invited her up here to live with me.
There wasn't a response for a few minutes and I was
freaking out---
"I think that'd be good."
Allison is selling or giving away everything that won't fit in
that crappy Mazda she still owns. She is giving notice at
her work, giving up her life in Sacramento, and moving up
here to Portland and it will either make us closer than we
have ever been or it will drive us apart for good...

April 28, 2015

I know I bitch and moan about Lodi but Rocklin is even worse. I have a "three to five day" gig here and it's just a wasteland. I am spoiled having lived in Portland with all the green and awesome old buildings and character. Rocklin is just a vomit of earth tones and box stores and traffic.

I am writing this in a McDonalds of all places. I am trying to avoid fast food but I am broke and too tired after working to cook anything. Everything is a chain in Rocklin---it's really just fucking ghastly. Teresa would argue that Barstow is worse; I remember how disgusted she was with Barstow when we were on the way to Phoenix. The thing about Barstow is it became a shithole and Rocklin is that way by design. I mean, it's not poor and seedy like Barstow but it's soulless. There's no imagination in any of the buildings, everyone is rushing around in an SUV--it just feels soulless. Rocklin. Roseville. Natomas---they're all the same. If you are ever in the Sacramento area I seriously recommend you avoid those towns.

I am a mess over Allison; I am getting more and more scared that she will be another Jackie Bonner. We hook up from time to time and sometimes it seems she has deep feelings for me or maybe that's just wishful thinking. I say that because most of the time she is very cool with me, and doesn't seem to have the time for me. A keeps saying that wants to keep things casual leaving me to struggle with playing it cool like I agree while inside I am totally falling for her. Is this God's revenge for how I hurt Emily? Maybe. It's murder wanting to be around someone all the time, almost feeling desperate for them to want you and having to pretend you're keeping what's going on between the two of you light and unimportant. It isn't unimportant to me though I wish it was because I can see I am going to get hurt big time. I am losing myself in my feelings for Allison; it's almost like an obsession. The fucked up thing is that there are times when A and I are together and I could swear I am picking up on her falling for me--and then she backs off...and I can't. I am out there, man; I can't just go deeper into whatever is between us and then return to the shallow end like she can or forces herself to go or whatever it is. With Jackie Bonner it was never like we were on the path to being "boyfriend and girlfriend"; she wanted to get laid and I was there and nothing more. With Allison we have been on the path to being boyfriend and girlfriend, it has even come up in conversation. Sometimes she brings it up and seems fine with it but sometimes she brings it up and acts all claustrophobic like I am smothering her or something. But I am laying all this on her, who knows if I could make a commitment if A decided she wanted one. Maybe I am into her because it's safe; I *know* she doesn't want anything serious (most of the time). Maybe it was the same with Jackie Bonner---was I into her because she was unavailable/uninterested and consequently had zero interest in being my girlfriend? The sick thing is in both cases I am pretty sure both maybes are true.

September 10, 2016

This morning I was sitting in a restaurant with Kimberly and Alec. Sitting in the booth I felt so weak and disoriented I was amazed I got there under my own power. They sat on either side of me. K and A could tell I was a wreck and were holding one of my hands; it was kind of weird, it was kind of sweet. I could smell food cooking and for a couple of minutes it was touch and go.

"Guys, if I drop your hands real fast it means I am about to puke and I need to get out of here and run to the bathroom." Both of them squeezed my hands; it was kind of sweet, it was kind of weird.

I ordered food I was not sure I could eat. When it came I ate it with a vengeance.

"I've seen that before."

After saying that Alec giggled like a schoolgirl. It was kind of weird. Kimberly elbowed me playfully.

"You're full of shit, but I love you."

"What do you mean?"

"You talked a lot about Jackie Bonner last night--"

"You cried; it was kind of weird but it was kind of sweet." Alec seemed to be reading his hash browns like tea leaves when he said that.

"Sorry, guys; I was really drunk." I looked over at Alec. "*Really* drunk."

"We learned that JB was never going to go with you cross country earlier this year."

"Yeah, I never even asked her."

"Are you scared the feelings you had for her will come back?"

"Probably not, I was probably just afraid of rejection. More importantly I wouldn't do that to Allison; she's already jealous regarding that situation."

"You love her a lot, don't you?"

"Yeah, unfortunately."

"It'll work out, Ike. It might take a couple of years but it will."

"After Jackie I'm just scared, you know?"

Kimberly took my hand again. I wanted to go back to her house and lie with her, have her hold me. Nothing sexual, I was too far gone for that and Alec would expect to be involved, schoolgirl giggles and all. It would have been nice, though. K is such a dear person; a great agent but even more so a great friend. I can see us being good friends for a long time though I see some rough patches down the road--I could see a showdown between her and Maggie.

"Jackie was living in Sacramento two years ago, wasn't she?"

"Yeah."

"But you wrote about visiting her in San Diego around then..."

"We weren't even communicating that summer. I was pissed off about her disrespecting me in a bar and she was pissed off about me bailing on her."

"I am doubtful you guys could ever be friends without a lot of weirdness on the edges."

"You're a woman so I will go with your guess; women have a better understanding of this sort of thing."

"It's sad---you guys sound like you've been great friends in the past but your falling in love with her fucked it up."

"Yeah. I know."

June 28, 2017

Emailed Mom this morning to wish her a happy birthday.
She would have preferred a phone call but I wasn't in the
mood to talk to her. The last time we talked on the phone
she just went on and on about how I was wrong and she
knew what I should be doing---
OK, I am shutting up now; you don't want to read this and I
don't want to write it.

It is getting closer to the time when Mom can no longer
work. She has been missing work because of severe pain in
her neck and back and I wouldn't be surprised if she has to
retire by the end of the year. What then? She can't survive
on just her Social Security; she will lose her rental house
unless I help her out. My head is barely above water right
now but I am her only child so it's up to me. It pisses me
off--not helping her, I am happy to do that, it's that she is
completely oblivious about my feelings or at the very least
does not respect them. She always drags out a new spin on
that You Know I'm Right bullshit--
Sorry, fell into a rant again.

Marija played tonight at the Crystal Ballroom. I bought a
ticket three weeks ago and I'm glad I did because the show
sold out. Most cities she half fills small halls or large clubs
but Portland digs her. I took the 15 downtown and lined up
outside the Crystal Ballroom wondering if Marija would
remember me.

I stood up front while they set the instruments up. Marija
walked on stage to check her effects pedals but I didn't flag
her down; before a gig the last thing you need is someone
flagging you down for a chat. Marika didn't look my way
before walking back off stage. A minute later a staff
member in a black shirt walked up to me.

"Hey, Ike, long time."

"Yeah, how you been, Darren?"

"Good. Marija wants to see you after the set. I'll come by later and tell you where to go."

"It's not the same place?"

"No, there have been some changes."

Marija just had a bassist and a drummer backing her up. Her guitar playing had really evolved. Not technically, technically she was still mediocre, but technically great players are a dime a dozen. She plays like sociopathic/paranoid Edge from U2 or like an in tune Sonic Youth with a little more funk. Her sound is all scratchy and soulful and kind of yowly like a deranged cat trapped under an oven. On stage, braless in another sweatshirt, Marija is sexy but sexy like a homeless physics major who dropped out of school to live by her wits in some city. Sexy in a way that bites your head off after mating just to have something to write another song about.

After the set Darren led me to a small room where Marija was drinking a local beer and looking antsy to smoke. I was surprised when she walked over and hugged me as a greeting, she was wet with sweat and her body odor was strong.

"I need a cigarette; where can I smoke?" She asked.

"I know a place."

We went to an outdoor area where she wouldn't be bothered.

"So, you live in Portland?" She asked.

"Yes. Your English has really improved."

"Actually, it's gotten worse; sometimes I just pretend to not speak it, you know?"

We talked about music a bit and played catch up on what had happened the past year to both of us. It was a good talk but after fifteen minutes her manager came out to fetch her.

"Good seeing you again, Marija."

"And you, Ike. I'd go home with you instead of the hotel but you're too old for me, you know?"

I had no idea what to say. Her manager was a few feet away pretending not to listen. Marija lit another cigarette. "It took me a few days to figure that out when we were on tour last year. There was something sexy about your songs. Not normal sexy, forlorn sexy. But you are too old for me to want you as a man, it took some time for me to figure out it was not for me, you know? I just wanted to let you know that at least you crossed my mind that way. Maybe in a few years I will be old enough to not think I am too young for anyone."

"In a few years in a sane world you'll be huge, your music is amazing. I have no idea why you aren't huge already."

"I could be huge, Ike; I could show more of my tits and do all the shit they suggest and let other people produce my music but I don't want it. Look how *huge* has destroyed so many musicians."

"Yeah, it wrecked a lot of people."

The manager gave her a dirty look. She flipped him off, snubbed her cigarette, and gave me a kiss. It was a real kiss full of nicotine and beer. Breaking away, she studied me for a few moments and I could tell she was restraining a smirk.

"Sorry Ike; still too old."

Marija smiled, winked, and walked back inside with her manager on her heels...

"Sometime"

Yun started chattering excitedly as we approached the city.
She went on and on about all I was going to see and do and
all the people I'd be meeting. It was kind of annoying but it
was also kind of sweet and cute. If you've been reading this
blog you know that Yun is my guide here in China. Maybe
she works for our mutual employer, maybe she works for
the State, maybe both. She is adorable and yet formidable;
all smiles and business suits with something steely not far
below the surface. Her eyes give her away; a certain
intelligence, a certain calculation. We get along, though, so
I'm not bothered. There have been cell phone conversations
that end abruptly when I approach, there was the time that
whiskey loosened my tongue and Yun shook her head and
put a finger to her lips.
Oh baby, just you shut your mouth.
I have no idea who she is. She appeared in my sleeping
berth one night, all polite fury and teasing kisses.

A couple of hours later a stern looking man somewhere
between thirty and fifty was leading us through the train
station. A porter with Downs Syndrome pushed the cart
with our bags as he hummed an old David Bowie song.
The station was crowded in a manner I have only seen on
documentaries. Everyone was walking fast and carrying on
clipped phone conversations. Nobody smiled. We ended up
at a dark blue Mercedes 600 from somewhere around 1969.
The sun was out but in the distance there was the crack and
snarl of thunder.

A stern man drove that work of art perilously fast through
gaps in traffic I did not see until they were in the rear view
mirror. Yun was holding my hand like a trap not fully
sprung, her skin reassuringly warm.

We ended up in the parking garage of an impossibly tall building. Yun explained that I would be taken to my hotel after meeting with Mr. To. The stern man remained behind the wheel of the car as we walked into a high speed lift that moved disconcertingly fast like elevators that have had featured roles in my nightmares. I lean over and kiss Yun as floor after floor falls beneath us. I am kissing her but I know I am really kissing Allison or Emily or Jackie Bonner or any other woman I have ever loved or will love. I understand at that moment, in a strange city in a strange country, that time is meaningless. We all live forever beyond the frailty of our bodies. Most times we just don't remember who we were, who we really are and have been and always will be. It's one of nature's mercies---not cursing us with the memory of all the people and dreams we lost the other times around, all the heartache and confusion, all the broken wandering wondering if we will ever find a place to call home. Forgotten. Anything else would not be kind and nature is strangely kind.

We ended up in an office on the top floor of the highest building in the city, maybe in the world. I could feel it swaying but I was not afraid. I understand that life is an illusion and the time between lives is the length of a flash from a gun. Mr. To greeted us, an impeccably dressed man somewhere between forty and sixty. I felt shabby in my best clothes. He seemed to sense that and started paying all these compliments about my writing and I couldn't help but feel reassured. It smelled like jasmine in that office, jasmine and cigarettes right after you open a new pack.
"You belong here, Ike. You would love this city."
"No disrespect, Mr. To, but I love Portland."
"We have places like Portland here."
That seemed unlikely but I did not want to be disrespectful. Mr. To seemed to sense that.

"We can give you anything you want, Ike. You will no longer have to worry about money. You will no longer have to worry about how you are going to support your mother."

He looked at me meaningfully. The walls of the office had disappeared and surrounding us were the endless vistas of the desert. The Slabs. It could be Mr. To or it could be Maggie or it could be Pete who said he could get us some peyote three days ago. Identity is an illusion...

March 4, 2018

Going on that date with Marilyn was a mistake; I really
need to learn how to say **_no_**.
One---what did we have in common?
Two---I am deeply in love with someone else.
So why did I go on that date? Because a female friend of
mine was insistent that I go on it because she thinks Allison
is a disaster and wants me to be with someone stable.
Marilyn is 45 and an optometrist; a serious grown up
person with a grown up career who probably eats fruits or
vegetables with every meal and never got drunk more than
every few months. What would she want from a guy like
me? What would I want from a woman like her?

Like I said, I was kind of bullied by good intentions to go
on that date so I agreed to meet Marilyn at this bar. I have
already forgotten the name and I just got back from it two
hours ago; just another trendy bar in the Hawthorne district.
Normally I wouldn't have gone within a block of that joint
but Marilyn really likes the place so I agreed to meet her
there.
I really have to stop being so agreeable.

The place was jam packed so we stood at the bar and
struggled to carry on a conversation that would have been
awkward in the best of circumstances. Part of me wanted to
sabotage the "date," tell her I had lesions on my penis or
something, but she was a nice woman and also it would get
back to my friend and she'd be pissed off at me. I decided
to just let the "date" run its course and about the time I
made that decision Ram showed up (not that I recognized
him at first). I worked on one of his scripts a couple of
years ago and the movie ended up being a blockbuster. If I
had points on that fucker I'd be rich but I was just the script

doctor---and it needed a lot of doctoring. If I remember right it took three of us to get Ram's script shoot worthy. He comes up with these amazing film concepts that are usually huge but his actual writing is shit. I shuddered reading that script.

And you will soon understand why I am so "openly" critical of that smug prick.

I have no idea how he recognized me, how he picked me out in that crowded bar, but he walked up to me with the grin of a man who talked a shark into giving him its fins.

"Ike!"

"Do I know you?"

He introduced himself and explained that I had been a doctor on one of his scripts. In the interest of continuing to have a career I am not saying the movie nor "Ram's" real name.

"Hey, congratulations, man, that movie was huge."

"*Is* huge, bro. It may be out of the theatres but home sales are blowing up."

"Awesome, good for you."

I introduced Marilyn to Ram and explained our working relationship leaving out the bits about my labors to adorn a turd with gold spray paint.

"I didn't know you worked on scripts, Ike."

"Only when he's slumming," Ram laughed metallically.

"Hey, how is the latest novel doing anyway? I heard sales in Romania are almost encouraging."

Marilyn, not stupid, could tell Ram was trying to make me feel small; I could see it registering on her face and she didn't like it. Maybe she was okay after all. I had no idea why Ram was making the effort to be a dick to me---here is a guy worth tens of millions with this amazing career most writers would sacrifice their children to Satan for picking on a nobody cult writer.

"Hey, I love my Eastern European readers," I smiled.

"You know, I love my house and boat and all that but what I would really like to be is taken seriously like you," Ram leaned forward and dropped to a confidential tone. "I mean, money is easy to come by but to have people think you're some kind of deep genius, now that is some great reward."

"Yeah, I don't think anyone thinks I'm a genius, Ram."

"If they don't they'd have to be stupid, Ike. Maybe most of the world is just too stupid to get what you do---"

"Whoa, no, I don't see it like that at all---"

"Hey, what do I know? I'm just a cheesy screenwriter, right? I mean, you think our movie is a piece of shit, right?"

Whoa, where did he---Maggie. Drunk Maggie. Shit shit shit.

Ram could eliminate any shot I have of getting any more screen work.

This is a fucking disaster.

Before I could object Ram got bored with us and walked off to harass a waitress.

*Shit shit shit **shit**.*

October 17, 2017

Malo and I had been emailing back and forth when I was
planning my second promotional trip to Europe. When the
dates were set we agreed to meet up for two or three days
and work on his demos.

Today was our first day in the home studio he jury rigged
in the spare room of his apartment. Considering how well
the boy band he was in did, I was surprised how grotty his
apartment was. Lots of modern but cheap furniture and
empty tequila bottles. I guess he read my face because he
has probably seen my expression many times.
"Not where you'd expect a big pop star to live, huh?"
"I know management often screws teens in bands, it
happens."
"A couple of the others did well." Malo shrugged as he
poured another tequilia. "I was more stupid, you know? I
didn't care, I guess, I was having a good time. There were
lots of girls."
"It happens too often. In a band there is always at least one
guy savvy with the money side of things. You guys were
young, right? Like 17 or 18?"
"I was 16."
"Right. See---what the fuck do most 16 year olds know
about business?"
Malo had plowed through half of his tequila. I know all
about that sort of drinking, know it all too well.
"Do you ever wish you had made it big in music, Ike?"
"Maybe twenty-five years ago, but I always knew the stuff
I do is outside the mainstream. I got older and my reasons
for doing it changed."
"Me too. When things fell apart I found I had little money
even though they told us we were selling millions of
singles. But it had been so fun I couldn't be serious, you

know? We were getting to see these amazing places and being treated good and fucking these amazing girls, it was good. It was so good it was impossible to think it could go bad. It's a drug, you know? But the drug wore off and I had to withdraw a bit."

"How did you survive?"

"I got another manager and he found me gigs."

Malo told me of all these wretched, squalid gigs and it broke my heart considering the level of fame he had and the venues and all the girls he had experienced. His group was not as big as the Backstreet Boys, but not that far off. One year they were playing in stadiums and getting mentions in Billboard magazine and the next he was playing strip malls and third rate travelling amusement parks.

"But it's just the business side isn't it, Ike? Life goes on; I have these new songs and we will make a great demo and my manager can take it to labels."

I just smiled and nodded. I love Malo; he is such an awesome person, a real sweetheart, but his songs are a flat line. They aren't terrible and he still has a great voice, but they don't have any spark to them. Some songs haunt you, some annoy you, and you want either or both--especially when you are a 34 year old who has been dying for a comeback. And I *hate* saying that, I hate talking shit about those songs because he was pouring himself into them, but I am trying to be honest. I am going to do what I can. I am coming up with parts on various instruments and counter harmonies and other stuff but it's all uphill, you know?

January 11, 2016

This chapter begins a couple of days ago. I was sitting in my room stressing about Europe or, more accurately, stressing about all the money it will take to get there. Stress is toxic. Stress is something that opens people to cancer. Having that realization led me to think about Tiyo. If you have been reading this blog you may remember that Tiyo was a cancer survivor I met two years ago in San Diego. We had an amazing couple of days and then fell out. A week doesn't go by without my thinking of her. What happened to her? Is she still okay? Did she relapse? In my darker moments I believe she relapsed and died. Being around her was addictive. People who have faced death and stared it down have something to them I can scarcely define.

As I was saying I got to thinking about Tiyo a couple of days ago, her shooting the van and being so blase about it. For a second I was pissed off about how blasé she was about what could have been a disaster but the moment passed and I realized how small the hole in the van was compared to cancer or many things we all face in life: Growing older. Losing friends. Raising kids.

I know why I hadn't texted Tiyo before two days ago: Rejection. When we fall out with friends, reaching out to that person is so much harder than reaching out to a stranger. It's hard to be the brave one, the bigger person, because if the other person ignores you it's like reopening a wound that was just beginning to heal. This is why although I think of Tiyo on a regular basis I couldn't reach out to her.

A day passed with no response and I was going between being sad ("She must be dead.") and angry ("She is just being a bitch, blowing me off again.").

Two days have passed now. She has not responded to my texts and my instincts tell me she never will for whatever reason. Some friendships are not designed to last a lifetime. Sometimes we're really close to people for a few days or even a few hours and that's all there is and all there was ever supposed to be...

May 12, 2018

If you have been reading this blog you know of Miguel, my Spanish stalker. He wrote these bizarre, lengthy letters on peach colored paper that reeked of old lady perfume. He showed up at a book appearance a few months later all intense stares and tension, shoving his hand in his jacket like a part time assassin. You may remember how much I worried the mad fucker would stab me—
It would appear he moved on and stabbed or at least attempted to stab someone else. You remember "Ram"? That cunt that tore into me in that bar a couple of months ago? For some reason he became the latest object of Miguel's attentions. I don't know whether to be relieved or offended. I mean, did Miguel think Ram's writing is as obsession worthy as mine? The story I heard is that Ram knows some sort of martial art and was able to subdue Miguel and rid him of the knife we all knew he had.
It was one of those rare times I had been rooting for a psychopath.

Got an email from R this morning. R was the first person I almost dated in Portland five years ago. There was a miscommunication and she asked me to never contact her again so I didn't and it was over five years before I heard from her again. That was a sad situation. We only went out twice but I had already been falling for her and it broke my heart a bit. Mentally and physically I was into her and I thought she was into me---I guess I was wrong. I have no idea why I fall for some women so easily: R, my ex-wife, Jackie Bonner. With R as with Jackie Bonner I did the cliché/stupid thing and numbed myself with alcohol and less idiotic throwing myself into my job and writing and selling the first book. It's all you can do in those situations. Still, every time I passed R's apartment building or the bar

467

we hung out in those two times or walked the streets I walked her home down it just hurt. It got easier as the days became weeks, but sometimes I still feel sad in those places. There are some roads and buildings we call *haunts* for a reason.

When R cut me off I was pissed off at myself for wreaking whatever chance I had with her because she seemed incredible to me. Not perfect, perfect doesn't exist and if it does it scares me, but she was smart and sarcastic and beautiful in a geeky/socially awkward way. But I fucked it up like I have fucked things up with a lot of people. All that sadness---I was the one who walked into the shop and bought it. All these ghosts in these haunted houses that are our lives we drug them out and keep them from moving on. It's just sad like many things in life are equally sad and pathetic. You have to take it slow with people but unfortunately my heart is made to race. The truth is I have no middle ground; either I love people and would do anything for them or I could care less if they live or they die. I made the leap with R and it was just this disaster inside me that spilled out and made a fucking mess and she smelled it and got disgusted and told me to go away and that's all there is...

March 12, 2014

The night I met Teresa I knew we'd play an important role in each other's lives. As we lay in bed somewhere between midnight and dawn, I knew that we'd fall in love and eventually get married.

We separated three years ago. Fortunately both of us wanted out so neither of us was left holding the bag. I am grateful for that. I had been unhappy for years, felt trapped, but we went through so many hard times together I didn't want to abandon her. She seemed to get more bitter, I know I drank more, our happiness became more and more infrequent and always dark around the edges.

The break was clean and amicable and I had hopes for our remaining close friends. Sadly it didn't end up that way; Teresa expected me to research getting a divorce and when I didn't complete my assigned task she got snippy. Both of us were unemployed. She resented how I never snapped to it and I resented her for putting it on me and being oblivious to the things I was dealing with. During the Summer of '13 she cut me off entirely and we were estranged for several months until she was able to start divorce proceedings. Even after that she was still resentful of how I had let her down in that regard.

We had dinner together tonight at Jerry's Diner on Thomas for old times sake. I picked her up at the condo she shares with her longtime friend Justin out in Peoria. When she opened the door I was reminded of how fond of her I was; I will always have a lot of love for Teresa. Maybe it's not "wife" love but it's as deep as it ever was even if it has become impossible for us to be friends. We lived in each others' pockets for over seven years. There were a lot of hard times we faced together, probably too many hard times. How many hard times can any relationship survive?

I drove us over to Jerry's. Teresa put her feet up on the dash just like old times and started going on and on about some co-worker and was still talking about it when we walked into the restaurant.

"So, your book is coming out next year?" I asked.

She had been looking at a text on her phone and seemed annoyed by my question.

"Hold on."

"Sorry."

I hated those flashes of impatient anger, but like so many times in the past I held my tongue and cooled my heels until she was ready to answer my question.

"They are planning on putting it out on May 8th, 2015," she said.

"Awesome---I'm proud of you."

"Thanks. How's it going with your agent?"

"Nothing yet."

"Sorry."

"It'll happen," I smiled.

"You've always been so certain. I've always been amazed at how certain you've been as long as I've known you. It was hard sometimes."

"I know."

The waitress came by and we ordered.

"Has your publisher requested a lot of changes?" I asked.

"Not too many."

We ate our meals and talked about Phoenix. The two of us recollected our two rental homes and the van we drove from Sacramento to Phoenix. It's hard because I want us to be really good friends but maybe that is unreasonable. When you are as close as two people can be and then separate, maybe it's impossible to ever have any sort of closeness again. I know Teresa felt something similar because I could feel her disengaging, talking less; staring out the window and checking her phone. I kept looking out the window at my van, feeling a desire to put a lot of distance between Phoenix and myself.

I drove her back in near silence even though it took thirty minutes to get her back to the condo. I dropped her off; she just got out of the van, looked back to say goodbye, and didn't look back a second time as she made her way to the front door. After I made sure she got inside I drove around aimlessly, thinking of how in love we had been, our wedding, the night we met---so much history and history is just an army of ghosts. We had fought in so many wars, side to side, back to back, and in the end we turned on each other. I drove to this coffee shop thinking of ghosts, thinking of how everything, no matter how beautiful, how deep in your blood it is, has an expiration date.

April 15, 2017

I don't know if I'll ever publish this chapter. It's personal
and regarding a sensitive matter. A couple of days ago I
wrote that Maggie and I slept together but nothing
happened; that was a lie I had to tell partly out of respect
for Maggie's privacy and partly because that sort of
honesty has a tendency to backfire on me. It is also
emotionally charged enough I struggle to articulate it, even
in my own head. I was also a lot more sober than Maggie
so part of it is also that I feel guilty.

Maggie reminds me of Jackie Bonner, a smart, strong
woman who has moments of weakness: Pain. Frustration.
Self-destruction. I can't help but care for her, care for both
of them. They're both amazing people I feel a combination
of love, frustration, lust, admiration, and concern for.

This reminds me of the Spring of '13 when I was up in
Portland for the second time. Jackie was fighting cancer
and going through chemo. I had come back here to
Portland, in part, to forget about her or at least get past
being in love with her.
And then I found out she had cancer.
Things were weird between us that Spring. Not in a bad
way--things were kind of sweet and almost loving in our
own strange way, but they still a bit *weird*. I told her how
beautiful I found her and how much I loved her because I
wanted her to have something positive in her life; I wanted
her to understand that someone genuinely loved her and
that she had more than the casual attentions of the people
she was meeting in bars. J sent me sexy pictures: Her in a
towel, her in a skimpy tank top, her topless wearing just
panties. It was confusing because she had always made it
clear that I was just a buddy, that she didn't want anything

472

else from me...and then she sent those pictures. I kept looking at those pictures; she had a particularly sweet smile in the one with the tank top, a dark sort of sweetness only J could pull off...dark or maybe just complex. I got a little lost in those pictures like a child wandering around a haunted house and began wondering if we could ever be a couple---if she could ever desire me, if Jackie Bonner could ever fall in love with me.

Four years later I shudder at the memory. I feel foolish remembering how I fell back in love with Jackie that Spring, wandering around Portland thinking about her. Writing haikus and poems for her that I never sent because I didn't feel they were good enough. But how could I not love her? She was sick, she could have died. Later I found out---thankfully---that the cancer was caught early and she has since recovered completely but I didn't know that at the time. J never even used the word *cancer*; she said she was going through chemo and that was it. For all I knew she was really sick; for all I knew it wasn't that bad. So, I allowed myself to fall for her again, wandering the rainy streets of Portland thinking of her. Sitting in bars surrounded by strangers who were surrounded by friends. My only companion was this intense, confusing, beautiful, cursed love for someone who wasn't in love with me. Like I said, I shudder at the memory of those times, how stupid I was.

I couldn't fall in love with Maggie; I am already in love with someone else (Allison), but I have a lot of love for M. She is one of those people you meet and it feels like a continuation, like the two of you are picking up from another life. There is no awkwardness, no struggling to build a relationship because it is already there and has been for many years. I've had a few other friends like that and can't help but believe in reincarnation. Allison is one of

473

them--we talk about chasing each other through the centuries and it is as matter of fact as discussing the weather.

September 27, 2018

"So you're actually doing it?" Allison asked.

"Only if it sounds good to you."

"It's not my money, Ike."

"You know what I mean; we've been over this."

Allison says nothing.

"Do you have the money to buy it and keep the studio and pay bills?"

"I wouldn't do it unless I did."

A is worried because she hasn't found work yet in Portland; she is not the sort of person who can deal with feeling vulnerable like most proud people who have been made to feel small many times in their lives.

"So what are you going to do with this land---build a house?"

"Eventually. There isn't the money now."

"But they're making a movie out of one of your stories and you get points off that, right?"

"Yeah, but you know how it is; it could do well or it could flop, you never know."

"It'll be huge."

When she says that I am overwhelmed a little with this deep, hopeless love for her and it takes me a few seconds to get it under control and not just blurt out how I am completely mad for her.

"I'm glad one of us is confident," I say.

"You're confident, you just feel you have to deny you are sometimes because you worry about people seeing what an egomaniac you are."

There is a smile in her voice when she says that so I say nothing. We were walking down Division and passing a large, loud group waiting in front of one of this week's hipper bars.

"So, it's going to just be dirt and trees?" She asks.

"I want to buy an old RV or maybe a school bus to take up there until we can afford to build a cabin."

"I knew a school bus would come into the equation at some point---"

"And when we have the money I want you to help me design the cabin."

Allison says nothing for over a block. When she speaks again her voice is soft and I can tell I struck a nerve--- hopefully in a good way.

"I can't design a house."

"Not a house, a cabin; a lot smaller and a lot less complicated."

"It still involves plumbing and wiring and things like that."

"It's not that hard to design that stuff," I reply. "I've done it before. The hard thing is actually putting the plumbing and wiring in---that requires hiring other people."

Allison comes to a dead stop and the energy coming off her changes completely. I had the feeling she had just closed herself off to me; I recognize that closing off feeling because I have experienced it many times with her. I stopped a couple of feet from her, unsure what to do or say. I hate those moments; utterly *hate* them.

"Give me a second, Ike. I am a little freaked out."

A bus passes and for some reason I hone in on the sound of the tires kicking up spray off the pavement. When Allison continues speaking her voice is shaky but warm, as warm as the Fall evening is becoming chilly.

"I just realized I have to ask you something, something huge, something so big it freaks me out," she says quietly but firmly.

"Yeah?"

"Yeah. And I know you know what it is."

"I do."

"Are you saying 'I do' because you understand or are you saying 'I do' as your answer to what I am asking you?"

"Both."

476

We are standing in front of one of our favorite bars. I take her hand and we walk inside...

www.ingramcontent.com/pod-product-compliance
Lightning Source LLC
Chambersburg PA
CBHW072016020726
47501CB00006B/1829